She grabbed at the paper again, and this time Galen released her wrist and let her take it. "You have not told me yet," Galen said tightly, "where you got this."

Meredith's own anger began to resurface, but she held it in check. There was no sense in losing her temper again, she told herself, and anyway, she was more disappointed than she was angry. "You're bluffing, aren't you?" she growled. "You don't know what this writing means any more than I do. I think you'd better leave."

She stared determinedly into Galen's face, and he stared back. Those fierce blue eyes deepened, searching hers. She blinked, feeling suddenly dizzy, and his hands reached out, gently gripping her bare shoulders.

"Meredith." His voice was mesmerizing, a soft, husky croon. "Tell me what I wish."

He drew her closer, and Meredith did not resist. To take her eyes from that dark face had become impossible. She felt something in him reach out for her, and something in her answered.

It rose up in her like a tide, compelling beyond reason or thought. She lifted her arms and slowly put them around his broad shoulders. He tensed, as if she had startled him, then his whole body seemed to envelop her as he pulled her against him and lowered his lips to hers. . . .

Books by Jessica Bryan

BENEATH A SAPPHIRE SEA
DAWN ON A JADE SEA
ACROSS A WINE-DARK SEA

BENEATH A
SAPPHIRE SEA

Jessica Bryan

BANTAM
NEW YORK   TORONTO   LONDON   SYDNEY   AUCKLAND

BENEATH A SAPPHIRE SEA
A Bantam Fanfare Book/September 1993

ISBN 0-553-56221-5

Published simultaneously in the United States and Canada

PRINTED IN THE UNITED STATES OF AMERICA

RAD 0 9 8 7 6 5 4 3 2 1

To my lover and husband,
Stephen,
and my sister-in-law and best friend,
Pam
—my two most relentless critics.

CHAPTER
1

The Mediterranean Sea in the year 1974

Help me.

The boy sent the desperate plea out of his mind and into the gloom of deep waters. Pain sliced through him, firing the length of his body like the venom of a thousand sea snakes. Struggling to clear his vision, he blinked again and again. The abode of the clan that lived in these waters was not far. His senses, dimmed though they were by the relentless agony, kept telling him it was near.

Gasping, the small gills on his neck fluttering madly in the monochrome shadows, he forced himself onward, trying to swim in the smooth, undulating movement of his kind. But the pain attacked again. This time when the spasm passed it left him motionless.

The currents took over, catching up the boy's limp body

and moving it into their ceaseless flow. The abode he had been trying so hard to reach loomed in the distance, a great dark mass growing out of the ocean floor, its forbidding aspect softened by the glitter from the thousands of tiny luminescent fish that flitted and danced about its rocky crags.

As the boy drifted away from the haven it offered, a dozen sleek forms shot through the water, racing toward him with a precise flowing power. Surrounding the unconscious boy, they propelled him back to the abode, moving him far more swiftly than he could have moved himself. Within moments they had him inside.

As the huge chamber that allowed the abode's inhabitants access to the sea emptied itself of water, the tallest of the group swung the boy's sagging body into his arms and carried him toward two massive doors of black coral inlaid with alabaster. Long-limbed and powerful, the man strode purposefully, splashing through the water that had already dwindled down to his ankles. His tanned, fine-featured face was taut with concern, and his companions flowed after him, their hands moving over the boy with worried reassurance.

All of them, male and female alike, were unclothed, their only adornment the elaborate necklaces sparkling about their throats. Wan light from secret places in the rough-hewn walls washed over the gleaming black pearls of the leader's necklace as one of the women pulled the lever that would allow them to leave the chamber.

With a grating roar the two great doors separated, and the bright, coral-tinted glow of a wide corridor burst upon the group. The spacious hall was crammed with people, so many that they were pushed against the smooth, glimmering walls of alabaster and coral. As the man carrying the boy strode forward through the press, questions and comments were thrown at him with the persistence of anxiously clicking dolphins.

"What's happened, Galen? Who's the boy?"

"Why, it's Alaric. I know his kin."

"What's wrong with him, is he hurt?"

"No, he seems ill. But how can that be? We're never ill!"

The rough voice of the one called Galen cut across the clamor. "Summon Cleonith the Elder. She's traveling these waters. If anyone can help him, she can."

Hours later, Galen stood in one of the abode's guest chambers. Like all living spaces in this vast and ancient structure that had been home to his kin since the beginning of time, it was a magnificently appointed room, filled with the exquisite and intricately detailed murals, sculptures, and furnishings so dear to the hearts of the beauty-loving merfolk. Galen took not the least notice of the beauty that surrounded him, though. He watched impatiently as Cleonith, the most senior of all Elders and a woman noted for her extraordinary healing powers, rose from beside the bed in which the boy lay.

Her robe of high office whispered over the polished jade floor as she crossed the room, the garment's long folds the same snowy shade as the thick coil of hair that lay over one shoulder. She stood tall and straight despite the passage of more centuries than anyone could count, but the deep lines that grooved the Elder's face bespoke a wisdom and power gained through lifetimes of experience.

She halted before Galen and looked up at him gravely. Her eyes were deep brown, a dark contrast to his, for Galen possessed the coloring that marked him as a close relation to the royal house: jewel-blue eyes and jet black hair.

"Well?" he asked in a low voice. "How is he?"

She glanced back at the bed. "He will live."

A burst of relief swept through Galen, but at the look on Cleonith's austere face it quickly faded. "Tell me what's wrong, Cleonith," he ordered quietly. "You do not stare at me like that without reason."

The Elder did not answer right away. "It might have been better if he had died," she said at last. "My skills preserved his life, but they could not prevent what this unknown illness has left in its wake. His gill slits have closed, Galen. As if they were never there."

"What?" Galen thought he must have misunderstood. "How can that be? I've never heard of such a thing happening before!"

"You have not been swimming the Mother as long as. I have, youngling." Cleonith's voice was quiet, full of a foreboding that made the muscles in Galen's neck tense. "I once heard tales about a sickness like this. I was no older than you are when I heard them, and even then the stories were grizzled with age, so old that many among the Elders believed they were an exaggeration. Now, though . . ."

Her gaze went to the still figure in the bed. "The little one is doomed," she said flatly. "He will awaken from his fevered sleep, but what will become of him then? Your abode is so far beneath the waves that no creature who lacks the Mother's gifts could ever reach the surface alive. And the pressures of the Midnight Sea itself—even inside this dwelling they may still kill him. Despite all the powers I possess, I cannot tell you what caused this. But if a strong young one like Alaric can be struck down . . ."

She did not finish her thought. She did not have to. His mind reeling, Galen stared at the young unconscious merman. Within him, disbelief warred with horror at the Elder's words. Alaric appeared so peaceful, so deceptively normal as he slept. Galen knew the boy's kin; several times he had stayed at their abode in the sea that landfolk called the Aegean. Obviously Alaric had decided to embark on one of the wanderings common to all their people. With disastrous results.

"His clan doesn't know yet," Galen murmured. "With my mother and father no longer among the living, I am head of this abode now, so it falls to me to tell them." Grief shadowed his eyes as he stared at the boy. "Two more seasons and he would have been ready to go on his dream-walk."

Cleonith's dry, calloused fingers touched his arm. "In the nine seasons since your parents made the transition from this world, you have done well with your new responsibilities," she said gently. "You will deal with this just as capably."

Galen turned away from the sympathy in her face. His thoughts were distant and throbbing with loss. To speak of his parents was to bring them back, alive and vibrant in his mind. Yet it brought back as well that terrible day when his life and his destiny had changed forever. The day his parents had died. No, his mind corrected him—the day his parents had been *murdered.* The reminder sent flames of rage and hatred firing through his brain, emotions he could not afford to indulge, at least not now.

The weight of his responsibilities lowered upon him, and he turned back to Cleonith. "I will sit with him awhile," he said quietly. "There is little else I can do for one who came to my abode seeking refuge."

A day later, Alaric's condition had not changed. Sitting with Cleonith as the two maintained a silent vigil beside the boy's bed, Galen did not know whether that lack of change portended good or ill. Neither did Cleonith, and she had just finished saying so when the carved chamber door swung open.

A woman poked her head inside. At the sight of her, Galen came instantly to his feet. She was a kinswoman of his, and one of the dozen or so lookouts who regularly patrolled the ancestral waters of their clan. She would not be there unless something serious was afoot. Her words confirmed this. "Galen," she said urgently, "Toklat of the Selkie folk is here, and he is very upset. He says he must speak with you and any Elder present, and at once."

Galen and Cleonith exchanged glances.

"What now?" Galen muttered.

Toklat was waiting for them in a small meeting chamber. Dispensing with the usual ceremonies of greeting, he strode forward swiftly to meet them.

"My people are dying."

The squat muscular man spoke hoarsely in a tone of controlled desperation, gazing at the two merfolk with eyes that seemed to belong to a seal rather than a man.

Galen met Toklat's bleak stare with shock. He and Toklat were the closest of friends. They had grown to adulthood together, swimming the endless seas of a shared domain, part of an alliance between merfolk and Selkies—an alliance that dated back to the very beginning of time.

"It started three turns of the tide ago," Toklat continued, including Cleonith in his dark stare. "First a mother and her pup, then a young bull, strong and in his prime, the same age as me. Now two more of us are gone, and our healers can do nothing."

"What were their symptoms, Toklat?" Galen asked the question sharply, his gaze meeting Cleonith's.

Toklat began to pace, gliding over the smooth coral floor with a grace belied by his squat build. He was at least a head shorter than the smallest of the merfolk, but after the innumerable wrestling matches they had engaged in over the centuries, Galen was keenly aware of the enormous strength contained in that stocky man-shape. The Selkie spun about to stare at them, a look of anguish on his blunt-featured face.

"It is the shapechanging," he cried. "The afflicted ones try to change from seal to human, as we always have. Only something goes wrong and they can't finish it. They turn into a dreadful combination of the two, instead, and screaming in pain, they die." In mute appeal, he lifted a broad hand, the thin webbing between each finger extended. "It is horrible," he said brokenly. "Horrible ..."

"Gently, young one." Cleonith spoke softly, her voice casting a balm over the distraught Selkie. "And your father," she went on when Toklat had calmed a little, "why is he not here? As ruler of the Selkies it is his place to bring us word of something so serious."

Toklat's barrel chest heaved with the deep breath he drew. "He cannot, Lady. He died this morning, screaming like the others before him."

"Toklat, brother-friend." Galen was at the other's side in an instant. Grief stabbed him with the sharpness of a sea scorpion's sting as he gripped the Selkie's hairy shoulders. He had loved the venerable seal king, had always thought of him as a wise old uncle. "We sorrow for the end of your father's reign." He spoke the ritual words with heartfelt sincerity. "Yet may your own be as long and joyous."

"I fear it will be neither." Toklat's hoarse voice shook. "But your abode is closest to my ancestral waters, so I've come to you as my father would have if he were alive. Back when Mother Ocean was young, a Selkie saved the life of a merwoman. Your people and mine have been friends ever since. I call upon that ancient debt now. Compared to other sea folk our numbers have never been great. If you cannot help us, there will soon be no Selkies left in all the waters of the seas."

"We will do what we can," Galen said, then added softly, "For our sake, as well as yours."

"For your sake ..." Toklat looked around him. Caught up in his own crisis he had not noticed the strange expression upon the faces of his hosts. He noticed it now, and he frowned. "What do you mean, Galen?"

"Yesterday one of our young ones—a boy as strong and healthy as any of us—fell mysteriously ill. Merfolk are never sick, Toklat, you know that." Galen looked at Cleonith again, the enormity of what had happened to Alaric sinking in anew. "He is not going to die like your unfortunate kin—at least not right away. But he will never swim the Mother's waters again. His gill slits are gone."

The Selkie's eyes grew larger. "By the Mother," he whispered, "what is happening to us?"

Cleonith opened her eyes. Around her the great cavern sprang into focus, its gloom hiding nothing from her keen gaze. Shadows drifted up from the pool of volcanically warmed dark water in which she sat, steamy curls that wreathed about the faces of the other Elders who sat with her. Their features were gaunt, gray with exhaustion and strain.

Mirror images, Cleonith thought wearily, of how her own face must look. Traveling into the realms of the Seeing was never easy. This mind journey had been particularly draining, weighted as it was with the sense of foreboding that pressed down upon them all.

"So." Cleonith's voice echoed off the cavern's rock walls. "We are agreed, then. The visions were the same for all of us."

"They were the same," said one of the men. "But I would not say we are agreed. I have never believed a scroll from the Time Before exists, and the Seeing was not as clear about that as I would have liked."

"It was clear enough," the man next to him said. "We have no choice but to act upon it. Now."

One of the women shook her head, her face troubled. "Yes, but how would a Terran woman know anything about the scroll? It makes no sense. The visions could be directing us along the wrong current, or we could be misinterpreting them. Even with all our powers, we are not infallible."

"Perhaps not," Cleonith said. "But still"—she paused to stare around the circle, her gaze stabbing each solemn face in turn—"aren't we forgetting the most important thing? Our people sicken while we sit here debating. The boy Alaric is no better, and now Morat, an adult in his full strength, is ill as well. Then there are the Selkie folk. Their condition is even worse than ours. The Seeing told us this is all connected, and the scroll may provide the answers—"

"May!" snapped the first man who had spoken. "That is all we know, Cleonith. Only that it may!"

"And that is all we have!" Cleonith shot back. "This is no time to argue, my fellow Elders. Our skills could not prevent or heal what has already happened, but they have provided us with the only weapon we have for stopping it before it goes any further. The visions showed us where the landwoman is now. None of our historians are on or near this island the Terrans call Karpathos, so someone must go to her and find out what she knows. Someone who is strong as well as subtle, who can act without raising a lot of questions and suspicions."

She gazed at her companions, her dark eyes filled both with pleading and determination, and she saw the consensus—though it was reluctant on the faces of some— that finally attended her words.

"Very well," someone said. "Whom should we send?"

Cleonith answered without hesitation. "Galen."

The Greek island of Karpathos two days later

The dream visited again that night, creeping and curling into the outer edges of Meredith's consciousness the way waves whisper delicately on the beach at dawn. It carried with it the smell of the sea, the iodine-scented strangeness seeming to come not only from the ocean's salty embrace, but from the body of the man who held her.

In strong and tender arms the dream man rocked her. His deep, melodic voice was a gentle murmur, blending with the sound of wind and waves until it formed an indistinct lullaby in her ears. Before she could see the man's face, the dream slipped away, leaving her to awaken in unfulfilled yearning, the taste of salt inexplicably upon her lips.

Groggily, Meredith pushed the hair out of her eyes and sat up. The weightless freedom of rocking back and forth in the sea still enfolded her, and she felt disoriented and confused—momentarily uncertain of where she was. Moonlight slanted onto her face through the opened bedroom window, revealing the silvery black expanse of the Aegean as it shimmered under the stars, brooding over mysteries only it knew.

Propping a pillow behind her, Meredith leaned back against the ornate wooden headboard of the large bed, hand-carved decades earlier by some unknown master craftsman. Eventually she would be able to sleep again, but the dream had come often enough for her to know it would not be yet. For months the dream had been visiting her, this haunting vision conjured up by some part of her mind she had not known existed.

She had had vivid dreams before, but never anything that lingered with so strong an impression. The warm breeze of the Greek night whispered over her naked breasts, and restless, she got out of bed. She looked down at her body, half expecting to find it dripping wet as though she had just emerged from the waves.

The mirror atop the bureau gave back her reflection, and absently Meredith gazed at herself. A finely featured face looked back at her, dominated by high cheekbones and

large black eyes. Tousled by sleep, the curly dark hair she
had pinned atop her head for coolness had come loose, tumbling in a soft lion's mane about her muscular shoulders.
Lost in thought, she began to pin it up again.

The sea. It was a force that had long possessed her
thoughts. Now it had pulled her to this remote Greek island
and the house that sat in whitewashed solitude overlooking
the Aegean. Here on Karpathos, a place brushed only
slightly by time, she was determined to find answers, to
prove beyond all doubt that what she believed was true.

Her mind was filled with her work, awash in ancient stories, in the myths and legends she had collected single-
mindedly for the past year. But which legend was it that had
begun to haunt her sleep, even in her native Midwest,
where she was hundreds of miles away from the sound of
the sea? It was late when Meredith finally fell into sleep
once more. A sleep that was deep and, this time, without
dreams.

The village of Olympus faced the endless sea, a collection
of white churches and brightly colored houses clinging stubbornly to the tall mountain from which they had sprung
long ago. For Meredith, to enter this village was to pass into
another time.

Women walked through the streets or gathered at wells
far older than the town itself. They stepped lightly in
brightly colored shoes and stockings, triangular scarves
wrapped about their heads, their sturdy bodies clad in
handwoven white dresses clasped by wide belts and overlaid by embroidered blue vests. The steady music of the
sound that ruled their days—the rhythmic clack of the
loom—rose into the hot air as they smiled and called out to
the lone American woman in their midst.

Returning their greetings in fluent Greek, Meredith

walked through the village's main street, passing the
kapheneia, where old men sat around rickety outdoor tables
with demitasse cups of strong coffee, then past the taverna,
the rural inn she had left in favor of the more private house
by the sea. She exited the village, and the dusty street
quickly became a rocky path that paced the jewel-dark sea
on one side and the steep hills on the other.

Her destination, the secluded stone hut of the old woman
known to everyone on Karpathos as Flijanou, sat on a cliff
overlooking the sea. Flijanou had been given her name because of her astonishing ability to read fortunes in the dried
grounds left in a coffee cup: the *flijani*. Every village in
Greece had its share of elderly women reputed to be able to
predict the future in coffee grounds, but Flijanou was more
ancient than most—and considered more accurate than
most as well.

When she had first arrived in Olympus, villagers had told
Meredith that the old woman was a treasure trove of information about the sea and the local legends surrounding it.
Meredith had quickly introduced herself to Flijanou. Despite the twin gaps of culture and age, she had immediately
felt an uncanny rapport between them, a rapport that
Flijanou apparently also felt. In a surprising departure from
the usual reticence with strangers, she had invited the
American woman who called herself a "folklorist" to visit as
often as she wished.

As Meredith approached the little hut, a quavering voice
came from the shadowy recesses of the house, and the
black-kerchiefed head of Flijanou appeared in the doorway.
A delighted smile wreathed the leathery face with its wrin-
kled pathways of a long and hard life as she beckoned to
her caller. "Come inside, child," she called in Greek. "Get
out of that hot sun. I've made coffee, *gliko*, the way you like
it."

The invitation was a courtesy only. From previous visits

Meredith knew it would be no cooler, and far more stuffy, in the one-room hut crowded with walnuts, corn, tomatoes, and pickled fish—offerings left by clients in exchange for Flijanou's fortune telling skills.

Pouring small cups of thick, sweet coffee, the old woman offered her guest the better of the hut's two chairs, then took the other. She sipped her drink in silence, smiling a little, watching as Meredith drank her own coffee and opened her shoulder pouch to take out a small tape recorder and a thick notebook.

"Flijanou," she began, "today I'd like to ask you about—"

The old woman shifted on the unsteady chair. Leaning over, she peered into her guest's empty cup. "Come," she said. "I will read the *flijani* for you."

Meredith glanced at her in surprise. "I've been visiting you for two weeks and you've never wanted to before. Why now?"

"It is time."

Taking the cup, Flijanou held it with reverence, staring intently at the grounds on the bottom. "You are alone but will not remain so." The Greek woman's voice had fallen into a low singsong, and her head was bent so far over the cup that Meredith could not see her face. "He is alone, too, but he comes for you. As a dolphin sweeps after a fish, he will find you, for only you can help him. Only you."

Meredith stared at the black-kerchiefed head and felt the hairs on the back of her neck rise. *The dream.* The hunched over form of Flijanou wavered before her eyes as the familiar nighttime sensations reached out for her, their power even more intense in the hot light of day.

"What man?" She heard the harsh note in her voice and realized with a jolt that it was fear. This was ridiculous, she told herself. Nothing more was going on here than an old woman gazing into the dregs of a coffee cup. When Flijanou remained silent, though, Meredith said more sharply than she had intended, "Flijanou, answer me."

The Greek woman looked up. "You have shared your blood with the sea, haven't you?"

Meredith cocked her head. "My blood?"

"Yes, child." The old one's voice held a touch of impatience. "Your blood."

Meredith sat back in the creaking chair. She remembered the legend about that now; it was one of the first she had ever recorded. If a person was cut and even a drop of his or her blood fell into the sea, that one's soul would belong to the goddess of the sea forever. And she remembered something else as well.

During her first evening on Karpathos, she had gone for a walk along the beach, carrying her sandals in one hand as she splashed through the gentle waves. In the uncertain light of dusk, she had cut her foot on a rock. It hadn't been a bad cut. In fact, she had not even noticed it until the sting of salt water had made her glance down to see bright spirals of red rippling off through the clear water. The small wound had healed cleanly and she had forgotten all about it.

Until now.

"I did cut myself," she whispered. "On my first day here."

Flijanou nodded wisely. As she looked at Meredith her black eyes were suddenly keen, probing as knives, filled with an ancient and secret knowledge. Then just as quickly, a veil seemed to fall over those eyes. "That is all," she said. "The telling is finished."

Meredith fought to gather her thoughts. She had a trained mind, she reminded herself angrily. She listened to ancient beliefs and strange stories all the time. Why should this be any different? But it was, and no matter how she tried to rid herself of her uneasiness, it would not be banished.

Flijanou touched her hand. "You go now, child," the old woman murmured. "I am tired. I do not want to speak of the old stories today."

Almost relieved to have their session brought to such an early end, Meredith rose from her chair and helped Flijanou up. Clasping the younger woman's hand, Flijanou walked with her to the door. "Come back tomorrow, in the morning. We will talk then."

Meredith smiled at the other woman. "I will," she promised. "I'll look forward to it."

As she started down the rocky path something made her glance back at the little hut. Flijanou had remained in the doorway. It was obvious the woman was watching her, but there was too much distance between them for Meredith to see the expression on her face. She went on along the path, then looked behind her again. The old woman had not moved. Like a statue, she was still standing there. Watching.

CHAPTER
2

The full moon rose over the Aegean as night fell, proclaiming the time when the pull between the forces of land and those of the sea were at their greatest. On this night—alive with power and magic, as such nights have been since the world's beginning—Flijanou went down to the sea. She wore not her customary black but a loose white robe, and she went alone, casting many glances about her to make certain she was unobserved.

Karpathos was not a heavily populated island, and though in cosmopolitan Athens the hour would still be considered early, most of the people here were long since asleep. Those who weren't would not have interfered with Flijanou, even if they had seen her. They would not have dared. Deep within the consciousness of the people who inhabited Greece's remote islands, the old ways still held sway. Flijanou, in whom those ancient powers were said to reside, was not one to anger by spying.

Facing the sea, with the waves singing secret songs to accompany her, Flijanou carefully piled several flat rocks together. Slowly, her knees creaking in protest, she knelt before this simple altar and took three white candles from her robe. Placing them upon the flattest of the stones, she lit them reverently. Then she waited.

The giant moon rode the star-bright sky, the waves splashed and teased about the old woman's bare feet, and suddenly he was there. No splash announced his coming. The waves simply seemed to move aside, allowing first his dark head, then his torso to slip through the surface.

The rest of him followed, his smooth wet skin glimmering under the silver light of the moon. Tall, lean, and powerful, he strode through the shallows, appearing to Flijanou's dazzled eyes as one of the true gods—the ancient ones who had ruled the seas since time immemorial. She knelt, and he gestured at her impatiently, the ornate necklace about his neck flashing in the harsh moonlight.

"Arise," he said in Greek. "You do not need to do that every time we meet. It is neither necessary nor required." He put out a hand to help Flijanou to her feet. "It is arranged?"

She nodded. "Yes, lord. Since your coming to me last night, I have seen the young woman. She will visit my house again tomorrow morning, and I'll introduce you to her then. I plan to say you are a friend of mine who knows about the old stories she is so interested in."

He regarded her with approval. "Cleonith has proved her wisdom once again in advising me to seek you out first," he said warmly. "You have the gratitude of the merfolk, venerable woman of the land."

Flijanou ducked her head, embarrassed by the praise. "It is little enough," she mumbled. "Your Elder did me great

honor in allowing me the opportunity to uphold the obligation my family has owed the gods of the sea since the days
when my ancestors, the Amazons, rode free. Your king
helped my foremothers then. I only wish I could do more to
help you now."

"Believe me," he said, "you have done enough. More
than you know."

Flijanou gazed at him worriedly. She was feeling very
torn. There was no question that the weight of her ancient
lineage dictated she must do as the sea god asked. A bond
had been forged between her and Meredith as well, though,
a bond Flijanou herself did not fully understand. She did
not want to see the child hurt. The god had assured her that
he meant the young American woman no harm, but he had
not explained why Meredith was so important to him. and
his powerful kin. He had not done so when he'd appeared
at her door late the night before, and apparently he did not
intend to do so now.

Instead, he was turning to go back into the sea. "I will be
at your house at first light," he said over his shoulder.
"Farewell."

"My lord." Flijanou hesitated as he paused, glancing back
at her inquiringly. All the questions she wanted to ask tangled together, sticking in her throat before his penetrating
gaze. "Will ... will this woman be able to help you?" she
asked in a rush.

He was silent a moment. "That is what the powers of the
Elders say," he finally answered. "And by the Mother, I
hope they are right."

"There is one thing more." Caught up in the compelling
magnificence of her visitor, Flijanou had forgotten until now
what she had planned to tell him. "This woman," she said
hastily. "I read the coffee grounds for her today. I know
that is a weak magic compared to yours, but it does have its

truths. The grounds told me, and so did the woman herself, that she has shared her blood with the sea."

"Has she."

The deep strong voice gave no hint as to what the god was thinking. Lowering her eyes, Flijanou nodded. "I thought you would want to know," she said.

She looked up again, eager to see his reaction. Only the rippling sea met her eyes. The sea god had gone.

Seated at her dining table, Meredith sipped absently from a glass of wine and stared out the long windows she had flung open to the moon. She was not especially fond of Greek wine, but tonight the resinous aftertaste that bit her mouth with every sip was welcome. The presence of the dream hung heavy in the little house, its power called up and strengthened by her session with Flijanou. It left Meredith unsettled, far from eager to seek her bed, and deep in thought.

She had worked hard to get to this place in her life, and now it all seemed clouded, threatened by forces that were eating away at her concentration, leaving her distracted when she should be focused and intent. The answers she sought lay on Karpathos. She was convinced of that, had felt it the moment the ferry had brought her here. But something else lay here as well, and its force was growing stronger with every passing day.

She exhaled a deep breath, not quite a sigh, and refilled her glass. An incident that had occurred when she was studying for her doctorate came back to her, the words jabbing at her as sharply now as they had the day the professor had spoken them.

"You gentlemen," he had said to a lecture class in which Meredith was the only woman, "have a lot of traveling to look forward to. And to some rather lonely and uncomfortable places. However, that's the price you must pay for being a folklorist. The unusual, exciting knowledge that sets a man apart in this field is only to be found in the more primitive spots of the world."

In the front row of the lecture hall, Meredith — with an almost straight-A average and a master's thesis other professors had termed "brilliant" to her credit — had shifted angrily in her chair.

The professor, seeing the expression on her face, had smiled. "Our lone representative of the gentler sex apparently feels left out," he'd said dryly. "Well, I won't mince words. This is not a career for women. They aren't built to withstand the physical hardships, and there never has been, and never will be, a female with the mental discipline required of a serious researcher. Nothing will ever change that. *Gentlemen.*"

If she lived to be one hundred, Meredith would never forget his patronizing tone, nor the looks thrown her way by her male classmates. Some of the glances were slyly delighted, others embarrassed or sympathetic, but all of them added up to humiliation. Then and there she had sworn to make that professor eat his words. And she had. She was the first woman to ever earn a doctorate in folklore at the University of Wisconsin — Madison, and one of the few students to achieve it with a nearly flawless academic record.

That record, coupled with a relentless determination to succeed, had gained her a position in the department that had granted her degree. Though still at the bottom of the seniority ladder, she had published several research articles in scholarly journals and those articles had earned her considerable recognition in the field of folklore. In the past year the resentment of her male colleagues, who'd been uncomfortable enough with a woman invading their bastion, had turned to downright hostility. It was one thing to be a brilliant student, she had quickly learned, and quite another to be in competition with her former teachers.

Those who were not hostile were condescending, an attitude Meredith found even more irksome. Her department head fell into that category, especially with regard to the theory Meredith had advanced as her reason for requesting this sabbatical: to collect folklore regarding the existence of a city that predated the empires of the Egyptians, the Phoenicians, the Babylonians, a city inhabited by a race of superior people now extinct.

"Not more of this Atlantis nonsense," the man had interrupted with a groan. "It seems to be the latest thing—that, and aliens from outer space building the pyramids of Egypt. But I wouldn't expect a member of this department—even a female one—to jump on the bandwagon of such foolishness."

He looked her up and down with a jaundiced eye. "You're one of those girls who call themselves feminists, aren't you? Don't answer that. I know you are, otherwise you wouldn't be so damned insistent about traipsing all about the world instead of finding a husband and settling down to have kids." Without waiting for a reply, he went on. "Well, that's what comes of this women's rights garbage. Next thing I know, you'll be telling me the Amazons really existed too."

Seething, Meredith forced herself to remain silent. He was right, she barely managed to keep from telling him. She *was* a feminist, and though it had nothing to do with the matter at hand, she believed the Amazons had once existed, as well. However, the goal was to get permission for her sabbatical, so she refrained from arguing either point.

The strategy had worked, though more than once Meredith found herself wondering at what cost. It was struggle enough to be taken seriously by her colleagues, and the news that she was pushing a "crackpot" theory was most definitely not a step in that direction. In fact, she strongly suspected that the only reason her leave request had been granted so quickly was because her fellow professionals were eager to see her make a fool of herself!

Setting down the half-empty wineglass, Meredith let her gaze drop to the carefully wrapped parcel that lay in front of her on the table. Instantly, as though it were alive, it seized her attention—the precious object she had brought with her from Madison. The secret thing that lay behind all her theories. The whole reason for her being there.

The scroll.

Galen's head broke the surface of the Aegean, followed a moment later by Toklat's.

The sun was just beginning its ascent, gilding the rippling water with gold as it rose like a huge orange ball, seeming to come from the depths of the sea itself. Just ahead loomed the dark mass of the island, its bulk still cloaked by silvery night mists. The flat, winding beach protected by the little cove they swam in lay in shadow, not yet illuminated by the dawn. Behind it rose the towering mountains, as unchanged in the half-light, Galen thought, as they had always been.

"I don't know about this." Toklat's hoarse voice was strained as he and the merman floated effortlessly in the ocean's embrace. His wide eyes darted back and forth ceaselessly. "Are you sure this Flijanou woman can be trusted?"

"She's a friend, Toklat. One who thinks of us merfolk as gods. These days there aren't many of them left."

Toklat bared sharp white teeth, an odd sight, since he was still in his human form. "As far as Selkies, and our animal brothers and sisters the seals, are concerned," he said energetically, "there have never been friends among the land folk. They kill us every chance they get, either to eat us or wear us. Why, in older times, when we gathered beneath the full moon to dance in our human shapes, Terran men would try to steal Selkie women! I have no use for them, Galen, none at all. I hope you don't expect me to go upon the land to see this woman with you."

"No, brother-friend, I understand your feelings," Galen told him. And he did, though his own attitudes tended to be more enlightened.

Despite ancient merfolk traditions, such as historians visiting the land and the king taking a Terran as mate, the disdain of merfolk for landfolk had always been entrenched. Only within the last few thousand years had this long-lived scorn softened. That it had changed at all was due to one of the more celebrated ruling pairs of the merfolk, Dorian and Thalassa, as well as to a distant kinswoman of Galen's named Rhea, who had not only taken a Terran as mate but had brought him back to the sea with her.

These bold ones had challenged old beliefs and shaken the contempt many held for those who lived upon the land. Galen, born seven hundred years ago, had grown up in this new and more generous spirit. But now in the late twentieth century, the destructive grip of landfolk was tightening, not only upon their own world, but upon Mother Ocean Herself. As a result, many merfolk were returning to that earlier contempt, even to downright hatred.

"We, too, see the wisdom of being cautious around Terrans," Galen assured the Selkie. "However, this landwoman may be the only chance we have, and with Flijanou arranging my meeting her, I'll arouse far less suspicion than I would otherwise."

He frowned as he remembered the sad meeting with young Alaric's clan in their abode several days' swim from Karpathos. "Alaric is no better, and neither is Morat."

Toklat shivered despite the brightening sun. "But how do we know that a scroll from the Time Before even exists? Or if it does, that it contains any answers to what's happening to your people and mine? What if the legends are nothing more than mist and moon-talk?"

"Cleonith believes it exists," Galen said. "And all legends have their basis in some sort of fact."

Toklat snorted. "You sound like an Elder yourself."

Galen scarcely heard him. "By the Mother," he said softly, "I hope the Seeing was right, and this woman has what we seek."

With so smooth a motion he might never have been there, he slipped beneath the waves. But Toklat's keen Selkie eyes marked the merman's passage as he undulated toward the shore.

His gaze followed Galen for a long time.

Midmorning found Meredith climbing the path to the stone hut of Flijanou once again. She had finally shaken off the previous night's mood, though not without the aid of another glass of wine. The wine had helped her sleep. It had even kept away the dream, and now she felt refreshed, newly charged and ready to work.

Halfway up the trail she paused to admire the radiant tapestry of the Aegean spread out below the cliffs. Sun-shot and glittering with diamonds in the merciless light of morning, the sea moved to a gentle rhythm of its own, distracting Meredith momentarily with its beauty. Absently she tucked some loose strands of hair into the ponytail she had worn against the heat.

"I hope Flijanou's in a better mood today too," she muttered, then smiled at hearing herself voice the thought aloud.

She talked to herself often, a habit that had followed her from the time she was a child. "A quiet and unusually thoughtful child," her father had frequently remarked to her mother, a slight frown of disapproval on his face as he said it. The other children—always quick to notice anyone who acted differently—teased her unmercifully whenever they heard her mumble out loud. By her adolescence, a painful time during which Meredith's feelings of not fitting in were reinforced all too cruelly by her peers, the habit had become entrenched. Now at the age of twenty-eight, she no longer tried to break herself of it, just as she no longer cared what other people thought.

Flijanou was nowhere in sight when Meredith reached the hut. She was about to call out to announce herself when the familiar bent figure appeared from around the side of the house.

"Flijanou." Meredith stopped short. "You startled me."

"Hello, child. You're here at last." The woman gave her a preoccupied smile. "Come, I want you to meet someone."

Outlined in the harsh sunlight, a black-haired man strode from behind the hut. He was clad in worn khaki shorts and a faded red tank top, and his eyes—the most intensely blue eyes Meredith had ever seen—were fixed intently upon her.

"This man is known to my family."

Flijanou's quavering voice had taken on a note that Meredith found oddly formal. She glanced at the other woman and saw that she was even standing formally, as straight as her age would allow, almost as though she were introducing royalty.

Meredith turned back to look up at the man, and that in itself produced an unexpected sensation. Standing close to six feet tall without shoes, she was far more accustomed to looking down at or being at eye level with the men she met. She had always been tall, even as a child—another reason for the teasing she had endured, especially as a gawky and ungirlishly athletic teenager.

Unlike most Greek men who were short in stature, this black-haired stranger was taller than she. He had to be at

least six feet four, or even taller, Meredith mused. Everything about him bespoke strength. The shoulders and arms
revealed by the loose tank top were massive. And his eyes,
she thought in bemusement, his eyes were the exact color of
the Aegean. She suddenly became aware that she was staring at him, and equally aware that he was returning her
scrutiny just as closely.

She tore her gaze away as Flijanou went on. "His name
is Galen." Taking Meredith by the hand, the Greek woman
drew her forward. "This lovely child"—her voice was suddenly soft as she looked up into the tall man's face—"is
called Meredith."

"Meredith." Galen's eyes were still locked with hers. "I
am honored. It is a pleasure to meet you."

Meredith took the hand he offered. She possessed a
strong handshake, which sometimes disconcerted men
meeting her for the first time. This man wasn't disconcerted,
though. Long, calloused fingers curved warmly around hers,
his grip polite but filled with a controlled power as forceful
as the man himself. Meredith drew her hand back and regarded him.

Galen was an odd name for a Greek, if that was indeed
his heritage, for he spoke the language with a slight accent
she could not identify. His slightly rough voice also held an
elusive, seductive quality that she found almost hypnotic. It
made her think of the sound the waves made as they
washed along the beach below her house. . . .

Belatedly she realized that Flijanou was speaking again.
"The two of you will get along well together. This child"—
she turned to Galen—"has come all the way from the land
of America just to study our old stories about the sea. She
calls herself a folklorist, and for one who is not of our people, and young besides, she is surprisingly wise."

"Is she." Galen gave Meredith a speculative glance from

out of those fierce blue eyes. "I had that very thought when first I saw her."

He smiled, and Meredith felt an astonishing surge of intimacy, as if he had suddenly run his large hands up and down her body. Those electric eyes seemed to delve into her very soul, leaving her vulnerable—emotionally naked—all her secrets opened to his sapphire gaze. It was disquieting, more than a little alarming, yet there was a *rightness*, a feeling of unexpected familiarity that bewildered her as much as it shocked her.

With an effort she regained control of herself. She had spent too many nights alone in the house by the sea, she thought, had allowed herself to be caught up in the persistent call of the waves and the grip of too many dreams. Forcing polite interest into her voice, she asked, "Do you live on Karpathos too?"

His gaze had not left her face. "No, I came to see Flijanou."

"I asked Galen to come here, child," Flijanou explained, "so you could meet him."

"Me?" Meredith looked at her, startled.

"Of course. You want to know about the old stories, don't you? Well, he can help you. A young woman like you should not be alone with a man who is not her husband, but Galen is not like other men around here. He knows even more about the old stories than I do, and you may trust him not to do you harm."

"But . . ." Meredith's gaze flicked back and forth between the old woman and her towering friend. It seemed unlikely that this man, who only looked to be in his early thirties, could possibly know more about folklore than the venerable Flijanou. And for some indefinable reason, the thought that he might made her uneasy. "There's still a great deal I'd like to learn from you, Flijanou," she protested. "Our visits have just begun."

"Yes, yes." The Greek woman waved this aside. "They can continue, if you like. But Galen has a boat. He can take you to secret places that most do not know about, even those who have lived here all their lives. The things I can only speak to you of, he can show you. Is that not what you are seeking?"

Meredith thought about it. It was exactly what she was seeking, though she had intended to conduct such explorations by herself. However, could she really afford to pass up a chance to be with someone who knew these islands and could reveal things she might otherwise miss? In her three weeks on Karpathos she had come to trust Flijanou, who now vouched for this man. Surely the disturbing effect he'd just had on her was the result of last night's wine, combined with an overactive imagination.

She contemplated him as he stood beside Flijanou, completely at ease, waiting patiently for her to make up her mind. He seemed as serene as the sea that day, she thought, and felt a little smile steal across her face. "Well, if you're sure it's no trouble," she said to him, "it would be invaluable if you could show me around."

That dazzling smile lit his tanned face again. "It is no trouble," he said in his deep voice. "No trouble at all."

"Ah," Flijanou said happily. "Then it is settled."

"I guess so." Meredith pushed away the last lingering doubt, and in its place felt a surge of eagerness sweep over her. She gave in to it, her mind flying to the task ahead. "Would you both excuse me for a moment? I'd like to look through my notes and jot down some places Galen might know about."

Galen's stare followed Meredith as she walked around the side of the hut, lingering on her as she sat down in the shade of the doorway and tucked her long bare legs beneath her. He watched her flip through a notebook, his calm expression giving no hint of the astonishing effect she'd had upon him. He could not make himself stop looking at her, could not pull his attention away to focus it as he needed to.

Who was she? Where had she come from? His inner eye told him she was as unlike other landwomen as a seal was from a Selkie. If only this were an older time and place, with no danger looming over his people. Then he could wait until she was alone on some quiet strand and come to her for a few hours pleasure, as his people had done for eons when they saw a Terran who aroused their desire. Would he have then been able to leave her, though, been satisfied that he had plumbed the mystery of her?

Flijanou spoke, breaking into the turmoil of his thoughts. "Is she what you expected?" the old woman whispered.

Frowning, he continued to stare at Meredith. "No," he said shortly. "She is not."

"So she won't be able to help you?"

He heard the disappointment in Flijanou's voice, as well as the overwhelming curiosity. "I did not say that," he said evenly. "Thank you for bringing her to me."

"She keeps asking me questions about the sea," the old woman told him. "And remember what the coffee grounds said, lord. She has shared her blood with Her—the Goddess of the Waves."

Galen sighed. Despite his reassuring words to Toklat, he never, until this illness struck, would have conceived of a day when merfolk would be turning to Terrans for help. In the long history of the two peoples, those of the sea had always come to the aid of their savagely primitive cousins. Yet no matter how reluctant he was to place his trust in landfolk, he could not deny the extraordinary pull of Meredith herself.

"Lord." Flijanou was looking up at him, awe mingling

with apprehension on her lined face. "What do you plan to do?"

Meredith unfolded her long, elegantly muscled legs and stood up. A small smile tugged at the corners of Galen's mouth as she came toward them. "I will merely walk her home," he murmured to Flijanou. "Nothing more than that."

CHAPTER
3

Galen did not look at Meredith as they walked down the stony path from Flijanou's house. He didn't have to. Now that they were alone his awareness of her was even greater than it had been in the presence of Flijanou.

Yes, there was something about her, something he could not identify, that went far beyond the initial attraction her beauty alone had held for him. On some inner level his senses were reacting to Meredith as though she were not a landwoman.

But of course she was exactly that, he reminded himself, astonished that the question should even come into his mind. What else could she be?

"Where are you from?"

Galen didn't realize he might have asked the question too abruptly until he did not receive an answer to it. He looked at her to see a frown on her arresting face with its high cheekbones and smooth olive skin. Inwardly he cursed himself. He needed to befriend this woman, take her off her guard, so that he could quickly extract whatever information she possessed. Immediately he gave her his friendliest smile.

"I'm sorry," he said, switching to English. "Did I sound as if I were interrogating you?"

Her watchful look remained, though it was mingled now with surprise. "As a matter of fact, you did," she said in the same language, then added thoughtfully, "Your English is excellent." She regarded him for a moment, and when he did not speak, went on herself. "I'm from a city called Madison. It's in the midwestern part of the United States, in Wisconsin."

"Ah." Galen searched his seven centuries of memories for recognition of the place, but without success. He had visited the American continent several times, but not in two hundred years had he gone any farther than the lands along its ocean borders. "Is this Wisconsin near the sea?" he asked.

She grinned, and unconsciously Galen drew in his breath at the way her great dark eyes tilted upward with a merry glint. "No. In fact, it's about as far away from the sea as you can get. We have freshwater lakes, though. Two big ones right in Madison itself. In the winter they freeze solid and you can ice-skate to work—"

She caught herself with a little laugh. "Listen to me rambling on. You've probably never even seen a frozen lake, much less skated on one."

He nodded a bit impatiently. "Your name," he went on with determination, "is an interesting one. And rather unusual, no?"

Meredith gave him a puzzled glance. He had a way of asking simple questions as if the whole world spun on her answer. She shrugged mentally. Maybe he just had trouble making small talk. "My name is not that unusual," she told him. "Not in America, anyway."

"Do you know what it means?"

He asked *that* question as though he were quite certain she did not, and she took a small measure of satisfaction in replying, "Yes, I do. It's from the old Gaelic and it means 'protector from the sea.'" Turning the tables on him, she said, "Now you tell me something. How did a Greek fisherman learn to speak English so well, and also become so knowledgeable about Gaelic names?"

He was scrutinizing her with that odd intensity again. "Because one lives in a simple manner," he said with a quiet and severe dignity, "it does not follow that he is simpleminded."

"Of course not," she retorted, stung by his tone. "That's not what I meant at all. It's just that I've spent a lot of time in out-of-the-way places, both in Greece and the Middle East, and you're the first person I've ever come across who knows about old Gaelic."

"Then we are a surprise to each other."

His dark voice was soft and even, and Meredith had the strong impression that it was not names or out-of-the-way places of which Galen spoke. She met his gaze, and his blue eyes deepened until they seemed to be reaching into her very soul. They had almost reached the bottom of the path and the village of Olympus lay in the distance. Only the sound of the sea broke the silence that abruptly fell between them.

Looking into his eyes, which had become almost black, Meredith experienced again the sensation she'd had on first meeting Galen—that vivid and disconcerting *searching* of her. It was even more powerful, though short-lived, lasting no more than a few seconds. This time, Meredith broke it off by forcibly making herself look away.

Frowning, inexplicably embarrassed, she took a step to the side of the path, surprised to find she was slightly dizzy. It must be the heat, she thought. "Damn," she said, wondering at the shakiness of her voice. "That sun is hot."

Glancing back at Galen she saw that he, too, was frowning. *Scowling* was actually a better word for it. In fact, he was staring at her with an expression that coupled amazement with outright displeasure, a look Meredith found utterly bewildering. And annoying.

"You know, you're a very strange man." She matched his angry look with a direct stare of her own, pleased that her voice sounded even again. "Do you always look daggers at people you've just met, the way you're glaring at me?"

The frown stayed upon his face. "I do not. And as for being strange, I could say the same about you. Even more so, for you are . . ."

"I'm what?" she demanded when he didn't finish. "Not like the other women you know?"

A sudden smile twinkled unexpectedly in his eyes. "Exactly."

Meredith sighed. So that was it. It had not taken her long to find that male disapproval could come not only from her peers, but was a predictable reaction on the part of men who lived in the remote places to which she traveled. This last, however, was something she expected. She had encountered it so many times that she was used to it and had learned to conduct herself accordingly.

Why, then, was she annoyed at Galen? Perhaps because he had seemed different. In reality, he was no different at all. The last of her earlier excitement at finding a guide evaporated. In the past she had tried to glean information from local men who felt as Galen obviously did, and it had rarely worked out. His supposed knowledge aside, she had enough on her mind without trying to establish a working relationship with a man who disapproved of her.

"Listen," she began carefully. "I know Flijanou wanted you to help me, but maybe it's not such a good idea after all."

"Why is that?" The twinkle in his eyes vanished. He regarded her closely, the frown back on his face.

"Well, I think it just might be better . . ." Her voice trailed off. Galen was no longer paying attention. Instead he was gazing past her, those startling blue eyes fastened on the sea, his features stilled as though he were listening to sounds only he could hear.

"I must go," he said in a remote tone. "I will come for you tomorrow morning."

"Wait, I'm trying to tell you—"

He was already striding away from her toward the glittering white strand, and all Meredith could do was stare after him in exasperation.

"Okay," she finally muttered. "Come if you want. But it doesn't mean I'm going anywhere with you."

Galen walked rapidly along the diamond-bright sand until the village of Olympus was left far behind. The fishing boats of the Greeks were distant black dots on the bosom of Mother Ocean when he reached the spot where he had emerged from Her depths that morning.

Swiftly he stripped off the tank top and shorts, replacing them in the waterproof pouch he then fastened about his waist. Always, when he visited the land, this was the moment he looked forward to, the moment when he freed himself of Terran encumbrances and returned to that which was his. This day, though, his thoughts were not with the waiting sea, or even with Toklat, who had called to him and now waited beyond the breakers in the place where the waters began to grow deep.

Instead, Meredith filled Galen's mind. Meredith. Eyes as black and fathomless as the Midnight Sea, high-breasted, long-limbed—and possessing an inner power that surged like the waves. A strength that rivaled his own. He shook his head, and with a quick glance to make certain no one was watching, dove into the sea.

Toklat's restlessness flowed out to meet Galen long before the Selkie himself did. As further evidence of his impatience, he even surfaced, something he never did when Terrans were anywhere in the vicinity.

"You were so long away," he barked, his harsh voice coming out as if he were in seal form, rather than human. "Something went wrong, didn't it?"

Galen did not answer immediately, and that obviously worried Toklat even more. "Tell me of the landwoman," he urged. "Did you find her?"

"Yes," Galen said at last. "I did."

"Well? What happened?" Breasting a large swell that came rippling into the cove, Toklat leaned forward eagerly. "Does she have knowledge of the scroll?"

"I don't know!" Galen's voice was harsh, filled with so many shades of frustration, puzzlement, and even anger, that Toklat stared at him in astonishment.

"What do you mean you don't know?" The amazement in the Selkie's voice matched the bewilderment on his round face. "She's only a Terran. Surely you used your powers—"

"Twice I tried to probe her mind," Galen cut in roughly. "The second time, even more strongly than the first. Both times the woman rebuffed me. I cannot understand it. I've been over and over it in my mind, and I still can't make sense of how she did it. My mental abilities are my gift, Toklat. They are very great, they always have been. Only an

Elder is capable of withstanding me, and yet *she* did. Easily."

Toklat gaped at him. "She knows about you?" he asked in horror. "Something did go wrong, then! I knew it, I knew—"

"Of course she doesn't!" Galen threw him a shocked glance. "To her, I am a simple fisherman, a friend of Flijanou's. She doesn't know the truth about me any more than she grasps what she's done in pushing my mind away."

He stared out over the shimmering lapis water, frowning at the island, this piece of foreign world that held the enigmatic woman called Meredith. "Astounding and troubling, isn't it?" he muttered. "That she has absolutely no inkling of what she's done."

"I'd say more troubling than astounding." Toklat followed his friend's gaze, only he glared at the island with unconcealed hostility. Terrans called the place Karpathos, but merfolk and Selkies had a different and far older name for it, referring to it as "island of grottos where the seals come." Only most of the seals were gone now, shot by landmen with their guns, or drowned in the nets those same landmen used to catch more fish than anyone could possibly eat at one time.

Toklat was deeply concerned over this latest development. A landwoman who possessed abilities no landwoman should possess. There was danger here, his instincts had warned him of it from the moment he and Galen had arrived. Now he was sure.

"I don't like it," he declared. "No good ever comes from the land. It even reaches out to taint those parts of Mother Ocean unfortunate enough to be anywhere near it. This woman—"

"Her name is Meredith," Galen interrupted quietly, "and

she is not tainted." He was silent for a moment. "The prospect of spending more time on the land is not one I'm overly happy about, but it seems I have no choice. I will not leave until I have what we came for.

"But you, Toklat." He turned his head to meet the Selkie's dark gaze. "It is not safe for you to remain so near the haunts of landfolk for too much longer. I can pass among them, while you obviously can't."

"You'll get no argument from me there," Toklat said sourly. "But I'll stay anyway." He shook himself. "Danger circles us on the wind, Galen," he added in a low growl. "I smell it, as would you, if your thoughts weren't so caught up with this woman. Normally, I would flee, and warn you to do the same. But . . ." He hunched his massive shoulders. "Find out what you need to know quickly, my friend."

"Have some more of my *Demestika*, Meredith. It's the best red wine you'll taste on all of Karpathos."

Meredith smiled dutifully as Mr. Xanapoulos, owner of the one general store in Olympus, refilled her glass. After filling his own glass and that of his wife, he leaned his chair back against the stone wall of the enclosed courtyard and beamed at her happily.

Mr. Xanapoulos, along with the other villagers, had originally been suspicious of her, an American woman, unmarried *and* unnaturally educated, who had come there to write a book. But Flijanou's acceptance had brought about an immediate change, helped along even more by Meredith's excellent Greek. Now she found herself the recipient of friendly curiosity, a certain protectiveness, and more meal invitations than she had either time to accept or room in her stomach to accommodate.

Today, though, she'd been relieved to hear Mr. Xanapoulos call out an invitation to dinner when she'd passed his shop on her way home after Galen's abrupt leave-taking. The impact of meeting the tall stranger had remained, and Meredith was finding that she could not shake free of the inexplicable feelings he had loosed in her. Relentlessly they coiled about her. The peculiar way he had left her, though, bothered her the most.

She took a sip of the homemade wine, although her thoughts were swirling in so many directions she scarcely tasted it. "Flijanou introduced me to a man named Galen today," she said, accepting a plate of sliced cucumber, feta cheese, and olives from Mrs. Xanapoulos. "She says he can help me with my research."

"Galen?" Mrs. Xanapoulos looked thoughtful. "It is not a Greek name."

Meredith felt a stab of disquiet. "So you don't know him."

It was more a statement than a question, and Mr. Xanapoulos shrugged as he washed down a bite of fish with a mouthful of wine. "It is not important that we don't," he said, gesturing at his wife to bring more bread. "Flijanou knows many, many people. She is famous for her powers, our old one. They come to her from all over, from other islands, from the mainland, even from the mountains near Turkey. This man is probably someone like that."

"I see." Meredith ate some of Mrs. Xanapoulos's fish, a fresh red snapper baked in olive oil and herbs, but she was not yet ready to drop the subject. "Is there anyone else on Karpathos who might know him?"

Mrs. Xanapoulos bustled back to the table with another loaf of bread. "If we do not know him," she said positively, "then no one does."

"You needn't worry, though," Mr. Xanapoulos added. "If Flijanou introduced him to you, then he is, as you say in

40   JESSICA BRYAN

America, 'okay.' Flijanou likes you, and those she likes she
takes care of. Those she doesn't . . ." He rolled his eyes and
drew a hand across his throat. "Well, it is better if she likes
you," he concluded, and turned his full attention to eating.

After a dessert of fresh melon, peaches, and the ubiqui-
tous Greek coffee, Meredith said her good-byes and started
to leave. Mrs. Xanapoulos walked her to the door.

"You should not be staying in that house by the sea," the
woman said softly, touching Meredith's shoulder. "Nikos
should not have rented it to you when he went to Rhodes."

"Why?"

In the evening dusk, the other woman's face looked troubled. "It is so far away. You are alone there, with only the
sea to keep you company."

With only the sea to keep you company.

The words ran in Meredith's mind, each word vibrating
as if it possessed a life of its own. The arms of the dream
man tightened about her . . .

She twitched her shoulders. Hard. "I'm fine in the house,
Mrs. Xanapoulos," she said. "Really. It's very comfortable,
and the view is magnificent. I need the solitude to work on
my book. That's why I didn't stay on at the taverna."

The shopkeeper's wife shook her head. "It is not good for
a woman to be so alone. You're a stranger here. There are
many things you don't know."

"But that's why I've come here," Meredith reminded her.
"To learn about those things. And to give them the honor
they deserve."

Mrs. Xanapoulos was silent, gazing up at the American
woman who stood so much taller than she. "It is better that
you be among people," she finally said. "And some things
are better left unlearned." She made a surreptitious gesture
with one hand, which Meredith—well-versed in the practice
of old customs—recognized at once. "Our sons are married.

They have their own houses now. If you don't like the taverna, you could stay here, with us."

Touched, Meredith impulsively clasped the woman's hand. "That's very kind of you, Mrs. Xanapoulos, and I thank you. But you really don't need to worry about me. My work requires me to spend a lot of time traveling, and I've learned to be alone. I know that must seem strange to you, but it's what I'm used to." She smiled wryly. "Compared to some of the places I've been, Nikos's house is a veritable palace."

No answering smile lit Mrs. Xanapoulos's face. She shook her head, a sad little motion. "Well, perhaps you will change your mind," she murmured.

About to leave, Meredith paused in the doorway of the courtyard. She gave the woman a long, thoughtful look. "Mrs. Xanapoulos, does your wanting me to stay with you have anything to do with Flijanou's friend, Galen?"

Mrs. Xanapoulos's eyes widened. "No," she said promptly. "As my man said, Flijanou herself introduced him to you. I don't know why I'm talking about this now. It—it is just a feeling I have. On this island we are far from the rest of the world. Here, among the mountains with the sea all around us, we all have such . . . feelings, from time to time."

She laughed a little as she said this, but Meredith saw her fingers move furtively again in the same gesture she had made a moment earlier.

Mr. Xanapoulos appeared from behind the large oleanders that shaded the courtyard. "Why are you keeping the girl so long, woman?" he demanded of his wife. "Her manners are too good for her to tell you she wants to leave. If you don't let her go, she'll have to walk that steep path in the dark."

Meredith finally took her leave and headed home. The sight of Mrs. Xanapoulos, though, fingers twitching nervously at her side, nagged at her mind, a disturbing picture that would not go away.

The shopkeeper's wife had not crossed herself as so many Greek villagers did when speaking of things for which they felt divine protection was needed. The gesture she had made was one that predated Christianity by thousands of years. It was the sign against the evil eye.

CHAPTER
4

The eastern sky had not yet blushed pink when a lone figure emerged from the singing darkness of the Aegean and waded onto the deserted beach. The warmth that persisted even before dawn in this part of the world enveloped his body as he dressed himself. After shaking the water from his wet hair, he headed for the meandering path that led up from the strand.

Deep in a dream, Meredith and the faceless man were making love. His voice was a whispered singing in her ear, the words indistinguishable and yet somehow familiar. His arms, wet from the sea, curved around her; his legs smooth and muscled, intertwined with hers. She tasted salt on his lips as he kissed her, arched against him as he surged inside her, fierce and gentle and demanding all at once. Like the sea itself.

Her eyes jerked open.

Dazed, Meredith sat up in bed trembling from the intensity of the dream and her body's reaction to it, and wondering what had awakened her. It hadn't been the dream, though it had visited her with more power than ever before, mesmerizing her so greatly that she longed to have stayed asleep. For an instant she had had a feeling, as though someone were coming. But that was impossible. Her sleep-blurred vision told her it was still dark outside.

Glancing around the dim room, she swore under her breath. God, she had slept abominably, falling into a light sleep from which she'd wakened often. What was worse was her uneasy sense that the conversation with Mrs. Xanapoulos was in some way responsible. Rest had come at last, along with the dream. It seemed she'd slept deeply for only a few minutes, though, before this new thing—whatever it was—had awakened her.

Sighing, she crawled out of bed, and without bothering to slip on her robe, padded over to the long open window. The stars had faded and the moon had set. The sea appeared almost black under a sky that had not quite let go of night, had not yet given way to dawn.

Meredith propped her elbows on the windowsill. She had no concerns about someone seeing her naked. Even during the day, this stretch of beach saw few visitors, and at this hour there was no chance of anyone being about. Bearing a hint of the approaching morning, a warm breeze ruffled through her hair. With it came the salt tang of ocean, and Meredith smiled, letting her eyes drink in the sight that always soothed her no matter what her mood.

She had not grown up near the sea. In fact, she had never seen one of those vast bodies of ceaselessly moving water until the age of sixteen, when she visited Florida with her parents for the first time. She could not explain why she loved the ocean world so, but she had from the first moment her gaze had fallen on a limitless waterscape of rippling waves whose only horizon was the sky. She sighed again, gazing out over the silver-dark Aegean, welcoming the magic that its quiet, ever-changing beauty worked upon her.

Coming around the side of Meredith's house, walking with his noiseless tread, Galen froze. Framed in an open window, the landwoman stood gazing out to sea, her expression of yearning unlike anything he'd ever seen on the face of a Terran. She was unclothed, and his eyes drank in the sight of her, easily piercing the darkness around her. Her body was like an elegant poem created in flesh, punctuated by breasts proud and shapely.

Without the restricting cover of garments, Meredith was even more beautiful than he had dreamed. Her skin was dark, partly from the sun and partly from its own deep olive tint, and she looked strong—lean and muscled in the manner of women warriors from days long past. He could not take his eyes from her, though he was quite aware that *she* would have a different reaction if she saw him. Nudity did not come naturally to her people, as it did to his. And truthfully, he had not meant to spy upon her. She had taken him by surprise, standing at the window and gazing out at his world with such love.

Lifting her arms, she ran her hands through the thick mass of hair that lay tousled and loose over her shoulders. The movement was lithe, flowing with a grace that seemed easy and unconscious. Her breasts rose with her raised arms.

So did Galen's manhood.

No! he told himself. He fought down his arousal, tearing his gaze away from the woman who had sparked it. He was disturbed and angry with himself. It was not the wanting—who could not see such beauty without feeling desire? It was the strength of it, the overwhelming urge to stride forward, take her in his arms, and press those lovely breasts against him.

This was neither the time nor the place for such things. He was a seasoned adult, not some inexperienced youth discovering the joys of pleasure-making for the first time. He had sought this landwoman out for grave reasons, serious reasons. The survival of his people, as well as that of another folk, depended upon what he did here. How could he let himself forget that purpose, even for a moment?

He looked back at Meredith and saw a change washing over her face. The rapt expression was gone, her body had lost its grace, and she was tense and stiff, frowning. Had she realized —? With the quickness of a cat, Galen stepped into the screening cover of an oleander bush a moment before her eyes flashed to the spot where he had been standing. He frowned himself, wondering how she had known he was there, then he slipped around to the front of the house and rapped firmly on the door.

Startled, Meredith swung around. Gooseflesh shivered over the skin of her arms. Just a second ago she'd had the strongest sensation that someone was outside, and now someone was. Unbidden, the dream flashed into her mind, and with it, the troubled face of Mrs. Xanapoulos.

"Don't be so jumpy," she ordered herself aloud.

Still, the painful awareness that whoever was out there might have seen her naked at the window persisted. With her olive complexion Meredith rarely blushed, but now her face burned as she threw on her robe, sashed it tight at the waist, and turned to the bed table. Swiftly she drew out the small gun she had learned to shoot when she first began going on research trips. So far, she had never had to use it. But, she told herself grimly, there was always a first time. Holding the weapon with practiced ease, she strode to the door as the knock sounded again.

"Who is it?" she called out sharply.

"Galen."

Meredith stared at the blank wood. At the sound of that

deep rough voice, her blush intensified until she could feel it burn from the roots of her hair all the way down to her breasts.

"Meredith?" he said with a touch of impatience. "Are you still there?"

She exhaled and swore under her breath. "Just a minute," she snapped. Returning to the bedroom she replaced the gun, then went back to the door. She yanked it open. "What are you doing here?" she demanded before he could speak. "Do you have any idea what time it is?"

Galen's towering form filled the entryway. He looked down at her, his gaze searing her. He *had* seen her, she thought in consternation. Then again, maybe he hadn't. He had such an intense way about him, it was hard to know for certain.

"You are not ready," he said without preamble. "I told you I would come this morning."

"This morning!" Caught between astonishment and growing anger, Meredith peered past his broad shoulder. "It's not even dawn yet!"

Unruffled, he glanced behind him at the dark expanse of water. "It will be soon. I assumed you would want to get an early start."

Meredith leaned against the doorjamb and glowered. The arrogance of the man was incredible. But behind his looming form, a shadowy vision was taking shape: Mrs. Xanapoulos making her furtive gesture of protection.

"I tried to talk to you about those arrangements yesterday," she said coldly, hiding her disquiet. "But you went marching off as if I wasn't even there."

He gazed at her, his expression unreadable. "I suddenly remembered some urgent business I had to attend to." He flashed a smile. "I'm sorry if I took my leave too abruptly."

Meredith eyed him. Dressed exactly as he had been the day before, he looked well rested for the early hour. He was even wet, as though he had gone for a swim before coming there. And, she realized, he was just as compelling, and therefore just as unnerving, as she remembered. His physical presence was overwhelming, even more so with the nagging speculation that he might have seen her at the window.

The thought made her flesh tingle, alive with fresh uneasiness. Those piercing blue eyes seemed capable of burning a hole right through the thin silk of her robe. She could almost feel his gaze brush against the hint of cleavage revealed by her robe, and the heat that suffused her made her feel as if she were indeed standing in front of him naked. Hurriedly, she drew the edges of the robe together.

It was hard to admit to herself that this man had her rattled. Something in her rebelled even more strongly at letting *him* know that he could have that kind of effect on her. Still, she could not allow anyone or anything to interfere with why she was on Karpathos.

"Look, you're obviously very busy," she said. "It's not fair of me to take up so much of your time. After all, you only offered to do this in the first place because of Flijanou. I'm sure she'll understand if I explain to her that it didn't work out."

He held up a hand in a manner Meredith could only describe as imperious. "I would not have offered if it were inconvenient," he said, his tone matching the gesture. He put his head to one side, studying her. "You do not feel easy with me." It was a statement of fact. "Perhaps you would feel better if I told you the truth about myself."

She straightened against the door. "The truth?"

"Yes." He was looking into her face, his expression open and straightforward. He sent her another dazzling smile. "You needn't look so apprehensive. I was only going to explain that I am more than a fisherman. I spend a great deal of time here, yes. But I work also at the University of Athens. As an archaeologist. Flijanou knows this, which is why she asked me to help you."

"Why didn't you say so in the first place?"

Galen met Meredith's suspicious gaze squarely. Now was the time to bluff a little, to probe and see what lay beneath the rocks on the ocean floor. "For the same reasons you are not anxious to advertise your own true purpose for being here," he said softly. "You are conducting research on things you would rather not discuss openly. So am I."

Ah! So he had struck a nerve. Galen felt a thrill of discovery that overwhelmed even the powerful desire Meredith aroused in him. At last he was getting somewhere.

It might be true that this Terran woman possessed inexplicable powers she was not aware of, but an unreadable countenance was not among them. Her shock was mirrored plainly on her face, so plainly that Galen smiled again, taking care to keep his own reactions well in check.

"I have not shared my speculations," he assured her. "Nor will I. I mention this only to convince you that we should work together. We are probably the only two educated people among these islands, and since our fields of study are complementary rather than competitive, we can be of use to each other. Don't you agree?"

She looked at him a moment longer, then stepped back from the door. "Come on into the house," she said in a businesslike tone. "It won't take me long to get ready."

He followed her inside, his gaze sweeping quickly around the house's interior. He did not often enter the dwellings of Terrans and he always found them interesting, though in this case, his interest was not one of idle curiosity. He was searching for some sign that what he sought was there.

"I'll get dressed."

She looked away from him as she spoke, and Galen kept his face impassive, forcing back the image her brief statement evoked, of her *un*dressed at the window, her skin shimmering in the darkness. Perhaps his expression was not neutral enough, though. Meredith suddenly glanced back at him, and their eyes met. Her face turned several shades brighter.

"It'll be just a minute," she added, and retreated into the bedroom, closing the door behind her. Firmly.

Galen wasted no time. Immediately he began prowling about the living room of the little house, careful not to disturb anything. Books and papers lay scattered in profusion over the long dining table, along with half a dozen notebooks and the tape recorder he had seen her carrying the day before. Here was where she apparently worked. But the crowded table held no scroll or anything that resembled it.

She must have it somewhere else in the house, he thought, frustrated. Or perhaps she didn't have it at all. Perhaps he was mistaken about her altogether, and with so much hanging in the balance, he was swimming along with the wrong current!

Savagely he muttered a curse in his own tongue. He was turning away from the table, when something caught his eye, jerking him back as though a hand had reached out and grabbed him. A piece of paper was sticking out of one of the notebooks. Only part of it showed, but there was enough for Galen to see that it contained a number of words.

Words written in the language of the merfolk.

Incredulous, Galen pulled the paper free and held it up. The words were crudely depicted, as if someone had traced them out without understanding their meaning. They formed part of a sentence, copied over and over . . .

"What in the *hell* do you think you're doing?"

Meredith, dressed in loose shorts and a sleeveless cotton top that ended at her midriff, stood glaring at him from the doorway of the bedroom. Her dark eyes blazed as she stomped over to him.

"How dare you go snooping through my papers! Especially after that speech about telling me the truth so I'll trust you. Is this how they conduct research at the University of Athens? By stealing someone else's work!"

She snatched at the paper, and Galen's hand closed around her wrist.

"Where did you get this?"

His voice was low and controlled—too controlled, containing a fierce undercurrent that Meredith might have noticed if she hadn't been so angry. "None of your business!" She tried to yank her wrist free, and a part of her noted the warmth of his hand, as well as its strength. He held her with surprising ease, and that observation only fueled her anger.

She grabbed for the paper again, and this time he released her wrist and let her take it. "Do you know what these words mean?" he demanded in that same low tone.

"Why?" She glared up at him. "Do you?"

"Yes," he said simply. "I do."

A wave of stunned excitement smothered Meredith's anger. For more than a year—ever since the scroll had come into her possession—she had been trying to decipher the language it was written in.

She had friends among the faculty in the archaeology department at her university and, without explaining where she had gotten the materials, she had asked these friends to examine several samples she'd laboriously traced out on paper. All had told her that the strange characters belonged to no tongue developed during the ancient civilizations—none of the great ones or any of the lesser ones. Obviously, whatever she had taken her samples from was a fake, they said sympathetically. Someone was playing a trick on her, trying to make her think she had found something of value.

Unconvinced, Meredith had gone to the head of the archaeology department himself, a man renowned in archaeology circles for his knowledge of ancient languages. He told her the same thing. Still, something deep inside Meredith refused to accept that the inexplicable characters were meaningless. And now, this stranger was telling her they did indeed comprise words, and that he understood them!

"What do they mean then?" she asked. "Tell me."

He looked down at her without answering, and for the first time she saw the flames glittering in his eyes, the muscles bunching in his jaw, as though he could barely keep himself under restraint. "You have not told *me* yet," he said tightly, "where you got this from."

Meredith's own anger began to resurface, but she held it in check. There was no sense in losing her temper again, she told herself, and anyway, at this point, she was more disappointed than angry. "You're bluffing, aren't you?" she said. "You don't know what these depictions mean any more than I do. I think you'd better leave."

She stared determinedly into his face, and he stared back. As had happened the day before, his fierce eyes deepened, searching hers, growing so dark they became almost as black as her own. She blinked, feeling as dizzy as she had on the path, and his hands reached out, gently gripping her shoulders.

"Meredith." His voice was mesmerizing, a soft, husky croon. "Tell me what I wish to know. Tell me . . ."

He drew her closer, and Meredith did not resist. To look away from his face had become impossible. She felt something in him reach out for her, and something in her answered. It rose up in her like a tide, compelling beyond reason or thought. She lifted her arms and slowly put them around his broad shoulders. He tensed, as if she had startled him, then his whole body seemed to envelop hers as he pulled her against him and lowered his lips to hers.

His arms were like bands of steel, the thud of his heart deep and powerful as a drum, beating in a wild rhythm that echoed the same frantic cadence of Meredith's. His lips seared hers. His breath was hot in her mouth, and the hard muscles of his bare upper thighs thrust against her lower belly, the bulge between them only lightly concealed by the thin material of his shorts.

Then, as quickly as their lips had come together, they parted.

Galen stared down into Meredith's face, his arms still locked around her slim, strong back. He was deeply shaken, far more than he cared to admit, even to himself. He had been totally focused on probing the landwoman's mind once and for all. Where had the driving urge to kiss her come from, descending on him with a need so strong, it had overridden everything else?

He dropped his arms. "That was a mistake," he said, frowning. "I—"

"You're right." Whatever had taken hold of Meredith vanished like the "pop" of a soap bubble, leaving her feeling as though she had fallen headfirst into a cold sea. "It *was* a mistake," she said quickly. "Mine. Now if you'll just get out of here, we can both forget this unfortunate incident ever happened."

She stepped back from him, and Galen saw the anger in her eyes and, held deep below that anger, the hurt. It stung him. None of this was her fault. Whatever forces she exerted upon him, he was convinced she was completely unaware of them. He was equally certain she had no idea of the scroll's significance. To her it was simply an impressive artifact, a rare find that would no doubt gain her great recognition in this folklore profession of hers.

He could not allow that, of course. But the methods he had expected to succeed with her had not worked. He could try again—the very thought of pulling her back into his arms was a seductive one. It played on his senses with heady anticipation, shocking him at how easily this woman could distract him. He would have to find another less physical means of discovering where the scroll was.

"I did not mean it that way," he began in a gentle tone.

Meredith shook her head, refusing to be mollified. She was as taken aback as he by what had happened, and deeply chagrined, as well. The fact that she had enjoyed the kiss—no, that was too calm a way of describing it. Galen's mouth had sent rivers of sensations coursing through her, sensations she had not known existed, and that just made the chagrin worse.

"I don't care what you meant," she said in a voice as stiff as her posture. "I've asked you to leave. I don't want to tell you again."

"Meredith, wait." He stepped forward, stopping just short of touching her. "I'm sorry about . . . I did not mean to lose control. And it won't happen again. But I still want to work with you. And whether you admit it or not, you need me."

"Need you?" Her tone grew frosty. "I don't see how."

"Then you don't see very much," he snapped. He paused to draw in a deep breath, then continued in a placating tone. "Who else can interpret the language on this sheet of paper for you?"

Meredith eyed him. If he was telling the truth, if he really could make sense out of those characters, then despite the problems he presented, he was an answer to her prayers, to this obsession that would not let her go. She bent and picked up the fallen piece of paper.

"Prove it." She held it out to him. "What does this say?"

He ignored the paper, staring steadily at her. "We will work together, then?"

She frowned as she returned his stare, trying to probe whatever lay behind his handsome face. "Why is it so important to you that we do? I can see why you might think

I need you, but what do you get out of this? What do you want, Galen?"

He took the paper from her. *"The season of destruction will soon be upon us and our city,"* he read deliberately, *"but I may have found a way to save some of us, we who were once among the most powerful in the sea. Near the long and narrow island that is but a stone's throw from Crete, the island split by Mother Ocean into two halves ..."*

He stopped. "It ends there." His voice was low and fierce, as fierce as his gaze, which seemed to reach out to grip her. "Are you satisfied now? Or do you require still more proof?"

CHAPTER 5

Meredith tore her gaze free of his. Taking a step back, she turned away so Galen would not see her face.

He did know!

The realization set off a storm of conflicting emotions so powerful, she almost wished he didn't. Abruptly she was transported back to the last days of her mother's life. More than a year had passed, yet the sights and smells of sickness that could not be cured were still painfully vivid. The picture of a once vibrant woman ravaged by cancer lying wasted and in pain in a hospital bed was indelibly carved in Meredith's memory.

Her mother had refused the drugs that might have made her more comfortable at the end. She had talked to Meredith instead, even when her strength had begun to fail with ever-increasing speed, telling her only daughter of the lead-lined strong box she was leaving her, and of what the box contained: a scroll passed down from mother to daughter for so many generations, with the origins of the tradition having long since been lost.

It's our only true heirloom, she'd said with a wan smile, and worth several fortunes, not only because of its antiquity and the hieroglyphics that were as much a mystery as the scroll itself, but also because of what those hieroglyphics were carved upon. Fifteen sheets of gold, beaten into a paperlike thinness through a skill that had been lost eons ago.

Torn with grief, tears clouding her eyes, Meredith had listened as her mother explained that no one knew what the scroll said. Any attempts to decipher it had long since been given up. All that mattered was that it stay in the female line, guarded from the eyes of others, including husbands and sons.

Meredith could still recall the smell of the sickroom, the rasp of the dying woman's breathing, and the confusion in her own mind as she tried to understand this sacred inheritance her mother was using the last of her strength to describe. But why? she had asked, the scholar in her rising up despite her grief. To keep something like this a secret when it might have enormous historical value—

Her mother's eyes had flashed in a resurgence of her old vibrancy. "It is a trust," she said. "A trust we have to keep. The scroll is an obligation held by our family alone. God forgive me, I should have talked to you about this sooner, but I didn't want to burden you as I've been burdened. To take on the responsibility of the scroll is to take on a weight you'll carry for the rest of your life. I can't explain it, but it must never be shared, never . . ." She had grown so agitated that Meredith had hastily dropped her questioning and promised to do as she wished.

Her mother had done one other thing before slipping into the sleep that would later become the coma from which she would not awaken. Asking for paper and pen, she had scrawled out several lines of unfamiliar symbols. These phrases had survived through the years, she'd whispered. Where on the fifteen sheets of gold they came from was not known. But somewhere during the passage of time these characters had been translated. She'd handed the paper to Meredith and told her their meaning.

It was what Galen had just read.

Meredith had herself traced and retraced those mysterious symbols out onto the piece of paper he now held. For him to have read word for word the sentences her dying mother had whispered to her during their last hour together was proof beyond doubt that he was telling the truth.

"Meredith?" There was a note of concern in Galen's voice. "Are you all right?"

She forced her features into what she hoped was an expression of composure, and slowly turned back to him. He was scrutinizing her, his face tense. Clearly, he had his own secrets, she thought, and she wondered what they were.

"These words mean something to you," he said flatly. "Do not try to tell me they don't."

She looked at him without answering.

"They are the same sentences, copied over and over." He threw the paper onto the dining table, the simple movement filled with a subtle, leashed violence. "Show me something else, and I will translate that for you as well."

She shook her head. "That won't be necessary. You've convinced me."

The consternation of Galen repeating the same words her mother had was fading as her earlier excitement returned. He truly would be able to unravel the scroll's ancient secrets! If only she could accomplish it without telling him about the scroll itself.

Galen watched the hunger for knowledge flare up in her eyes, and saw also that she was trying to hide it. Sea and Sky, but she was the most maddening and incomprehensible of women! Here he was so close to his goal, only to find himself thwarted by a Terran woman with powers she had no business having!

"Good," he said, his face a careful mask.

She stepped over to the table. Picking up the paper, she stared at it, then lifted her thoughtful gaze to him. "I've shown this to other archaeologists," she said slowly. "One of them is the head of the department at my university. He's widely regarded as one of the leading experts in the world on ancient languages. He told me these were nothing but a bunch of meaningless symbols. In fact, he stopped just short of accusing me of having made them up. How is it that you can make sense out of this and he couldn't?"

Galen met her eyes steadily. "Not knowing the man, I cannot answer that. All I can tell you is that I, too, have been fascinated by this language. I have ... studied it for some time—"

"Where?" she interrupted sharply. "Where else have you seen it?"

He was silent for a long time. "On tablets deep within the sea," he finally said.

Meredith's eyes, her whole face, came afire, blazing with such a light that Galen would have been driven to take her in his arms again if so much were not at stake.

"Which sea?" Her voice was slightly hoarse in her excitement. "*Which sea, Galen?* When did you excavate them? Can I see—"

He shook his head. "You must trust that I believe as you do," he said quietly. "But I have my own reasons for not answering your questions right now." He gave her a sharp look. "Just as you have for not answering mine. However, there is a place off the coast of this island that you may find interesting. It's an underwater cavern located in a cove. I can take you there, if you wish."

He watched as she tried in vain to curb the zeal that lit

her eyes. That driving need to learn, to know more, was something she could not disguise. Yet he could see that she was wary of him, confused and puzzled by his knowledge. As he was of hers, he said silently to himself.

"You still haven't answered the question I asked you before," she pointed out, frowning. "What is it *you* want, Galen?"

He made himself shrug. "The same things you want. Learning, wisdom, the solving of ancient mysteries." He spoke softly. "We are kindred spirits, you and I. Engaged in the same search."

"Are we?"

"Yes. I have a boat waiting down on the beach. We can go now. This place might shed light on what you seek."

She was still cautious. "I haven't said I'm seeking anything," she reminded him. "Except for stories and legends about the sea."

"You are searching for evidence to support that," he said, pointing to the piece of paper. "I am interested in the same thing. All I ask is that we work together."

Meredith hesitated. Common sense was shouting at her to stay away from this troubling man, but common sense no longer seemed to have any place here. Something far stronger was drowning it out: the sea, and all the mysteries that it contained.

"All right," she said. "Let's go."

Galen smiled.

Driven along by a stiff breeze, the caïque, single-sailed and gaily painted, made its way along the coast of Karpathos. The island's shore was long and narrow, deeply indented by countless coves and bays, each fringed by a broad swath of golden beach. Overhead the sun burned in a sky as hard and glittering as blue glass.

Seated in the bow of the boat, Meredith impatiently watched Galen's skillful handling of the sail. Like most caïques these days, the small boat had an outboard motor. Galen had disdained to use it, though, saying the wind would be quite sufficient to bring them to their destination. Meredith, however, would have preferred the motor, if only because it might have meant getting there more quickly.

On any other morning she would have been content to laze along, drinking in the beauty of the jewellike bay over which they sailed, delighting in the feel of sun and wind and spray upon her face. But today all she could think of was what Galen knew and what he might show her. And of what she had to keep from showing him, she reminded herself uneasily.

Keeping the scroll a secret had not been a difficult task when everyone to whom she showed the sample of text called it worthless. Galen, however, presented a new and troubling complication. He not only believed as she did, but had information of his own. That made him both an ally and a threat. How could she find out more without dishonoring the vow she had made to her mother?

Looking over at him, she found herself momentarily distracted by the smooth play of powerful muscles beneath his tanned skin. She glanced away, but was unable to keep from watching him out of the corner of her eye. His presence alone was enough to make her lips burn with memories of the fiery kiss they had shared at her house. As hard as she tried to shut those sensations out, to push them away, they slyly popped up again, haunting her with every move he made.

Though he had been quiet since she had agreed to go with him, she often felt the heat of his gaze brushing against her. Apparently he was having as hard a time not looking at her as she was with him. She wasn't sure if that thought consoled or troubled her.

"Tell me about this cavern," she said abruptly. "Where along the coast is it?"

Galen's face was unreadable in the intense sunlight that shone off the glistening waters of the bay. "Off the island's southernmost tip," he replied. "The waters in which it lies are very deep."

"I see." She gazed out over the water, her impatience eating at her. "And the evidence you spoke of. Are there tablets inside, or engravings on the cave walls?"

His attention was on the boat's rudder. "There are many stories about this cave," he murmured in a neutral voice. "It will be easier to explain them when we arrive there."

Another twenty minutes dragged by, though to Meredith it seemed more like hours, before the caïque entered the cove where Galen said the cave was located.

"The entrance to the cavern can only be seen through those rocks," he began explaining, then abruptly fell silent.

His tanned face underwent a transformation so profound, Meredith could scarcely believe she was looking at the same person. As though he had completely forgotten her presence, he leaned forward, staring past her, his features twisted into a mask of fury, his gaze as narrowed and glittering as the edge of a sword.

Astonished, she swiveled around to find the cause of this change in him. All she saw were the sparkling crystal waters of the cove. "What is it?" she cried, turning back to Galen. "What's wrong?"

His face still set in that terrible expression, he did not reply. It was as if he had not even heard her.

Meredith looked out at the cove again, trying to see what he saw. This time she caught a glimpse of a swimmer, a distant figure whose pale blonde hair shone wetly in the harsh sunlight.

"Is it the person who's out there swimming?" she asked. "Galen, answer me!"

His eyes focused on her. "You see him?" he hissed. "You *see* him?"

"Of course," she said, confused. "What of it?"

He stared out over the water again. "Can you see him now?"

"Yes." She was beginning to lose patience with this inexplicable behavior. "Just barely, but he's still out there. He's obviously some tourist who decided to go for a swim. What in the world is wrong with you, Galen?"

He jerked the rudder so hard, the caïque heeled about sharply, throwing Meredith forward. "Hey—" she began in astonished anger.

Savagely Galen yanked at the cord that controlled the motor, and a harsh sputtering filled the air as it growled to life. An instant later, he sent the boat racing over the waves.

Straight toward the bobbing head of the distant swimmer.

Within seconds it became apparent to Meredith that he was heading for the man deliberately, as though he intended to drive the caïque right over his head!

"Galen." Her anger and bewilderment were rapidly changing to concern. "You're going to hit that guy if you're not careful!"

He ignored her.

The boat shot closer, enabling Meredith to get a better look at the swimmer. He was a handsome man, with pale blonde hair that caught the sunlight, hair so long that it snaked wildly over his shoulders. Treading water, he watched their approach. Instead of moving out of the way, as he had ample time to do, he inexplicably stayed in the path of the oncoming boat. Meredith stared in disbelief.

The man was smiling.

"Galen!" Now she was really worried. Had both he and the swimmer out there gone completely crazy?

Still, Galen paid her no heed. His strong hands drove the caïque forward with deliberate and deadly skill. Before

Meredith could try to stop him by lunging across the small space that separated them, they were upon the man in the water.

At the last possible instant the man dove, although she could not be sure, everything was happening so fast. Then they were past, and Meredith was grabbing at Galen's arm, an arm that felt like ridged iron beneath her fingers.

"Have you taken leave of your senses?" she yelled at him. "You could have killed that man!" She swung around, anxiously searching the waters behind them. "My God, maybe you did. I don't see him!"

"He is alive." Galen's deep voice was frigid. "You need not concern yourself over him. It would take more than this puny vessel to kill that one."

"Good Lord!" Astounded at his callousness, Meredith gaped at him for an outraged second. Finally she found her voice. "I came out here to do research," she exploded, "not to watch you and some lunatic tourist play chicken!"

He frowned, slowly seeming to come back to himself. "Chicken?"

"Yes, chick—oh, never mind! How do you and that man know each other? And what possessed you to do such a thing?"

He looked at her without speaking, as if weighing his response. Frustrated by his silence and still upset over what she had just seen, Meredith snapped, "What the hell is it with you? Do you have some kind of feud going on with him?"

His eyes turned to blue ice. "One could say that."

"Well, even so, that hardly gives you the right to try to murder the man!"

"He is no man." Galen spoke in a low voice that sent prickles up her spine. "He is an evil. Nothing more, nothing less. As for rights, you know nothing of the rights I have where he is concerned."

It was an enigmatic statement, as enigmatic as the man himself, and nonplussed, Meredith stared at him. Then she looked around again, expecting—hoping—to see the blonde swimmer stroking safely toward the beach. All that met her eyes was an unbroken expanse of rippling waves. Nowhere did a blonde head push through to disturb the shimmering surface.

"We have to go back," she told Galen, tense and anxious. "I don't see him. Galen, you may have really hurt him."

Galen was concentrating on her, though, and not on the swimmer. "How did you know he was out there in the first place?" he suddenly asked her. "He was very far away. Too far away for your eyes. How could you see him?"

"You saw him!" She was disconcerted by his accusing tone of voice, by his fierce scrutiny, and most of all, by his complete lack of concern for the man in the water. "Anyway, what difference does it make? We have to find that man and make sure he's all right!"

Galen shook his head. "We are going back," he said. "Now."

"Wait a minute—!"

"Do not argue with me, Meredith. I am sorry, but we must go back."

Under her furious, uncomprehending gaze, he started the motor again, more sedately this time, and sent the boat puttering back the way it had come.

Toklat lingered restlessly in the waters around Karpathos. To human eyes the quiet coves and bays appeared serene, but for the Selkie's taste, they were far too crowded. He longed to dive beneath the waves and strike out for open sea, rushing away from the fishermen who plied these waters and distorted the Mother's surface with their ugly little boats.

Instead, he prowled along the shoreline where Galen had headed in toward land early that morning. When he saw his brother-friend bring a landwoman to the small boat Galen had obtained the day before, Toklat growled deep in his throat.

"So that's her," he muttered, unimpressed. "I don't see any power in her. She looks just like any other Terran female. I wonder where he's going with her."

He watched as, with Galen working the vessel's one sail, the two set off. Personally, Toklat disapproved of boats, of that artificial means of traveling over the Mother. But in the myriad centuries that the sea people had shared the world with those who lived upon the land, many of the merfolk had taught themselves to sail boats, more out of amusement than for any other reason. Galen was among them. And he could hardly, the Selkie reminded himself, swim off with the Terran woman.

Toklat sighed, then in the time-honored Selkie tradition of always keeping one's belly full in times of trouble, he decided to remain in the area and go hunting while Galen did whatever he needed to do with the woman.

Eating was an act of wisdom, the old ones said. Eating brought strength, and strength meant survival. But it did not bring peace of mind, Toklat reflected as he swam after a school of darting silversides. It did not remove the nightmarish pictures of the hideous things his people had turned into before they died.

Toklat had not shapechanged since the terrible morning of his father's death. Three had recently tried it, only to suffer the same agonies as the others before them. Twisted and screaming before their helpless kin, they had writhed in anguish until the kindness of death released them.

Now everyone swam in the shape he or she had had when the plague first appeared, afraid to switch from seal to human and back again with the careless ease that had once been theirs. They were terrified and they looked to Toklat, their new king, to find some cure for this affliction that had come out of nowhere to ravage them.

Though he could not allow them to see it, Toklat was as afraid as they. There was a bitter similarity to what faced his people and what their allies, the merfolk, suffered. Locked in one shape, the Selkies were prisoners of this evil as much as Alaric and Morat, who still lived, but without their gills. They were locked in Galen's abode, shut away from the sea that was their heritage, their very life.

Brooding on these thoughts, Toklat caught up with the silversides. Moodily he shoved several of the small fish into his mouth. He did not particularly like hunting in his human shape. He felt it made him slower, though Galen always laughed and argued that it did not, that merfolk were as fast as Selkies in their seal shape during any turn of the tide. Abstracted, thinking about Galen and the landwoman, Toklat followed the school of fish as it descended into deeper and deeper waters.

You should be more careful, Selkie. Hungry sharks could easily catch so inattentive a meal as you.

Toklat jerked to a stop, the silversides forgotten. The words that came into his head had been sent telepathically, but the coldness in them was as clear as if they had been spoken aloud. He stared at the merman who had appeared from the depths.

Anastas.

Toklat knew him, and he knew what had happened to him. Who in all the oceans did not? But he had changed so much, the Selkie scarcely recognized him.

Long yellow hair floated about the merman's shoulders, unkempt and tangled as no mermen or women of Toklat's acquaintance would ever allow their hair to become. Like all his kind, Anastas was tall and heavily muscled. But no necklace glittered around his neck to indicate the ancestral clan to which he belonged. His pale green eyes were sunk deep in circled hollows that, despite the power of his muscular frame, made his face seem emaciated. There was a look in those eyes—a look Toklat had never seen in the eyes of any creature before, yet recognized deep in his bones. If he had been in seal-shape he would have bristled.

I will not speak with you, he sent out. His hostile gaze went past Anastas to include the five mermen who hovered in the shadows, all of them as wild and disheveled as their leader. *Neither you, nor those with you.*

He turned his back and began to swim away. Like the sharks the yellow-haired merman had spoken of, the six shapes darted forward to surround him. Toklat drew himself up. Rage poured through his veins, driving away even his preoccupation with the state of his people.

Do you intend to attack me now? he sent, blazing. *Are the crimes for which you were banished from the abodes of your people not enough to satisfy you? Well, come ahead then. But I promise you you'll regret it!*

Dry laughter rippled into his mind from Anastas. *Calm yourself, Selkie,* he sent. *Sea and Sky, you people are excitable! I suppose it comes from switching between shapes all the time. Still, I have no quarrel with your folk. I never did.*

Toklat lost none of his alertness. *Then what do you want?*

Only to ask you some questions. The merman's gaze was hooded. *As you know, none of my own people will acknowledge me anymore, much less talk to me or these loyal friends of mine. Indeed, my own kinsman just tried to run me over with one of those cumbersome Terran boats.*

So Galen had already seen him! Toklat's derisive snort was not telepathically sent, but blown out into the water as he bared his teeth in a grimace of contempt. *With good reason too. He should have killed you. Both you and these "loyal" friends of yours should have been killed long ago, I think.*

How interesting of you to say so, Anastas replied coldly. *Be-*

cause something is trying. Two evening tides ago, one of our little group took sick. One moment he was fine, the next, he was sick— the merman waved a hand—*just like that.*

Astonished, Toklat stared at him. So the illness had struck again. That it was one of these evil ones—the only merfolk in uncounted eons to ever warrant banishment, the worst of all their peoples' punishments—mattered little. It had happened again, and Galen must be told. At once.

But, Toklat's thoughts raced on, he would first have to extract as much information as he could from these outlawed mermen. According to merfolk law, neither Galen nor any other member of his people was allowed to speak directly with them. And in Galen's case, that was probably wise. Toklat knew his brother-friend very well. Seeing Anastas while in a boat and in the presence of a Terran was one thing, but it would not be a good idea for Galen to meet up with his former cousin in these waters. Not a good idea at all. He wondered if Anastas realized that too.

What happened to him? he cautiously asked the blonde merman.

I told you, he's fallen sick. He's in great pain, and most puzzling of all, his gill slits seem to be growing smaller. If it continues, there will be no hope for him, of course. We could take him to an abode where he might have a chance—Anastas's hollow eyes blazed—*but all such havens are closed to us. They are as good as killing him, my noble people. Do you know how Ladru will die, Selkie? He'll drown, like some inferior Terran.*

You cannot blame the merfolk for this, Toklat shot back. *They, too*—

He clamped down on his too hasty thoughts. His goal was to obtain information, not give it. All his instincts were jangling a warning against letting these creatures know too much about what had befallen merfolk and Selkies in these last days.

The damage had been done, though. Glances flew back

and forth between the mermen, and Anastas's pale eyes glittered craftily. *I see. So they are affected as well. That is some consolation at least. What about your people, Selkie? Are they also falling sick?*

Toklat glared, as furious at himself as he was with Anastas. By the wind, he gabbled as foolishly as a largemouthed grouper! He was simply no good at being devious. None of his folk were; it was just not in them.

Anastas shrugged. *Never mind. The answer is there in your face.* He gestured to his companions. *We can return to Ladru. I've learned what I needed to. For now.*

They left Toklat, undulating off through the depths as silently as they had come. He watched them go, and when even his sharp eyes could no longer discern their shapes, he shot off in the opposite direction. To find Galen.

CHAPTER
6

The merman groaned, one hand going to his neck in a feeble, clawing motion. "Malk," he gasped, and the rasping whisper bounced eerily off the dank walls of the little cave.

The man beside him leaned forward anxiously. "I am here, Ladru. It grows worse?" His voice was low and worried, the expression on his face one of frustration as he touched the other's forehead.

Ladru moved his head. "Pain," he mumbled. "My neck."

Malk stared down at his only brother, helpless. Merfolk never fell sick; in fact, he could not recall a single instance when anyone he knew had ever done so. Wounds, yes, cuts, scratches, stings, bites, all of those could be dealt with. But this? He had not the least idea what to do.

As Ladru's condition worsened, it had become impossible for him to swim. Indeed, to Malk's tormented eyes, it seemed as though Mother Ocean Herself was turning upon this child of Hers, denying him his birthright, the birthright of all merfolk, which Malk had thought even banishment could not take away.

Yet the water that their people breathed as easily as those of the land breathed air was crushing Ladru, painfully draining the very life from him. It had been Malk's idea to come to this tiny undersea grotto, where temporarily out of the sea, his brother might be able to recover from the mysterious malady attacking him. To some extent, it had worked.

Ladru was no longer at the point of death, but the forlorn hope that sheltering in the little cave might heal him completely was disappearing as inexorably as the stricken merman's gill slits. What would happen if they closed up completely? How could Ladru go out into the sea that was his home? What would become of him?

Malk resolutely pushed such terrifying speculations from his mind. "If I brought you food, would you eat?" he asked gently. "You have not had nourishment since you became ill. You must try."

Muttering, his hands plucking at his neck, Ladru seemed not to hear him. Malk sighed and fell silent. He could think of nothing else to do but stay beside his brother, watching over him and waiting for he knew not what. His keen eyes pierced the gloom of the cave with ease, and he saw all too clearly Ladru's unnatural pallor, as well as the sweat beading on his naked body despite the grotto's coolness.

Ladru. Always so healthy and strong. If they had stayed in the abodes of their people, would he be well now? It was Malk's fault that they were here instead, here in this dark cave that smelled of dead fish and old seal dung, with Ladru tossing in pain, drifting slowly toward an unknown fate.

"Oh, little brother," Malk murmured. "This is my doing. It was I who convinced you to leave our home waters and come to see Anastas. I, who let myself be seduced, and then saw to it that you were seduced as well. If only I could put things back the way they were. If only . . ."

He broke off and looked toward the grotto entrance. The others were returning. One by one they slipped through the narrow tunnel that connected cave to sea and pulled themselves up onto the damp, rocky floor.

Anastas was first. Walking over to where Ladru lay on the flattest portion of the floor, he gazed down at the sick man. His face was impassive, revealing no trace of concern. However, the five who had come in with him hung well back, staring at their ill companion with nervous, shifting eyes, and whispering to each other in barely perceptible undertones.

"He is no better."

Anastas said this as fact rather than question, and Malk shook his head.

"I'm not a healer," he said tersely. "I can't say. He's better than when he was in the water, but the problem with his neck is unchanged."

"The gill slits are still closing?"

Malk nodded miserably, and Anastas leaned over, peering closely at Ladru's neck as if to verify this for himself. Whether it was because of the blonde one's presence or the sound of his voice, Ladru came out of his stupor and smiled weakly at him.

"Lord," he rasped. "I am beginning to recover. Except for my neck. Something is still wrong with my neck . . ."

Anastas ignored him. Straightening up, he said in a casual tone, "At this rate, the gills will soon be gone altogether." He rubbed a hand over his chin and went on thoughtfully, "What will we do with him then?"

Malk fought to hold on to his temper. It was hard to believe he had once been so enthralled by the beauty and power of this man that he had willingly betrayed the ancient traditions of his people. They would tear down outmoded ways, Anastas had said, green eyes blazing like lamps, and replace them with new ones—ways of power and strength. They would rule the land as well as the sea. . . .

Well, here were those new ways, Malk thought, a taste like bile in his mouth. Banishment, utter loneliness, and horrible suffering for the brother he loved above all else. Was that why he suddenly saw Anastas in a new light, because Ladru was ill and because Malk was growing increasingly convinced that he would not be if they had not all been cast out?

"Lord," he began. The title of respect stuck in his throat, but he forced it out. "I have been thinking. Perhaps we could seek help from our people—"

"They are not," Anastas corrected him coldly, "our people. Not any longer."

"But they were once." Fear for his brother drove Malk on. "None of us are skilled in the Healing Strata, and there is nothing we can do for Ladru. But a healer could help him, I'm certain of it. We could go to an abode and beg for aid. Just this once, the Elders might relax the Banishment long enough to heal him. After all, this illness is something that has not been seen before. Surely, they will wish to know about it."

"Yes," Ladru put in, his voice gaining strength. "I am well enough to wait for a healer, Lord. Or with help and enough stops along the way, I could even travel to an abode myself."

Both brothers paused, waiting for Anastas to speak, but the blonde merman was silent. "Please, Lord," Malk added desperately. "Ladru is all I have left to me, especially after—after all that has happened."

It was the wrong thing to say. Anastas's pale eyes turned even paler. "You are fortunate to have had him then, even for so brief a time. I have no one. Everything has been taken from me. And from the rest of us. If we have nothing, why should you be any different?"

Malk could not answer him. A soft sigh rose from Ladru, and Malk's throat closed in fear at the resignation it contained.

Bron, one of those hanging back by the water's edge, spoke into the stillness. "What harm would it do to try? The waves know *we* can't cure Ladru of whatever is ailing him. If you don't want to go, let Malk take him. And I"—he drew a deep breath—"will go along to help."

A look of surprise came into Ladru's glassy eyes, and Malk threw the merman a look brimming with gratitude. Stocky and powerful, Bron had always been known for his strength rather than his wits. He was a taciturn soul, even in happier days, and the seasons of banishment had rendered him even more so. But he possessed more courage, Malk now realized, than he had ever given Bron credit for.

Anastas was regarding Bron pensively. "And aren't you afraid of being taken ill with the same thing?" he asked in a silken voice.

Bron shrugged. "Of course. What sane person wouldn't be? But the way I look at it, Ladru may be the luckiest of us all. What do the rest of us have to look forward to? More endless tides of *this*." He jerked a thick arm up to indicate the cave. "If this strange plague is going to send me from the world, I'd just as soon go in an abode. I'd like to enter an abode one more time before I die." He glanced around defiantly. "And so would the rest of us, even though they won't dare say that to your face, *Lord*."

"Is that so." Anastas's gaze was flat and hard. The tone of Bron's voice bordered on insult, even on direct challenge. With a rancor he never would have exhibited in the early tides of their exile, Bron returned his leader's gaze for several moments before reluctantly dropping his eyes.

The longer this accursed banishment dragged on, Anastas

thought bitterly, the harder it was for him to maintain the leadership that had formerly been his. The unswerving admiration he had taken for granted, the obedience once vouchsafed him without question, were all growing slippery in his grasp, seeming more and more in jeopardy with each tide that dragged by.

Only nine seasons had passed since he and his followers had been cast out. To the long-lived merfolk, that was a span of time hardly worth noting. To exiles cut off from family and friends, from merfolk life itself, all the time knowing there would never be any change in their terrible fate, nine seasons seemed more like nine centuries.

Sunk in upon himself, Anastas had not called up his unique powers since before the Banishment. Now he realized what a mistake that had been. The seductive skills he possessed would not control everyone, but they had controlled these followers of his, or they would not be there with him now. It was time to exercise those powers again.

Ladru's sickness was surely a gift from the Mother, Anastas decided. What else could it be but the means by which he would regain both the loyalty of his followers and the position he had lost—or rather the position that had been taken from him? As for those who had done the taking . . . He smiled. Ah, his revenge, when it came, would leave a sweetness in his mouth that would linger for eons. They would be sorry they'd cast him out, and Galen, in particular, would be sorry indeed. . . .

The last shreds of Malk's control parted as he watched the smile creep across Anastas's face. "What do you smirk at?" he cried. "My only brother lies in pain while you stand there grinning. He and I followed you into this oblivion, and look at what's become of him! Well, no more. I do not ask your leave to take Ladru to an abode. I tell you now, we will go, with or without your permission. And once we reach an abode, I'll beg and plead on my knees—"

"Malk."

The name was spoken in a new voice, one Anastas had not used in a long time. The fine hairs along Malk's arms rose at the sound of it. He turned to Ladru, focusing his attention once more on his brother. "Don't worry," he said in as reassuring a tone as he could manage. "I'll get you help. I promise."

He could feel the power building behind him like a great wave, and stubbornly he kept his back to the source of it. But Anastas's insidious voice penetrated the barrier of flesh and bone with chilling ease.

"Malk, my faithful one. Look at me."

Malk shivered. Near the tunnel entrance, he could hear the scuffling of bare feet as the other mermen shifted uneasily on the damp floor. They, too, knew that voice, at one time or another had all experienced what came from it. Ladru gazed up at him pleadingly, and Malk stiffened his spine. He would not give in, he told himself, for his brother's sake, he would not.

"Malk."

Another shiver went through Malk, so hard that for a moment he thought he might be coming down with Ladru's illness. He almost wished he were. Anything was better than taking on Anastas while his brother lay helpless and suffering. If only he could gather up Ladru and flee without looking into those green eyes, without engaging in the struggle it would take to hold on to his will once he met that gaze. If only . . .

He found himself facing Anastas with no recollection of having gotten to his feet and turned around. The blonde merman gave a slight nod of satisfaction.

"I see you are coming to your senses," he said. "And that is good. For we must talk of Ladru, you and I."

Caught in the glittering depths of the other's eyes, Malk felt the familiar disconnected sensation start to come over him, and he called upon every shred of determination to resist it.

"Yes, let us speak of Ladru." He fought to control his thoughts, to steady them in the face of Anastas's power, his terrible will. "I want to save him, but you do not. If you did, you would not try to stop me from taking him to an abode."

"Why do you think I am trying to stop you?"

The voice was silken, stroking over Malk's jangled nerves like some vast, gentle hand. "I—" He fumbled, searching for the words. The truth was there, hovering just beyond his reach as the power of Anastas erected higher and higher walls to block him from it.

"Brother," Ladru said, his voice strained.

"You want him to die!" Malk got out triumphantly. "You do not want us to go begging for help from our people because it would shame you. You would rather let my brother die than permit that, wouldn't you? *Wouldn't you?*"

Anastas was silent, smiling gently at him. His eyes deepened, seeming to reach into Malk's brain like the curved talons of the huge sea eagles that fished the northern seas. And indeed Malk felt like a hapless fish caught by one of the great birds of prey, writhing frantically, yet unable to flee the grip of those ruthless claws.

"Malk, I am not ready to die," Ladru whispered, and the sound of that pain-wracked voice stabbed Malk to the bone.

"Please." He stretched out a hand in pleading to Anastas. "We must seek help for him. Don't you see?"

"Of course I do. No one wants to help Ladru more than I, Malk. You're exhausted from the strain of your vigil and that is why you spoke to me as you did. But I know how worried you are, and so I forgive you."

The soft, purring words seemed to be coming from inside Malk's head, sent there by those gleaming eyes. Ladru had fallen silent. Weakened by his illness, he was the least able of all to resist Anastas. Malk himself swayed dizzily, and behind the leader's tall form he could see the other mermen sway also. Even without facing the power of that gaze, they were tangled as tightly as he in the net of Anastas's irresistible voice.

But it was not their brother whose life was at stake! he reminded himself. Yet was that really the case? Anastas wanted to help Ladru. He had just said so, hadn't he? Anastas never lied. He was good, kind, he took care of those who followed him, he always had. Whatever misfortunes had befallen them were the fault of others, not Anastas.

"Look at Ladru, Malk. See how little he resembles a merman any more."

His jaw slack, Malk obeyed. Ladru appeared before him as though through a haze. His pallor had intensified, and his hair clung to his face and throat in lank strands. He no longer even tried to pluck at what remained of the gills on his neck. Grief flooded Malk's soul as he stared at his brother, and there was no strength left in him to resist the great voice that beat at his soul like wings.

"To take Ladru to an abode would only increase his suffering. Our former people are cruel. They care nothing for his pain, or yours. Do you think the interlocking chambers of even a single abode in all the seven seas will open to us? You are wrong."

A thin voice came to life in Malk's head, struggling to warn him, to be heard over the force of that other voice. He tried to listen, but Anastas went on, his words pulsing and throbbing in rhythm with each blink of his glittering eyes. The tiny voice floundered beneath that mighty cadence, like the cry of a gull caught in a storm.

"The stone doors will remain closed, as unyielding as the hearts of those within. They will laugh, Malk, *laugh* as your brother chokes and screams in the Midnight Sea, and as you beg for their help. But if that is what you want, go then. Take Bron and your poor brother and go. You will see, to your sorrow, how right I am."

Swaying, Malk put a hand to his forehead, and Anastas's voice crackled off the walls of the grotto. "Well, what do you stand there for? Go!"

Malk shuddered. "Please—"

The terrible voice grew gentle. "You no longer wish to leave us?"

"No." Malk's own voice was near a sob. "I don't know what to do for him, I don't know . . ."

"Shall I tell you?" Anastas asked softly, beguilingly.

Malk nodded, his tear-filled eyes eager, and Anastas sighed. "Good." He gazed at the distraught merman, allowing the desperate silence to drag out for a few moments more. Malk was wholly in his power now, and Anastas was enjoying the sweetness of it. "There is a way by which you can prove that you are still part of our brotherhood, while helping Ladru at the same time." He paused, letting his gaze hold Malk's. "Do you understand me?"

Malk shook his head that he did not.

"Ladru's gills are almost gone, and without them he is no longer one of us. He can't travel, he won't even be able to hunt his own food. We'll have to do it for him. He'll be nothing but a burden, and we do not need burdens. There is only one solution. I can do it, of course, but it would be more . . . appropriate for his brother to act in my stead."

Malk stared at him, still without comprehension. Suddenly, from behind Anastas, there was a shuffling as Bron started, momentarily dragging himself out of the hushed stillness that bound them all. "You cannot mean this," he protested, trying to shake loose the cobwebs miring his brain. "Ladru is not that far gone. Malk, listen to me—"

"Be silent!"

Anastas thundered out the command, whirling around to impale Bron with his blazing gaze. The stocky dissenter quailed, his own eyes glazing over as they met those of Anastas. When he, too, had fallen back into the trance that held the others, Anastas turned to Malk again. "Are you ready?" he asked sternly.

Malk's head moved slowly up and down. "Ladru." His voice was tentative, his gaze vague. "Ladru. What must I do, Lord?"

Anastas smiled, the same smile that had sent Malk into a rage such a short time before, a smile that would have now set ice around his heart had he been in the proper frame of mind to see it. "Take Ladru out into the sea," the pale-haired one said, "and let the waters do their work. He is useless to us, and to himself. It will be better for everyone with him gone. He'll be happier too."

"He will?" Something in Malk strove to rise up and deny that, but it flopped back helplessly in the face of Anastas's strength. "Truly, Lord?"

Anastas beamed at him, and hesitantly Malk returned that beautiful smile. How magnificent he was, the merman thought, how wise and thoughtful. To be so concerned with Ladru's welfare, when so much else must surely be weighing upon his mind. Truly, he was a man worth following! Relief and gratitude washed over him as Anastas responded.

"Why, of course, he'll be happier, my faithful one. He will be at rest, sent there by the hands of you, his beloved brother. I would never lie to you, would I?"

"No." Malk's smile widened. "I know you would not."

"Then"—Anastas gestured toward Ladru, whose pain-filled gaze met his blankly—"go and do as you must. We will wait for you here."

That would be a further show of his power, Anastas thought. His strength was so great, Malk would now murder his own brother without Anastas even having to be present to ensure that he did.

Malk bent to Ladru. Slinging an arm around the sick

man, he pulled him gently to his feet, though Ladru made an incoherent sound of protest. Anastas's stony gaze silently ordered the other mermen to stand aside as the brothers moved slowly toward the tunnel. Suddenly Ladru seemed to regain his senses.

"Where are you taking me?" he asked weakly. "Out into the sea? Are we going to an abode, then, to ask for help?"

"Shhhh," Malk hushed him. "Be at peace, my brother. You will be happy soon. Anastas has said so, and Anastas always knows what's best."

"Mal—"

The name became a gurgling plea as Malk dove into the black waters of the tunnel with Ladru slung over his shoulder.

The silence in the grotto was deafening.

Anastas studied the five mermen who stood clustered near the waters that still rippled with the brothers' passing. His gaze moved over the faces of each, and all of them looked away. He settled at last on Bron.

"You," he said calmly. "Go after him. But do not interfere. Return and tell me when it is done."

It was another test to send Bron, the only one besides Malk who had dared defy his power. The slack fear Anastas saw in the stocky merman's eyes sent a pleasure surging through him that was warm as seed spurting from a swollen penis. He watched contentedly as Bron slipped into the tunnel.

In a little while he was back, the huge muscles in his arms quivering uncharacteristically as he pulled himself out onto the rocks. The fear on his face as he looked at Anastas had intensified to terrific respect.

"Ladru is dead," he whispered. "Malk took him to the ocean bottom and left him there. Ladru tried to follow as he swam away, but he could not. He stretched out his hands, begging in mind-speak for Malk to come back. But—but

Malk only smiled." Bron closed his eyes. "He even laughed, telling Ladru that now all was well."

"And Malk?" Anastas questioned. "Where is he now?"

Even as he spoke, a splashing announced the return of Malk. He came out of the tunnel in a great rush of water, the haze already leaving his eyes, the beatific expression of peace utterly gone.

"My brother," he gasped in an anguished wail. "He floats outside at the bottom of the sea. He's dead. What happened? I—I seem to remember that I took him there. Tell me I did not. Tell me I did not!"

"Why, Malk," Anastas said gently. "How can we tell you that? For you did, of course. You killed your only brother."

Galen's features were rigid as a stone wall as he listened to Toklat. "Are you certain?" His voice was a near whisper, its softness belied by the expression on his face. "The gill slits were closing. That is what he said?"

"By the Great White's tooth!" Toklat snapped. "I may have the mouth of a grouper, but I still have a Selkie's ears!" He sighed. "I'm sorry, Galen. I should never have allowed myself to be drawn into conversing with *that* one in the first place. He's more crafty than a pod of hunting orcas."

Galen shook his head in disagreement. His eyes were on fire with a light that rivaled the hot stare of the afternoon sun burning down on them in the little cove. "Don't blame yourself, brother-friend. It's good you talked with him. How else would we know the sickness had struck someone else?" He was silent a moment, his flaming gaze turned inward. "By the Mother, I wish it had been *he*, and not one of his lackeys, who took ill."

Toklat glanced toward the brown and green bulk of

Karpathos, its pine-clad hills glistening in the brightness of midday. "Where is the landwoman now?"

"I took her back," Galen replied absently. "I could not risk having him whose name I will no longer speak see her any more closely, or her him." He thought a moment. "She did not want to go. Indeed, she was quite angry about it."

The thick hair on Toklat's bulky shoulders lifted as though it were fur. First a landwoman possessing abilities no landwoman should possess, and now the appearance of Anastas and his ilk. But he should not really be surprised, he told himself. It made sense that the banished ones would choose to wander among these islands, they who belonged nowhere else in the sea. Things were growing more complicated and more worrisome by the minute. He listened wearily as Galen went on.

"Brother-friend, I think it would be a good idea for you to go back to my abode and tell Cleonith of your encounter with *him*. She must hear everything he told you, every detail about the one who's become ill."

Toklat assented immediately. Despite his assurances that he would stay with Galen, the chance to head away from land and from the danger he was so certain loomed all about him came as a distinct relief.

"I can do that," he said. "But what about you, Galen? I'm sure the banished ones are still in these waters. If I leave, you'll be all alone."

When Galen did not answer, Toklat drew a deep breath. He had vowed not to speak of things that would only cause more pain, tearing open wounds that had scarcely had time to scab over. The flames in Galen's eyes frightened him, though, driving him to break that vow.

"Galen," he said deliberately, "Anastas killed your parents in revenge for the declaration by his father, old King Lugarion, that Anastas was unfit to rule. Now that Lugarion has transitioned from this life, the kingship of your people still sits vacant.

"And I *still* say Anastas should have died for what he did. My people have never agreed with you merfolk about banishment. It removes the person but not the evil. Galen, if Anastas finds out that it is you the Elders are considering as the new king, he will kill you, too."

The flames in Galen's eyes became an open fire that blazed out into his voice. "Let him try," he snarled in that scorched, deadly voice. *"Let him try!"*

CHAPTER
7

Hugging her elbows, Meredith paced up and down the long veranda behind her house. She was furious. Galen had left her several hours ago, morning had lengthened into the breathless heat of afternoon, and her anger had not abated one bit.

She slammed a fist into the trunk of the large oleander tree that dominated the courtyard, as she remembered how the expedition that had begun in such hopefulness had ended in such failure.

Completely ignoring her protests, Galen had motored the caïque back to the beach below her house, maintaining a grim silence that nothing could penetrate. Adamantly, he had paid not the slightest heed to her questions, her demands, or her pleas that he turn around and continue on to the cave. His jaw set, those brilliant eyes looking inward, it seemed to her that he had scarcely known she was there. Certainly, he had acted as if he did not.

Unceremoniously, without a single word, he had dumped her on the beach, practically pushing her out of the boat in his eagerness to be gone from her. She hit the unoffending tree again.

"I knew I shouldn't have gotten mixed up with him," she muttered out loud. "I *knew* it!"

The heavy fragrance of oleander blooms surrounded her, and she drew in deep breaths of their sweetness, trying to let them calm her. Through the thickly flowered branches she could see the Aegean, its waters gleaming gold in the late afternoon sun. The bright glow reminded her all too sharply of the mysterious swimmer Galen had tried to run down.

She worried again about the swimmer, as she had been doing since she had returned. No answers came to comfort her, though, only speculations that left her more concerned than ever.

Was he dead? Galen had insisted he wasn't, not only when the incredible incident happened but on the way back. In fact, the one time he had deigned to speak to her at all had been to gruffly tell her so. But how could he know? The look on his face when he'd said it had indicated all too clearly that he would like the exact opposite to be true.

Meredith resumed her pacing, then paused. Her anger was finally beginning to cool, and as it did, her mood was turning distinctly uneasy.

Although she had thought Galen odd from the beginning, she had not thought him dangerous. Until that morning. The events of the morning had stamped his face in her mind, his handsome features fixed in a look of hatred and rage more overpowering than anything she had ever seen. It blurred the earlier picture of how he had looked when he had kissed her such a short time before, clouding that sweet and disturbing memory. Truth be told, Meredith could not say which picture disconcerted her more.

Slowly she started walking again, her bare feet softly slapping against paving-stones that felt hot even under the widespread shade of bushes and trees surrounding the veranda. Suddenly she was glad the expedition to the cave had ended so precipitously and that she was there alone, and felt relieved, as well, that Galen was as anxious to be rid of her as she now was of him.

But what about the scroll? She sighed. If his knowledge was genuine—and she believed it was—then dangerous or not, she did not really want to be rid of him. Not yet anyway.

Deciding abruptly what to do, she turned toward the house. She would go to see Flijanou. If she hurried and did not extend her visit too long, she could head home before nightfall and not have to negotiate the narrow, twisting path in the dark. She went inside to pull on her sandals and a hat, and within a few minutes was on her way, striding purposefully toward the village of Olympus and Flijanou's hut.

As she walked Meredith acknowledged that what she was doing was a long shot. The idea of going to see Flijanou to ask her about the odd episode in the caïque was born as much out of her need to do *something* as out of any real faith that the Greek woman could actually be of help. Yet there was a chance that she might be able to provide some insight regarding Galen and why he had acted as he had. Even more crucial, Flijanou might know something about the blonde swimmer, since she seemed keenly aware of every person, either native or tourist, who resided on Karpathos.

Flijanou's sources of information were as far-reaching as those of any spy network, Meredith thought with a wry smile. Then her smile faded as the unsettling vision of a blonde-haired body washing up on the beach filled her mind. Galen had said the swimmer was unharmed, and

Lord, how she wanted to believe him. But what if he was wrong?

She squared her jaw, unaware of how much, in that moment, her face resembled the grim sternness of Galen's that morning. "If he's not alive," she said to the sea below the cliffs, "then my next stop after Flijanou will have to be the police."

Flijanou was as happy to see her as always, but puzzled, glancing back along the stony path as though she expected someone else to be coming.

"Greetings, child," she called, then asked quickly as Meredith came closer, "But where is Galen? Why is he not with you?"

"Actually, Flijanou, that's why I'm here." Meredith paused. "I'd like to talk to you if I may."

The expression on Flijanou's seamed face was curious and, to Meredith's eyes, a little wary. "Come inside then. I'll make coffee."

Meredith sighed inwardly as she followed her host. The last thing she desired in this heat was coffee, or the interminable courtesies that always preceded a discussion with Flijanou. The old woman would not be hurried, though. In fact, the only time Meredith had seen her dispense with her usual ceremony had been when Flijanou had introduced Galen to her. Meredith now found herself wondering why.

"All right, child," Flijanou finally said when they were settled in the stuffy little hut. "What's wrong? Clearly, you are troubled."

Meredith studied her. "Yes," she said at last. "I am. Tell me something, how well do you know Galen?"

"Why, quite well." There was the briefest hesitation, then the old woman went on firmly. "I have known his people all my life, and so has it been with my mother and her mother and her mother before her, as far back as we can remember. Why do you ask me this?"

Meredith set down the demitasse of coffee. Starting with the moment she and Galen had set off in the caïque, she told Flijanou what had happened that morning, though she carefully left out—for different reasons—both the conversation about the phrase he had translated and the kiss which that conversation had ignited.

Sitting very straight in her rickety chair, Flijanou listened without comment as Meredith described the blonde man in the water, Galen's rage, and how he had tried to smash the boat over him.

"I don't understand any of it," she finished. "And other than insisting that the man was alive, Galen absolutely refused to tell me why he behaved in such an incredible way."

She paused for breath, gazing intently at the older woman and trying to decide if she really saw wariness on her face, or if it was just the shadowy interior of the hut. "Do you have any idea?" she asked when Flijanou did not speak.

"Well." Flijanou poured more coffee. "If Galen told you the man was not hurt, then I would believe him. Galen does not come of a people who are violent. Indeed, they are of the most peaceful nature. Very unlike the rest of us."

"You keep mentioning his people," Meredith said. "You mean his family?"

"Yes, yes, his family."

"Who are his family, Flijanou? They aren't from Karpathos, so where are they from?"

"Many places," Flijanou said vaguely. "They are very well traveled, Galen's folk. They have never cared to stay in one place for very long."

"I see." But Meredith really did not. There was no doubt that Flijanou was being evasive. The question was *why*.

As if she had read her mind, the Greek woman said, "You must forgive me for not speaking more openly to you, my child. But Galen's . . . family is very private. They do not like others to discuss their business. It would be better if you asked Galen about these things yourself."

"I tried." Meredith's mouth tightened. "He was not very communicative, to say the least."

"Perhaps you should try again. He is quite taken with you, you know." Flijanou's black eyes twinkled, growing even merrier as a flush rose in Meredith's cheeks. "I'm sure he would not be happy if he knew how upset he has made you."

"Flijanou"—Meredith sought to keep the impatience and anger from her voice—"it's more than a question of being upset. I really think Galen tried to kill that man!"

"Then he must have done something to deserve it." Meredith started at the hard note that had entered Flijanou's voice, but after another slight hesitation, the woman swiftly continued. "However, I know that the man you speak of is not dead."

"You do?" Meredith leaned forward. "How?"

"Because I saw him. You said he is blonde, didn't you?"

At Meredith's nod, she smiled. "Then he is fine. A man who looks as you describe is staying on the other side of the island. He's a tourist. I saw him near our village early this afternoon, which would mean, of course, that he did not drown under Galen's boat, after all."

Meredith pondered this. She wanted to feel relieved at Flijanou's disclosure, but a lingering apprehension was still eating at her. Other than an occasional scholar like herself, tourists were not common on Karpathos. Those few who did make it as far as this remote island almost always stayed on the southern side, with its larger population and better roads.

Getting to the northern side of Karpathos was difficult, and as a result, not many tried it. However, some of the more adventurous tourists did sometimes take it into their heads to undertake the journey, first catching a boat from the city of Pigadia to the fishing village of Diafani on the coast, then braving the long and bouncing bus ride over the mountains, all so that they could visit the picturesque village of Olympus. From Flijanou's account, the blonde man had to be one of those.

"Are you sure?" she asked. "You actually saw a man with long blonde hair this afternoon?"

"Yes, child." Now it was Flijanou's turn to be impatient. "How many men with yellow hair are there on this island, eh? You tell me that."

Meredith sighed. "It's just that I'm worried about whether or not he's okay." She said this last word in English, since "okay" did not translate into Greek.

Flijanou understood anyway. "Well, there's no need," she said briskly. "Not all strangers have the high regard for our ancient ways that you do, my child. Sometimes foreigners come to our islands and behave poorly, without respect for the traditions and customs we hold dear. This man is probably someone like that. Perhaps he offended Galen in some way, and when Galen saw him this morning, he decided that he needed to be taught a lesson."

"Maybe," Meredith said doubtfully. "But I can't imagine him doing anything so terrible that he would deserve what Galen tried to do to him."

Flijanou shrugged, a vast and expressive gesture that was purely Greek. "Who among us women can ever make sense out of the ways of men? Their tempers run as hot as their passions. Our men are perhaps more hot-blooded than those you know in America. What Galen did does not seem as strange to me as it does to you. Such things often happen when two men are angry, and more often than not one of them ends up leaving the world of the living after it is over.

"Now." She peered out the open door at the lowering sun, then rose and held out her hands to Meredith. "You are welcome to stay for supper—so long as you are home by nightfall, for it is not seemly for a woman to be roaming about alone after dark."

"Thank you, Grandmother," Meredith demurred politely, "but I think I'll be on my way."

Leaving the hut, trailed by her hostess, she paused in the blast furnace that was the tiny front yard. Putting on her straw hat, she gave Flijanou a preoccupied smile. "I appreciate your letting me stop by like this to clear things up for me, Grandmother. I really do."

The other woman regarded her shrewdly. "But you still aren't easy in your mind, are you?"

"Well ..." Meredith gazed abstractedly past the stony cliffs. "I'd be lying if I said I wasn't still disturbed." She glanced back at Flijanou. "You didn't see Galen's face this morning."

"Don't worry yourself, child." Flijanou patted her shoulder. "Everything is as it should be. Do not search for trouble where there is none. Galen is a good man. As upright as a god, child! Believe this."

A god? Meredith turned to the Greek woman in amused surprise, a chuckle coming to her lips. The teasing comment she was going to make faded before the fervency blazing in Flijanou's face. Those lined features held such intensity, such feeling, that she held her tongue and thought better of saying anything further about Galen.

"All right, Flijanou," she said. "If you say so."

She started down the path, her doubts eased somewhat by the news that the blonde man was unharmed. The doubts were not gone, though, not entirely.

Flijanou stood watching her. "A god!" she repeated, although Meredith was already out of earshot. "Remember what I say, child. A god!"

She shifted worriedly from foot to foot as the young woman passed from view. Had she done the right thing? She hoped so. It had bothered her, lying to Meredith that way, but what else could she do? She had to protect the sea lord. Her vow of loyalty left her no other choice.

However, there was one thing she had not lied to her visitor about. She truly believed that whoever had been foolish enough to arouse the sea lord's anger had more than deserved the scare he had gotten that morning. Whatever the lord had done, Flijanou told herself firmly, he had his reasons, and no doubt they were very good reasons, certainly not ones for her to question.

Meredith had her worried, though. She had not left in as reassured a frame of mind as Flijanou would have wished. Flijanou shook her head and went back inside to start her evening meal. All she could hope for now was that at least the American woman was reassured enough not to start questioning others in Olympus about the blonde man. If she did, she would find out that no one but Flijanou had seen him. And she would surely wonder, then, if he had been seen at all.

Deep, deep waters lay just beyond the friendly coves and inlets of Karpathos. Three thousand years earlier a Phoenician ship carrying a cargo of marble columns had gone down there, the victim of a violent storm. Now, from one of the many hiding places created by the lichen-encrusted columns and the even more ancient boulders on the ocean floor, Anastas watched Toklat's powerful shape sweep past, heading into the distance.

What is he *up to?* a thought-voice muttered into his brain.

Anastas turned his head to look at Gilkon, the one who had mind-spoken. As their eyes met, the latter quickly averted his gaze.

It had been only a few hours since Anastas had led his newly chastened followers out of the little grotto. With the memory of his power so fresh in their minds, not one of them was eager to do anything that might even hint at a challenge, including Malk, who hovered on the outskirts of the group, silent and utterly defeated, his spirit crushed.

That, Anastas replied with exaggerated patience, *is what we need to find out. My guess, though, is that his rushing off has to do with what he found out from us, and we from him.*

You mean Ladru, said the thought-voice of a sullen-faced merman called Tovash. Once Tovash had basked in the coveted position of being Anastas's second-in-command, eagerly awaiting the moment when Anastas would become king and he, Tovash, could wield the unlimited power the golden-haired one had promised him. Now these hopes floated lifelessly, as dead as Ladru. Tovash still held his place, though surely no one envied him for it any longer.

What of it? he went on, unable to keep the despondency from his thought-voice despite the fear of offending his leader. *It won't affect us a hair if all the peoples of the sea rush back and forth babbling to each other about this sickness until the very waves dry up. I hope they all die of it,* he added savagely.

Anastas clenched his teeth in disgust. With the exception of Malk, who was too dazed and destroyed to show much of anything, the grim and bitter resignation expressed by Tovash was mirrored on the face of every man in his little band. A wave of impatient anger rolled through him.

Why are all you so stupid? he snapped.

He struck one of the ancient columns with his fist, sending a flurry of tiny creatures scurrying out into the deep. *The illness that struck down Ladru is affecting other merfolk as well. They will certainly be seeking a cure, and we must find out what that cure is. Otherwise, we might as well sit here waiting to drown, just as Ladru did.*

Well, they're hardly going to share any knowledge they find with us, Lord, Tovash pointed out carefully. *You know that better than anyone. Even if there is a cure we'll no more be able to avail ourselves of it than the whalefolk could go back to living upon the land. If the sickness strikes again we are doomed.*

Anastas barely managed to keep from hitting that surly face. *You don't see because you are as blind as the creatures who live on the bottom of the Midnight Sea,* he mind-shouted in return. *Don't you understand that if we obtain the cure for this illness we'll possess a power beyond challenging? Our people will be helpless. They'll have to deal with us, or else watch the gills of every man, woman, and child close up the way Ladru's did. We can make any demand we wish, and they will have no choice but to obey!*

Memenon, who had not spoken before now, sent his thoughts into the discussion. *But how do we know there is any way of stopping this illness, Lord? What if the cure you speak of simply doesn't exist?*

Anastas did not reply. He turned away from his watching followers, his thoughts flying back to earlier that morning, when he had seen Galen.

He had paid little attention to the distant boat at first. To him it had been just another Terran vessel clogging up the waters, until his merfolk vision had picked out who was at the helm. He had set off to follow it, alone at the time and glad that he was, for tension enough existed between him and his followers without their seeing Galen to exacerbate it further.

He and the dark-haired merman were grudge-mates, a thing seldom seen among their people. The flames of a special hatred leaped between them, and because of it there was more than a little resentment toward Galen on the part of Anastas's fellow exiles.

The Elders were the ones who had thrown Anastas from his high place as heir to the throne. But it was Galen who had been given the right to decide his fate. Through many a long midnight tide Anastas had brooded about that decision, and about the various ways he would one day demand retribution from the one who had made it.

However, he was far from being a fool. Hate Galen though he did, he was well aware of the murderous rage Galen bore him in return. Anastas was not eager to confront that rage. The terms of banishment forbade merfolk from acknowledging, much less conversing with those so punished, but such restrictions might not be enough to stop the savage-tempered Galen should he ever come upon his grudge-mate alone.

Indeed, Anastas often suspected that the only reason Galen had called for The Casting Out rather than execution, was because he wanted that very thing to take place. He *wanted* to catch Anastas alone one day, so that he could exact a death far more terrible than any the Elders would have allowed.

That morning, though, a perfect opportunity to torment Galen without fear of reprisal had presented itself. For reasons he had yet to discover, the black-haired one was obviously pretending to be a Terran. He could hardly throw off that pretense to come roaring into the waves after his grudge-mate, even should the latter swim up to the very edge of the boat itself. And the landwoman accompanying him, Anastas had seen once he had taken his eyes from Galen, was beautiful—extremely beautiful.

Heat had pierced through his loins as he'd noticed this. It had been a long time since he had shared pleasures with a woman. No merwoman alive would now have anything to do with either him or his followers, and since merwomen were as strong as mermen, there was no question of using force to change that attitude. Besides, in a society where the concept of sexual violence did not exist, the consequences of resorting to it were beyond imagining, even for those who already bore the ultimate weight of banishment.

There were always Terran women, of course, an alternative Anastas's fellow exiles had availed themselves of more than once. Anastas himself had not. Now that the legs of merwomen were forever closed to him, he had come to look upon land females with something akin to loathing.

They were weak creatures in his eyes, poor substitutes for the sweet flowing power of the women of his own kind. The fact that becoming king would have required him to take a woman from land as his mate mattered little. Anastas no longer bothered to concern himself with the logic of his hatreds.

Galen's Terran companion was interesting, though. Not only was she magnificent—particularly for a Terran woman—but she held another, far more compelling attraction.

Galen wanted her.

That much was obvious, Anastas had decided. It showed in the way Galen's body inclined toward her, in the way he looked at her. Indeed, so intent was he upon the woman, he had not noticed Anastas, a lapse very out of character for the usually keen-sensed Galen.

Anastas had positioned himself so that the woman's back was to him, then held himself upright, treading water, as he waited for Galen to catch sight of him. It had provided only the smallest of consolations to bedevil his enemy in this way. But small consolations, Anastas knew, often led to bigger ones. In any case, it had been well worth it to see the look of ungovernable rage on Galen's face when he'd glanced up to see his grudge-mate smiling at him over the waves.

Of course, he had had to flee after Galen tried to run him down with that ridiculous boat, but that did not matter. First the Selkie, then Galen, Anastas now mused. There was friendship between those two; if they had come to these waters together, then Galen must surely be searching for a cure to the illness, with Toklat helping him.

His thoughts were interrupted as he realized that Memenon was repeating his question. *What if a cure doesn't exist, Lord?*

It does. Anastas stared off in the direction Toklat had taken. *It has to. And that Selkie knows something about it. I want you to go after him. All of you. Find out where he's going and what he knows.*

And you, Lord? The now-chastened Bron asked the question with careful respect. *What will you do while we are gone?*

Anastas continued to stare off into the distance. *I have a visit to make. To a certain landwoman.*

He smiled, and each merman who saw that smile was exceedingly glad that he was not the target of it.

CHAPTER
8

Toklat did not realize at first that he was being followed. So caught up was he in reaching Galen's abode, and in doing so as rapidly as possible, the thought did not even occur to him. By the time it did, it was too late.

With ominous swiftness his pursuers burst upon him. Mermen, Toklat saw. The banished ones who followed Anastas—only, Anastas was not with them. They raced to surround him, even as he shot up from far beneath the ocean surface into the soft purple and crimson warmth of sunset in a desperate attempt to evade or at least confound them long enough to make his escape.

"Where are you going to in such a hurry, Selkie?" asked one, whose way of holding himself proclaimed him to be in charge.

Toklat stiffened, glaring around him at the circle of watching faces. Danger pulsed in the sweet, salt-tanged air of early evening, and with a sickening insight he suddenly understood that the menace he had been sensing since he and Galen had come to Karpathos was from *them*, these banished ones.

There was no one about to come to his aid. None of his own people were within range of a call for help, nor were any of the friendly dolphin-folk—allies of merfolk and Selkie alike—anywhere nearby. He would have to deal with this alone.

"The last time I looked," he snarled, "the mother seas were still free to all who wish to travel over them." He met his antagonists' eyes, taking refuge in anger, and in bluff. "And you address the ruler of the Selkie folk. So treat me with the proper respect, you who are but gull dung upon the waves!"

The circle of faces sneered at him. "We owe respect to no one," said the first merman. "Not any more."

"That much is obvious." Toklat stared coldly at the one who had spoken. "Not even to he who once led you, apparently. What did you do, kill him, so you could lead this pack of misbegotten algae scum in his place?"

"Never mind about Anastas," snapped the burliest of the group. "We came here to have you talk to us, not the other way round." He gestured to the leader. "Let's get on with it, Tovash. We're wasting time."

"Quiet, Bron," Tovash ordered. "Let me handle this. You," he said to Toklat, "will now tell us everything you know about a cure for this illness that has attacked the merfolk."

Toklat's lips curled back, revealing the long animal teeth that Selkies retained regardless of what shape they were in. "Why do you think I know anything at all?" he asked with contempt. "And if I did, why in all the tides, would I tell misbegotten creatures such as yourselves of it?"

Another merman lunged forward. "Listen to me, you miserable shapechanging beast!" he shouted directly into Toklat's face, his voice thickened by self-hatred and grief and pent-up frustration. "My brother died of that illness. He was the only person left in the seas that I cared about anymore, and now he's gone. I don't care if you're king of the Selkies, the starfish, or the entire sea and sky. I have no intention of drowning in agony the way Ladru did, while my former people stay safe in their abodes availing themselves of a cure!"

"Malk," one of the others broke in, "be quiet. This is getting us nowhere. Anastas told us what to do if he would not tell us willingly. Stop your spuming and—"

"I'm in charge here!" Tovash broke in. The realization burst upon him that he *was* in charge, at least for the moment, and without those pale green eyes to sap his will. A measure of courage suddenly returned to him. "A curse on Anastas!" he shouted boldly. "We would not be cast out today, if not for him!"

Shock rippled through his companions at his words, and Toklat saw his chance. Hurling himself at Tovash, he struck in the blink of an eye, sinking his teeth deep into the merman's throat. Flinging the wounded merman aside with powerful arms, he plunged through the opening he had created in the circle that surrounded him.

If only he were in his animal shape, Toklat fumed as he fled. He did not care what Galen said; seals *were* faster than merfolk.

Selkies in their human form, however, were not. He could feel the closeness of his pursuers in every nerve as they swept after him. Racing as fast as he, they were on top of him in minutes.

He would not allow himself to be surrounded like a helpless pup a second time, Toklat decided grimly, and wheeled around to fight.

"Don't kill him!" Tovash called. "We need him alive!"

Toklat noted with a brief spasm of satisfaction that the merman's voice was thick with blood, as well as rage. But he also felt a pang of disappointment. He had wanted to tear out the accursed one's throat, not just wound him. If only there had been time! His enemies were closing in on him, though, and Toklat had no chance to think of anything else.

A full-grown Selkie in the prime of his or her strength was never an easy opponent to overcome. Few in the seas, save the cold-eyed great white sharks, or the powerful and keenly intelligent orcas, cared to try—and even their preferences ran to prey that did not suddenly and unexpectedly change form on them.

This confrontation, though, was not about the natural and accepted law of survival that called upon all denizens of the sea to hunt or be hunted. This was an obscenity, perpetrated by merfolk who no longer had the right to call themselves merfolk.

Toklat, who had never in his life raised a hostile tooth to a member of the race of sea-people, now found himself fighting these exiled ones with a rage he had not known he possessed.

He flung two of his attackers back, slashing them viciously before they could dodge his lethal teeth. The other three tried to seize him and he went after them, too—slashing, chopping, tearing, and whirling in a dozen different directions so that it was impossible to either lay hold of him or avoid the menace of his powerful jaws and pounding fists.

The five mermen were thrown back by the sheer fury of his attack. They recovered rapidly, though, and urged on by Tovash's bloody-voiced exhortations, they hurled themselves back into the fray.

Toklat met them with undiminished savagery. The waters churned wildly as the mermen sought to grab hold of him.

The air rang with their cries and curses as Toklat doggedly kept laying their flesh open to the bone.

His enormous strength, coupled with his equally enormous determination, stood him in good stead. Yet, despite the courage of the beleaguered Selkie, the battle could have but one end. Two merman, perhaps even three, and the outcome would have by no means been assured. But there were five to Toklat's one, although by the time the struggle reached its inevitable conclusion, each of those five bore wounds he would not soon forget.

Tovash was hurt worst of all. A bright carpet of blood coated his entire chest as it flowed from a badly slashed neck. Toklat had made a second attempt to tear his throat out, and only the lightning reflexes native to his people had enabled Tovash to keep his jugular vein from being ripped open. However, even his quickness had not saved him from suffering wounds that would have meant the death of a Terran man.

Tovash was not dead. But he was in pain, and he was wild with fury. Pressing one hand to his mangled throat, he choked wordlessly, glaring at Toklat while using the other hand to help his compatriots hold the Selkie captive. It was several minutes before he could speak.

"You will pay for the blood you have drawn here," he finally gasped. "We had planned to make you tell us what you know and then let you live. But now you will not only spill every shred of knowledge that stubborn beast brain of yours contains, you will die afterwards. And be glad of it!"

Toklat, gripped tightly by five sets of implacable hands but still undefeated, bared his teeth. "It is you who will pay, exiled one," he snarled. "You will learn nothing from me. My *beast* brain is stronger than the five of yours put together. And as for harming me, go ahead, do so. My people will scour the seas looking for you, and when they find you you'll wish they hadn't."

One of the mermen, whose torn shoulder and chest ran with blood, looked nervous as he tried to hold on to their prisoner and stanch the flow of blood from his own wound at the same time. "The Selkie king has a point, Tovash," he panted. "There has never been violence between his people and ours. We have troubles enough already without also having the Selkie folk thirsting after our heads."

"That's right," another said breathlessly. "Anastas made no mention of killing. I don't think he would want us to—"

"Anastas, Anastas," Tovash said in disgust. He spat out a thick glob of blood, his boldness heightened both by the pain of his wound and the absence of their leader. "In another season, all of you will be whining that we need his permission before we so much as piss into a sand dune. We have to learn to think for ourselves. Do you want to end up with your spirits destroyed, like Malk? Or worse yet, like Ladru?"

He looked into Toklat's dark blazing eyes, then smiled at his companions in a manner eerily reminiscent of the one of whom he spoke so disparagingly. "If the Selkie is dead," he said in his blood-thickened voice, "how can he accuse those who killed him? I certainly have no intention of saying anything to enlighten his people, and unless someone here wants the entire shapechanging tribe of them to come roaring down upon us, you'll keep your mouths shut as well."

This cast-out merman was as mad as Anastas himself, Toklat thought. Stunned, and with disbelief, he listened to the words of his death sentence fall around him like pellets in an ice storm, and found himself irrelevantly wondering if Tovash had always been unbalanced, or if the exile had driven him to it.

"Anastas won't care if the Selkie dies," Tovash was assuring the others. "All he cares about is that we find out what he knows. By whatever means necessary."

He paused, waiting for someone else to raise dissent over his plans for Toklat. No one did.

"Good," he said with another of those chilling smiles. "Then let us begin."

The new morning dawned hot and hazy. A sharp, dry wind skittered relentlessly through the air, stinging the eyes and fraying the nerves of every creature, human or animal, that it brushed.

The *meltemi.* That was what Greeks called this stiff wind, and it was the bane of the Aegean islands, as well as of the mainland. Tourists hated it, for it tore at beach umbrellas and towels until they were shredded, and whipped grit into food and eyes without mercy.

The best that could be said for the *meltemi* was that it reduced the humidity. It was not a cooling wind, however. Meredith likened it to regular blasts from a hot oven with an open door, and took the only protective measure one could who wanted to be outside when it was blowing: she wore wraparound sunglasses.

She was wearing them now as she walked beside the sea and gazed up at the sky. There was no season that was free from gales in the Aegean. Storms could strike at any time and did, especially in the summer, when thunderstorms were a frequent occurrence. There would be a storm that day, Meredith thought, maybe more than one, judging by the look of the clouds building up over the horizon.

It was a good day to stay inside transcribing notes, and that was what she had decided to do after she walked off her restlessness. The sea had called to her before first light, though, as it had been doing more and more, and she could not resist that call. In fact, she scarcely tried any more.

She had slept poorly again the night before, though she had not really expected to do otherwise. There had been no sign of Galen, and she had not really expected that, either. But he did not need to be present to disturb her. Taking out the piece of paper containing the phrase he had translated, she had sat for hours beside the window that looked out over the sea, brooding about Galen and the blonde swimmer.

When she had finally fallen asleep, her dreams had not been the usual ones. Instead, the faces of both men had swirled through her consciousness, and the images they had evoked were even more upsetting than the actual events of the day. She had awakened often, sweating and uneasy, and each time she had, she had looked out at the sea. She'd kept having the feeling that eyes were upon her, persistent and watchful. But of course, no one was there.

"Good morning."

The voice was unfamiliar, though deep and pleasant, as it called out the words in Greek. Not in the dialect of Karpathos, but with a formal, more ancient sound, such as Galen spoke.

Galen. She did not want to think about him right now.

Wondering who was out on her usually deserted beach so early, particularly on a morning like this, she turned to face the man who had greeted her, and froze, her mouth falling open and staying that way.

A man stood looking at her. No sunglasses protected his eyes from the irritating wind, and he was barefoot, wearing only a pair of ill-fitting cotton pants that were obviously too small for him. But his hair . . . Spun by the *meltemi*, it trailed over his shoulders in waves of gold, so long it almost seemed as if he wore a shirt. It was blonde hair. Blonde! Could he be—?

"It's you," she breathed.

"Me?"

He smiled, as though something amused him, and she stepped forward hastily.

"Were you—are you all right?"

The smile broadened. "And why should I not be?"

"Because . . ."

She hesitated, then plunged ahead. "Were you the one who was out swimming yesterday? The—the one we saw?"

"Yes, my lady," he said evenly. "I am."

She drew in her breath, but before she could speak, he said, "You certainly did not seem concerned about my welfare then. Nor did your companion. What has brought about this change?"

"It wasn't me," she began indignantly. "It was—"

"The man who was with you," he finished for her. "I saw that it was he who drove the boat. Straight at my head, I might add. Was it that neither of you noticed me?" he asked with feigned innocence.

Meredith winced at the knife-blade sharpness underlying that smooth voice. "I don't know what to say." He was watching her with the palest green eyes she had ever seen, and she resisted the urge to look away. It was mortifying to see him, to think about what had almost happened to him, but it was an even more overwhelming relief to see him at all. "I'm so glad you're all right," she said impulsively. "And I'm so sorry. Please accept my apologies. For myself, as well as for my companion."

"I doubt that he would wish you to apologize for him," the man said softly, that strange, secret smile on his face once more. "But it pleases me to hear it nonetheless. I accept."

Meredith sighed. Now that her fears about what had become of him could be laid to rest, she found herself looking at him more closely. He was very good-looking, almost too much so, as if such perfection were somehow unnatural. He was also tall, nearly as tall as Galen, and powerfully muscled in much the same way that the dark-haired Greek was. But there, all resemblance ended.

Perhaps it was that long, unkempt hair, or those pale, pale eyes, but the man was unsettling—and not in the blood-pounding, dizzying way that Galen was. This was different. Something peered out at Meredith from behind those light green eyes, something challenging and strangely cold. It set her teeth on edge, making her want to look away, yet at the same time look deeper, even though an inner voice whispered that the risk of losing herself in that gaze was very great.

Instinctively, she reacted as she always did when faced with a challenge. She stared directly into his eyes and said with determined courtesy, "I understand you're a tourist here. My name is Meredith." She put out her right hand. "And you are . . . ?"

To her surprise, he drew back a step. A scowl crossed his features, and his eyes were suddenly fierce, with that disturbing something that she had glimpsed flashing savagely bright for the briefest of instants. Then it was gone, and he was replying smoothly, "My name is Stassi, and I suppose one could say that I'm a tourist."

He fell silent, studying her, and she tried again. "Is this your first visit to Karpathos?"

"No."

"Oh. When were you here before?"

"Long ago." He said this impatiently, as though tiring of her questions. "And you?" he asked. "What are you doing on this island and in the company of a man who tried to dash a boat over me as though I were nothing more than a strand of sea kelp?"

"I'm a folklorist," she said, deciding to respond only to the first part of his question. She could see the word meant nothing to him. "I study ancient legends and stories," she elaborated. "I've come to Karpathos to write a book about some of them."

An indefinable expression passed swiftly over those per-

fect features. "How interesting. And what might those ancient legends and stories be that you have come to write
about?"

"Oh, various ones," she said, being purposely vague.
"Mostly stories having to do with the sea."

"How cryptic you are," he said softly. "Is there some reason for your secrecy?" Before she could reply he continued,
"And you have not yet answered my question about what
you were doing with the man in the boat. Do you belong to
him?"

"Belong?" Meredith forced a laugh, hoping it would hide
the uncomfortable rush of heat that raced through her. "No,
I don't *belong* to him, or to anyone else for that matter. He's
just someone who was supposed to help me with my research. What a peculiar thing to ask." She eyed him. "His
name is Galen. How do you and he know each other?"

"Why do you think we know each other?"

"It certainly seemed that way. Especially from Galen's
end." Meredith frowned. She had to ask him, had to find
answers to the questions plaguing her. "Forgive me for prying, Stassi, but when you saw the boat coming at you, why
didn't you try to get out of the way? Why were you smiling,
of all things?"

"Ah," he said thoughtfully, in a surprised voice. "You saw
me smiling?"

"Yes. Why do both of you find that so odd?"

"Both?" he repeated.

"Galen was amazed that I saw you out in the water, I
mean really amazed. Look, I know this is probably none of
my business, but I was very upset by what happened yesterday. Galen is Greek, and Greek men can be hotheaded.
Maybe if you told me what happened between you two, I
could talk to him, try to patch things up—"

"You are right," he broke in calmly. "It is none of your
business. At least, not at the moment."

Resigned, Meredith decided to drop the subject. There seemed little point in pursuing it any further. "Your name sounds Greek, too, Stassi. Where are you from?"

"Here and there." He smiled his secretive little smile. "You see? You are not the only one who can be cryptic."

"I'm not trying to—" she began, then stopped, quickly drawing in her breath.

Behind the blonde man's shoulder she saw a tall figure stalking down the beach. He was headed straight toward them, his long legs taking such powerful strides that a shorter man would have been forced to run in order to keep up with him.

"Uh oh," she muttered before she could stop herself.

Stassi glanced behind him to see what had caught her eye. When he turned back to her, his smile was back in place as though it were a permanent fixture.

"I see we are about to have company," he said blandly. "The man to whom you say you do not belong would appear to have other ideas."

CHAPTER
9

"I doubt that I have anything to do with this," Meredith said grimly. "It might be a good idea if you left."

"Why?" There was an odd, sharp note beneath Stassi's pleasant voice. "I was here first."

Meredith looked at him in amazement. "What difference does that make?" she snapped, exasperated. Men and their ridiculous posturings, she thought with disgust and more than a little worry, as Galen drew nearer. "I don't want a repeat of what happened yesterday—"

"That will not happen," Stassi assured her, still smiling. Meredith was beginning to find that smile very annoying. "For he has no boat today, does he?"

Before she could think of an answer to that, Galen was upon them. Meredith felt the blood drain from her face as she saw his expression. Without a word he lunged forward, and not pausing to think about it, she threw herself in front of him.

"Wait a minute, *wait a minute!*" she ordered.

She pushed both hands against his broad chest, all but naked under his deeply cut tank top. The heat of him reached out to surround her, its source rising from his rage as much as from the smooth flesh beneath her palms.

"Calm *down*, Galen," she said in a low voice.

He could have easily thrust her aside, and given the way he looked, she fully expected him to do so. For some inexplicable reason, though, he did not. He stood still, his chest heaving under her hands, and glared past her at Stassi. She had no idea what the expression on the blonde man's face was, and she did not dare take her attention from Galen to find out.

"What," Galen snarled in a voice she barely recognized, "is he doing here?"

"He has as much right to be here as you or I. Now stop acting so crazy!"

"Yes," Stassi said. "Please do control yourself."

Meredith felt a tremor run through Galen at the other man's words, and it was not a trembling that came from fear. "Stop it, both of you," she said quickly. "What is it with you two, anyway?"

She heard, rather than saw, the smile in Stassi's voice. "Tell her," he said to Galen. "I'm sure she would find it most interesting. She studies such things, you know. Ancient stories and legends, she told me. And with you helping her. How sweet."

Meredith was not aware of Galen stepping around her. Suddenly, he just had. She swung around after him, her eyes widening as she saw him surge forward, his hands reaching for Stassi's throat.

"Galen!" she screamed.

A part of her noted with a shameful twinge of satisfaction

that the blonde man's annoying little smile had been replaced by an openmouthed gasp of astonishment mingled
with fear. At the same time, an absurd thought flashed
through her mind: Why is there never a cop around when
you need one?

Galen picked up Stassi by the neck as though the other
man weighed no more than a handful of sand, and threw
him. Under Meredith's horrified and disbelieving gaze, he
landed an impossible distance away and lay motionless.

"Oh my God." She started after him, only to be brought
up short by a long-fingered hand that coiled around her arm
and held it like a vise.

"You will not," Galen growled in a voice that sent shivers
of anger as well as shock up her spine.

"Let me go!" she said. Before she could try to fight free
of him, Stassi clambered slowly to his feet, apparently unharmed, at least so far as Meredith could see.

"Leave this place," Galen roared at him. "Now!"

Swaying a little, Stassi stood looking at them, one hand
clutching spasmodically at his throat.

"Stassi, are you all right?" Meredith shouted, tugging fu-
tilely, furiously, at the hand that held her.

He nodded, though his pale gaze rested not on her but on
Galen. The latter took a step forward.

"I will not tell you again," he said, and the quiet of his
deep voice was far more terrible than his roar had been.

Stassi turned and stumbled off down the beach, pausing
only once to look back at them. When he did, Galen moved
toward him again, his hand still imprisoning Meredith's
arm. Only when the blonde man's tall form had disappeared
behind the clumps of brush and rocks farther up the strand,
did he release her.

Meredith spun on him. But furious as she was, he was
even angrier. "By all the forgotten gods," he exploded be-

fore she could even open her mouth, "what were you doing with him!"

Meredith stared, outraged and incredulous at once. "What in the hell business is it of yours?" She drew a deep breath, fighting for control in a situation that shifted beneath her feet as rapidly as quicksand. "Not that I owe you any explanations," she went on, "especially after the way you've behaved. But I was trying to make sure he was all right after you tried to kill him yesterday. And I was apologizing—"

"Apologizing!" Galen's piercing eyes, unprotected by sunglasses as Stassi's had been, shot blue flames. The tendons in his neck stood out in ridges. "To that one, you would—"

"He deserved an apology," she said through clenched teeth. Stassi had said Galen would not wish her to apologize on his behalf. That, she thought, was the understatement of the year. "He said you wouldn't want me to apologize for you. And he was certainly right."

Galen still stared at her. "What else did he say?"

"Nothing that would shed any light on why you turn into a complete madman whenever you see him," she snapped. "Stassi is just a tourist here, Galen. If he's offended you in some way, I'm sure it was unintentional—"

"Stassi," he interrupted. "He told you that was his name?"

She rolled her eyes. "Isn't it?"

"It doesn't matter." He looked away from her. "He is dangerous, Meredith." His voice was calmer, though only slightly. "Very dangerous. You must understand that, at all costs."

"Excuse me, Galen," she said angrily, "but you're the one who seems dangerous. And as for what I understand, all I understand is that twice now I've seen you try to kill a man without provocation, and it scares me. *You* scare me."

She paused, suddenly realizing how true that was. With an inward shiver she recalled the terrifying and violent ease with which he had picked up Stassi, who was certainly no small man himself, and tossed him through the air like a rag doll. "Flijanou may think the world of you and excuse your actions," she finished grimly, "but I don't share her high opinion—"

"Flijanou?" Galen said sharply. "What has she to do with this?"

Meredith shook her head. "I went to see her yesterday, hoping she could enlighten me about you and Stassi. But other than telling me he was a tourist—and that she'd seen him in the afternoon, so he hadn't drowned as I'd feared—all she did was defend you." She made a disgusted sound in her throat. "Do you know what she compared you to? A god. Some god. Going around attacking innocent people."

"Meredith." Slowly, almost tentatively, Galen put out a hand to touch her, then drew it back. "Do not be afraid of me, I beg you." He spoke in a changed voice, so different from the way he had sounded with Stassi, it was hard to believe he was the same person. "I would never hurt you," he went on quietly. "You must believe that."

"How can I?" She forced herself to meet his gaze. "After the way I've seen you act, how can I?"

"There is good reason for what I have done. You would not question me if you knew—"

"Then tell me." She kept her gaze on his face. "What is it, Galen? Tell me, and maybe I can help."

She waited, schooling herself to patience, and was not entirely surprised when he shook his dark head. "I cannot. I wish I could, but . . . no, it would only put you in more danger from him than you already are."

His eyes were suddenly pleading. "Promise me, Meredith," he said in an urgent tone, "that you will have nothing more to do with him. Promise that if he seeks you out, you will not let him near you, that you will flee as far and as fast from him as you can."

Completely frustrated, Meredith turned away. She was strongly tempted to tell Galen that she had sensed something in Stassi that rubbed her the wrong way, but she held back. Surely to tell him that would only encourage him in his obsession, and that was the last thing she wanted. Truth be told, though, she was not particularly anxious to see Stassi again. And Galen, did she want to see him again? She no longer knew.

"I have to go," she said shortly.

"Where?"

She stiffened at the note of interrogation in that one word. "Back to my house," she said with exaggerated politeness. "To wash the sand from this damn wind out of my hair, and then to get some work done. I've had quite enough excitement for one morning," she added. "Enough for the rest of the week, in fact."

"It's probably best," Galen said. "The *meltemi* will make traveling over the water in a boat most unpleasant, and the sea and the air speak to me of storms."

An unwilling smile tugged the corners of Meredith's mouth at the poetic way he described this cloudy, windy day. "Well, good-bye."

She started toward the path that led to her house.

"Wait," Galen called after her. "The weather will be better tomorrow, and perhaps we can go to the cave I told you of, yes?"

She paused but did not turn around. "I don't know, Galen. I don't know."

Galen watched her walk down the beach, straight-backed and beautiful. His heart twisted with an anxiety and a rage so intense, it made him feel physically ill. Rigidly, he began to stalk up and down the white-hot sand that, whipped by the wind, swirled stingingly around his ankles.

How dare Anastas show up smirking and grinning with a veiled threat plain behind his eyes, obviously thinking that in the presence of a Terran, his grudge-mate would not risk giving way to his feelings!

Unfortunately, he had been right, at least in part. If Meredith had not been present, Galen would not have stopped with merely tossing him down the beach, but beyond a doubt would have twisted the very head from his body.

Yet there was more to Anastas's showing up there than a desire to taunt him. Galen knew that with a certainty that chilled his blood. Anastas's warning had been unmistakable.

You have an interest in this woman, those reptilian eyes had said. And now I have found her as well.

The disharmony and evil that had found such a welcome home in Anastas had washed toward Galen like a polluted tide as he'd glared at the blonde one over Meredith's head. In some peculiar way he had grown stronger in his banishment, Galen had realized, but more and more unbalanced. It was a dangerous combination.

He clenched his fists, ignoring the grit-filled gusts of wind that swept up to batter his face. To one who had killed his own cousin's parents, what would the taking of a landwoman's life mean? Nothing. Especially if his twisted mind told him there was something to be gained from it.

And what of Flijanou? Had she really seen Anastas as she had told Meredith, or was she only covering for the one she called sea lord?

Galen hoped and suspected it was the latter. It was unlikely that Anastas would have shown himself to the old woman and told her what he was. Without an Elder to advise him of Flijanou's status, as Cleonith had advised Galen, Anastas would have no way of knowing about the Greek woman's special relationship to the merfolk.

Meredith, however, was not so lucky. By seeking her out so openly, Galen had put her in danger. He could not have known that the banished ones were in these waters, but his ignorance of that changed nothing. Meredith had been seen, and now it was up to him to protect her — and just as important, the knowledge she carried.

All through the long hours of the previous night he had hovered in the stretch of the sea below her house, on guard in case Anastas or one of his minions came ashore in an attempt to get to her. He would have been utterly unsurprised if they had. Destruction was what his onetime kinsman lived for, and it would provide Anastas special pleasure to rob Galen of a landwoman he thought the latter wanted, perhaps killing her in the process.

And Galen did want her. That was the misery of it, and the truth. It pulsed beneath the fear that had kept him in the quiet sea through the long dark hours, watching and waiting.

His merfolk gaze had fastened on Meredith with ease, and with a persistent longing he kept trying to push from his mind, as she had sat beside her window, gazing out at the star-silvered sea. Much later in the night he had seen her appear and reappear by that same window, clearly unable to sleep.

He had left only when Toklat's distant call had come to him just before dawn, and torn as he was by his desire to protect Meredith, the decision to go had been difficult.

The Selkie had departed the previous afternoon, immediately after he had found Galen and told him of his meeting with the banished ones. Like all his kind, Toklat was a fast and powerful swimmer. By morning, he should have been far advanced on the journey to Galen's abode and Cleonith. Too far away to send any sort of message, owing to the fact that the telepathic powers of Selkies were not as great as those of the merfolk.

The call Galen had heard had been very faint, but that it had come at all was reason enough to respond. The need to find out what his brother-friend wanted had to come first, and though Galen had hesitated, he had left quickly, albeit reluctantly, to swim in search of Toklat.

However, the distant hail had soon faded, then disappeared entirely. Galen had circled for a while, waiting for it to come again. When it did not, he had turned, troubled and dissatisfied, back toward land.

As he'd neared Karpathos, the sense of Anastas had crashed out to meet him like a great dark wave. The blonde one had strength enough to cloak his presence from other merfolk, even his powerful grudge-mate, and that was apparently what he had done until then. Perhaps he had even arranged for one of his followers to imitate a Selkie call so that Galen would be lured away from his guarding of the landwoman.

Galen had not been able to reach the wide strands of Karpathos fast enough. He had come ashore and thrown on his clothes, the gusting sweeps of the *meltemi* drying his body almost instantly. Then he had raced down the beach, intent on cutting off Anastas before he could encounter Meredith.

He had been too late.

Galen's restless strides grew longer as he recalled that heartstopping moment when he had seen Anastas standing close to Meredith, so close that he could have easily reached out and pulled her into his arms, and then on into the sea.

Absently, Galen picked up several small rocks and closed his hand around them in a fist. With one of Anastas's followers sick, and with the information Toklat had unwittingly provided about other merfolk being affected by the same malady, it might be that Anastas's interest in Meredith

went beyond the simple desire to hurt whatever or whom-
ever Galen took an interest in.

"That one must *not* find out about the scroll," he muttered. "He must not."

Unconsciously, he tightened his hand, and when it
opened, the rocks had been crushed into dust.

Anastas cursed savagely, a stream of the most vile words
in the merfolk tongue spitting from his mouth as he swam
deep below the sea, letting the currents take him along the
western coast of the island. His neck felt like one great mass
of pain, and he knew that even with the natural vitality of
his people, it would take some days for the deep bruising to
heal.

Galen's grip was not something to be taken lightly. Of
course, Anastas was well aware of the dark merman's
strength, but he had been supremely confident that if his
grudge-mate showed up and found him with the Terran, he
would not risk revealing his strength in front of her. How
wrong he had been.

The realization that he had miscalculated only added fuel
to the fury already possessing him. His hatred for Galen, his
craving for revenge, throbbed as fiercely as his injured
neck, and they were helped along even more by the frustrating encounter with the landwoman called Meredith.

He had thought to use his powers on her, reducing her to
nothingness as he probed her mind to discover what, if anything, she knew about Galen. Then he had planned to seduce her, marking her so irretrievably as his that she would
never look at Galen, much less any man of her own
blood, again.

It should have been easy. The strongest Terran mind was
no match for even the weakest of merfolk, and Anastas was
far from weak. Indeed, he had been as supremely confident

of his ability to conquer the landwoman as he'd been certain Galen would not dare harm him before her eyes. At worst, if Galen came upon them together, he would put off his seduction for another time, after planting the anticipation of it deeply in Meredith's mind, of course.

But he had been wrong about her as well.

She had resisted him! Anastas snarled wildly in the darkness of two hundred feet down, thrashing at the water as though it were his enemy, heedless of the school of damselfish that darted out of his path in a frenzy of terrified motion.

That puny, inferior land female had resisted him and won. He, who was capable of exerting such control over those of his own kind that brother would kill brother at his command! Yet that woman had kept him out of her mind as easily as a sea otter's fur kept out the cold.

It was infuriating, impossible to understand, and more and more maddening every time he tried to make sense of it. Perhaps Galen, too, had sought to use his powers upon the creature, with the same result, and this was the secret of his fascination with her. But with a mysterious illness attacking the merfolk, and his grudge-mate's devotion to the foolish concept of selflessness, it seemed odd that he would be taking up time with Meredith when a cure cried out to be found.

Unless, she was somehow connected with that cure.

The furious pace of Anastas's swimming slowed as that idea occurred to him. An interesting notion, but surely not one worth considering, he decided in a fresh wave of disgust. Despite her peculiar reaction to his power, the landwoman was, when all was said and done, only a landwoman. Of what possible help could a mere Terran be to the vastly superior people of the sea?

Anastas increased his speed again, angling off in the direction his followers had taken the previous day when they had set off in pursuit of Toklat. It was time they were returning, he thought impatiently. After all, how long did it take to overcome a Selkie, when there were five to his one?

I should have gone myself, he muttered in mind-speak. *Even at my worst tide, I am more capable than all of them combined.*

He swam on through the morning, stopping to make a meal out of some shrimp he came across, then continuing on his way without pausing to linger. The day was half gone when he finally sensed the approach of his band.

At last, he growled to himself, and sped up his pace to meet them.

Their shapes moved toward him through the gloom of deep waters, slowly becoming more distinct as they drew closer. Tovash was in the lead, with the others forming a ragged phalanx behind him, Malk bringing up the rear. Even at this distance, Anastas could see that they were tired. And wounded. In spite of himself he was impressed by this observation.

Well, the Selkie was a better fighter than I would have given him credit for.

With a powerful kick of both legs, he shot forward, coming face to face with Tovash. His second-in-command halted instantly, and Anastas saw that despite his obvious exhaustion, he had a satiated look about him.

It must have gone well, he observed. As his gaze drifted to the gaping wounds borne by Tovash and each of his three companions, he added, *Though all of you look somewhat the worse for wear.*

Tovash curled his lip, remembering just in time to be respectful. *The Selkie fought, but he did not win, Lord. We did. You were right in having us go after him.*

Anastas stared at the other merman until Tovash glanced nervously away. *Of course.* He sent the two mind-spoken words out on a layer of ice. *Else I would not have sent you. Now tell me. What did you learn?*

There was a brief flurry of glances between Tovash, Bron, Gilkon, Memenon, and even Malk. Then Tovash answered.

Lord, he sent, *there is a scroll ...*

CHAPTER
10

Storms billowed up later that day, arriving in great dark clouds over the Aegean and whipping up the waters beneath them before they finally blew onto land. They were unusually fierce storms, even for that time of year, heavy with thunder and lightning, and laden with rain that fell from the troubled sky in streams, pounding against the tile roof of Meredith's house like a million enraged fists.

Afternoon sank into evening, with Meredith scarcely noticing the change, so dark and wild had the weather turned. At her favorite window she leaned against the rain-spattered glass, watching as daggers of lightning stabbed viciously at a roiling black sea, and against her will, thought of Galen.

Neither he nor Flijanou had ever mentioned where he stayed on the island. With all the inexplicable events that had happened since she had met him, Meredith had not thought to ask. Now she found herself wondering about it, hoping that wherever it was, he was there and out of the violent path of the storm.

"Though it would serve him right if he got the drenching of his life," she muttered, and reluctantly turned away from the wild beauty of the night, back to the table where she had spread out her work.

It had not been a very productive day, she thought, staring glumly at the jumbled piles of paper and cassette tapes. The scene between Galen and Stassi had left her too wrought up to concentrate. Even a bath followed by a late breakfast had not helped, though she had fervently hoped it might. Still, she had been determined to put that morning out of her mind, and after clearing the remains of her meal, she had gone to work transcribing tapes.

She had not made a great deal of progress.

The tapes that needed to be transcribed were all of Flijanou. They contained lengthy conversations with the Greek woman as she described old sea superstitions, some of them dating so far back, Flijanou herself could not say where they had originated. Normally Meredith would have enjoyed the transcribing. Having accepted the Americana fully, Flijanou needed no urging to speak, and with the younger woman as a delighted and respectful listener, the old one would ramble on happily for hours.

Her recitals, and the depth of knowledge that gave rise to them, were mesmerizing. That afternoon, though, the sound of that ancient voice had continually sidetracked Meredith, distracting her into remembering their conversation of the day before, about Galen. From there, it was all too easy to call up her most recent emotions about this dark, puzzling man: confusion, anger, and most disturbing of all, the feel of his smooth, warm skin beneath her palms, mingled with the intimate surge of heat that swept out to enfold her whenever he was near.

By the time the first of the storms had arrived just after

midday, they were almost a welcome diversion. But now, after hours of listening to the rain beat a steady counterpoint to her thoughts, Meredith decided to make another attempt at getting some work done.

She flipped on the tape she had last been listening to and sipped absently at the rapidly cooling cup of tea she had made a short time earlier. Flijanou's creaky voice filled the room.

". . . superstition, belief, or whatever you wish to call it, my child, that beneath the fur and flesh of a seal there is actually a woman. That is why the older ones among us do not care for swimming. The sea does not belong to us, you know, she only tolerates us. *We* are not her true children, no, not at all. Her true children, well, that is something else again.

"Ah, but where was I—oh, yes, the seals. There is an old, old fear that if someone swims out too far, he runs the risk of being seized by this woman in the shape of a seal and strangled."

There was a brief silence, then the old woman cleared her throat with a loud hacking sound before resuming. "The creature then carries the lifeless human body to some distant shore and weeps over it. That is why we have the saying that, 'when a woman sheds false tears, she cries like a seal' . . ."

A crack of thunder boomed, followed by a burst of wind that slashed at the house until the windows rattled in their frames. The rain was falling even harder now, so hard that Meredith had to turn up the volume on the tape player to hear over it. As a result, she did not at first hear the voice outside.

"Meredith!"

She jerked up so abruptly, her tea sloshed over the notes she had been struggling all day to make. She swore at the spreading brown stain, shaking the wet pages, and wondered if she had really heard her name or if it was just the cry of the wind.

Her name was shouted again. This time it was unmistakable, and so was the deep voice that had called it out.

Hastily, the wet notes forgotten, Meredith jumped up from the table. What in the world was Galen doing there, and on a night like this? She went to the door, but just as she was about to fling it open, she stopped. Uncertainty raced through her so powerfully that she shifted from foot to foot, her mind filled with a hundred screaming doubts. Was it entirely wise to let this man in?

The memory of his violence toward Stassi coiled uneasily through her mind, and she stood with her hand on the knob, torn by two conflicting pictures: Galen's dark, beautiful face frozen in an expression of terrible rage, and later, how he had looked when they were alone and he had pleaded with her to be careful. That same face had been tense with concern then. For her.

The two images chased each other, each struggling to remain uppermost in her thoughts. Suddenly she realized that the only sounds she heard now were those of the storm. Galen had not called out again.

The second picture abruptly won the fight in Meredith's mind. What if he was hurt? No one should be out on a night like this. . . .

Worry overriding everything else, she pulled open the door. Just to make sure he was all right, she told herself.

A blast of wind-driven rain promptly hit her in the face. She shook the water droplets from her eyes, peering hard into the darkness as she battled the storm's furious efforts to slam the door back in her face. Lightning arched across the sky, and in its flicker and dazzle she thought she glimpsed a figure on the path that led down to the beach.

"Galen!" she yelled.

Thunder roared over her words, and though it seemed

impossible that she could be heard in the tumult, the figure turned around. Through flashing spears of light it made its way across the yard, then suddenly Galen was there before her.

Now that her decision had been made, Meredith was eager to get in out of the storm. She ducked back into the house, forcing the wind-battered door to stay open until he could follow her inside.

"Good Lord." She brushed a sopping strand of hair from her eyes. "*What* are you doing out there on a night like this? Are you crazy?"

Galen shrugged. He was soaked to the bone but seemed singularly undisturbed by it. In fact, it looked to Meredith as though he was not even aware that he was wet. He made no attempt to shake the water from his hair or body, but stood calmly, letting the drops cascade down him onto the parquet floor.

"I was worried about you," he said quietly. He stepped close, gazing down into her face. "And as for the storm"— his fierce eyes took on a deep, startling glow—"it is beautiful, is it not?"

"Yeah." Meredith forced herself to step back, covering her reaction to his nearness by adding gruffly, "But not when you carry it in with you and drip it all over my house. Let me get you a towel."

It was a relief to have an excuse for turning away from that jewel-bright gaze. She went into the hall, to the wooden chest where the house's owners had laid in a supply of linens for her. Pulling out the largest towel she could find, she came back. "You're absolutely drenched," she said, handing it to him. "How long have you been out there?"

"For some time." He gave the towel an amused glance, then took it from her and dabbed politely at himself. "I apologize for the puddles. Being wet does not bother me. Indeed, I enjoy it. I always have."

"Well, you certainly picked a good night to indulge yourself," Meredith said wryly. She scrutinized him through narrowed eyes. "Did you come all the way out here just because you were worried about me?"

"Yes."

"Why?"

He met her eyes, the towel now dangling forgotten in one large hand. "I felt very bad about how things were left between us this morning," he said in a careful tone. "I did not—I mean, I wanted to set things right, Meredith." His brow furrowed in a troubled frown. "Are you truly afraid of me?"

She did not reply at once. Then she sighed. "I was this morning."

"And now?"

"Now, I don't know." She gave him a small ironic smile. "I suppose I'm not too afraid, or I wouldn't have let you in the door. Although I'd have to believe you were a real monster to leave you outside on a night like this."

As if to punctuate her words, a peal of thunder boomed overhead, adding its rumble to the steady rain pounding on the roof. She grimaced. "So far, the roof hasn't sprung any leaks, but if this keeps up—"

"It will." He spoke with indisputable authority, as if the sky itself had whispered some secret to him. "At least until dawn," he added. "By sunrise, the storms will have moved on." He looked past her to the dining room table where she had been sitting. "You have been working today, I see."

"Trying to." She glanced disgustedly behind her at the table. "I haven't accomplished as much as I would have liked."

He threw her a keen glance from beneath thick black lashes. "Because of what happened this morning?"

"Of course." She heard the testiness in her voice, but made no apology for it. "What else would it be?"

Without answering, he walked over to the table. He stood there for some moments, his attention wandering from the tape player to her tea-stained notes.

She watched him curiously, though with little concern. All of her notes and writings about the scroll, as well as the scroll itself, were safely tucked in a case under several other cases, all of them stowed carefully beneath her bed. She walked over to join him.

"I've been listening to Flijanou," she explained. Reaching past him, she rewound the tape and turned the cassette on to the part she had been listening to before. Flijanou's voice came into the room, relating the legend about seals actually being women.

Galen stood motionless. A slight smile appeared on his face as he listened, widening into an outright grin when Flijanou reached the part about the seal-woman strangling hapless swimmers if they went too far out into the sea. The way that grin transformed his face so entranced Meredith that she paid little heed to the tale she was already familiar with, until Galen murmured something under his breath, so softly she could not make it out.

"What did you say?"

He was still smiling. "Just that there are many I know who would disagree quite strongly with this story. They would either laugh or be angry." His smile grew a little sad. "Poor Flijanou. Do you think she believes what she told you?"

Meredith bristled at the subtle note of condescension in his voice. "I admire Flijanou a great deal," she said stiffly. "She's a very wise woman who's lived a long, long time and has seen more than you and I put together. A person as old as she is deserves my respect. And it's not for me or you or anyone else to sit in judgment of what she does or doesn't believe."

Galen seemed unoffended by her tone. "She would be

pleased at hearing you defend her," he said gently. "And it is good to find that someone as young as you has such respect for age."

"More than you, apparently." She turned off the tape player. "You know, you never answered my question before."

He was watching her now, instead of the cassette deck. They were standing close together again, as close as when he first had entered the house, and even though he did not move nearer to her, Meredith suddenly felt as if he had.

"What question was that?"

"About why you were worried about me."

"Ah." The grin vanished so completely from his face, it was hard to believe it had ever been there.

"I don't know why you would be," she went on quickly. "No one in his right mind would think of going out in a storm like this. Except," she added wickedly, "someone like you, who gets his kicks out of waiting to be hit by lightning or washed away by a wave."

"Being washed away by a wave is not a thing I concern myself with," he said, and his voice was as changed as his expression, which had become as distant and cold as a rock facing out to a northern sea. "And there are others beside myself who do not fear going out in storms."

She frowned at him. "You're not talking about Stassi, are you?"

"He is not what he seems, Meredith. I beg you to realize that."

"And what about you, Galen?" Frustration boiled up inside her, seizing her with a force that surprised her, despite the anger and confusion she had been wrestling with all day. She was so fed up with this man and all the mystery he surrounded himself with! "Are you what you seem? Because I have as many doubts about you as I do about Stassi."

Galen let her wrath slide by him unnoticed. "So you are

wary of him after all," he said with obvious relief. "Good. To hear that you at least have some doubts is a hopeful sign."

"I have more doubts," she said tightly, "about you. Or haven't you been listening? Since I've met you, you've done nothing but cause me trouble and interfere with my work." Even as she said it, she knew it was not entirely true. She'd been having trouble long before that. But wound up by her anger, she was not particularly interested in acknowledging that technicality.

"First you pass yourself off as a simple fisherman," she continued hotly. "Then you tell me it was all a ruse, and you're really an archaeologist from Athens. Well, maybe you are and maybe you aren't, but you were able to translate a language one of the best experts in the world couldn't fathom, and you claim to know a lot more. Only when it comes to showing me some of that supposed knowledge, like that cave yesterday, you back out right when we get there because of some stupid feud with a tourist."

She paused to catch her breath, then finished in a determined rush. "Well, I'm not interested in whatever it is you and Stassi are fighting about. It doesn't concern me. And what's more, I'm sick and tired of this mysterious act of yours. Right now, I don't care if you're an archaeologist or a spy for the Russians. I've got work to do. If you really do know something and want to help me with that work, then we can talk. Otherwise, I'd just as soon have nothing more to do with you, and I mean nothing! Do I make myself clear?"

She was baffled to see Galen smile at her with what she could only term admiration. He had listened patiently to her tirade, completely unaffected by her ire. She had not expected that reaction, and it frustrated her more than anything else. "Maybe you take this lightly," she began on a fresh wave of irritation, "but I —"

He shook his head, his face grave. "No, Meredith," he said quietly. "I do not take this lightly at all. You have no idea how serious all of this is to me."

"Really?" She refused to be mollified. "That just sounds like more of your mysterious act to me. Stop playing games, Galen. You said you had a cave to show me, so go ahead, show it to me."

He watched her a moment, then seemed to come to a decision. "When?"

"Tomorrow morning," she said without hesitation. "You said the weather would clear, didn't you? If your powers of prediction are that good, then there shouldn't be a problem."

"You said you were afraid of me," he reminded her. "Doesn't it concern you, the idea of going out alone with me to a remote place?" He watched her closely as he spoke, his expression at once curious and intent.

"I'm alone with you now," she pointed out. "And I'm not concerned."

She was shocked to realize this was true. Whatever apprehensions and fears she had felt toward Galen had evaporated as she'd finally given vent to her anger. But there was something else as well.

Just as she had sensed a quality in the blonde tourist that was "off" in some inexplicable way, she also felt in a deep part of herself that Galen—enigmatic and annoying as he was—meant her no harm. She could not say why she felt this, only that she did, and more strongly than at any other time since she had met him.

"The only thing I'm afraid of," she said, "is that we'll run into Stassi again and I'll have to try to keep you from acting like you've lost your mind. But as long as you can control yourself, I'll be okay."

As long as he could control himself. An appropriate choice of words, Galen thought. That was what he had been trying to do from the first moment he had entered her house.

He loved storms and the wild weather they brought; he always had. They exhilarated him, fired his blood, leaving him subtly, and sometimes not so subtly, aroused. Tonight, with so much else preying on his mind, it was the former. The arousal was still there, and Meredith's nearness only enhanced it.

The burdens he carried—the fears for his people, the hatred for Anastas and worry over what he might do to Meredith, the frustration of dealing with Meredith herself—all of those were still with him, weighing him down like the deepest, blackest level of the Midnight Sea. But here in this land dwelling, with the heat of the storm racing through his blood, there was surcease. At least for a little while.

Meredith was temporarily safe. After what had happened that morning, Anastas would not dare to come near her as long as Galen was present. As for Toklat, he was well on his way to Cleonith by now. The storm would have little effect on his journey, for Selkies were as comfortable with Mother Ocean in all her moods as were the merfolk.

So for this short space of time, Galen could rest. And who knows, a calculating voice whispered in his head, perhaps the time could be put to use in seeking the knowledge about the scroll which this landwoman possessed but would not share.

However, more was driving him than just the desire to accomplish that objective, important as it was. There was the woman herself.

His senses, far keener than those of any man who was chained to the land, tormented him as he looked at Meredith. He was aware of everything about her, as though he sensed her in every pore. The rhythm of her breathing, the rise and fall of her breasts beneath the loose, soft top she wore, even the very pulse of the blood moving through her veins, teased him, calling out to him as relentlessly as the tide.

He could not take his eyes from her. Her legs and arms were bare, her long neck as graceful as a water bird's. In the golden-orange light of the lamps her sun-browned skin had a velvety sheen, and she had freed her hair to lie loose over her shoulders. Hanging down in a silky, dark mass, it seemed to capture and hold the flickering lightning in its depths. It captured him as well, so that he yearned to catch handfuls in his grasp, testing its softness against his face.

To keep from doing exactly that, he moved a few steps away from the table. She was watching him. He could feel her dark, dark eyes upon him, and he almost saw the questions forming in her mind before she asked them.

Unfortunately, her curiosity and yes, her wariness—even her frustration—were all too understandable, given the behavior she had witnessed on his part. Curse his temper! If he had been able to ignore Anastas when he surfaced yesterday, things might have turned out very differently. Or they might not have. It was useless to speculate about that now.

"Galen." Meredith leaned a hip against the edge of the table and folded her arms across her chest. "Where are you staying on Karpathos? You've never said, and neither has Flijanou."

"Perhaps because it is with her that I stay whenever I visit this island."

"With Flijanou?" Meredith was surprised. "Her house is so tiny! I don't even see where there would be room for you to sleep."

He shrugged. "I make do. My requirements in such matters are small."

Meredith thought for a moment about it, a pensive frown drawing her eyebrows together. "It seems odd, but"—it was her turn to shrug—"as you said, your requirements are small."

"Yes," he said slowly. "In other matters, however, they are not so small."

He fell silent, and to Meredith, it seemed that his eyes had changed color, taking on a deeper hue, like the sea at twilight. Thunder snarled through the room, loud enough to drown out any attempt at speech. He appeared to listen to it, a smile teasing the corners of his mouth. When the thunder had rumbled on, he gazed out the broad window to where spears of lightning still dueled with one another over the Aegean.

"I love the sounds," he said dreamily. "The music of this night."

"The thunder?" Meredith's own gaze grew distant. "Or the sea?" She, too, was listening as she spoke. Her attention was suddenly distracted, leaving her unaware of Galen for the first time since she had let him in.

Unlikely as it seemed, she truly could hear the sea's voice in the midst of all the wind and rain and thunder. Perhaps it was only in her head, for what she heard was not the wild roar of breakers crashing against the land, but something farther off, a keening song, one moment high, the next moment low. It was a familiar song, one that haunted her dreams and tugged at her soul without ceasing, filling her with a nameless longing she could never seem to grab hold of or satisfy.

She realized that Galen was staring at her, a strange new intensity in his face. He moved nearer, and his eyes were aglitter with all the twilight colors of the ocean. "How is it"—his voice was deep, drawing her as much as his eyes, as much as a tide flowing out to sea—"how is it that a woman of the land can hear the voice of the sea in her blood?"

"I—I don't know." She watched him come closer, unable to move, and unwilling to. "I always hear the sea." Even when she was trying not to, she thought. But she did not say that aloud.

"Always?" He was standing in front of her, looking down into her face.

She nodded. A lassitude had come over her limbs at his nearness, weighting her down as though he were deep waters and she a rock, falling, falling . . .

She pulled back. It was the storm, she told herself. This night was having a strange effect on her, and having the equally disturbing Galen with her certainly did not help.

He was still staring at her, his eyes blazing with all those entrancing, constantly shifting colors of the sea.

"Beautiful Meredith," he said softly. "I think you are not what you seem, any more than I am."

She drew back even farther. "I don't know what you mean," she said sharply, more sharply than she had intended. "What are you talking about?"

He did not seem to hear her. "Who are you?" he asked, still using that soft, low voice, a voice that again made her think irrationally, wildly, of the distant calling sea. "Who are you, really?"

CHAPTER
11

Meredith was thankful for the thunder that boomed at that moment, forestalling any attempt to respond. In the daylight, under the clear hard sun, she would have laughed, made some light, inconsequential answer to such a question. In this golden-lit room, though, that was little more than a tiny glow dwarfed by the night and by the unleashed magnificence of storm and sea, and in the presence of this enigmatic man—in whose eyes she saw the sea, in whose voice she heard the ebb and flow of the tides—she could not find the words, glib or otherwise.

For rising from some deep, frightened part of her soul, the same question thrummed throughout her entire being, torturing her as it had ever since the scroll had come into her life. A question she dared not acknowledge to herself, much less to Galen.

Who was she?

"I have no idea what you're getting at," she said, and peered at him suspiciously. "And what do you mean, 'woman of the land'?"

He came closer again, slowly, as if he didn't want to frighten her. "There are those who belong to the land, and"—he glanced toward the window—"there are those who belong to the sea."

Meredith followed his gaze. In her mind's eye she saw the sea—surging, calling, sending white-foamed breakers onto the land, breakers that sought her out and only her, that tried ceaselessly to draw her back with them in their eager return to the depths.

"But how do you know," she whispered, and a despair she was not aware of cried out in her voice, "which one you belong to?"

"For those who are of the sea, there is no question. Only the knowing."

She brought her back to him. "Where do you belong, Galen? With the sea or with the land?"

"Is it not obvious?" he asked in a curious tone.

She nodded vaguely, still entangled in the mood that refused to leave her. "I can see the sea in your eyes," she said, and wondered at the note of certainty in her voice, wondered that she had said it at all.

He smiled. "And I can see . . ."

His voice trailed off, and he stared hard into her eyes. Abruptly, he turned away from her. "It *can't* be," he muttered. "It can't be."

The mood that had held Meredith motionless vanished like mist upon the waves. She shook her head, feeling as though she had been dreaming and had just woken up.

"What is it?" she demanded. "What can't be?"

He spun around and, before she could move back, he took her gently by the shoulders. "Meredith, have you always lived . . . in this Madison place?"

She heard such an aching need in his question that she answered without trying to pull away. "Yes."

"Always?" he persisted. "Since you were born?"

"Yes." She looked up at him, trying to fathom his expression. "I've told you that."

As gently as he had gripped her, he released her. "There is no sea in this Madison," he said slowly, "is there?"

She shook her head. "No, there isn't. I've told you that before too."

"So you have."

He looked at her as though he would say more, and she watched him, noticing how his hands tightened at his sides. That simple movement, eloquent with frustration, awoke a strong feeling of sympathy in her. If there was one thing she was familiar with lately, it was frustration.

"Galen." Her voice was as gentle as his touch upon her had been. "What's wrong?"

"Everything," he said. "You are not what you should be, what I expected. You are filled with secrets, and I must know those secrets. You must tell me . . ."

Once again his deep voice trailed off, and they looked at each other. It seemed to Meredith that the night had closed in around them, wrapping her house up in stormy arms, leaving them the only two people on Karpathos, in the whole world.

"How can I tell you what I don't know?" she burst out. "There's so much I don't understand. About me, about you—"

"Tell me." His voice called to her, reminding her jarringly of the voice in her dreams. "Tell me what you seek."

She almost did, for she was tempted, oh, how she was tempted. But she did not. She could not.

"I'm sorry," she said. And she was.

He sighed, a soft exhalation of sound she heard in her bones despite the clamor outside. He did not speak, though.

When the silence and the weight of his gaze upon her had become too much, she finally spoke herself.

"Well," she began awkwardly. "It's getting late—"

"You wish me to go?"

"Back out into that?" She gestured at the rain-swept window. "Don't be ridiculous."

"I do not mind," he told her, a smile lighting his somber face. "The storms do not—"

"Bother you," she finished for him. "I know. But they do bother me. I don't like to think of you walking all the way back to Flijanou's house in this weather."

She made herself meet his eyes and put all the briskness she could into her voice. "Flijanou will probably have a fit when she hears about it, but it looks like the only thing to do is to have you stay here."

He was staring at her in a way she found impossible to fathom. One thing, however, was obvious. There was desire in those twilight-sea eyes. She could see it clearly, so clearly that she wondered what had possessed her to extend the invitation in the first place. It was out of the goodness of her heart, she told herself wryly, although she knew, whether or not she could admit it to herself or to Galen, that there was far more to it than that.

For a quick moment she was sorely tempted to rescind her spontaneous offer—to shut the door she had opened between them by her words. But there were other qualities in Galen's deep gaze besides desire, and she saw those just as clearly. The sea was speaking to her from his eyes, and it was those swirling deep visions of distant places and wild feelings that decided her.

"You can sleep on the couch," she said. "It's quite comfortable, and—"

"I will be fine." He continued to smile at her. "It is kind of you to ask me. But are you certain you don't mind?"

Unbidden, an answering smile tugged at Meredith's lips.

She was crazy, a voice whispered, completely out of her mind to let a man who affected her as this one did stay in the same house with her, whether on the couch or anywhere else. Unless, of course, she *wanted* something to happen. . . .

"No," she said. "I don't mind."

Far out at sea, the waves towered to wild heights, leaping up at a sky that sizzled with lightning before they crashed down to batter and then lose themselves upon the breast of Mother Ocean.

A forlorn figure drifted upon those dark waters, his blood seeping out to mingle with the wind-tossed foam. He was oblivious to the storm—heedless, in fact, of everything but the need to move, to swim steadily on.

Long ago, he had stopped thinking. Over the past few hours, he had even ceased to remember why it was so important that he continue moving. Though his thoughts were no longer functioning, however, his torn body forced itself doggedly on its way, stroking toward a destination his mind no longer had any connection with.

The waves played with him, tossing his bleeding form this way and that without mercy, throwing him savagely into the air, only to catch and crush him in their salty embrace when he hurtled down. He paid little heed to their fury. He let them do as they wished, allowing them to vent their spleen on him, then moving on, always managing to swim in the same direction.

The flame of life that burned within him had grown faint. With the passage of this long and storm-filled night, it was close to flickering out completely.

There were many in whom that flame would have long since turned from embers to ashes, many whose lifeless bodies would now be floating upon the waves. However, this poor battered traveler was strong, and he came of a strong people. He would not give up until that tiny light no longer burned at all.

So he swam on, some dim, barely conscious sense leading him forward, on toward the island of Karpathos and the one there he had to reach.

Galen stretched out his legs and propped his elbows behind his head. As Meredith had said, the couch was comfortable—for a piece of Terran furniture—but it was barely long enough to contain his length. His feet hung so far over the armrest that he had at last tossed the cushions onto the floor and laid himself down there instead.

He would have preferred his true bed, the moving cradle of waves that had lulled him to sleep for centuries. Yet one night's slumber was a paltry thing to give up in exchange for being in this house and so near the puzzling, frustrating, and enormously compelling Meredith.

He was all too aware that she was as wide awake as he. Perhaps the storm was keeping her from sleep, or maybe there was another reason for her wakefulness. His presence, perhaps?

Galen stared into the darkness. He hoped so.

She had closed the door to her bedroom before retiring, but that made little difference to him. His ears picked up every sound she made. He could hear her breathing, listened with ease to every rustle as she tossed restlessly in her bed. In his mind's eye he could see her long legs entwined in the covers, could feel the smoothness of the sheets on which she lay, could feel it as keenly as though they were beneath his own body. He was fired by a yearning that demanded he throw open the door that separated him from her and join her in that lonely bed.

Yet he held himself back, sensing that if he waited long enough, she would come to him. And in truth, that was what he wanted. How ironic it was, he thought, touched by a sudden wash of sadness. He was capable of seeking to probe this woman's mind without her knowledge or consent. Indeed, he had already tried to do so. But to share lovemaking with her was another matter entirely.

Whatever happened between them in that regard must happen of her own free will. Still, he wanted it to happen with every fiber of his being and for reasons far beyond the physical lure of her. Perhaps through making love, her secrets would finally be revealed to him. Perhaps then he would understand . . .

He shifted on the cushions and stared out the window, listening to the sea.

Meredith rolled over on her back. Lightning flashed against her closed eyelids, followed by a steady roll of thunder that shook the bed. She sighed and opened her eyes to gaze up at the shadowed ceiling.

The storm did not seem to be letting up at all, a fact that at least made her feel she had done the charitable thing in insisting that Galen stay the rest of the night. What it had done for her, was questionable.

Galen's powerful presence imbued the entire house, including the dubious sanctuary of her bedroom, closed door and all. There was no denying him or the pull he exerted upon her. The only question was what she was going to do about it.

What indeed?

She sat up and threw off the light coverlet. Sleep did not seem likely just now, not with *him* lying only a door's width away on her couch. She propped her back against the headboard, her eyes drawn as always to the view outside her window.

Lightning still skittered through the black sky, and outlined in its fitful illumination, white-foamed breakers continued to lash at the land. Running through the storm, mingling with the sound of wind and waves, the distant keening voice of the sea called to her more persistently than ever.

Listening to that far-off song, watching the sea and the storm, and thinking of Galen on her couch, Meredith lost track of how long she had sat there. She only knew that gradually her eyes grew heavy, her head listed to one side, and then—she was dreaming.

It was the old dream, the familiar one, in which she and the faceless man were making love. He murmured to her in a voice as deep and compelling as a midnight tide. His body felt safe, that of a friend as well as a lover. It joined with hers. Their blending together was sweet and all-consuming, like the satisfying of a long-held thirst. It aroused a feeling of trust in Meredith's soul, as much as it did a deep and wild delight.

She awoke sharply, a low cry trembling on her lips— whether from shock at the dream's vividness, or from its pleasure, she did not know. Disoriented, she turned her face to the door, feeling in every thread of her soul the tread of swift, light footsteps down the hall.

"Meredith," a deep voice said softly. "Are you all right?" *That voice.*

Still caught up in the mists of her dream, Meredith swung her legs over the edge of the bed and stumbled to the door. As she put her hand on the knob, she felt a deep, tolling awareness that if she opened that door, she would be doing more than just opening a door. She would be flinging away a barrier, crossing a threshold that once crossed, she could never return from. She turned the knob.

Looming up in the dimness of the hall, Galen stood looking at her. He had taken off his rain-drenched shirt and wore only his shorts. His naked upper body seemed to gleam with a light all its own, sending out a heat that found itself answered in Meredith's pulse, her very heart.

She put out a hand, then drew it back just short of touching him.

"You," she whispered more to herself than to him.

He stared at her, questioning, waiting, but utterly silent.

She reached out again, and this time she touched him. Her fingers were featherlight on his bare chest.

"Are you—?"

It was a whispered question she did not finish.

Galen's hand closed gently over the fingers she had laid on his chest. The heat between them ignited sharply, flaring up with the inevitability of the lightning racing across the sky over their heads. Neither of them would ever know who moved first, but suddenly they were in each other's arms and the hows and whys of it no longer mattered.

Galen gathered Meredith to him, closer and closer, as though he would press himself through her skin and into her very soul.

He had not been prepared for this, and the intensity of his desire was all the greater because of it. An hour ago he had given up hope that she would come to him and had decided it was probably for the best. He had resigned himself to lying on the couch cushions alone, waiting for the morning to arrive.

Then Meredith's soft cry had rung through the night. A man of land would not have heard it in the tumult of the weather outside, but to Galen, that small sound was as loud as if she had shouted in his ear.

He could not have said what he was expecting when he padded down the hall to her room. Whatever it was, he had not been ready for Meredith to fling open the door and stand facing him in the shadows of her bedroom.

Her eyes were huge black coals in the night-blanched outline of her face. She was close to being naked, clad only in a sleeveless loose white top that ended at the tops of her thighs, creating a startling contrast between the pale material and the long tanned legs beneath it.

The recognition in her eyes as she had stared at him! And the strangeness. All of this had registered on Galen's mind in an instant. But now, with her in his arms, whatever questions he had would have to wait.

Her lips were hot and sweet against his, her breasts barely separated from him by the flimsy cloth of her shirt. He kissed her, striving to be leisurely, determined to call up all the experience and control his long centuries of learning The Pleasures had given him.

Yet for the first time in his adult tides, he found that experience giving way to something else. Meredith's urgency, underlain by an amazing strength, flowed into him. *She* was not interested in control or expertise. Something else was driving her, something so deep and powerful, it swept away everything else.

She wanted him, and Galen, who had hoped she would come to him that night so he could gently seduce her, discovered that it would not be a seduction after all.

Her lips never leaving his, Meredith's slim strong hands grasped his shorts, pulling them down over his hips. He stepped out of them as his own hands slipped up her body, underneath the loose top.

Meredith gasped deep in her throat as those broad palms, warm and calloused, slid over her thighs, her belly, and up to her breasts. The feel of him was like a burning in her veins, driving her to want more and more.

Yet, incredible as it seemed, it was not a stranger she held in her arms. The body of this man was familiar, known to her through uncounted nights of dreaming.

Later, she would wonder about that, even worry over why it should be. But not now, not with this fierce need flaming through every fiber of her being.

She had no memory of how they ended up on her rumpled bed, but suddenly they were there and her nightshirt was gone, leaving their bodies as free to explore each other as their hands and mouths already were.

Meredith was ready when Galen entered her, more than ready. She cried out eagerly, her legs wrapping themselves around his back. He said something, and her world tipped crazily, for his voice, the low murmurous sounds, and the way he held her, so possessively and yet so tenderly, all of it was her dream made even more real.

Caught up by those forces that threatened to overwhelm her with a supernatural intensity, Meredith froze. The questions she had been content to push away before now demanded to be acknowledged. But the demands lasted for an instant only.

Galen's body, so gentle for all its muscled strength and power, began to rock her, and the movement of him within her was of the sea, of quiet waves on a peaceful sunlit day. She gave herself up to it, and in some deep part of her she felt him give himself up to her in return.

They moved together, their bodies flowing in a dance as old as the sea herself. And when the rhythm changed, became stronger, faster, in concert with the steady beat of the night storm, they were both ready and eager for the change.

Galen's thrusts grew faster and faster, and Meredith welcomed him, meeting every downward stroke with an eager lifting of her hips against his. She felt her contractions begin, starting deep, deep in her belly, and she cried out in pleasure, feeling herself constrict against the hardness moving so inexorably within her softness.

Her climax pushed him over the edge. He cried out himself, a wordless cry that trembled on the edge of a roll of thunder overhead. His movements were no longer the rocking of a gentle sea. He drove himself into her like the waves lashing at the beach outside.

Meredith urged him on. His release burst through her, so

strong that even though she had already experienced her own satisfaction, she went with him yet again. The ecstasy seemed to go on forever, and they took equal glory in it, each pushing the other on.

When it was over at last and they lay entwined in the bedcovers and each other, Meredith turned her head to look at him. His eyes were open and they glowed into hers, as unfathomable as the night sea in the dimness of the room.

He seemed to sense that she was about to speak and shook his head.

"No," he said softly. "Let us not talk now. Sleep, and remember the pleasure."

She studied him a moment longer, then laid her head on his shoulder, releasing a little sigh. Outside, as they drifted off to sleep, the rain was still falling. In the distance, Meredith could still hear the voice of the sea calling.

Only now it was louder.

CHAPTER
12

Morning poked hesitantly through the heavy clouds, a pale lightening of the iron-colored sky that hinted of clearing weather. The angry storms that had possessed the night were finally losing their power. The winds still blew, but the thunder and lightning had moved on, leaving only a steady rain in their wake.

The wounded traveler was drawing nearer to his destination, although he scarcely realized it. The island of Karpathos wavered before his foggy gaze, drifting in and out of a blood-colored haze that had nothing to do with the approaching day. He struggled onward, through rippling wind-driven waves. They were somewhat calmer than they had been the night before, though they dragged at him still, feeling as heavy as mud against his exhausted arms and legs.

Ahead of him, the island lay sheathed in layers of mist.

None of the Terran boats so routinely present in these waters were anywhere in sight. Likely they would not be until the winds had died down and the weather had cleared still more. For the moment, the swimmer was alone.

A few miles out from the coast, the last shreds of his stamina began to give way completely, and with that fading strength his consciousness threatened to leave as well.

Only fierceness of will had gotten him this far, yet the swimmer knew all too well that the struggle to reach Karpathos would be for nothing if his awareness deserted him now. His enemies must not find him in this terrible and desperately vulnerable state, floating bleeding and unconscious in the sea, utterly at their mercy.

His torn limbs trembling, he tried to send out a call for help. The effort cost him dearly, and even so, the call was so weak he dared not hope that his friend had heard.

He tried again, but this call was even weaker than the first. Somehow, he would have to hold on long enough to reach a place of safety, and in this part of Mother Ocean there was only one haven to which he could go. Thank the Mother, it was not far, though in his condition any distance, no matter how small, was torture indeed.

Galen had been right in claiming that the next day's weather would be better. The rain was still falling, but it was fading into a drizzle that would probably stop within the next few hours, if not sooner.

It was a strange thing to be thinking about, Meredith decided as she gazed out the window. Lying in bed ruminating about the weather while a beautiful, disturbing, and most enigmatic man slept beside her.

Only he was not asleep. She suddenly realized that, though she could not say how she knew it. He had not moved or made any of the small sounds one normally makes when coming out of sleep.

"You see?" He spoke softly, a smile in his voice. "The storms are passing on."

She rolled over to look at him. He was lying on his side, and the sight of him, black hair tousled, his broad brown chest dark against the sheets, those depthless eyes glinting at her through heavy black lashes, sent a strange, tight lurching through her chest.

"I know," she said, trying to cover the shyness that suddenly swept over her. "But what I'm wondering is, how did you know they would?"

He shrugged, a gentle movement against her. "My kin have a sense of storms and winds and tides. It has always been so. One could say it is . . . innate."

"Because you belong to the sea, as you said last night."

Meredith tried to speak lightly, but somehow the words did not come out that way, perhaps because of how he was looking at her.

"Yes," he replied gravely. "Because I belong to the sea."

They gazed at each other without speaking, and just when the silence had begun to grow too intense, Galen reached out a hand and traced the line of her hip.

"So," he murmured. "Do we leave this comfortable bed and begin our journey to the cave, or do we wait?"

"Well." Meredith felt an inward shiver at the touch of that large warm palm, a sensation at once delightful and disconcerting because of the memories of the previous night's lovemaking that it aroused. With an effort she made her tone sound as if she were carefully considering the matter. "I did want to get started at first light."

"Yes, but it is barely that. It's raining and there will still be mists along the shore. We should let them lift before we get started."

"I see."

She found that her eyes had focused on his mouth. As if her gaze were an invisible string drawing him toward her, he eased forward until his lips hovered just beyond hers, his breath stirring against her face.

"There are several ways I can think of to while away a bit more time," he said, and he kissed her.

It was a gentle kiss, as light and soft as a dawn breeze, but it deepened swiftly at Meredith's response. Her earlier shyness vanished in a sweep of new desire, and her own breath sighed into his mouth as her tongue began a slow, tantalizing duel with his. He pressed against her, his hands seeming to stroke and enfold her at once. She felt his erection brush against her thigh as though it had a life of its own, and her pulse quickened in anticipation.

Suddenly, with no hint of warning, Galen stiffened in her arms. His entire body went rigid, and he lifted his mouth sharply from hers. Lying with her still wrapped in his embrace, he jerked his head up, his whole attitude one of intent and terrible concentration as he stared out the window.

"Galen." Bemused by his abrupt change, her physical arousal still firing her blood, Meredith shook her head and then gave him a little shake. "What is it? Did you hear something?"

He did not answer at once. "I—yes," he finally muttered in an uncharacteristically abstracted way. Abruptly Meredith found herself alone in the bed, as with a single, swift motion he put her from him and rose. "Forgive me," he said in that same distracted voice, "but I must go. Now."

"No, you don't." With a quickness of her own, she jumped out from under the covers and stood facing him. "Not without me, anyway."

"That is not possible."

He was already heading for the door, and she hurried after him, snatching up his discarded shorts from the floor.

"*Galen*, where do you plan on going naked as the day you were born?" she asked, thrusting them at him.

He paused, glancing back impatiently. "I don't—" he began, then pulled the shorts from her and yanked them on.

Meredith did not waste time watching him. She was already at her closet, hastily throwing on the first clothes that came to hand, some shorts and a top. Grabbing her sandals, she caught up with him in the living room.

"It's not only possible," she continued as though there had been no break in the discussion, "it's decided. I'm going with you."

She met his glare with a hard stare and spoke before he could. "I thought we resolved this last night." Frustration, anger, and hurt rang out in her voice, and she did not seek to hide any of them. "I thought you understood that if we were going to continue on together there wouldn't be any more secrets between us. And especially after last night . . ."

He was staring at her with those enigmatic sapphire eyes that seemed capable of reaching into her soul, and she found that she couldn't go on. Still, she continued to glare at him, refusing to drop her eyes before his penetrating gaze. "I thought things were different now," she added in a softer, though no less heated, tone.

She saw a slight flinch of his broad bare shoulders, as though she had struck him with more than words. An indefinable look came over his face, a strange, wild expression composed of hurt and wonder and things unsaid, all of it overridden by his driving need to be gone from her house.

"And so they are," he said at last. "They are very different. More than you can possibly know. But Meredith—"

She shook her head. "No, Galen, I don't want to hear any more lame excuses, and I've had enough subterfuge. Take me with you. Or don't bother coming back."

He stared at her a moment longer, the tension in his face and body so intense that it seemed to vibrate throughout the room. He made his decision. "Very well, then. But you must do exactly as I say. We will take the caïque, but when I go into the sea, you must promise me that you will stay inside the boat and wait for me. No matter what, do you understand?"

She nodded briskly. "Of course."

It was not until they were well down the path to the beach, with the light rain drifting over them and Meredith having to stretch even her long legs in order to keep up with him, that she had a chance to ask the questions that were nagging at her. "Why are you so sure you'll have to go in the sea? Where are we going?"

He didn't appear to have heard her, but he finally said, "A friend has need of me. I must go to him quickly."

She was confused. "But you said something about going into the water. Is he hurt, in danger of drowning? Did he have some sort of accident?"

Galen's voice was fierce and distant. "Yes, to all that you ask."

More questions sprang to her lips, uppermost among them how Galen had *known* his mysterious friend was hurt, particularly since that awareness had appeared to come just when he was about to make love to her!

She was having a hard enough time keeping up with him as it was, though, and even if that had not been the case, something about her companion's face made her hold back the rest of her queries. Until later, she told herself.

Galen hurried her into the caïque and had it launched into the waves within moments. He was right about the mists, as he seemed to be about everything that was weather-related. White shrouds clung to the long lean flanks of Karpathos, obscuring the land from Meredith's view as the boat raced out to sea.

The sky, though, was clearing rapidly despite the rain. Streaks of blue had widened a path through the iron-gray clouds just since they had left the house. However, the winds were still stiff and they blew hard from the south, fighting the progress of the little boat as though determined to push it back to land.

Galen, though, was as determined as the winds. With a strength that left Meredith in awe, he disdained the motor, unfurling the single sail instead and tacking straight into the wind. Fiercely he kept the caïque under an iron control as he headed it out to sea, then along a course she thought familiar.

"Are we going toward the cave?" she shouted at him over the steady drone of wind and waves.

He nodded, his eyes on the sail overhead.

"Why?"

This time he spared her a brief glance. "Because my friend is there."

"But how do you know?" She looked out over the heaving water, straining to see with the clarity of vision he must surely possess in order to be so certain. "How can you possibly—"

"I know," he broke in roughly. "That is enough."

She stared at him but said nothing more. They went on in silence, driven swiftly forward by Galen's skill and the capricious winds, which had changed and now seemed eager to help them reach their destination quickly. In far less time than Meredith remembered the first ill-fated trip taking, they neared the cove where Galen had told her the deepwater cave lay.

She remembered these waters as they had appeared two days earlier—hard to believe it had only been two days!— peaceful and shimmering with a blue- and diamond-sparkled invitation to explore their depths. This morning the waters were different from how they had been on that other day, when Stassi's blonde head had poked through their surface. They were darker, tossed into irritable whitecaps by the wind, and somehow imbued with an ominous quality that made her glance nervously at Galen, almost as though he were the source of the foreboding that had taken over this once peaceful cove.

He was scowling at her, and for some reason she was not entirely surprised that he was. As their eyes met, he muttered something under his breath. She could not make out the words, but the sight of his lips moving, coupled with the look on his face, sent all too familiar feelings surging through her where this man was concerned: irritation, along with a healthy dose of worry.

Leaning forward, she raised her voice so that it would carry over the cracking of the sail and the sound of waves splashing against the boat. "What did you just say, and why are you looking at me like that?" she shouted.

His face changed, though the terrible concern she saw rippling through his eyes did not. Nor did he ease his white-knuckled grip on the rudder. Yet he answered her, and his deep voice seemed to cut through the noisy morning with a peculiar strength, reaching her ears as intimately as though she and Galen still lay cozily entangled in her bed.

"I was saying I should not have listened to you," he said honestly. "I am angry at myself, not you, *philtate*. I should not have brought you along, for it is not safe."

Bemused by the Greek endearment, a word that meant "beloved," Meredith said the first thing that came to mind. "So why did you?" Recovering herself, she added, "Am I so persuasive?"

"Yes." He said that one word in an odd tone. "The question is why. I am not a man who is easily persuaded . . ."

His voice trailed off as his head jerked around, his gaze fastening on a spot far distant from the caïque. Meredith turned to look, but saw nothing.

The next instant Galen was hurling the vessel toward the shallower waters near the shore. In a single motion, he flung out the anchor and rose to dive, saying to her, "The water is not as deep in this spot, the anchor will hold the caïque and keep you from drifting. Wait here for me."

"Galen—"

"*Wait here for me, Meredith.* Do not leave this boat."

He was gone, his dive over the small boat's side so smooth, so utterly without effort, and yet so completely controlled, that scarcely a splash signaled his going. Meredith, however, was far too preoccupied to admire her companion's swimming prowess. Knotting her fingers together she stared out at the spot where he had obviously seen whatever or whoever it was he sought.

The rain had all but stopped and the sun was making a stronger effort to slice its way through the clouds. It lit the undulating waters with uneven streaks of brightness, bringing bursts of steamy heat that passed over her, then were pushed away by the driving breeze.

Meredith shifted restlessly. She *hated* inactivity, and hated even more the feeling of helplessness that went with it. Despite Galen's stern injunction that she remain there, she was strongly tempted to go after him. If he did have a hurt friend out in the cove, then he would need help getting him to safety, and she herself was a strong swimmer.

Yet she could see all too clearly that there was no sign of any boat other than Galen's in the cove. If someone was out there in the water, he would have surely drowned by now, wouldn't he? The thought sent chills chasing each other up and down her spine, though she was growing increasingly convinced that this was precisely what had happened.

"Poor Galen," she said aloud, and at that moment she saw a dark head break through the surface of the waves at a spot far distant from the caïque.

Impossibly distant.

•   •   •

"Lord!"

Anastas jerked awake.

Blinking eyelids that felt as if every grain of sand from the beaches of Karpathos had gathered on them, he glared up at his visitor. He had spent a horrible night and was groggy, ill-tempered, and in a generally foul mood.

Ever since the beginning of his exile he had come to hate storms. Almost as much as he hated Galen.

They represented no danger to him, of course. But every time the sky turned dark and the waves wild, he thought of his former people gathered in abodes throughout the seas to wait out the storm, laughing and eating and making love while the weather raged outside, and while he and his few followers swam aimlessly through it.

More than anything else, storms had come to symbolize the reality of banishment, and when they struck, Anastas, in turn, sought refuge from them. Last night that refuge had been this cave. The fact that it was the same cave in which he had dominated Malk into taking his brother Ladru to his death mattered to him not at all.

Yet he had rested poorly anyway. Despite his exile, he was still a merman to his bones, which meant that like all his kind, he was keenly sensitive to the weather and all its changes. The storm had throbbed through his brain and his blood during every long hour of the afternoon and night, and now, with an annoyed frown, he regarded wide-eyed Tovash, who had come bursting up through the cave entrance.

"By the sperm whale's balls, what is it?" he growled. "You had better have a good reason for disturbing me."

"The Selkie ..." Tovash drew a deep shaking breath. "He is ..."

"What? *What?*" Anastas hauled himself to his feet. "Stop your spuming and spit it out! What about the Selkie?"

"He is alive." Having said it, Tovash gulped and fell silent, staring with huge, distended eyes at the blonde merman.

Anastas might feel nothing at being in that particular cave, but the same could not be said for his lieutenant. Tovash remembered all too clearly what had happened there, and the thought that those terrible powers might be turned against him for bringing this news made his knees quake. He dropped his gaze, unable and unwilling to meet that deadly green stare.

"You told me he was dead," Anastas said softly. "How do you know this? You had better speak quickly," he added when the other did not answer him at once.

"We saw him," Tovash explained miserably. "Bron and I. Just this morning." He did not mention that Bron had flatly refused to come with him to tell Anastas of what they had seen.

Anastas considered this. "What of it?" he said after a moment. "He was far from these waters when you caught up with him, and I possess the information he carried, thanks to you." He shrugged, concluding, "Therefore, he is of no further value."

"Yes, but . . ." Tovash gulped again, then stammered desperately, "He has come back! We left him for dead, but somehow he made it back to these waters, and—and—now Galen might find him!"

Silence.

Cringing, waiting to feel the terrifying power of Anastas's thoughts whip into his brain, Tovash finally dared a glance at his lord. Anastas's face was rigid; only the eyes were alive, and they were fixed on a point somewhere beyond him, blazing with sickening force at that invisible sight.

"Where?" he asked in a poisonous whisper, then flung up a hand in a gesture that made Tovash start with fear. "Never mind. Take me to where you saw him. At once."

He strode to the tunnel that led into the sea, with his lieutenant crowding anxiously behind.

"Oh, and Tovash," he said in a conversational tone that was all the more menacing because it was so mild, "we had better find him before Galen does. Or I will be highly displeased. Highly displeased."

Tovash shuddered and said nothing more.

CHAPTER
13

"Galen!"

Meredith muttered his name aloud. How could he have gotten out there so quickly? Without even coming up for a breath of air, at least so far as she could tell.

The realization came to her that she had not seen him at all since he had dived off the boat, had not seen his powerful shoulders breaking through the water in the crawl, the breaststroke, or any other swimming stroke she knew about. He simply could not have gone all that way underwater, she thought in a welter of confusion, then forgot about those speculations when she saw what looked to be a limp form rise slowly beside the dark bobbing shape that was Galen.

She squinted, staring with all her might to make sure she had seen correctly. She had.

Galen had found his friend. Now the crucial issue was, had he found him too late?

There was only one way to find out.

There, Lord, I see him! He's far away, but it looks as though he isn't moving. Perhaps he died already.

Relief swept through Tovash. He started forward, his eyes fixed on the figure in the distance, eager to ascertain if the troublesome Selkie was truly dead. If he was not, Tovash would finish him off once and for all.

A curt gesture from Anastas stopped him. *We are too late,* the blonde merman sent out sharply. *Do you not see Galen coming toward him as well? Keep still, you fool, or he will discover us, and I'm not ready for that, not yet. Now stay behind the rocks.*

Tovash obeyed reluctantly. The sight of Toklat, dead or very near to it, had greatly restored his equilibrium. With it, his courage in dealing with his lord was beginning to return.

The Selkie looks so far gone I don't think it matters now whether Galen finds him or not, he persisted. *He won't be able to tell who did this to him, Lord. And there are two of us against only Galen, for the Selkie is worthless if it comes to fighting. Why don't we take your old kinsman and discover what he knows about the scroll?*

Anastas shot him a quelling glance. *Because then we would have to kill him, and right now he is of more use to me alive. The Selkie didn't know where the scroll was. Obviously, neither does Galen or he would no longer be in these waters. There's no point in going after him until he does know.*

Tovash made as if to protest, but Anastas silenced him with another sharp motion. They watched as Galen reached Toklat, pulled him gently into his arms, and started for the surface.

Now why is he doing that? Tovash wondered in mind-speak. *It would be faster for him to travel at this depth.*

Anastas did not reply, although he was wondering the

same thing. Slipping around from behind the rocks he began to follow his enemies, taking care to keep a safe distance between himself and them and sternly motioning at Tovash to do the same. They soon saw why Galen had gone for the surface.

Driven by an impulsive and unquestioning need to help, Meredith yanked off her sandals and was on her feet in an instant. The caïque swayed and bucked at her abrupt motion, but she paid little heed.

Her dive was not as smooth and controlled as Galen's, but it was skilled. The water closed around her, welcoming her with warmth despite the blustery winds that still rushed through the gray and blue morning.

Her light top and shorts barely impeded the strength of her swimming as she set off toward the two distant figures. She swam swiftly, using a smooth Australian crawl. Fortunately she was going with the wind rather than against it, but though she plowed her way steadily through the tossing waves, she quickly found that her speed could not begin to match Galen's.

To her astonishment, he met her more than halfway across the distance that separated them, despite the fact that he was towing an unconscious man along with him. She pulled up as he approached, treading water and waiting until he drew closer before she tried to speak.

Looming up out of the waves, Galen's face was a study in several different emotions, all of them roiling over one another so vehemently that Meredith could not decide which one to try to identify first. Then she got a look at the man he was carrying so protectively, and all other thoughts promptly fled her mind.

"Oh my God."

Her eyes widened until it felt as though her eyebrows

were climbing into her very hair. Involuntarily her arms and legs froze, sending her bobbing below the waves. Hastily she paddled herself back into the treading-water position. Her mouth still hung open in horror and disbelief, and a wave washed into it, making her cough.

The distraction did little to ease her shock.

In her travels through remote countries, she had often seen horrible sights, some of them truly gruesome. But never had she seen anything to equal this beaten, ravaged, and torn figure, so mutilated he scarcely resembled a human being anymore.

"G-Galen ..." she stammered, and fell silent, not knowing what else to say.

The man was not moving, she could not see any sign that he was even breathing. Beyond a doubt, he had to be dead, but from the tender way Galen was holding him, she wondered if he had either realized or accepted that fact yet. And who or what had done this to him?

"I told you to wait in the caïque," Galen said harshly. "Do you always do the exact opposite of what is wise?"

Under other circumstances Meredith would have come back with a sharp rejoinder, pointing out that he was hardly the judge of what was deemed wise. The pain and worry beneath his angry tone was so obvious, though, that she only said, "Let me help you get him into the boat. With two of us it'll be easier."

"No." Galen's tone was forceful, brooking no dissent. "Go back to the boat. I will join you there when I can."

"But what about ... ?" She could not believe she had heard him correctly. "You can't—I mean, where are you taking him?"

He ignored her. Turning, his big body cutting a powerful swath through the tossing water, he swam carefully but swiftly away from her, cradling his burden in one strong arm as he went. A burden that Meredith now saw was leaving long trailing smears of red in its wake. She saw also that Galen was headed in the direction of the cave that he had pointed out to her the other day.

Setting her jaw, she sent her body knifing through the water after him, not pausing to question her decision to do so any more than she had examined the impulse that had led her to leave the boat in the first place. But perhaps she should have, she suddenly thought. Perhaps she should have questioned that, and more.

For Galen was moving fast—very, very fast. In fact, he was racing away like mist blown over the sea by a sharp wind, slipping through the cove with a speed that made her want to stop and rub her eyes to see if they were deceiving her. There was no way she could hope to catch him, or even keep him in sight, unless . . .

Tovash popped his head out of the sea and quickly dropped back under. *They are leaving, Lord. That landwoman can swim,* he added in a tone that mingled admiration with more than a little lust. *She moves well, considering she's a clumsy Terran.*

Anastas raised out of the waves just enough to see for himself. Eyes narrowed, he stared at Meredith as she plowed strongly through the water in the awkward way of her kind.

He had surfaced before, when Meredith first left the boat to swim to Galen, and he'd watched intently as the dark-haired merman met her. It appeared that they had argued, although from a distance it had been difficult to tell.

At least his concern that his former kinsman would detect them had lessened. Galen was plainly distracted, as much with the landwoman as with the Selkie. For Anastas, just seeing Galen and the woman together brought back the feel of Galen's steely fingers around his throat. Unconsciously he touched his neck, where the bruises from the previous morning still lingered, and his gaze narrowed again as he stared out at what was taking place in the distance.

Galen had turned from the landwoman and was racing away with the Selkie still gripped in his arms.

"Come," Anastas said. "We must follow and find out where he is taking the Selkie."

"Perhaps we should also take the Terran woman," Tovash suggested hopefully. "See how he has left her behind. She must be the one the Selkie told us about, the one you went to find yesterday. Isn't she?"

"Don't be so anxious," Anastas admonished, his gaze still on Meredith. "We'll let Galen get farther away before we . . . introduce ourselves. Where are the others of our group?"

Tovash shrugged. "Hunting, sleeping, wandering. Do you wish me to summon them?"

"No," Anastas snapped, exasperated. "Galen may be preoccupied, but he is not mindless. He'll certainly hear any call you send out. We'll handle this ourselves. But slowly," he cautioned. "I don't want to get too close too fast."

Suiting action to words, he dived. Undulating forward at a slow, almost leisurely pace, he stayed just below the surface, guided by the sight of Meredith's sleek form kicking its way into the distance.

Tovash followed him dutifully, setting his speed to Anastas's, though the latter could feel how his second-in-command chafed to go faster. Tovash's interest in the landwoman apparently went beyond her knowledge about the mysterious scroll, Anastas reflected, and smiled coldly.

Apparently Meredith had decided to follow Galen, though she had not a chance of catching him. Anastas watched her legs flutter and splash through the watery layers that lay between them and made no attempt to go any faster himself.

Suddenly she paused, her legs hanging down for a moment as she trod water. Then she lunged underneath the waves and, as Anastas and Tovash stared in stupefied amazement, she began to move in a new way, speeding off through the depths in a motion startlingly similar to their own!

Meredith drew a deep breath and ducked below the waves. At once, her body fell into an almost instinctive motion that was far more natural to her than the crawl stroke she had been using. Easily and with greater speed, she slipped through the warm water, staying just beneath the surface until her lungs cried out for air, then lifting her head only long enough to grab a gulp of oxygen before continuing on.

Through the clear waters of the cove she caught glimpses of Galen's long naked legs ahead of her as he raced swiftly toward the place where the cave must lie. Long streaks of red still marred the crystal clarity of the water, and that bloody reminder of the condition of Galen's friend drove Meredith on even faster.

Suddenly Galen dove, and Meredith faltered as she watched him descend. The waters in this part of the cove had grown very deep, and he was dropping an impossible way down.

Even with her own unusual ability to hold her breath—an ability she had never been able to explain, even to herself—she could never, she told herself incredulously, take enough air into her lungs to follow him that distance.

But how could he? Perhaps he came from a family of sponge divers, she thought in resigned frustration as she kicked up through the surface. Greek sponge divers were famous for their diving prowess, capable of traveling down to incredible depths in their search for the precious sponges that comprised their livelihood. Yet what could Galen be thinking of, to take his friend to that deep cave?

Water sprayed up in her face as with a great rush of splashing waves, Galen rose before her.

His appearance—like some mysterious god of the deep—was so utterly without warning that she gasped and let out a little shriek.

It was all she had time for.

"Keep your mouth on mine," he ordered.

Banding her to him with arms that seemed as hard as rock, he fastened his mouth over hers and dropped below the sea, pulling her with him.

Colors shattered around Meredith, bursting inside her head and behind her eyes with the brilliance of a thousand exploding firecrackers. She noticed them only vaguely. She was hardly aware of anything save Galen's steely grip and the force of his mouth over hers.

The instant he'd seized her a kind of stupor had dropped over her. A dark, heavy sensation that left her dazed and disoriented, as though he had enfolded her in a net of thick cotton batting. She wanted to breathe, her body told her to breathe, but even this deepest and most compelling instinct for survival was overwhelmed, stifled by Galen's hold, his mouth.

They were dropping through the water at an incredible rate of speed, down and down and down, until not even the slightest vestige of the sunlit world above remained.

To dive this fast and this deep was impossible. It was death. Meredith knew it, knew her lungs would have already contracted so hopelessly, they could never withstand the return to normal pressure. It was far more likely, however, that she would drown first from lack of oxygen.

Even this knowledge, though, was overshadowed by the

inexplicable spell that had been cast over her. In some way that she could not even begin to understand, Galen was keeping her alive.

His mouth, pressed so closely over hers, was breathing for her; the astounding strength of his arms was protecting her against the drop in pressure that would otherwise have killed her. It was a bonding that she never could have accepted with her head clear, yet it was a bonding more intimate than anything she had ever known.

They were approaching a great mass of rock so rapidly that even in her dazed state Meredith was certain Galen was going to dash them both to pieces against its unyielding surface. At the last moment, he angled them in toward a gap between several huge boulders.

The gap turned out to be an entrance that gave way to a long tunnel so narrow, its wet, rough walls scraped against the side of Meredith's body that was not protected by Galen. The sea in all its force sang through this tunnel and it pushed them through the passage, the saltwater leaving a stinging wake along the scrapes in Meredith's hips and legs.

The tunnel ended abruptly in a wide jagged hole. Before she realized what was happening, Galen had thrust her up through it, following close behind her.

Dizzy, her senses still reeling, she staggered, trying to find her footing on the slick rock surface. Galen's long-fingered hand steadied her, and when she could stand by herself, he released her.

Her eyes adjusted to the gloom as her head slowly cleared, and she looked dazedly around her.

She had been in a few underwater caves before. Small ones that were little more than grottos, easily reached by a short swim and a quick dive. This one, though, so far beneath the sea, was big—a cavern really. Its ceiling arched far over her head, forming a dome shape so perfect, it seemed impossible that nature had sculpted it rather than some ancient group of stoneworkers.

Waves washed in and out of the tunnel entrance, their splashing echoing against the walls with an eerie, hollow monotony. The sound fell right into sync with the hollow fear in the pit of Meredith's stomach as the reality of how she had gotten there crushed down upon her. Something else came to life also, coiling in her stomach along with her fear. She did not know what it was, could not put a name to it.

A dark pool lay at the far end of the cave. Turning to look at it, she saw Galen kneeling by the still form of his friend who lay beside the edge. He murmured something, and though he spoke in a whisper, the cavern magnified the sound into a sibilant hissing off its dank walls. Meredith drew in her breath sharply as the battered man's torn mouth opened and he answered in a deep throaty groan that trembled with pain.

His words made no sense to her, but she stared in shock as with infinite care Galen lifted the wounded man and laid him in the dark, rippling pool, arranging him so that only his head was out of the water.

Automatically she started forward. "What are you do—"

Galen spun around. "Leave him! This is not your concern."

She halted in her tracks. Her eyes wide, she gazed at him, bewildered, frightened, and utterly at a loss. Too much had happened too quickly for her to take it all in, much less assign a logical explanation to any of it.

Galen felt a stab of guilt at her expression, but he pushed it aside. He himself was nearly speechless, though his state of mind had evolved for vastly different reasons.

All the questions he had hoped might be answered by entering this woman's body as well as her mind had only doubled back on him, twisting and turning like one of the great

whirlpools that sometimes appeared at certain spots within
Mother Ocean's seas. Meredith had only drawn him further
into the web of fascination she had spun about him, revealing nothing of herself except more mysteries!

He had brought her there, protecting her with the ancient
method known as the Breath of Life, because he could not
leave her alone, particularly after his senses had warned him
that Anastas and his followers were in the area. But the
sight of her following him was burned indelibly in his brain.
That following was, in itself, bad enough, but it was the *way*
she had been coming after him: in the undulating motion of
his folk!

Oh, not exactly to be sure. Her movements had been
awkward and she had to keep surfacing for air, but it had
been close enough to cause his world and his perception of
merfolk and landfolk within that world to sway crazily upon
its moorings.

Terrans did not swim like that; they could not. The way
the sea-people swam had evolved over millennia, based
on their long association with other folk of the sea: the
whales, the dolphins, the seals, and of course, the Selkies.
Perfected over time, it had gradually become a genetic
trait, inherited from generation to generation, just as gills
were. This woman should not be able to achieve even an ap-
proximation of that subtle undulation!

"Where did you learn to swim like that?" he demanded.

Meredith brushed several locks of wet hair from her eyes
and stared at him without answering.

Old feelings of embarrassment flowed to the surface,
coming from a place of hurt that lay deep inside her. With
them they brought painful memories of reactions from other
people who had seen her swim as Galen had, throwing them
into sharp focus as if those unhappy experiences had happened yesterday instead of years ago, when she had been
younger and more foolish.

She had since learned that it was better not to let anyone
see this peculiar ability she had. For the truth was, she had
absolutely no idea how she did it. It was just something that
came to her, as naturally as breathing.

"I don't really know," she said defensively. "I told you,
I'm a strong swimmer."

"You weren't swimming in the way your people swim!"

Galen roared this with an explosive violence that made
her blink, stunned at the inappropriateness of his outburst.
Staring at him even harder, she took a step backward.

"I told you," she repeated uncomfortably. "I don't know.
Why are you getting so upset about this?"

He stood and followed her, thrusting his face into hers,
his eyes shooting blue-hot flames as he bent over her. "I
asked you a question, and by all the lost gods, you *will* answer it! How did you move through the water in that way?"

Meredith had finally had enough. Her nerves were
stretched to the breaking point and she was shaking in every limb, but she held her ground, refusing to back away
from that terrible gaze. Straightening to her full height, she
glared back at him.

"You can stand there and interrogate *me*, after the way
you brought me here? I should be dead! What are you,
Galen?" Her voice shredded, teetering on the edge of hysteria. "What are you? How is it that *you* swam the way you
did? The speed you were going and the way you dove down
here was unhuman! And what's this about the way *my people*
swim? Who are your people? Fish or seals? Or mermaids,
maybe!"

He looked at her for an interminable moment that seemed
to drag on and on, like the waves washing slowly in and out
of the cave. "The proper word," he said at last, "is merfolk."

CHAPTER
14

Meredith did take a step back then, several of them. A dozen possible responses sprang into her head, but all of them froze on her lips before Galen's cold measuring stare. She still saw the sea in his eyes, but it was an arctic sea now, penetrating her with knives as sharp as icicles formed in the dead of winter.

"Like hell," she finally said. When all else failed, she thought, unable to stop her trembling, try bravado.

One of his black eyebrows rose. He studied her as if undecided whether to laugh or become even angrier.

"Are you unfamiliar with the legend?" A hardness underlay his voice, subtle, but as cutting as his eyes. "You who study such things? In ancient times, there were many who told the story. Foolish men they were, like all Terrans. Sailors who fell overboard from their awkward vessels, only to be saved from drowning by some woman of the sea who took pity on them and breathed life into their weak landman lungs."

He looked away from her. "Of course, that was long ago. But we still remember the method."

"And you're saying"—her knees felt as wobbly as her voice sounded—"that that's what you did?"

His gaze flashed back to her face. "As you so aptly put it, you should be dead. Explain to me then how you are not."

Meredith was silent. Of course she was familiar with the legend about good-hearted mermaids rescuing hapless sailors. It was only one of many that had grown up about the sea since the dawn of the earliest civilizations, when men had begun venturing out to challenge the vastness of the oceans in their tiny boats. But those were legends, a voice cried in her mind, they were not meant to be true. They weren't real. None of this was real, it couldn't be.

"Those are only stories," she whispered. "There's an explanation for it. There's always an explanation."

His gaze did not leave her face, giving her no relief. "Yes," he said quietly. "There is always an explanation. But that is not what we're talking about, is it? For I have already given you an answer, more than one of your kind has heard for centuries. Can you accept it? I think not."

She wrapped her arms across her chest, a gesture both of protection as well as denial. It was damp in the cave, though not cold, yet her shivering threatened to swamp her. "You can't mean what you're saying," she insisted desperately. She was ashamed of the weak thready way her voice came out, but could do nothing about it. "You can't possibly be a . . . that. Anyway"—she felt incredibly foolish, but stumbled on regardless—"they have tails, like fish!"

"No," Galen said sardonically. "Your people always did get that part wrong. Although in younger times, Terrans had a better idea of who we were. The Greeks you came here to study, for example, knew we had nothing so ridiculous as fish tails."

A moan came from behind them, soft and penetrating in the echoing stillness of the cave and the even more profound stillness that lay between Galen and Meredith.

Galen swung sharply about. In two strides he was kneeling beside the pool. Reassuringly he enfolded the groping hand of the wounded man in both of his and said something in the same unrecognizable language he had used before.

Trying to control her trembling, Meredith stood listening. She tried in vain to connect his words to one of the dozens of dialects that abounded throughout the Greek islands. It sounded like none of them. In fact, she could not get the thought out of her mind that if one of the ancient tongues she had studied—the truly ancient ones, Babylonian or older—were to be spoken, it would sound like Galen's murmurings to his friend.

The idea sent a new rush of chills chattering up her spine.

The other man spoke now, and Meredith was amazed to hear that in the short time since Galen had brought him there, his voice already sounded much stronger. And even more odd than she had first thought. She drifted toward the pool and the two figures there. Absorbed in their conversation, neither took any notice of her. She drew closer and stared cautiously over Galen's shoulder.

She blinked as she saw the man's face. The light in the cave was poor, but despite that her eyes could not be deceiving her. His face was *healing*, the bloody scabs and deep gashes sealing themselves as if in some incredible demonstration of slow-motion photography.

Meredith gasped in disbelief. Galen glanced up with a startled frown, and the man in the pool opened his eyes. Huge, far too large for a normal face, those dark luminous orbs looked up at her. Completely brown, almost a liquid black, with not even a sliver of white visible around the rims. And they were round, perfectly, perfectly round. Not the eyes of a human man at all. Neither were his features, she saw now. Squat and blunt, they reminded her of . . .

Meredith felt the walls of the cave close in around her. A crazy thought slithered into her brain and stayed there, as persistently as the creature's eyes. He looked the way a seal would look if he suddenly took a man's form! But that was insane—

"Meredith." Still frowning, Galen got to his feet.

She stumbled backward, finally switching her shocked gaze from the figure in the pool to Galen.

"No," she whispered, then louder, "No! What is he? What are you?"

Galen's voice was oddly compassionate. "I have already told you, *philtate*."

The endearment that had given her such a feeling of sweetness when he had uttered it in the caïque less than an hour ago, now made her shudder. Whether it was out of re-action to what he had told her, to the face of the creature, or to the unimaginable manner in which she had been brought there, she could not say. It did not really matter.

She threw her hands up in a gesture meant to ward off Galen, the cave, the pool and its incomprehensible mystery—everything, in fact—and ran.

Tovash undulated in a restless circle, watching Anastas with wary eyes. How in all the seas had that Terran woman been able to swim in the fashion of merfolk? He and Anastas had increased their speed when she had begun moving in the astonishingly familiar rhythm, suddenly eager to overtake her. They were too far away, though, had allowed too much of a gap to open up between them and their quarry.

Without warning, Galen had shot up from the lower

depths, heading straight for her. They could only watch, Anastas gritting his teeth in frustration, as Galen caught her up in his arms and descended again, taking her with him. He had been bringing her to the deep water cave where he had obviously taken the Selkie, to the one place in these waters where the two mermen could not follow. And Galen knew it.

Tovash let his gaze slide away from Anastas. His lord was angry — no, furious was a better word, although, thank the Mother, that rage was not directed at him. Far better that it be directed at Galen. Which it was.

Tovash was exceedingly relieved that Anastas's thoughts were taken up with Galen, for the merman's rushing Toklat to this particular cave could mean only one thing: the odds were good that the Selkie would live. This did not bode well, especially for Tovash, but despite that fact, neither he nor Anastas dared go inside to halt the healing process that Galen would have surely instituted on the injured one by now.

This place, known as the Cave of Secrets, was forbidden to them. It had become so the instant the weight of The Banishment had been lowered upon his and his companions' heads. The penalty for going against that grave injunction was death, and if even some of the tales Tovash had heard were true, a horribly painful one.

So intense was the prohibition against entering this sacred spot, Tovash had succeeded in actually erasing the cave's whereabouts from his mind. It had taken Anastas — who never forgot anything — to remind him of it. Now that he knew, though, Tovash would have been just as happy to forget again. This mass of rock, with its long secret tunnel, made him uneasy. Very, very uneasy.

Tovash kept waiting for Anastas to show some sign of being ready to leave, but so far Anastas had given no such indication. Instead, he continued to float through the waters near the massive jumble of boulders, allowing himself to drift with the currents, moving only enough to keep from being pulled away from the target of his concentration.

To Tovash, it seemed a useless vigil. They may have been too far away to attract Galen's notice before, but that was no longer the case. He would certainly not bring the Terran woman or the Selkie back out of the cave, not with him and Anastas hovering about the tunnel entrance.

Lord, he ventured at last, *we should go from here. This place—*

—is forbidden to us, Anastas finished curtly. *I am well aware of that. But we are in these waters, as you see, and no harm has visited us yet, has it?*

No, Tovash replied tentatively. *Yet it seems unwise to linger. After all, there is nothing we can do here.*

Anastas's eyes glinted at him through the depths. *Thanks to you, my second-in-command,* he sent in a silky thought-voice that raised the hairs on the back of Tovash's neck. *I did not tell you to injure the Selkie so grievously. But since you did, you should have done it correctly and made certain he was dead before you left him. This was sloppily done, Tovash. Sloppily done.*

I know. Tovash's own thought-voice quavered. *I know that, Lord.*

He waited, trembling with terrified resignation, for Anastas's punishment to descend upon him.

Nothing happened.

Anastas had fallen silent again, brooding upon the opening in the boulders, which was now as solidly closed to him as though layer upon layer of the strongest, most impenetrable chain had been strung across it. He ground his teeth together again, this time until they ached.

He was furious with his incompetent lieutenant, and strongly tempted to vent that rage upon this follower who had failed in his task. Yet he knew he would not. He needed Tovash. He needed all of his followers, more now than ever.

At least until this mysterious scroll was securely in his possession.

Then there was the landwoman, with her unusual and totally unexpected abilities. He wanted her now too. Once he had her and the scroll, he would deal with Tovash. But in the meantime . . .

You're right about one thing, he sent. *There seems to be little point in staying here any longer.*

Jerking a hand roughly at his subordinate, he swam off, his undulation so abrupt and fraught with frustration that if he had indeed possessed the tail with which legend credited merfolk, it would have been lashing in fury.

Greatly relieved, not only to leave but to find himself unharmed, Tovash followed him with the speed of a shadow.

Meredith ran blindly. A long passageway opened up before her as though placed there expressly for her to flee down, and she took it. She had not the slightest idea of where she was going, but it did not matter. As long as the cave took her away from the pool and the two beside it, that was all she cared about.

"Meredith," Galen called behind her, a note of exasperation in his deep voice. She paid him no heed. The thick throaty voice of the one in the pool answered him, and that made her run harder.

"I frightened her," Toklat said sadly to Galen. His voice was still weak, but strengthening steadily as the healing waters worked their magic upon his terrible injuries. "I did not mean to."

Galen shook his head wearily. "I know, brother-friend. It's not your fault, it's mine. I was too hard with her."

"You were indeed." There was more than a tinge of condemnation in the Selkie's voice. "She was only trying to help, Galen. That's why she followed us. She was concerned—about me! I can never in all my tides remember a Terran having that kind of care for one of the Selkie folk."

"Toklat," Galen reminded him gently, "she did not know who you were until you opened your eyes. She thought you were a man of the land. As she thought I was, before I told her differently."

"Well, you had still better go after her."

"Yes." Galen sighed. "Although she'll come to no harm. There is no way for her to get out of this cave without me, and nowhere she can go that I can't easily find her. The one place I would be worried about is not a place she could discover by herself."

Despite his exhaustion, Toklat scrutinized him shrewdly. "You can act as unconcerned as you like, but I know better. I know *you*. Go find her. Anyway . . ." The water rippled as he gingerly shifted his hurt body into a more comfortable position. "I don't want to speak anymore. It's time for me to sleep."

Galen touched the Selkie's shoulder. "Sleep then, and let the waters do their work."

Toklat's eyes were closed even before Galen rose from the edge of the pool. His heavy stertorous breathing followed Galen as he went in search of Meredith.

Galen's thoughts, as he walked down the passageway she had run through minutes earlier, were as wild as her progress had been. In his brain he felt as if tidal streams were flowing out from the land, slamming head-on into waves pushed inward by the sea, with him directly in the middle of the two opposing forces. It was how he felt about Meredith.

He wanted to grab her, shaking her until her knowledge of the scroll and every one of the secrets he sensed in her were revealed to his gaze once and for all. He wanted to hold her, to kiss and comfort and offer reassurance until she no longer stared at him with that wrenching expression of fear and disbelief that had made him feel so sick inside.

He wanted to see his people healed, and Toklat's, and she was the only means by which to do it.

The passageway narrowed, then split off in two separate directions. One passage wound through the cavern in a wide circle that eventually led back to the pool, the other stretched out a long arm and ended in another split, at which point five smaller corridors tendriled out like spidery fingers.

Galen paused, frowning thoughtfully. In her panic, Meredith could have gone in either direction without caring where it led. He closed his eyes and called up his considerable powers of concentration, honed by his unique sensitivity, especially where she was concerned.

He could feel her presence strongly; she had passed this way only moments ago. The intensity of her terror and confusion clung to the damp rocks, echoing off the walls and ceilings like the distant cry of someone in pain. She had not taken the larger, more easily passable corridor, as he might have expected. She had instead run along the arm that divided into fingers.

Galen frowned with a touch of irritation. That choice would make it more difficult to find her, though of course he would. Of that there was no doubt. The most sacred part of this venerable cave—its heart—lay that way also, but as he had said to Toklat, it was not a place that a Terran would or could find.

Isn't it? a voice whispered inside his head. Look at how she had moved in the water, something no Terran was supposed to be able to do. If she could do that, what else was she capable of?

Galen began to stride faster toward the spot where the five tendrils branched out.

•   •   •

Panting, a stitch grabbing at her side, Meredith stopped to catch her breath. She leaned against the tunnel wall, and the rough rock that poked her back through the wet tank top was a welcome reminder that at least something in the world remained real and solid, unchanged.

Her breathing had steadied only slightly, but she went on anyway. She had to keep moving. It was better than standing still and letting herself think.

Running aimlessly through this cave could not shut off her thoughts, though, not entirely. It was in her nature to analyze and ponder; it was what she had been trained for. She could not push Galen from her mind or the things he had told her, could not erase the picture of the creature in the pool.

Selkie.

Unbidden the word popped into her mind. Beings who could turn from seal to human and back again. Flijanou's tale about the seal-women who strangled swimmers and then wept over them. Legends about seals and their possible human counterparts abounded throughout every part of the world where the sea touched the land, particularly in the Hebrides Islands, off the coast of Scotland.

Many a Scottish or Irish fisherman was said to have captured himself a wife by stealing the skin of a Selkie woman, holding her captive so long as he possessed it. Invariably, though, she would have her revenge. Finding her skin and clothing herself in it once more, she would return to the sea, usually taking her children—who had also turned into seals by this time—along with her.

The legends generally made Selkies female, although stories of male Selkies were interwoven among them. Before the scroll and its mysteries had come into her life, Meredith had planned to travel to Ireland and Scotland to research a

book about these curious beings who had held such a grip
on the imaginations of people for so many centuries. But
that had been before—

Her feet jerked her to a halt so suddenly, she stumbled
and almost fell. It was as if something outside herself had
brought her up short, shooting out alien hands to seize her
round the ankles. She put a shaking hand to her forehead.
It came away wet with sweat, as well as with sea water.

Given everything else that had happened, she could not
find it in herself even to be shocked by this latest mystery.
She stared around her and felt a new—only not so new—
strangeness come over her. It was the same uneasy sensation that had stirred, coiling in her stomach, when Galen
had first set her down in the cave. She could no more put
a name to it now than she had been able to before, but the
feeling had grown much stronger. It left her tingling with
dread and fear and, inexplicably, with a sense of wonder so
deep, it bordered on reverence.

She could not explain what was happening within her,
she was too exhausted and bewildered even to try. The
world as she knew it was dissolving under her feet like a
sand castle washed out to sea by the tide. There seemed no
choice but to let herself be pulled along by that inexorable
current.

Slowly she turned in a circle. The branch she had taken
off the main corridor had narrowed considerably, and as she
turned, new scrapes were added to the ones she already
had. She did not feel them.

Directly in front of her was a spot where the rocks comprising the tunnel wall came together in a subtle design. It
was little more than a tracery of boulder edges and shadows
in the dark corridor. She had not noticed it before and
would probably have never noticed it, if not for this outside
force pulling her toward it.

She started to reach out to touch the spot, then jerked

her hand back, hesitating as that storm of nameless fear gripped her. Tremors tore through her body until her teeth rattled.

Voices burst inside her head, calling and singing in that unknown tongue Galen had used. Waves thundered in her ears, and the sea and all its life swept through her. She felt and heard everything: the breathing of dolphins, the grunting barks of seals, the music of whales, the sizzle of rain hissing down to lose itself in the eternal waves.

Then the sensations were gone as suddenly as they had come. In their place was a curious calm. A sense of inevitability filled her, the serenity that comes with things finally decided.

She put her hand out again, slowly, but without hesitation this time. The rocks gave way at her touch, moving apart with a willingness that made them seem almost alive. She walked through the small opening they had created and did not even jump when the boulders closed behind her.

Instantly an explosion of color and sound surrounded her. The new cavern she had entered was half again, perhaps twice as large as the outer one to which Galen had brought her. However, unlike that chamber, this giant cave was lighted not with the dim shadowy light that comes in all but total darkness, but brightly, with a thousand shifting patterns of color that dazzled the eye and mesmerized the mind.

Entranced, her mouth falling open in wonder, Meredith stared around her. The walls and ceiling of this new cave were smooth, and they had been painted with mural upon mural, until there was not a square inch that did not contain some richly colored scene of incredible beauty.

So overwhelming was the combination of color, light, and music, she could not take it in all at once. She could not find the source of the beautiful dancing lights, but the sounds that filled her ears—a singing and rushing of countless watery voices—came from a huge fountain set directly in the center of the chamber. She started toward it, but paused, held by the magnificence of the paintings and what they showed.

Scenes spread themselves over the cave, and every one was of the sea. It was as if she had walked into some vast secret shrine to the life-force of the ocean. For that was what the paintings had captured: the sea in all her moods, along with the infinite variety of life that inhabited her depths, all of it depicted with a delicacy and reverence to detail that could be called nothing other than religious.

Even with the ringing music of the fountain, the cave had a hushed feeling about it, a sense of ancient and spiritual peace that Meredith had experienced only when walking into a cathedral or mosque or synagogue. But something in here, in these murals, called to her in a way that those places of worship never had. She drifted along one wall, staring, staring, devouring the pictures before her as if she could never get enough of looking.

Within her an emptiness she had not even known was there came to life, crying out in answer to this great cavern and what it contained. Those feelings that were so familiar, the silent yearning, the ache she had carried with her for so long that it had become an integral part of her, were, for the first time since she could remember, soothed.

She arrived at the fountain and craned her head back to look at the ceiling. She froze, a sudden stillness coming over her body as if it had been instantly encased in lead weights.

High above her, painted in sweeping dashes of brilliant color, an underwater sea rippled. In the midst of its midnight-blue depths, a group of beings swam. Larger than life—for the scene was huge, covering the entire ceiling—they swept through the water, exquisite and effortless in their beauty and strength.

Women and men. Naked except for flashing necklaces

hung about their throats, their bodies were sleek and muscled, their mouths open as if the artist or artists had caught
them in the middle of singing a tribute to the sea through
which they swam. Something about the way they moved
tugged at Meredith, reminding her . . .

Of Galen.

The songs in the fountain had grown louder. The grip
upon Meredith's limbs eased, and she found herself swaying
with the songs, keeping time to a rhythm that seemed to
come both from the water and from somewhere deep inside
herself. Her eyes closed. In the moment before she slipped
to the floor, she heard a voice, deep and familiar, call her
name, as footsteps whispered swiftly toward her.

"Meredith!" Galen cried.

But the music of the fountain drowned out the rest of his
words.

CHAPTER
15

In the season of the destruction

Marit brushed several locks of damp hair back from her forehead and heaved an exasperated sigh. No matter how she tried to keep her thick mass of dark hair confined, some of it always managed to stray loose. It was only a minor annoyance, but one that in this unusual season of heat made it all the more difficult to get any work done.

She picked up her stylus, then set it down, sighing again. Pushing herself back from the gold-inlaid table of marble and ebony where she did most of her writing, she got to her feet. Still toying with her unruly hair, she wandered out to the wide balcony that wound around her house.

As befitted her status as a lead historian, her home sat upon the highest hill of the five that ringed the capital city of the island kingdom her people called "The Land of

Gifts." It was an apt name for this country Marit loved so much.

The view that met her eyes was of a verdant land thriving with life. A far-flung tapestry of color stretched out past the walls of the city. Pastures of deep emerald formed oblongs or circles, each dotted with the dark specks of grazing horses and cattle. The deep gold squares of wheat and corn fields vied with the pale green of vineyards and the darker hues of tall groves of fruit trees and vast reaches of wild forest.

Roads wound through the land, broad and cobbled with whitewashed stone so that they glittered like ribbons of snow among the gold and green. Here and there, streams meandered through the pastures and fields, their waters so blue that it looked as though streamers had broken off from the sky and drifted to earth. In the distance, mountains tipped with a permanent dusting of snow loomed over the plains, guarding them in benign majesty.

The beauty of this land was eclipsed by one thing, though: the sea. She encircled the island as the walls encircled the city, as the hills encircled the walls, as the mountains encircled the island itself. There was nowhere that one could go, not even among the highest of the mountain peaks, and not be aware of the ocean's presence.

It was She who had created this rich island, the legends said, bringing it forth from Her darkest depth as a gift to the people who had settled it. A sign, many believed, that She did not hold any rancor toward these children of Hers who had left Her watery realms to live upon the land. But the legends also warned that only the Sea could take back what She had given, although after all the thousands of seasons that had passed, no one truly believed that She would.

Except for Marit.

She sighed, gazing down at the sparkling beauty of the graceful city enfolded in the embrace of the five wooded hills. There were other cities and towns in the Land of Gifts, but the City of Waves, as this one was known, was the largest and, without a doubt, the richest.

As with the other cities, every square inch of the City of Waves's walls and buildings had been painted with the brilliant colors and the loving attention to detail that was the hallmark of the artists who formed a large part of Marit's people. But unlike those other townships, the capital city was unique, coming by its name because of the theme that ran through its decoration.

Waves.

They were depicted on every available surface, from towering wall paintings to delicate courtyard mosaics. Each held visions of the sea's rippling surface in every conceivable mood and hue. One could walk through the wide tree-lined streets and glimpse those visions in all of their incarnations: gentle tides washing up on a quiet beach, walls of water hurled by storm winds into jagged mountainous peaks, dark masses of quietly undulating water under a setting moon. It was all there, as though the waves themselves breathed and whispered through this city.

Marit had often thought that the entire metropolis of her island's capital was a living masterpiece—a paean to the sea. She, with her own deep love of Mother Ocean, could not imagine living anywhere else, even on a fiery day like this one, when the walls that guarded the city seemed to shimmer and dance, as if they were about to melt in the burning glare of the sun.

Some of the most magnificent works of the entire city were displayed upon those great walls of sparkling limestone.

Over two thousand years before, when the City of Waves was first founded, the walls had been built for protection against possible invaders. In the minds of those founders it had been a precaution worth taking. Their own ancestors had been conquered by the renowned women on horseback, that fierce tribe of warriors who had then stayed to blend their strong and vital blood into the descendants who still inhabited that broad continent to the west. It was an offshoot of this new people comprised of Amazons and ex-merfolk, that had migrated to this island.

But all that had been long ago. Violence, in the form of warfare, had never visited the Land of Gifts. Indeed, violence in any shape was rare here. So the sturdy walls, built to withstand a possible siege, had instead become works of art.

It was a source of national pride to see that their colors were kept as dazzling as the day they had first been painted. Loving reapplications and constant tending ensured their brightness, so that from a distance on a windy day under a bright sun, the high, rounded buildings, the slender spires and conical towers, and the thick walls of the city, all seemed a piece of the living, undulating sea come to land.

The whitewashed stone walls of Marit's house, each with its own patina of brightly colored sea mosaics, were blinding in the midday sun. Even the tiles of the balcony floor, normally cool on even the hottest of days, seeped heat into the soles of her feet despite the protection of her sandals.

She walked over to the portion of the balcony that overlooked the sea. It was scarcely any cooler out here than inside the stifling house, but at least she could feel a faint breeze wafting up from below, a tiny respite sent by Mother Ocean in Her kindness.

Resting her elbows on the carved marble railing, Marit gazed down at the sea moving and whispering restlessly below. She was troubled. Always in the past looking at the sea had eased and reassured her when she was troubled, but no longer. Now looking at the waves washing up on the beach and rippling out to infinity only added to her sense of uneasiness, of danger that could not be seen but only felt.

The sea—the constant unchanging force that ruled her life and that of her people—did not even look the same any more. Not to her, although others disagreed, saying that she was worrying over nothing. Marit thought they were wrong.

Lately the waters that bordered their land, enfolding the island as closely as the balcony surrounded her house, had taken on an ominous brassy tinge. A hue that reminded her disturbingly of anger. The sea's voice sounded different to her, as well, calling out to those on the land but menacing them at the same time.

No, something was not right. The sacred harmony of sea and land was being disturbed. Even Marit with her highly developed sensitivity could not predict where that disruption, now that it had begun, might lead.

"Cherished one."

She turned at the sound of the rich voice, smiling at the man who had walked out onto the balcony. Her heart beat a little faster, as it always did at the sight of him. Twenty-two seasons since they had mate-bonded, and it was still the same: that sweet rush of warmth whenever he came near.

Jeram was somewhat shorter than the average male of their people. However, what he lacked in height he made up for in the burly power of his stocky frame. Neither did he possess the flawless beauty of feature that was almost an inherited characteristic among so many on the island. Despite that lack of perfect handsomeness, Jeram's craggy face held an attractiveness and love of life that had drawn Marit from the very first.

She particularly loved his hands. Big and powerful as they were, she had seen them cradle, with the utmost gentleness, a sick foal or the tiniest fish left stranded in a tidal pool. The same gentleness with which they touched her when they made love.

She held out her own hands to him now, and they exchanged the kiss of greeting. "You look as hot as I feel, beloved," she said, touching his sweat-soaked forehead.

He returned her smile tiredly. "I surely am. I've been out with the mares since sunrise. Three are ready to be taken to the foaling sheds, but with this heat, who knows how the birthings will go. The poor creatures are miserable, and so am I at the thought that I might lose any of them or their foals."

Marit nodded sympathetically but said nothing as she studied him.

In his appearance and in his consuming love of horses, her mate represented the new. He was the product of many generations of interbreeding between the original merfolk who had settled the great land farther to the west, and the powerful women warriors who had ridden there as conquerors and stayed.

Marit reflected, not for the first time, how odd it was that she and Jeram should have joined together. They were so different. He was tied inextricably to the land, while she, in so many ways, was a complete throwback to the old ways, to a far distant time when the sea and not the land comprised her people's whole world.

One would think she still had gills, her brothers and sisters had said as a gentle way of teasing her when they were children. They still repeated it from time to time, though by now it was a gibe that had become almost meaningless.

Once there had been some people who carried physical remnants of the unique heritage that had previously belonged to all the folk who lived on this vast island. But the last person with even a trace of gills had passed from this life into the next plane of existence several generations ago, and none had been born since.

The breathing slits that had made Marit's ancestors one with the sea were only a distant memory now, as was the extreme longevity they had once been credited with. Nevertheless, people here still lived far, far longer than those in surrounding lands. And they were equally known for their height and physical appearance, although, as Jeram's looks evidenced, that was changing too.

In other ways, though, the bonds with the past had been retained. Men and women ruled together as their remote ancestors had, in a totally egalitarian system headed by Elders of both sexes. The Seven Strata, with some minor alterations, were still practiced, comprised of healers, artisans, food-gatherers and growers, warriors, Elders, and historians, the last of which Marit belonged to.

Yet would the wisdom and kindness to one another, gained through adherence to the ancient ways, be enough to save them from what was coming?

"You look tired, love," Jeram said, breaking in on her thoughts. "You're still troubled, aren't you? Is it the dreams?"

Despite the heat and the stickiness of their bodies, she leaned against him, needing the reassurance of his physical presence. "They never leave me," she said wearily. "And neither does the feeling that something is terribly, terribly wrong. But the other historians will not listen to me." She smiled in a weak attempt at humor. "They think my brain is addled by the heat, and who knows? Perhaps it is."

"I don't believe that," Jeram said soberly. "And neither do you. You're wiser than the whole herd of them put together. What about talking to the Elders?"

"To tell them what?" She rubbed a hand over her eyes. "If my colleagues won't heed me, why should they? Anyway, I have nothing of the slightest substance to say to them. Only bad dreams and vague superstitions—that is how they would look at it."

He gripped her tense shoulder in silent sympathy. "I see you were working," he said in an attempt to change the subject. "Have you begun a new scroll?"

"No, it's the same one I started when the dreams first began. Although I haven't gotten very far with it." She closed her eyes and recited softly, " 'The season of destruction will soon be upon us and our city . . .' "

A chill swept over her despite the weight of the oppressive heat. She shivered and leaned farther into the comfort of Jeram's stocky chest. "That's all I've written, all I've been able to put down. The words haunt me, Jeram. They keep going through my mind, asleep or awake, over and over—"

"Hush, dearling." He smoothed a hand over her hair, but above her head his light blue eyes were grave, filled with a fear he was trying to keep from her as well as himself.

"Are you certain of this?" he finally whispered, unable to stop himself. "Is there no chance you could be mistaken? Perhaps you didn't see what you thought you did. Perhaps it isn't destruction after all."

"I am sure." Marit's tone was quiet, indisputable. "There's no mistake, beloved. Although I wish with all my heart that there were. I've prayed to the Mother of Life, She who is the Goddess of all the seas, to make me wrong in this."

"And has She answered?" he asked when she said nothing more.

Marit shivered again. "No," she said. "It's as though She has turned Her face away from me, away from this land. The waves no longer speak to me as they once did, Jeram. The sea is angry, and I tremble every time I think of where that anger might lead."

"But why?" Jeram's open face held both bewilderment and anger. "What have we done that the Mother should be displeased with us? We honor and worship Her as we always have. We fish and trade, raise the horses and cattle we're known for, create our art, and seek to learn and grow in wisdom, as we always have. Where is the harm in any of that?"

"I don't know, my love," Marit told him sadly. "I wish I did."

Later, as dusk approached and the relentless fireball that the sun had become was finally lowering into the sea, she and Jeram went down to a sheltered cove along the beach. It had long been their custom to bathe at this hour, even more so during this breathless weather, when the sea offered at least a slight respite from the heat.

Pulling off the short linen tunic she had taken to wearing since the hot days began, Marit waded naked into the cove. She stood still, letting the singing waves wash about her ankles, and looked hopefully up at the sky.

When rainstorms came, they normally arrived from the north. However, the sky in that direction, as well as in every other direction, was singularly unpromising. A net of high clouds had drifted across the pale burning horizon, but it was evident they would not thicken into anything more substantial. They were sterile clouds, wispy shreds turning pink and violet-gray in the softness of early evening, offering no hint of moisture, no sign of relief.

Jeram's footsteps splashed softly behind her. He pressed himself against her back, sliding his hands around to cup her breasts in strong, calloused hands. She leaned against him, feeling his manhood come to life, smiling a little as the beginnings of his erection prodded at her buttocks.

Both of them had come to regard this small quiet cove as their own private spot, and they always made love there, either before or after their swim. Wanting, needing to be receptive to this man she loved above all else, Marit tried to push the nagging fears from her mind.

It was not fair to Jeram, this constant worrying, she reminded herself. He was so patient with her, so kind, and here she was, so distracted.

Yet her eyes would not stay away from the sea that lay beyond the shelter of the cove. Ominous and hungry, it called to her, pulling her gaze toward it no matter how she tried to resist, speaking to her in ways that only became more disturbing, and more oblique, the harder she tried to decipher them.

She sighed, and above her head Jeram sighed too. "Do you see it?" she asked him, even though she knew she shouldn't, knew already what his answer would be. "Do you see how the sea looks?"

"No, love." He tried to speak patiently, but she heard the irritation he could not quite hide. "You ask me that every evening, and still I see nothing different. The sea looks as she always looks. Hazy from the heat perhaps, but nothing more."

Marit said nothing. She knew it was more than that. The strange brassy hue she saw from her balcony was even more striking up close. The ocean glittered; it had an uneasy metallic glow to its waters that came not from the sun but from somewhere below the surface. Subtle yet unmistakable forces were stirring beneath the waves, even beneath the placid surface of this little cove. Why was it that no one but she could see and feel them?

Jeram turned her in his arms. Bending his head he kissed her, lightly at first, then with more determination, sensing her distraction and trying to pull her from it. Marit embraced him back, wrapping her arms around his shoulders. She opened her lips to him, dancing her tongue into his mouth.

She wanted to respond, wanted to lose herself in sensation, not only for Jeram's sake but for her own. Entering the sensuous realms of the physical with her mated one was a way—perhaps the only way—that she could free herself, for a time, from the burdens that had descended upon her the same day the oppressive heat had first struck the Land of Gifts.

Linked together, she and Jeram slipped down into the gentle surf. The tide was coming in. Murmuring, it lapped around their bodies, bodies that were sweated and sticky with the effort of surviving another of the long hot days. It eased the perspiration away and washed it out into the waves, leaving a blessed coolness in its wake.

Honey flowed into Marit's belly as Jeram's hands slid slowly up her thighs, that delicious melting that was as sweet and familiar to her as the touch of his blunt fingers. So strong and yet so gentle, his hands probed and caressed between her legs, seeking the source of her female power, worshipping and arousing her in ways only he knew. His own eagerness taking hold, he finally entered her with a soft groan. They made love to the whispered music of the waters, their voices, as the passion within them caught flame, a fevered accompaniment to the ebb and wash of the waves.

The tide had flowed back out to sea by the time they had finished. Comfortably enmeshed in the easy way only long-time lovers have with one another, Marit and Jeram lay on the soft wet sand above the lowered water line, content to not speak.

Tired from lovemaking and the heat and a long day spent beneath the sun, Jeram soon fell asleep. Marit, although she was just as tired, could not follow suit. She lay awake in Jeram's arms, listening to the sea and to the soft rumble of her mate's snores.

Finally she extricated herself from his embrace. Jeram was usually a light sleeper, but on this evening her moving away did not awaken him. He only mumbled something incomprehensible, rolled over on his back, and went on sleeping. Marit smiled, touched him with one hand, then walked out into the sea.

Like all her people she was an excellent swimmer. The inhabitants of the Land of Gifts may have lost their gills, but they were still the descendants of merfolk, and their affinity for the water remained. With Marit this affinity was even stronger than usual. The sea had always felt like home to her, as natural a world as the island on which she lived.

She swam far out into the cove, stroking powerfully through the quiet waters, stopping only when the outgoing current began to exert a pull that threatened to drag her out past the bay and into the sea. The sun had sunk low in the sky, a flaming ball of pain hovering just above the horizon, its scarlet color promising another searing return on the morrow.

She turned around and began the long swim back to the beach. She had reached the shallows and, with the water reaching only to her waist, was splashing into shore, when a voice stopped her.

"Woman of the land, wait a moment."

Meredith's eyelids fluttered. She moaned, rising just to the edge of wakefulness, but not quite making it there. Then she subsided, going still as death once again.

Sitting beside her, the songs of the Dream Fountain cascading in his ears, Galen watched, mesmerized with wonder and disbelief, as he had been since he had found her there hours earlier.

He could not follow her to wherever she had gone. He would have given much to do so. She was in a deep all-encompassing trance. A dream-walk, he would have said, except that only merfolk embarked on that journey into the mind, as the final hallmark of their maturity.

But if it was not a dream-walk, what was it? And how had she found her way into one of the most sacred places known to merfolk, a place that only the initiated knew how to find?

Galen had long since given up trying to find answers. He simply sat with her, watching, and waiting for her to return. She murmured something, and he leaned forward.

A frown of concentration slashed across his strained features. He could not be certain, but he could swear she had spoken in his own tongue. The words were garbled, distorted with a strange accent, almost as though she were speaking a skewed version of the merfolk language. Yet he thought he had understood what she had muttered.

It had sounded like, "For me?"

Galen's frown deepened.

CHAPTER
16

It was a woman's voice, Marit realized. Low and musical, it had come from behind her, from the deeper waters through which she had just passed. She spun around in shock, a superstitious prickle dashing up her spine. For a wild instant she thought Mother Ocean Herself was speaking to her.

A moment later the one who had called to her appeared, a tall nude figure rising out of the waves, moving with an indescribable grace that was like a song. Long red hair snaked down her sun-dark back and shoulders, and a necklace of emeralds flashed about her throat in the dying sun's rays. Her eyes, as green as the stones of her necklace, were fastened upon Marit.

"I am called Kirta," the woman said. "And I have been waiting for you to come."

"For me?" Marit stared. Excitement and fear, mingled

with an almost stupefying awe, chased each other through her mind.

Clearly, this woman was of the merfolk. But not in the living memory of Marit's people had any person from the sea ever sought one of them out, for conversation or for anything else. All contact between the two races that had once been united had been broken long ago, when that distant band of rebels had chosen the land instead of the sea.

"Yes," the merwoman named Kirta said in a grave voice. "It is time we talked, the two of us, for the fate of both our peoples depends upon it."

Involuntarily Marit cast a quick glance at the beach, where Jeram still lay sprawled in sleep.

Kirta followed her gaze. "He will not awaken," the merwoman said. "While you were swimming I made a small magic to deepen his sleep. I am of the Healing Strata," she added, "and we are skilled in such things."

"Yes, I know," Marit answered bemusedly. She was dazed by her visitor, by the height and beauty and strength—both inside and out—that emanated from her. The merwoman was so utterly magnificent, she had such presence. Had Marit's people once possessed this aura of power? If so, how could they have borne giving it up?

"Our healers are skilled in that way as well," she went on lamely. Realizing what she had said, she gazed in silence at the merwoman. "Once," she said softly, "our people were the same."

"But no longer." There was an edge to Kirta's words. "Your ancestors betrayed their ancient heritage. And now you, their descendants, must suffer for it." She paused and gentled her tone. "That is why I have come."

A sense of relief poured through Marit, so deep she swayed with the force of it. *At last, at last.* "You know," she whispered, the words bubbling out. "You understand. You see as I have. I've been so alone. No one here will listen to me, to the things I fear. It's been so hard trying to get them to believe me . . ."

"Yes," Kirta said heavily. "It has been that way with me too."

Stunned, Marit frowned at the merwoman as the implications of what she had said sank in. "You—you have been having dreams?"

"I have. Bad ones that will give me no peace. But even the wisest and oldest of our Elders pay me no heed. To be blunt"—Kirta's jade eyes pierced Marit's dark ones—"they say that if destruction is indeed coming to your people, the choice was made long ago and you deserve whatever comes. You left Mother Ocean willingly, and they see no reason at all to help you now. I understand their feelings. I used to feel the same way myself."

"But you do no longer."

"No longer. Not since I have begun dreaming of my people, and of yours."

Marit held her breath, silent, waiting. Her heartbeat hammered in her ears, and on some plane deep inside her, where fear dwelt, she knew what the merwoman would say.

"Destruction is coming to this island you call the Land of Gifts," Kirta said somberly. "Beneath the island and around it, Mother Ocean is restless and angry. Soon She will release that anger on this land and all that live upon it. Nothing and no one will survive. People, animals, plants, nothing. My dreams have shown me this, and they've done it with such power that I know what I am telling you is true."

She paused to study Marit's face in the fading light. "You are not surprised. Have your dreams been the same, then?"

Marit nodded. "Not as clear as yours, Lady. But troubling, and filled with warnings that wake me from a sound sleep, leaving me trembling and afraid."

The two women regarded each other across the chasm of

time and heritage and the different worlds that now separated them. Then Marit asked with a ragged pain she did not try to hide, "But what has this to do with the merfolk, Kirta? You say your Elders don't care—"

"They don't. But they should care, we all should." Kirta closed her eyes. "My dreams have shown me something else. The destruction of your people will in time mean the destruction of mine. I don't understand it, not completely. But the dreams keep telling me the same thing over and over: that someday far in the future a plague will ravage the merfolk and other people of the sea as well. It will destroy us."

She opened her eyes, and when she spoke again, there was a note of pleading in her voice. "Only you can stop it, woman of the land. Only you."

Marit jerked back, startled from her grief by the merwoman's pronouncement. "Me! What can I possibly—"

Kirta continued on as though she had not heard. "You must survive what is coming, you must. Otherwise, we of the sea are doomed." She sighed and passed a hand over her eyes. "I wish I could tell you more. The dreams show me your face and the scroll you will write one day, a scroll that will contain a cure taken from all the healing knowledge that your people have amassed. But that is all I've seen."

"The scroll," Marit said excitedly. "I *have* started a scroll. But . . ." She paused, awed and confused and terrified. "I know nothing of healing or curing sickness. I'm a historian, Lady. I don't understand how I can help."

"Nor do I. Yet in some way you will, I'm convinced of it. If you live, that is. Which is why I'm here. To see that you do. Once the scroll is completed I will take it to a secret place, so that it will survive even after we are gone from the paths of this existence."

Despite the rapidly falling darkness, the merwoman's eyes took on a luminous glow, like moonlight over the waves. That silvery green light seemed to reach into Marit's soul.

"Three nights from now," Kirta said quietly, "come back to this cove, and bring along with you whoever else is willing. I will be here, with my mate and some others who take this as seriously as I do. We will use our combined powers to save you, to reawaken the abilities I believe still live within your kind, and bring you back to your true home: the sea."

She turned. "Now, I must go."

"Lady—Kirta, wait." Marit hesitated, then plunged ahead. "Do . . . do you know why my ancestors left the sea? Now that I have seen and talked with one of you, you are so powerful, so magnificent. How could my kin have given up so much to go to the land?"

Kirta faced her again, and the merwoman's voice was pensive as she answered. "It is said that they grew restless in the sea. There was a notable scholar at the time, a woman called Jabari, whose teachings they followed. She believed that our folk could thrive upon the land as well as in the sea, and could keep the gifts given them by Mother Ocean even though they left Her realms. She has long been discredited among us, but do you know, now that I have met and talked with you, woman of the Land of Gifts, I think that in some ways, she may have been right after all."

Kirta stepped backwards, moving deeper into the water. The last red tinge of sun had drowned itself in the sea minutes ago, and in the purple-blue darkness, her words came disembodied to Marit's ears.

"You have not lost as much as you believe, Marit. The shades of our common past glow in you yet. You may no longer be of the sea, but Her magnificence shines in you still. Now, though, it is time for you and yours to come home. Save yourself, Marit. Bring your people home. I only hope it is not too late."

There was no sound of a splash, though Marit listened as hard as she could. Then the merwoman's voice lilted out of the blackness of the sea, as eerie as one of the spirit beings that inhabited the stories one told to children on stormy nights to give them a delicious fright.

"Come home. Come home."

"We must," Marit insisted. "We must return to the sea and to the old ways we once followed. There is no other choice!"

In shifting patterns of orange and gold, light flickered over the faces of those who listened to her, cast by the dozens of ornate bronze oil lamps that lit the Hall of Elders. Marit glanced at Jeram, who stood stolidly beside her. Silently she beseeched him to lend her some of his rock-solid strength. He looked back at her, love and support shining in his eyes.

He had awakened groggy and disoriented after Kirta had left. It had not taken him long to get his wits back, though. Not once Marit told him what had taken place.

At least *he* believed her, she thought gratefully. Jeram, her cherished and beloved one who trusted her, had understood at last the gravity of the situation that faced them. She had not even needed to suggest that they go immediately to the Hall to summon the Elders. Jeram had urged it.

"I wish there were another way," she said, turning back to the Elders. "But there isn't. We must leave the land."

"Leave the land?" one of the Elders echoed incredulously. "You are mad, Marit!"

"Perhaps I am, but with what is coming it would be madder still to remain." She spoke firmly, her gaze steady and calm as it rested upon the faces of the men and women who formed the Circle of Wisdom.

Many had left their high-backed chairs to pace restlessly

about the large chamber. Others had gathered around to ring her in a circle of shock and disbelief and skepticism.

"Why?" another Elder demanded. Among the Circle she was a woman well known for her reasonableness and highly respected for her wisdom. Marit had counted on her as being one of the few who would listen and understand, but she found this hope fading as the woman went on.

"If destruction is coming, what good will it do to leave? We lost our gills more generations ago than any of us can count. We no longer have the means of surviving as our ancestors did."

She paused, her gaze wandering to the wide windows, where a three-quarter moon cast streams of silver down at the dark tossing sea. "Have you forgotten," she asked Marit, looking back at her, "you, who are a historian yourself, that there was, and still is, bad blood between those we spring from and those who remained in the sea?"

"Lady," Marit began, but the Elder held up a hand, cutting her off.

"Our kin left the sea amidst rage and acrimony and warnings that only disaster would result from their going to the land. The merfolk regard us as having betrayed our heritage. What reason would they have for helping us now?"

A shouted chorus of agreement met her words, but Marit's voice, ringing and razor sharp, sliced through it.

"Because they have said they would."

A silence as loud as the shouting had been met her pronouncement, and she hurried on lest someone interrupt her. "Last evening, as dusk was falling, a woman—one of the foremost merfolk healers—came to the edge between sea and land. She was looking for me, to offer her help. She has foreseen the disaster coming to our island, as I have, and she thinks she can help—"

"I will ask again," the Elder broke in. "Why?"

"She has had her own dreams to trouble her, just as I

have," Marit replied steadily. "Only hers speak of some terrible plague that will visit the merfolk and others of the sea in some far distant future. She believes the cure to this illness is contained in the healing knowledge we have amassed in our records. She wants to have this cure written on a scroll that will be kept in a secret and carefully guarded place, so that those who come after us will be able to avoid destruction."

"So she wants to trade," another Elder woman said thoughtfully. "Our knowledge in saving their people at some future time, in return for their aid in saving our lives now. Only how can she help us? She can't give us back our gills, can she?"

Before Marit could answer, one of the oldest among the Elders spoke. "There are ways," he muttered, more to himself than to his listeners. "Ancient ways. I have heard of them. From time to time, the merfolk have saved true Terrans from drowning, if the mood struck them to do so. The methods they use would certainly work even better with us, who were once of the sea-people ourselves."

"But we are no longer!" one of the younger Elders, a man of no more than three hundred seasons, cried in exasperation. "And how can one merwoman offer life-breath to a whole island full of people? Will all the merfolk in the sea that borders us come to help her?"

Marit fought the urge to fidget under the prodding of several dozen expectant pairs of eyes. She knew she had to answer the question truthfully, though the words stuck in her throat.

"No," she said at last. "She is having as difficult a time convincing the merfolk Elders as I am having convincing you. They will not help her. Not yet. But—"

"Bah!" The young Elder flung out his arms, sending the long sleeves of his robe billowing around him. "This is nonsense. The Land of Gifts has stood for millions of seasons and it will stand for millions more. Mother Ocean gave it to us Herself, the legends have always said so. You're allowing yourself to be too easily frightened, Marit. No one else sees the sea looking any different, only you do. And as for this merwoman, who knows why she came?"

"I know!" Marit tried to keep her rising temper in check. Fueled by her ever increasing worry, it was not an easy task.

She began again, keeping her voice calm with effort. "No merwoman or man has ever come to us before, not even in the land of our foremothers and forefathers. The very fact that this one did speaks for itself. And as for the legends: I'm a historian. No one is more familiar with legends than I am. Let me remind you that they also warn that Mother Ocean, and only Mother Ocean, can take away what She has given."

She looked around her. "Perhaps the time has come when She will."

"She's right," said a tall dignified Elder whose hair hung to his waist. "Yet," he added, "none are more skilled in the use and power of dreams than we who are Elders. If disaster approaches the Land of Gifts, why have none of us in the Circle of Wisdom been warned of it in our own dreaming?"

He sighed, as around him heads nodded in agreement. "You're one of our lead historians, Marit, a very wise woman in your own right. Surely you can understand that if we go about speaking of this without any real proof, the entire island will instantly be thrown into panic."

"Real proof!" Unable to keep still any longer, Jeram suddenly exploded. "What better proof do you need than the merwoman who came to Marit with the same portents she has been having?"

"Ah," the Elder said gently. "But you were asleep and

did not see her come, did you? Only Marit saw her, or says she did."

Jeram's eyes widened. "Are you saying that my mate, one of the foremost historians of our people, is *lying* about this?"

Marit laid a hand on her mate's taut-muscled arm. "All of these gathered here know me better than that," she said coldly.

"We do indeed," the same Elder said. "And I did not mean to suggest that you were telling falsehoods, my child. But this heat has placed a strain on everyone. Such weather can have a strange effect. It can play tricks with the mind, make us think we see things that aren't really there. Dreams, and who or what appears in them, can suddenly become very real. It has happened to me. I think it may have happened to you, earlier this evening."

Feeling her shoulders sag in defeat, Marit fought to keep herself standing erect. She had known this would not be easy. She had even warned Jeram of it when they ran straight from the beach to the Hall of Elders and set the chimes singing in the combination of special rings used only in times of emergency to summon the wise ones from their inner chambers.

Yet even she had not foreseen that it would be this difficult to persuade the Elders of the danger they and everyone else faced. The thing she had expected least of all was that they would tell her the appearance of Kirta was a figment of her imagination, brought on by a mind fevered by the terrible heat!

The weight of the new knowledge she carried was crushing in its horror. She had thought her old burdens, the ones generated by her dreams had been heavy, but they were as nothing compared to what rested upon her shoulders now. The fate of her entire people, as well as the fate of the people from which she and hers had sprung, hung in the balance.

If she could not succeed in getting the Elders—who were the wisest and most perceptive of them all—to accept what she was telling them as the truth, how could she possibly convince anyone else?

The Elders had fallen silent; those who had been pacing were now standing still. Beside her she heard Jeram breathing heavily, trying to control his wrath, wanting to protect her but not knowing how. She looked around at the circle of faces, all of them watching her, grave and intent.

"Does the Elder Luat speak for all of you then?" she asked quietly. "Does everyone in the Circle believe that what I have told you is nothing more than the ranting of a person overwrought from the heat?"

"Now, Marit," the younger Elder began placatingly. "We respect you highly, you know that—"

"Don't," she said sharply. "I am not a youngling or a Historian in her first season to be fobbed off and reassured by a few compliments. These are matters of life and death I speak of, whether you believe it is so or not."

"They will become matters of life and death," the younger Elder pointed out, "if you start running about predicting doom to people who have no reason to be frightened. You'll set pandemonium loose throughout the land."

Marit studied him. She realized suddenly that the Elder was afraid, and because of that fear he did not want to believe her. But he was only one among an entire circle of Elders, all of whom were older, more experienced, and by virtue of those qualities, presumably wiser than he. She looked from him to the others.

"How do you plan to prevent it?" she asked. "Will you imprison me? Stop up my mouth with rags?"

"Now Marit." The Elder woman known for her wisdom rebuked her in a gentle voice. "You know that is not our way. I hope, and I'm sure that everyone else does, that you will think about this further before you take actions that may cause you, as well as others, regret."

Marit clenched her hands into fists at her sides. "There's no time to think about it more. Don't you understand? What's more, there is no need. I know what I know."

Without a backward glance she swung about and strode from the hall, back out into the muggy embrace of the night. The voice of the sea met her. She could almost believe there was a thick note of triumph in the breakers hitting the beach, a gloating laughter.

They do not believe, they will not believe. My time is coming . . .

Jeram had come out right behind her. "They're afraid, dearling," he said with weary frustration. "If they acknowledge the truth you brought them this night, it will disrupt the tidy pleasantness of their lives. Fools! Can't they see that their lives will end more horribly than they can imagine if they don't listen?"

His voice rose. "Our world is at stake, Marit. Our world!"

She shook her head, stroking the bunched muscles of his shoulders, trying to calm him. "They're hardheaded, Jeram. But I knew that already, and so did you. They want proof, proof that we can't give them."

"What about the merwoman?" Jeram's eyes brightened as the idea struck him. "Perhaps if you went back to the cove and asked her to come to you again, she could go before the Elders. *That* would convince the mule-brained pack of them."

"She won't return for three days," Marit said. "And by then, it will be too late. I could go down to the sea and hope she comes, but I fear we would be wasting precious time.

"I think . . ." She straightened her shoulders and tried to suppress the shudder of apprehension that racked her. "I think our only choice is to find all those in the land who do believe, and three days from now take them with us. That's all we can do, beloved. Try to save whoever and whatever part of our world we can."

Jeram brooded for a moment, then he nodded. Taking her hand in his, he said briskly, "Well, what are we waiting for? Let's begin. We haven't much time."

CHAPTER
17

The next three days flew by, dawning and dying with terrible swiftness, running out, just as the life of the Land of Gifts and that of its people was running out.

To Marit, it seemed as though an evil spell had been cast over those numbered days. Some malignant power had toyed with the forces that ruled time, manipulating them so that hours sped past like minutes, and minutes flew by with the speed of seconds.

Since the flaming epidemic of heat had come to blister the island, she had been cursing the endless passage of every new day. How could she not, when they had dragged on and on, each hour sweating past the tedious progress of honey seeping from an open cask on a cold day?

Now she cursed for a different reason: the relentless determination with which the sun came up, allotting her a certain number of hours that were far too short for what she and Jeram had to do.

They had separated, going to different parts of the island in order to reach the greatest number of people possible. Yet it was not enough, it could never be enough. They argued and pleaded, reasoned and warned, until their throats were raw and their voices so hoarse, they could barely speak above a whisper.

It seemed to make little difference.

The Circle of Elders need not have worried over the pandemonium Marit and Jeram might cause with their warnings and pronouncements. Whether it was because the Circle refused to lend its weight to what they had to say, or that people simply could not admit that the end of their world was actually a possibility, few were willing to make a commitment that meant the disruption of all they knew as familiar.

Word still traveled rapidly for all that. From every corner of the Land of Gifts, people came to the City of Waves and the great Hall of Elders that reposed on the city's outskirts. Some arrived on their own, other were sent as delegations by cities and townships and distant farming villages. But all came for the same reason: to obtain clarification from those who were the wisest and most learned in the land.

A gamut of emotions ran through these gatherings of worried men and women who assembled before the Hall. People were puzzled and anxious, frightened, even angry, at the raising of a threat so vast that it defied comprehension. They wanted answers that would enable them to understand, but more than anything else, they wanted reassurance, to be told that there was nothing to fear, that above all, they would be safe.

And the Elders—perhaps because they wanted the same thing themselves—told them what was logical, what their people wanted to hear.

"Yes, we know what the historian, Marit, and her mate, Jeram, are saying, yet we ourselves have seen no evidence that it is true. Mother Ocean has not spoken to any Elder, in dreams or prayers or rituals. Nor has anyone from the merfolk come to seek us out. It grieves us to say it, but we do not think this merwoman who Marit speaks of actually came to her, though we believe that she believes it.

"To even consider deserting our homes, our possessions, our lands—our very world—just on the word of one person, is dangerous, as well as foolhardy. We are no longer of the sea. Even if we were to give credence to Marit's tale, to enter the sea now would mean certain death. We have no choice but to stay in the Land of Gifts. Here is our ancestral home. Here is where we belong, where we are safe."

"By the Mother," Jeram snarled, after a fruitless argument with yet another group of travelers, who, reassured by the Elders and on their way back to their homes, had stopped to advise him of what the Elders had said. "I've come to believe that the Elders, whom I've respected and admired all my life, are sentencing our people to their doom for no other reason than that they are jealous because the merwoman sought you out instead of *them*!"

With their tiny net of three days' safety nearly unraveled, he and Marit had rejoined each other once more. Back in their gaily painted house that overlooked the capital, they were—perhaps for the last time—in the large bedchamber in which they had known such happiness for so many seasons.

Marit rubbed her aching temples. "The three days are up tonight," she said desperately. "And there are five hundred people, maybe a few more than that, who say they believe us. Five hundred souls out of our entire land! In the name of the Goddess, what is to become of us?"

Jeram poured out two goblets of the pale rosy wine he had made from grapes grown in his and Marit's own vineyard, and handed her one. "I don't know, Marit." He drank deeply. "Maybe when the merwoman comes to the cove tonight, we can ask her to give us more time so we can try to gather more people."

"There is no more time." Marit spoke with sad finality. She knew from her dreams as well as from the hollow churning in the pit of her belly—a sick feeling that grew stronger with every passing hour—that this was so. "I think Kirta knows it too. Whatever is going to happen will happen after tonight. If we are still here, we will perish along with everyone else."

Jeram said nothing. He stared down into his wine, the same certainty reflected in his somber expression. It showed so heavily in his face, Marit felt a pang of empathy and grief clench inside her like a fist.

Despite the terrible realization that had become apparent to both of them over these last days, that the tragedy they were trying to avert was more powerful than they, leaving the land was not the same for her as it was for him. For her, buried far below all the pain and dread and sorrow, was a subtle excitement, an eager readiness to desert the land for what she considered, deep in some secret, singing part of her soul, her true realm.

She was deeply ashamed to acknowledge it, much less speak of it, for hand in hand with the eagerness went a tortured ambivalence. How could she experience even the slightest tinge of happiness in the face of her world's pending destruction? Her feelings were in themselves a betrayal, especially to Jeram, because she saw so clearly the heartbreak her mate was suffering.

After Marit and his family, what Jeram loved most in all the world were his horses. In a land where excellent horses were the rule rather than the exception, he was widely acknowledged as one of the best breeders on the whole island. His secret was simple: to him the horses he bred were not just animals, they were sisters and brothers and friends—equal beings who deserved to be treated with the utmost respect and love. It had long been a commonly repeated joke among the buyers and sellers of horses that, magnificent as Jeram's horses were, it took an intervention from the Goddess herself to convince him to sell any of them, so loathe was he to part with a single one of his prized equine children.

However, he would have to part with them now, and far more cruelly than he ever could have imagined in his worst dreams.

Marit ached for him, and ached with the helplessness of knowing she could do nothing to ease his torment. They both knew there was only one answer to the dilemma that faced him.

"At least our clans believe us," she said wearily, searching for the one bright spot in the darkness of this nightmare. "I don't think I could bear to leave if we had not been able to convince our own families of the danger we are in."

"Our human families, yes." Jeram's eyes, blue-circled from lack of sleep, were haunted. "But what of my dear ones, my horses?"

Marit sat down beside him on their bed. She held his hand silently, wishing she could find some words of comfort to offer. Language and its use were her gifts, yet she could find no phrases eloquent enough to ease the pain of this man she loved so much. It was a bitter feeling.

His fingers tightened around hers. "I know what I must do," he said thickly. "I've known since the merwoman came. I just could not face thinking about it."

Marit squeezed his hand in answer. "Would you like me to help you?" she asked softly. "Or I could do it for you, if that would make it easier. I give you my sacred word that I would be gentle and quick."

He shook his head. "No, dearling, I would not ask such

a thing of you, any more than you would ask me to destroy your scrolls. This is my responsibility, and I will deal with it."

Marit could scarcely swallow over the hot thick lump in her throat. It was said that merfolk could not cry, but the people of the Land of Gifts could, a legacy they had apparently gained in exchange for the loss of their gills. Marit had always said she would have preferred the gills. Now, though, she was glad for the tears that slid down her cheeks and those of her beloved, glad for this small release they could share together.

Words were her love, just as Jeram's horses were his. She could take her words with her, locked safely in her head. Jeram would have to leave his horses here waiting for death, unless he was kind enough and brave enough to release them quickly so they would not suffer.

"If only there were another way," she said.

He looked at her with hollow, wet eyes. "Yes, but there isn't." Hope flashed for a feeble second in those haunted depths. "Is there?"

Marit could not meet his gaze. "No," she whispered. "There isn't."

Darkness fell, a peculiar darkness, lit by the slow rising of a full moon that shone with a greenish yellow glow the color of seepage from a festering wound.

At sunset Marit had noticed that clouds were finally building over the sea. They were as odd-looking as the night, though, greenish yellow like the moon and coming from the east, a direction she could not ever remember seeing clouds come from. It was still searingly hot, and there was not a breath of wind, not even a hint of breeze, to lighten the sweltering darkness.

Sweating, Marit stood on the beach of the small cove

waiting for Jeram. He had left their bedchamber hours before dusk to go to his horses one last time. She herself was
alone. The hour for those few who had said they would embark on this tragic journey had not yet arrived.

She had not been able to stay in the house, though, with
its tapestry of memories accumulated over so many seasons.
The memories would only torture her. So she had bid her
home farewell and come here, though in some ways, waiting
at the cove was just as painful as waiting in her house. It,
too, held its share of memories, delightful and painful, to
torment her.

She paced restlessly on the flat sand, still so hot from the
day's sun that it stung the soles of her bare feet. Pressed
against her chest, wrapped in oiled cloth to protect it from
the water, was the one thing she had brought with her. The
scroll she had begun in what seemed another lifetime. She
had added to it, though only slightly. The words had come
to her that morning in the gray predawn, and they rang
again through her mind.

"The season of destruction will soon be upon us and our
city. But I may have found a way to save some of us, we
who were once among the most powerful in the sea. Near
the long and narrow island that is but a stone's throw from
Crete, the island split by Mother Ocean into two halves . . ."

It was all she had written, all she'd had time for. Yet there
was no doubt in her mind that the scroll would one day be
finished. The question was, what would it contain? How
could anything she wrote contain a cure for what would attack the merfolk of a future time, when she herself had not
the slightest knowledge of healing?

The sickly moon had traveled higher in the sky when the
first people began to arrive. Dark shapes against the darker
night, they converged upon the beach from different directions, some carefully descending the narrow footpath that

led from the hills above, others disdaining it in favor of a quicker scramble down the low rocky cliffs.

There was a preternatural quiet about their coming. Only the murmur of the waves washing against the shore and the slither of rocks dislodged by scores of feet broke the hot, still darkness. No one spoke. Not even the sound of tears came to Marit's ears as the men and women slowly gathered on the beach. There were children among them, but even they were silent, as though they, too, understood the irrevocable step that was being taken that night.

Marit was grateful for the silence. She was exhausted from the continual effort she had made over the last three days, worn out from searching for the right words to warn, persuade, convince. At any rate, the time for talk was past. Whoever was there would have a chance. Whoever was not . . . nothing more could be done for them now.

Jeram joined her at last. A fresh stab of pain contracted Marit's stomach as she saw his face in the wan moonlight. He had aged a hundred seasons in this one night. His once cheerful eyes were black caverns, filled with a suffering that he would carry with him the rest of his days.

"It is done," he whispered in a choked voice. "My wonderful horses. Gone, all of them gone. I hope they understand and forgive me." He said nothing more.

The people continued to come, arriving in small groups and in large. Still, it soon became apparent to Marit that not all of the roughly five hundred persons who had said they would leave the Land of Gifts were going to. Not surprisingly, some had obviously changed their minds at the last minute. The tiny fraction of those who might survive what was approaching had grown even smaller.

A voice broke abruptly into Marit's reverie, sounding louder than usual because everyone else was so quiet.

"Lead Historian."

It was the formal use of her title, spoken in a tone equally formal. Marit turned to see who had addressed her, and was astonished to find the head of the entire Healing Strata standing before her.

He was a man who had been a healer for so long, no one used his name anymore, if they even remembered it. He was known only as Chief Healer, and was among the oldest people on the island. He could have easily gone into the Circle of Elders had he wished to; they had offered him a place among them more than once. He had not done so, though. Healing was his love and strength and passion, he had always said, and the Healing Strata was where he belonged.

Calmly, this venerable one returned Marit's startled gaze. "I have come to go with you," he said. "I was not sure whether or not to believe you before, but I believe you now."

She regarded him in wonder. "Why?"

The wise old eyes went to Jeram's ravaged face. "Everyone in the Land of Gifts knows of your mate's love for his horses. When I heard he was killing them so that they would have a merciful transition into the next life, I realized the warnings you have been speaking of were real. I've know Jeram since he was a speck floating in his mother's womb—just as I've known you, Lead Historian. You are not given to hysteria, and Jeram would never sacrifice his beloved horses for a fantasy spun out of the web of this infernal heat."

"There are those," Jeram said bitterly, "who will insist that I did such a terrible thing because I have gone mad."

"Well, I am not one of them." The chief healer gestured behind him. "And neither are they."

Marit's gaze followed his arm. To her amazement, she saw a dozen or more healers sliding down one of the hills to the beach, their pale yellow robes making them look like spirit-beings in the eerie reflection of the moon. She and

Jeram exchanged stunned glances. All around them people were murmuring and pointing, both in surprise and relief.

The men and women approaching were the foremost healers of the entire Strata. Their presence lent a solemnity to the gathering, and many who had had their doubts, even though they had come, now found those doubts eased. It would have been better to have some of the Elders arrive as well, but these venerable healers were the next best thing.

Thin and dry as a sheaf of parchment, yet surprisingly strong, the chief healer's hand closed around Marit's elbow. "I see you have brought some of your work," he said, nodding at the parcel she still held clutched to her breast. "I have done the same."

Reverently he held up a bulky package wrapped in the same type of oilcloth Marit had used to protect her scroll. Behind him she saw that the other healers were all holding similar bundles, cradling them with as much care as parents cradled their children.

"These scrolls," the old man said quietly, "have been carefully selected with much thought, and a great many tears. They contain the most important wisdom and learning about sicknesses and their cures that the Healing Strata of this land possess. I, and all the other chief healers before me, have spent our lifetimes collecting this knowledge. It is far too valuable to be left behind."

His eyes fixed on her, dignified yet pleading. "Do you think there is a chance that they can be saved?"

Marit felt an unexpected lifting of her heart. For the first time she no longer agonized over the cure her scroll was supposed to contain. The Mother had surely heard her prayers, after all, she thought. That same Mother-Goddess had sent her daughter those terrible dreams, but She had done so for a purpose. Now She had sent salvation and hope for the future as well.

"Yes," she said, suddenly finding it difficult to speak. "Yes, Chief Healer, I know they can."

Meredith's eyes jerked open. She cried out wildly and tried to sit up, legs and arms flailing. She cried out again, this time in words, speaking the same twisted version of the merfolk tongue she had used before.

"They're coming. I can see them!"

Galen did not try to touch her. She was finally emerging from the spell that had held her for so long, but it was dangerous to hurry someone back to full consciousness. Even the slightest pressure of his hand could have devastating results if he was not careful.

He spoke to her, his voice the merest thread of sound, a breeze wafting to Meredith's ears. "Who is coming?"

She did not respond. He asked again, with the same result. Suddenly he realized he was using English, and on a hunch, though it seemed absurd, too incredible even to try, he repeated the question in the merfolk tongue.

Meredith's head turned slightly. In the many-hued lights of the chamber, her dark eyes were glazed, unseeing. "Kirta," she said distantly in that odd version of his language. "She is coming to save us, as she promised she would. And she is bringing others with her." Her eyes grew round with wonder. "So many others. They're so beautiful. Will I be able to swim like that?"

"Where is she coming from?" Galen whispered. It was an effort for him to hold his voice to the soft wisp of sound that would not disturb her. He could feel the blood pounding in his ears. His thoughts were as chaotic as his wild pulse.

Kirta was a merfolk name.

"The sea," Meredith replied. "She has come to take us home. And the merfolk Elders—she said they did not be-

lieve her, but they have come with her after all. They've decided to help us!"

Galen sat back against the rim of the fountain. Though he
knew he should ask more questions, try to discover as much
as possible from Meredith while she was in this state, he
could not. He was too stunned to do anything but stare at
her.

Under his incredulous gaze, she slowly rose. Swaying a
little, she lifted her hands to her neck. He stood as well,
watching closely, not interfering, as she began to move
about the chamber. Her face was transfixed, her eyes fastened on some point only she could see.

Lithe as she was normally, there was a grace about her
now that was somehow different. She seemed to float
around the chamber, her feet gliding smoothly over the
floor, her arms wafting at her sides in a gentle flowing
rhythm. Entranced, Galen had the sudden thought that she
was moving as though water buoyed her up rather than air.

Then, as inexplicably as she had begun her strange little
dance, she stopped. Her arms dropped limply, and a haze of
tears brightened the glaze in her eyes. An expression of
grief spread over her features, so deep, so utterly despon-
dent, it was like a bottomless well of sorrow. She blinked
several times, and the glazed look cleared. although the
tears remained. Dazedly she rubbed at them as though she
did not understand how they had gotten there.

"Meredith," Galen said. Recognizing the signs, he spoke
in English again. "You have come back. You are safe."

She shook her head, and agony was in her face. "But
they weren't," she whispered. "There was no safety for them
because they wouldn't listen. They died. So many died, and
she couldn't help them, no matter how hard she tried. Such
a waste, such a terrible, terrible waste." She put her hands
to her face, shoulders shaking.

Galen went to her, but before he could reach her, she

lowered her hands. The tears had dried up as quickly as they had come. He saw in her face a dignity, an awareness that had not been there before. She had altered in some indefinable way. Forced to put a name to it, Galen could only say that an aura clung to her that made her seem older, though physically she looked no different.

"I understand now," she said in a calm, strong voice. "I understand everything." She paused. "Or almost everything. For the first time in my life, I know who I am."

He stared down at her. "And who are you?"

She looked back at him, and knowledge, fierce and unshakable, blazed out of her eyes. It struck Galen like a beam of dark light, piercing him to the core of his heart.

"One of your people, Galen," she said without a tremor, without even a tinge of hesitation. "I'm one of yours."

CHAPTER
18

A great silence filled the chamber, as deep and vast as the sea, broken only by the steady, indifferent music of the fountain.

"That is impossible," Galen said at last, and wondered if it was Meredith or himself he was trying to convince. "There are no merfolk upon the land. Once there were, yes, but that was long ago, long even for us. And they are all gone, destroyed by the wrath of Mother Ocean Herself, it is said, though the time in which it happened was so ancient, we have only the legends to tell us it was She who was responsible. But we do know that all who left the sea for the land died for their folly."

"Not all of them." That calm certainty had not left Meredith. If anything, it had grown stronger. "The legends are wrong, Galen. They've always been wrong."

She stepped closer, looking earnestly into his face.

"Those who followed the teachings of Jabari did go to that huge continent that was later destroyed." At the thunder-struck look on his face that *she* should know the name of that notorious merfolk philosopher, she spoke more quickly, her words tumbling out. "But they didn't all stay there. An offshoot of those people left before the disaster and mi-grated to an island they named the Land of Gifts."

Without warning, tears flooded her eyes again as the memory of that long-dead land surged through her. It was a part of her now, a legacy inextricably woven through her being, just as Marit, her distant, distant ancestor, was.

"Their new home was beautiful," she said softly, grief rustling through her voice. "It was a rich island, green and filled with life. They settled there and made themselves a world. It's true that in many ways they no longer resembled the merfolk. They had lost their gills, they couldn't swim underwater or mind-speak with each other or with other peoples of the sea, like the Selkies and dolphin- and whale-folk.

"But in other ways they stayed the same. They respected and worshipped the Mother-Goddess, and followed Her ways faithfully. They observed the Seven Strata, there was a Circle of Elders—men and women known for their wisdom—who all listened to . . ."

She paused and wiped angrily, sadly, at her wet eyes. "In fact, that was their mistake, that they listened too well. And the mistake of the Elders was that they didn't listen well enough."

Galen stared at her, utterly speechless. Things were fall-ing into place so rapidly and with such sea-shattering force, he felt as if he were bouncing on the crest of waves like those thrown up when a giant land mountain collapses into the ocean.

Could another branch of the disinherited ones have left to establish themselves in a new land? Based on Meredith's astonishing revelations, there was only one answer.

But how could such knowledge have escaped the merfolk for so long? It was incredible, yet he believed that what Meredith had seen was true, believed as completely as he had ever believed anything in his seven centuries of living in all the various worlds of the Mother.

He found his voice. "This island," he said hoarsely. "Did your visions show you where it was?"

She closed her eyes. "Near the long and narrow island that is but a stone's throw from Crete," she whispered, reciting words now burned indelibly into her brain. "The island split by Mother Ocean into two halves."

She opened her eyes, searching Galen's face. "She was talking about Karpathos. The Land of Gifts was once located in these waters, between the two islands that would one day be called Karpathos and Crete."

"Who, Meredith?" Galen's voice was harsh with excitement and incredulity. "Who spoke to you? Who told you this?"

She stared past her shoulder. "My ancestor," she said distantly. "The one I am descended from. She was a historian, her name was Marit. It was she who wrote the scroll you came here to find."

She looked back at him, her eyes sharp and knowing and sad all at once. "That is why you came to Karpathos, isn't it? To find the scroll. The merfolk have become sick, and the scroll is what will save them. The only thing that will save them."

"You know," he said in wonder, marveling at all that had happened and the implications that it held, marveling at her. "You know."

In that moment, he was in awe of Meredith, of what she had discovered, of this power held so deep within her for so long. He saw the strength in her, felt the newly awakened force that had broken free and was sweeping everything before it as it surged loose and wild toward some destination he could only begin to guess at.

She nodded. "I know. It was foretold to Marit by a mer-woman named Kirta. That's why Marit and the man she loved, along with a few hundred others, survived the volcanic explosion, and the earthquakes and tidal waves which followed, that broke the island into a million pieces. But it was such a small number of people who lived on, so small."

She sighed, her gaze drifting past Galen once more to a distant vision that only she saw. "And so ironic. The Land of Gifts destroyed in almost exactly the same way that the original land Marit's people migrated from met its end. One can't help but think that perhaps the merfolk Elders and all the legends that sprang up were right about at least one thing. The world of land just isn't meant for those whose blood is of the sea."

She shivered suddenly, her mind full of a far more recent memory. As if from another lifetime, it rose hazily in her thoughts. She remembered walking along the beach during her first evening on Karpathos, cutting her foot, watching the blood spiral red and swift out into the hungry, seeking sea. The sea, she now knew, that had been seeking her all along. Blood calling to blood. Was that how Galen had found her? Yet if it was, even he had not known who she truly was, any more than she had.

She shivered again as his hands grasped her shoulders and he turned her to face him. "Tell me all of what you saw, Meredith." His voice was low and urgent. "Share it with me. For now you understand why it is so important."

She told him then. Told him about Marit and about Jeram, about their futile efforts to save their people after Kirta's miraculous appearance from the sea, and then, of their even more miraculous return to that sea.

She hugged her elbows to herself as she described these

merfolk, who, through the choice of their ancestors, had become chained to the land. She spoke of how Kirta and the merfolk who had come with her had used their powers to help them find their lost heritage and be freed by it, released to enter the world that had once been theirs. Tears crowded back into her eyes as she talked.

"Oh, if only I hadn't woken up," she cried. "I was *with* them, Galen. With Marit, in her body. Swimming with them, exulting in the freedom of it, the joy." She fell silent. "And grieving for those left behind," she added in a voice torn with an ancient pain.

"The destruction of the island, Meredith," Galen said gently. "Did you see it?"

She shuddered. "No, but Marit did. I—I don't think that whatever happened to me is over yet. I can't explain it, but somehow I know I'm going to see more. It scares me—"

Impulsively Galen gathered her into his arms. She leaned against him gratefully, reassured by his warmth and the solid feel of the broad-muscled chest beneath her cheek, soothed by the steady heartbeat that told her he was real and not part of some unexplainable vision. He was a link—a lifeline really—to the world she had known before this incredible day, to a reality she still understood, at least in part.

"Lost ones," he said above her head, his voice thoughtful. "That is what you would be called. Lost ones who never found their way home."

"But we did." Her voice was muffled because she still had her face against his chest. She was very tired and it felt so good to lean against him. "Marit and Jeram and those who joined them went back to the sea. I told you that."

"Yes, but what happened to them after that? They could not have stayed there, or you would not have ended up on the land, in some barbaric place where Mother Ocean's voice cannot even be heard, possessing absolutely no knowledge of your past."

Powerful images wavered through Meredith's consciousness at his words. She pressed her cheek harder against his chest. "They did leave," she said slowly. "Not Marit and Jeram, though. They never again deserted the sea, which had been kind enough to take them back. But their grandchildren and the grandchildren of others who came with them did. Then their children's children, and generations after that."

Her voice slowed still more, the words spaced wide apart, as though someone else were placing them in her mouth. "All of them drawn to the land, knowing that their great-great-grandparents had once lived there and known happiness. The memories of the Land of Gifts were embroidered, made more beautiful with each telling, as it receded further and further into the past.

"The descendants of Marit and Jeram and the others grew arrogant beneath the waves. They felt superior to the merfolk who had known only the sea, because they themselves possessed a dual heritage that gave them the sea as well as the land. They left Mother Ocean often, pulled by some lure only they felt. They went to the land more and more often, staying there longer each time.

Spellbound, Galen listened, unwilling to speak lest he interrupt her halting flow of words. The lack of information about these lost ones was beginning to make sense.

If Meredith's distant relations had indeed taken on such an arrogant attitude about their origins, the true merfolk would have been enraged, particularly in light of the trouble they had gone to in rescuing these people. They might very well have told their ungrateful relatives to go back to the land, and good riddance, then allowed the course of time to conveniently erase all memory of them. But what terrible price might the merfolk of today be paying for the ire of their foremothers and fathers?

Meredith had lapsed into silence. Schooling himself to patience, he waited to see if more words would come from her. When they did not, he spoke, unable to hold back the questions that were gnawing at him.

"The scroll," he said urgently. "Was it ever finished?"

Dazed, Meredith shook herself. She lifted her head from Galen's chest, feeling as though she had just woken from a dream. "Yes," she said after a moment, and drew herself out of his arms. Under his intent gaze, she wandered over to the fountain.

Distorted by the ring and splash of the spraying water, her voice drifted back to him, strangely disembodied. "The head of the Healing Strata and the foremost healers he brought with him that night assured that what Kirta had seen in her dreams would come true. Marit used their knowledge, spent the rest of her life recording it, and just as Kirta had predicted, wrote the scroll.

"As for Kirta's other prediction . . ." She turned to look at Galen. "That is coming true now, isn't it?"

He had already moved to stand beside her, his eyes blazing so brightly, they rivaled the multicolored glow that lit the great chamber. "Where is it?" he asked. "You know, don't you? Tell me." His hands closed around hers, hard and hurting. "Tell me!"

Flijanou stood up abruptly, her joints creaking and complaining. What had begun that morning as worry had rapidly turned to profound uneasiness, and now, as evening approached, to downright fear.

Hobbling on legs that had grown stiff from sitting too long, she went to the doorway of her hut. For long minutes, she stood there, staring out at the stony path, willing a familiar figure to come walking up it.

She had not seen Meredith for two days. Of course, the storms that had struck the day before yesterday would account for one of those days, but what about today? It was unlike the young Americana not to stop by every day, if only for a short visit. Neither had there been any sign of the sea lord. The two absences taken together concerned Flijanou greatly.

The people of the sea had never brought harm to Flijanou's family. But it was *her* family they had never hurt. An ancient alliance existed between her kin and them, one that might not—no, did not—include Meredith. Flijanou had seen the way the sea lord had looked at the young woman, as though he had wanted to devour her on the spot. It had made her nervous then, and it made her even more nervous now.

He had looked at the beautiful Americana in the way a man looks at a woman. Yet Flijanou had glimpsed other things in that blue gaze that could pierce through a person like the swords of her remote Amazon ancestors. He had had some deep purpose in mind for seeking Meredith out. What if she had not cooperated with him as he wished? The powers of the sea-people were mysterious, great beyond reckoning. They were more than capable of blasting one lone human who dared to defy them. What if Meredith had angered the sea lord . . .

The small black and white cat who included Flijanou's house in her itinerary of stops where she knew she would receive a meal of fish scraps, some stroking, and a comfortable place to sleep by the hearth, paced around the side of the hut, her tail held high in greeting. She sat down companionably by Flijanou's feet and set about the important business of washing her face.

"I should not have brought her to him," Flijanou muttered to the cat, who paused in her grooming to listen. "I should not have deceived the child when she trusts me so. But what could I do? I have bonds, obligations. The honor of my family would be as nothing if I had not done as the sea lord wished!"

The cat looked at her with wise green eyes, and the old woman twisted her gnarled hands together. Guilt pricked at her, cutting as keenly as fishhooks embedded in flesh, and just as difficult to remove.

"What should I do?" she asked the cat and herself. "What should I do?"

Her washing finished, the cat rubbed against her legs and miaowed. Flijanou came to a decision. Hurrying inside, she snatched her black shawl off its hook on the wall and grabbed the plate that held her uneaten supper.

"Here," she said, setting the plate down before the surprised cat. "Eat well, little friend."

With a speed that belied her many years, she set off down the path.

"Don't you see?" Meredith said desperately. "Marit failed. But I can't, I won't."

Galen regarded her through narrowed eyes. "Failed? What do you mean?" His heart gave a dangerous lurch, feeling as though it had climbed into his throat. Did she not have the scroll after all, or worse, had her visions shown her something even more dire—that the scroll did not contain the answers he thought it did?

Meredith paced in front of him. So many emotions were plunging about in her, she did not know which one to give vent to first. A weight had lowered itself upon her, the same weight, she realized with a start, that her ancestor had once carried. Marit had passed it on to her through this long dreaming. She had passed on other things as well. They pulsed through her, vibrant with new life, leaving her confused and disoriented.

"There's so much I don't understand," she began. "But I

do know this much. The one great task of Marit's life was to save her people—those from the Land of Gifts *and* the true merfolk of the sea. The tragedy is that she felt as though she accomplished neither. Even the few who survived the island's destruction weren't content to stay in their new home, and that was communicated to their children, even to Marit and Jeram's. How terrible it must have been for her, to see her own children seduced away from the sea, starting up all those old patterns once again."

"If they hadn't," Galen said grimly, "the paths they followed would have been very different, and you would probably not have been born. And she didn't fail. She wrote the scroll, and her descendants, even though they had left the sea, kept the memory of it alive, otherwise, you would not now have it." He fixed his gaze upon her. "For you do have it, Meredith. Don't you?"

She nodded, a small solemn motion of assent. "I have something," she said gravely. "My mother told me it's been in our family on her side forever and forever, passed along from mother to daughter, further back than anyone can remember."

She caught herself as the truth of this struck her like a fist. Her mother. *She* might have known, might have had some idea. Or had she simply gone on protecting the secret without understanding any of it, as all the others before her must have done? As Meredith herself would likely have done, had Galen not entered her life.

She found herself talking to him, using her own words, not those sent to her by the shade of Marit. She described to him her last talk with her dying mother, told of how the box and what it contained had been passed on to her. It was a relief to speak of that sad, strange conversation. The pain and grief that had been with her since that day, the burden of sorrow laid upon her, had lightened miraculously, eased by the wonder and discovery of so much she had never understood.

"It's amazing," Galen said when she had finished. He took several long strides across the chamber. His eyes were bright, his tall body fired by excitement, restless as a flame. "All this time, and it has been kept safe. It seems impossible, almost too incredible to believe."

Meredith thought of the long sheets of carefully rolled gold, beaten so mysteriously fine they were like sheets of paper. "One reason it may have survived is because it's not a scroll made of parchment or papyrus, or even stone."

He turned to look at her. "What, then?"

"Gold."

His ebony brows rose. "Really. That was extremely wise of Marit, your foremother. Gold, if it is shielded and protected properly, can indeed last forever, or close to it."

"Yes, but why didn't she leave it in the sea with the merfolk where it belonged? How did it end up on the land?"

"You're asking me these questions? The visions were yours, Meredith. Didn't they tell you?"

She sighed and shook her head. "I didn't see the sickness Kirta warned Marit about either, but it's happened, hasn't it?"

When he did not answer, she yanked angrily at his arm. "You've made a lot of demands about what I know, Galen. Now you answer my question. The merfolk are sick, aren't they?"

He looked down at her, his eyes heavy with grief in a way that only eyes that were unable to shed tears could ever be. "Yes, and others beside them, as well. Your dreaming was all too accurate, Meredith. Far more than I can pretend to understand, or have ever imagined. I don't know why the scroll ended up on the land, and at this point it doesn't really matter. All that matters now is that it truly does exist."

His face grew pensive, filled with a dazzled wonder. "It

was supposed to be a myth, sea-spray and moon-mist. Most of us had never even heard about it, including myself. Only Cleonith believed the myth might actually be true, and even she had no inkling that those who had deserted the sea for the land could in any way be responsible for the creation of it."

"Who is Cleonith?"

"A very wise and powerful woman. One of our Elders. What she doesn't know about healing simply isn't worth knowing." His mouth twisted into a harsh line. "At least, that was the case until this plague came among us."

Watching him, Meredith asked carefully, "How—how many have died?"

"None," he said shortly. "At least, none that I know of. Yet. What has happened to them is worse. They will eventually die, but it will be a living death, one that will take a long, long time and leave terrible suffering in its wake. They have lost their gills."

He stared down at her. In the dancing light his eyes were fierce and wild beneath lowered brows. "There is no fate, no punishment more terrible to a creature of the sea than to take that away, their ability to be one with the Mother Ocean. When I left to travel here it had not yet affected a great many of us, but that will surely change, if it hasn't already. If this plague is not stopped, it will certainly spread, and when it does, there will soon be none of us left."

"I'm sorry," Meredith whispered. She was stunned by the enormity of what he had said, as staggered by it as she was by the revelations about her family's origins. Both were incomprehensible, but to discover in practically the same moment that she was linked to these mysterious beings of the sea, and that a disaster of horrible proportions threatened them, was almost too much to grasp at once.

"It's ironic," Galen went on as if he hadn't heard her

speak, "that someone who was of the land might have come up with the only means to heal and restore us to the sea."

His words struck her hard. She said quietly, "Marit was of the sea, Galen. It was her true heritage, and she never forgot that. Maybe that was why she was chosen by the fates or the Goddess or whatever forces we can name to write the scroll."

He was silent for a long moment. "Perhaps," he said at last, in a neutral voice. Then his tone changed. "I must have the scroll, Meredith. You understand what's at stake now. You have to realize how important it is for me to have it."

She met his gaze unflinchingly, her eyes calm and clear. "Of course."

"Where is it, then?"

"Back at the house."

Astonishment rippled over his features. "Truly? It's been there all this time?"

She nodded again, and had the grace to look a little shamefaced. "I've been keeping it well hidden, not only from you, but from anyone. It's beneath a bunch of stuff under my bed."

"Your bed," he echoed. He had made love to her last night, fallen asleep with her in that bed, and the scroll had been there the entire time, underneath them! He did not know whether to laugh or pound himself on the head for his stupidity.

"We can go and get it now," she said. She frowned, obviously puzzled by his preoccupied expression. "Don't you want to?"

Galen thought furiously. Toklat was healing, but he would need to be checked on and watched over while he lay in the pool. He would also have to be brought food once he awakened, since he would not be strong enough to hunt for some days yet. And once Galen took Meredith and left the protection of the cave, they would be vulnerable to Anastas and his followers should the banished ones come upon them. This was a matter that would have to be handled carefully.

"We will go," he said. "But not just yet."

Meredith studied him. Captured by the magic and power of all that had happened since she had entered this chamber, she realized something that had not occurred to her before. Galen knew a great deal about her now, whereas, other than his merfolk origins, she knew very little about him.

"Why?" she asked him. "What else is there that you haven't told me, Galen?"

He threw her a narrow glance. "You know about the scroll," he said, "and this terrible plague that has attacked my people. That is quite enough at the present."

It was not until a moment later that it struck Meredith. He had said *my* people, not *ours*. The realization left a painful gap in her heart, like the opening of a small wound.

CHAPTER
19

Flijanou knocked again on the door of Meredith's house. The sea was much closer here than at her little hut perched on its high rocky cliff. It thundered and shouted to her in the growing darkness, and she, who was sensitive to such things, paused in her knocking to listen. Surely some message was contained in the sound of those waves breaking harshly upon the beach; she just could not decipher what it was.

Tentatively she pushed at the door, then turned the knob. The door swung open, and a worried frown added more wrinkles to the creases that mapped Flijanou's face. Most of the native inhabitants of Karpathos never bothered to lock their doors, probably because many fit their houses with simple locks made of wood in a design so old, it dated back to the time of Homer.

Meredith, though, being a newcomer as well as a woman

alone, had told Flijanou that she never failed to lock her
door, whether she was home or not. The door's being unlocked was not a development that boded well in the old
woman's mind.

"Meredith?" she called into the house. "Are you
here?"

No answer.

"Child," she called again, and waited uneasily. She
could see no lights on anywhere in the house. Indeed,
there was an unmistakable sense of emptiness, the deserted feeling that a home possesses when its inhabitants
are gone.

"I'll just go inside to check and make sure everything is
all right," Flijanou told herself, and suiting action to words
she entered the house.

She knew the house well from when the family of young
Nikos had lived there, just as she knew every house on
Karpathos. As her eyes slowly adjusted to the gloom of the
shadowy interior, she began to peer about her.

She noticed several things at once. Meredith's tape recorder lay on the dining room table, notes spread all around
it as though she had been working. A half-full cup of tea sat
by an open notebook as if she had been interrupted in the
middle of drinking it.

However, what froze Flijanou in her tracks was what she
saw in the living room. A bed pillow lay on the floor beside
the couch, a sheet and blanket jumbled in an untidy pile
next to it. All the pillows from the couch had been pulled off
and clearly arranged to make someone a bed.

Meredith had had an overnight guest.

Nearly tiptoeing, feeling very much an intruder in the silent house, Flijanou made her way down the hall. Perhaps
she should leave, a voice in her head suggested. But she did
not leave. Intruding or not, she knew she would not be able

to rest until she had satisfied herself that Meredith was not lying in one of these rooms hurt, or worse.

The door to what was clearly the Americana's bedroom stood wide open. Cautiously Flijanou peeked through it. "Meredith?" she said softly. She wasn't really expecting an answer and didn't get one. She stepped carefully inside.

The bed had obviously been slept in. The covers lay in a wild tangle, as if the occupant had jumped out of bed rather suddenly. Occupants, Flijanou realized with a start. Both pillows were indented by the shape of heads.

A white pile of cloth lay on the floor by the bed, glinting at her through the gloom, and she stooped to pick it up. It was a loose cotton T-shirt, surely belonging to Meredith. Nearby, another piece of cloth caught her eye. She had not noticed it before because of its darker color, but now she picked it up too. Her eyes widened as she stared at it.

It was a red tank top, faded and very large, large enough to fit a big man. The sea lord. This tank top was what *he* had worn . . .

Flijanou stumbled back, dropping the shirt as though she had picked up a hot poker from her hearth. "Now calm yourself, old woman," she ordered out loud. "A shirt such as this, why, it could belong to any young man on Karpathos."

In her heart, though, she knew it did not. The sea god had been there. And he had been in Meredith's bedroom. But where was he now? And where was Meredith?

She turned in a circle, glancing wildly around the bedroom, almost expecting that if she looked hard enough, the answers would somehow be revealed to her. Her heart pounding, she stumbled back into the hall.

"Meredith, Meredith!" She ran through the house, star-

ing into every room, calling out the Americana's name,
knowing, of course, that it was futile.

A horrible thought occurred to her, and panting, she
rushed back to the bedroom. Lurching over to the closet,
she pulled the clothes hanging there aside with trembling
hands. To her relief, no young woman lay unconscious or
dead upon the floor. She stepped back out of the closet,
stared around for a moment, then, feeling unutterably foolish, she lowered herself to her creaking, protesting knees
and peered under the bed.

It was foolish to think that Meredith's body might be lying under the bed, crammed there as in a scene from one of
the mystery movies shown in Athens cinemas that she had
heard neighbors who had gone to that great city describe,
but had herself never seen. She looked anyway. She really
had no idea what else to do.

The bed was a large one, boasting a frame that stood high
off the floor, allowing a person to pile quite a bit underneath
it. This was what Meredith had done. Boxes and several
suitcases lay heaped in several layers. And what else?
Flijanou wondered in dread.

Stretching herself out, her body protesting the awkward
position, she began to pull things out, hoping that what she
feared did not lie behind them. She had dragged out the
suitcases and enough boxes to satisfy herself that it did not,
when she came upon a box that was different from the others.

For one thing it was heavier. Huffing and muttering
under her breath, she barely had the strength to lug it out.
When she had finally succeeded, she gazed down at it in
some confusion. Aside from the suitcases, the rest of
Meredith's paraphernalia consisted of small boxes and cases
that were filled with work notes: papers and notebooks
scrawled in English, which Flijanou could not read.

This case was of metal, though, and it had been wrapped

carefully in felt cloth. That, along with the way it had been jammed in between everything else, made it seem as though there was something secretive about it. Flijanou levered herself up and sat looking at it. Perhaps this mysterious box contained some clue to where Meredith had gone. It seemed unlikely, but worth a try.

She tugged on the lid, expecting the case to be locked. To her surprise, it wasn't. Inside lay a group of cylindrical objects, even more well wrapped in the same felt cloth that had enfolded the box. She lifted one of the objects out. It was heavy, unexpectedly so, and she had to quickly bring up her other hand to support its weight. Even then, it was almost too much for her, tired as she was from all her previous exertions.

She set the object on her lap and drew back its covering of felt. Her mouth fell open.

Meredith looked down at the man (man?) in the pool, and he looked back at her. Galen was kneeling beside the pool talking to him, but though he was listening to the merman, it was Meredith on whom his round, dark eyes were focused, not Galen.

She could no longer understand the watery murmur of Galen's tongue. Her tongue too, she thought angrily, feeling a keen stab of loss. It had vanished, along with the effects of the trance, as soon as she and Galen had left the singing chamber. But the memories remained with her still, and so did the presence of Marit. The fact that they did made the separation she felt from Galen all the more frustrating.

Suddenly the one in the pool spoke to her. His voice was husky, coming from deep in his throat and sounding exactly the way a seal—who Galen had indeed confirmed were his other people—would sound if he were given human speech.

"So," the Selkie said, "the woman of land is not so much of the land as we thought. This would explain a great deal." His large eyes turned meaningfully to Galen. "A great deal."

"How are you feeling now?" Meredith asked him.

The question seemed ludicrous in light of the situation they all found themselves in. But all she could think of were the hideous injuries, the gaping wounds that she had witnessed on his burly manlike shape when Galen had found him floating in the sea. She was astounded to see him coherent and talking, clearly recovering from what had seemed a certain death. In any case, the Selkie did not appear to find her question odd.

"Yes, Lady," he said with a curious, archaic politeness. "The Pool of Healing is doing its work. Which is why Galen brought me here, of course. It is the only thing that would have saved me—"

He was about to say more, but a warning glance from Galen cut him off. "And now that we know a scroll does indeed exist," he finished smoothly, "I am feeling better still. I am called Toklat. Galen has already told you I am a Selkie."

"Yes."

"And you are not frightened of me?"

She shook her head. "Astonished maybe. I've never thought Selkies—I mean, you, were . . ." She bit her lip.

"Real?" he asked, a weary, vaguely cynical smile hovering over his mouth.

"Well . . ." She shrugged helplessly. "Yes."

Toklat shrugged, too, a movement that caused him to grimace in pain. "No matter," he said, as Galen put out a restraining hand to keep him still.

"All that matters is the scroll," Galen said to her. "And since you are not frightened of Toklat—and there is no reason to be, anyway—you will not mind staying here with him while I go to fetch it."

"Wait a minute," she said. "I thought I would go with you."

"You can't." He softened his tone at the look on her face. Putting up a hand to forestall the objections he knew were coming, he went on before she could interrupt. "I won't leave until the morning, because Toklat must have someone who knows the secrets of the pool here with him in case he should suddenly worsen.

"As for you." He turned to the Selkie and spoke firmly. "You have done quite enough talking for now. You must rest. At dawn, if you are recovered enough to eat, I will bring you food and then I'll go. Meredith, though, will stay here until I have returned and you are strong again.

"That way," he added in the merfolk tongue to Toklat, "there will be two of us to protect her, if *they* happen upon us."

"If they are unfortunate enough to," the Selkie replied grimly.

Flijanou was exhausted, but breathing heavily she pushed herself along the path that led down to the sea. A soft rain was drifting out of the night sky, but the moon had broken through that light drizzle. It glimmered down on her, lighting the way ahead and shimmering over the white gown she had changed into after she had hurried back to her hut.

The night breezes caught at the loose folds of the ceremonial robe, sending them billowing about the old woman's bent form, as though seeking to lift her into the air and give flight to her weary feet. Grateful for their help, she moved a little faster.

Glistening in her mind, the image of what she had seen in the metal box beneath Meredith's bed floated ahead of her. Sheets of pure gold, covered with strange writings and so thin, they could actually be rolled up like long pieces of paper. A fortune in gold. A queen's ransom. So brilliant and shining they blinded the eye that gazed upon them.

How in the world had the young Americana obtained such unimaginable wealth? And was this what the sea lord had wanted from Meredith all along, why he had come to Flijanou for her help in bringing the Americana to him?

The answers to those questions could only come from one source. The sea lord himself.

Reaching her special spot on the deserted beach, Flijanou looked around for some of the flat rocks she always piled together to make her simple altar. They were difficult to find. During the storm, the wind-whipped sea had pushed far up onto the sands, leaving disarray in her wake when she had finally retreated. Flijanou had to search for some minutes to find suitable rocks, and this she took as a bad omen, one that caused her heart to beat in ever more painful thuds of apprehension.

Finally, she succeeded in gathering several flat stones. She arranged them quickly in the familiar shape, then took out the three white candles she had carried there in her robe, and lit them. It took several tries, for the light winds rustled about her, blowing out first the matches, then the first and second of her candles.

This, too, was an omen of ill portent, so grave a one that Flijanou hesitated before lighting the third and last candle. She was trembling with fear, longing for the feelings of awe mingled with divine protection that she always experienced when summoning the lords of the sea. Feelings that were mysteriously lacking on this night.

Secure in her family's ancient bond with the sea, Flijanou had never felt cause to fear the black powers that came alive with the hours of darkness. Yet it seemed to her now that shadows filled with menace hovered just beyond the line of her vision. The music of the waves had an evil voice in it, a note she had never heard before. She wondered if she should leave this place, leave it as quickly as she could, run back to the safety of her hut and leave Meredith to her fate.

"No," she muttered, squaring her thin shoulders. "It's my fault the child is wherever she is. The sea god must come to me. He must."

She lit the third candle, carefully shielding the flame from the wind until it had gained enough life to flicker on its own with the other two. Then she raised her arms in the ritual invocation and waited.

Minutes plodded by. The breezes whispered and played with the loose folds of her robe, and shadows danced in sinister shapes beyond the tiny glow cast by the three flickering candles. The waves pushed themselves toward her makeshift altar like long, reaching hands, and the subtle melody of evil below their rush and murmur grew ever stronger in her ears.

Flijanou's teeth chattered, though she continued to stand her ground with outwardly stolid determination. Inwardly, though, she was afraid. Oh, how she was afraid. And the worst part of it was that she did not know why. One thing she did know: it was taking a long time for the sea lord to show himself. Too long, far longer than it had taken the other times he had come to her.

Abruptly she became aware that she had been making the sign of the cross over and over. She stopped, wondering at herself.

Though raised under the auspices of the Catholic Church, as most Greeks were, in her heart she had always remained more faithful to a different and far older code. It was a measure of her profound uneasiness that she should resort to protection from a religion she had generally observed for form's sake rather than for any other reason. She looked around her and moved her hand again, not in the sign of the cross, but in a more archaic gesture that was to her mind more effective.

"Ah, how quaint. The sign against the evil eye. Do you think those paltry little gestures of yours will protect you, old woman?"

The words were spoken in perfect Greek. The voice was as velvet-dark as the night, and as menacing as the shadows.

Flijanou froze. The malevolent note beneath the waves had transformed itself into human speech, and unable to help herself, she shuddered. This one who had come to her was not the sea lord she had expected.

It took every ounce of courage she had to turn and face him, and when she had, the breath caught in her throat. Her eyes had adjusted to the night darkness—too well, she thought uneasily. She could see his form clearly in the pale phosphorescent light the moon cast off the sea, and in truth, she wished that she could not.

He was naked. No ornate necklace of jewels glittered around his throat as it had on the neck of the god who called himself Galen, or on the necks of the other gods Flijanou had met during her many years. Somehow the absence of such a necklace struck her as sinister, giving the tall, muscular god a forbidding and peculiarly menacing aspect she had not felt when meeting Galen.

He had appeared from the sea as silently as the lord Galen had, but there the similarity ended. Galen, tall and imposing, had aroused awed respect within her, a sense of reverent wonder. This god aroused only fear, a deep bone-wrenching apprehension that led every instinct she possessed to scream wildly at her to run, to run from him as fast as she could.

Yet such a course of action would be ridiculously futile should he choose to follow her. She knew it, and he knew it. And in any case, she must not forget her purpose. No matter how fearsome this strange lord of the sea seemed to be, she had to find out about Meredith.

"Lord," she began.

The silky voice cracked at her. "Have you forgotten how to show proper respect, Terran hag? Kneel to me!"

Trembling both in terror and in shock at how he had addressed her, Flijanou obeyed as swiftly as her aching joints would allow her. Unbidden, the memory of Galen gently reprimanding her for performing such an obeisance rose into her mind, increasing her deepening sense of this lord's evil. It also made one other thing abundantly, chillingly clear: she did not dare ask him about the Americana.

The sea god stepped closer, into the light cast by the candles, so that Flijanou got an even better look at him. His face had an icy beauty, like that of a statue. But his eyes, she thought, her heart hammering in her ears. His eyes. They were cavernous holes in the moon-blanched face, blazing with a light that stabbed at her like cold fire.

His hair, in another contrast to Galen, was long and unkempt. It trailed down past his wide shoulders in wet dark tendrils. Absently he wound one of these tendrils around his finger as he stood in silence, contemplating her. There was something almost seductive in the way he twirled and stroked the strand of hair, and Flijanou found herself staring at him as one stares helplessly at a snake that is poised and coiled to strike.

"So," the evil lord said at last. "You are the Terran who likes to help merfolk, or at least some merfolk. Tell me: where is the woman you brought to the one called Galen?"

"Lord," Flijanou whispered, quaking, "I do not know."

"I do not believe you," he told her pleasantly. "Shall I

twist the truth from you, along with your spindly, wattled neck?"

Flijanou's knees were paining her badly from kneeling so long. Perhaps it was the intensity of those shooting pains that gave her new courage, for the words shot from her mouth scarcely before she realized it. "It won't gain you a thing if you do. I don't know where she is, and I've been looking for her all day. That's the truth, lord. I swear it on the soul of my mother. In fact, that is why—"

She caught herself. She did not want this god with evil glinting about him like a miasma of death to know how worried she was about Meredith. She did not want to tell him anything about Meredith at all. He was shrewd, though, this strange lord of the sea. He studied her, his perfect features bone-white in the night, his hollow, moon-darkened eyes slitted.

"Why you came here? Go on, old woman, say it. Do you think I don't know that you came with your candles and your amusing little rituals to summon Galen? Only you got me instead." He chuckled, an odd harsh sound that had no humor in it. "How fortunate for me that he is otherwise engaged, though it may not be so fortunate for you."

He turned his head, gazing out over the silver and black sea. "She must still be with him," he said pensively, to himself rather than to her.

Flijanou tensed, her fear momentarily forgotten. "The lord Galen has Meredith?" she asked. "Where?"

His face took on a look that made Flijanou's blood chill to a sluggish flow of ice in her veins. "Lord," he repeated, and let out another of those mirthless laughs. "It is not your concern where. And *I* am your lord, Terran hag. You are here to answer my questions. And the first one is: where does Meredith live?"

"Why do you want to know that?" Flijanou whispered.

Two powerful hands seized her by the upper arms and

hauled her effortlessly to her feet, then completely off them. Holding her with her legs dangling in the air, her face suspended an inch from those terrible eyes, he said calmly, "I told you that you are here to answer my questions. Answer me."

Flijanou tried to free herself from that pitiless grip. Her feet kicked uselessly, inches above the ground, and all the while the cavernous holes of his eyes bore into her brain. He did not really need for her to answer him in words. The power of his gaze penetrated into her brain with a physical sensation of pain, slicing through her mental barriers as easily as a knife slashes through flesh.

Abruptly he dropped her, letting go of her arms without warning so that she fell bruisingly to the sand. Dazed, realizing he had read her mind as if it were nothing more than an open newspaper, she stared up at him. He met her stare with a surprised, speculative look of his own.

"Gold!" he exclaimed. "Who would have thought it would be written on gold? And that she would have it with her, given the greed of your kind. How very, very interesting."

He smiled to himself, then he reached over to the candles that had burned more than halfway down, and one by one pinched them out. Flijanou struggled to her feet. Her arms throbbed from the cruel pressure of his hands, and her head swam.

"What—what are you doing?" she managed to ask.

He turned back to her, that chillingly sweet smile still upon his face. "Why, I thought it would be obvious. They are not needed. Just as you no longer are. Indeed, it would be awkward if Galen learned about my coming here too quickly."

As the meaning of his words sank in, Flijanou let out a hopeless little cry. She lurched away, her instinct for life commanding her to run despite the futility of it. Playing with her, he actually let her go some distance up the beach before he caught her. The velvet voice spoke softly into her ear.

"You were very useful to me, old woman," he murmured as he lifted her once more. "So I shall be merciful in return. This will be quick."

It was.

CHAPTER
20

Toklat had fallen asleep again. In the dim light of the cave, his round face, propped on the edge of the pool, was peaceful. The rips and gashes that had disfigured it when Galen had first brought him there had completely healed.

Meredith sat on the damp floor beside the pool, watching him in silent fascination. After the mind-numbing things she had learned during the past several hours, it would seem that nothing and no one could ever shock, or even startle her, ever again. She was drained, utterly worn-out. Yet, tired as she was, she found herself mesmerized by the sight of Toklat: a living, breathing Selkie, a creature not supposed to exist outside the parameters of mythology and folktale.

No, not a creature, she corrected herself. Brief as her conversation with Toklat had been, it had left absolutely no doubt in her mind that he was a being with human feelings and with a human intelligence equal to, perhaps even superior to, her own. She wondered about the famed Selkie ability to change into the form of a seal. How incredible it would be to see that! To watch as, before her eyes, Toklat magically transformed himself into the shape of an animal.

The two of them had the cave to themselves for the moment. Galen had left, departing through the tunnel after telling her he would be back shortly.

At the time, she had wondered where he was going, but had not asked him. Toklat had lapsed back into sleep already, and as for Meredith, a great exhaustion had begun to steal over her. The tiredness she had felt in the singing chamber was growing harder and harder to deny, and it had been too much of an effort to question or argue with Galen any further.

Actually, she'd been relieved to stop talking, to simply sit down and rest beside the sleeping Selkie. It was quiet in the cave, peaceful. The only sounds were the gentle lap of the pool's waters whenever Toklat shifted an arm or leg, and the steady in and out whoosh of his heavy, regular breathing.

Meredith moved so that she could lean against one of the flatter sections of the rock wall that encircled the pool. The position was not the most comfortable, but she was too weary to care. Eventually, her head lolled to one side and she slept.

A hand on her shoulder woke her. It was a light touch, but it jolted her sharply out of a deep sleep. Startled, she sat up, confused and vaguely panicked, completely unaware of where she was.

"Gently, gently," Galen's familiar rough voice said. "It's me. Look," he went on as her gaze cleared. "I've brought you something to eat."

She rubbed her eyes. Awareness returned to her in a rush, and with it memory, splashing over her in a huge jarring wave of images and feelings. Dazedly, she stared at the unfamiliar items Galen was setting out before her.

"You need to regain your strength as much as Toklat does," he explained. "Experiencing the dream-walk is an exhausting business. It's always important to eat and rest afterwards, and for you it's doubly important. With us leaving your house so early this morning, you've taken no nourishment all day."

"Dream-walk?" She looked up from her perusal of what appeared to be some sort of purple seaweed.

He shrugged. "As near as I can guess, that is what happened to you. Although it should be impossible."

"Why?"

"Because the dream-walk is a ritual—a rite of passage, if you will. It happens only to the young men and women of my people when they reach a certain age. And by your standards, that would be several centuries."

The raw wound that had opened when they left the singing chamber and he had denied then her link with his mysterious people sent another sharp pang through her.

"Do you think that what happened to me wasn't real?" she asked, trying to keep the pain and anger from her voice. She had to speak softly so she would not disturb Toklat, who still lay sleeping. "How do you know that it wasn't a dream-walk? I may not be several centuries old, but I think this was *my* rite of passage. The final proof of my heritage, of who I really am."

She could see that she had struck a nerve. In the soft gloom of the cave, Galen's face was serious, heavy with the deliberations he had obviously been engaging in himself. He looked tired, she saw, almost as tired as she felt.

"I've thought of that," he admitted. "Indeed, I've done nothing but think about it this whole time." He sighed. "I said a dream-walk *should* be impossible, not that it isn't. There is no doubt in my mind that you are indeed descended from an ancient people who once belonged to the merfolk. But you must realize something, *philtate*. Despite that link, you are not a merwoman, you don't have our abilities—"

"I have some of them!" She straightened up, glaring at him. "All my life I've felt different. I've had dreams—especially since my mother gave me the scroll—feelings about the sea, that I've never been able to explain to anyone, including myself. You noticed it, too, even though you couldn't explain it any more than I could." Triumphantly she played her trump card. "And what about how I was swimming before you brought me down here? It drove you wild that I could do that. Well, now we know why."

"Yes, we know why. However . . ."

He leaned forward and pulled the hair away from the side of his neck. "Look," he ordered quietly. "What do you see?"

She stared at the small slit marring the smooth tanned flesh of his neck. It was something she never would have noticed if he hadn't called her attention to it. Now that he had, she knew, with some new and deep instinct, what that small slit was.

"I have one on the other side of my neck as well," he said.

"I know."

"Then you know what they are. And you know also that you do not have them. Without gills, Meredith, you are not truly of the merfolk. Without gills, you can never hope to survive in Mother Ocean, to be one with Her. As we are."

Tears sprang to her eyes, a further verification that what he said was true. Merfolk could not cry, she seemed to hear her ancestress Marit whisper in her ear. It was a sad whisper, as sad as the hurt in Meredith's soul.

Galen's long fingers closed around hers. "I'm sorry," he murmured. "I don't mean to hurt you, truly I don't. But there is so much here that I don't understand as yet. The scroll may provide the answers, but until it does I can't allow you to have a false sense of confidence about your heritage. It could be your undoing, and"—his voice lowered—"I could not bear that."

Stunned, Meredith looked at him. He stared back at her, his face inches from hers, his eyes burning with a glow that came from deep within, a hot blue flame that seared her with its need, its passion, its fierceness. Abruptly, he turned his head away, hiding from her that startling blaze of feeling.

"Come," he said brusquely. "You must eat. I know the food is unfamiliar to you, but you'll find it tastes better than it looks, and it will give you strength."

He picked up a spiny object and held it out. "This is a sea urchin. Eat the inside, the eggs. You'll discover they are quite tasty."

Hesitantly Meredith scooped out the bright orange substance he was pointing to. To her surprise it *was* good. Suddenly she realized how hungry she was. Her stomach had come roaring back to life, a voracious emptiness demanding to be fed. "This is delicious," she said, her mouth full. "It tastes just like caviar."

He nodded, a small smile curving his mouth. "Try this." He offered her the thick purple strands she had been eyeing earlier. "It's seaweed."

She ate that, too, then some more of the sea urchin, followed by yet more of the purple seaweed. Belatedly, she realized he was not eating. "I'm sorry." She gestured at the food. "You went to all the trouble of getting this for me, and here I am, gobbling everything up by myself. Have some."

He shook his head. "I gathered this for you, and for Toklat. He's healing to the point where he'll be wanting to eat soon too."

She nibbled at the meat from a spiny lobster that he had

cracked open for her. The flesh was raw, of course, but she ate it with enjoyment, the taste deliciously reminiscent of one of her favorite dishes, sashimi—raw fish prepared in the Japanese manner.

Finally her stomach signaled it had had enough. Satisfied, she leaned back against the rocks and sighed. "That was good, Galen. Thank you."

He gave her another of his small smiles. "How do you feel now?"

"Better, but tired, very tired." She scrutinized his face. "You look as though you could do with some sleep, too."

"I could indeed." He looked at her for a moment, then moved over so that he was sitting beside her against the wall. Stretching out his long legs, he put his arm around her and drew her to him, pillowing her head against his shoulder.

He was naked, having discarded his shorts at some point during this excruciating day. He was wet, too, from being in the sea, but through the saltwater moisture his body was warm, enfolding Meredith like a smooth blanket.

She snuggled against him tiredly, thinking that she had lost all sense of time since he had brought her to the cave. It seemed as though she had woken in her bed with him in another lifetime. It could be the afternoon of the same day, or the evening, or even two days later. She had absolutely no idea.

"Is it still the same day?" she asked sleepily.

"Yes, but it's night now. A warm cloudy night, with a faint moon."

His words called up a picture of the world outside the cave. In her mind she saw a hazy moon sailing through night skies lightened by swaths of dark gray clouds, the sea glittering and moving restlessly below it. She did not think of Karpathos, or of any other place on land, including her own home of Madison, so far from the sea. Mother Ocean filled her mind—the sea and all her mysteries, secrets that might forever be denied her.

"I wish," she said with tears in her voice, "that I had gills."

Galen held her closer, but he said nothing. What, after all, could he say?

At last, they both drifted off to sleep.

Anastas found his way to the dwelling of the landwoman Meredith without difficulty. The old woman had presented him with a clear mind-picture of where it was, and where, inside that house, the scroll was. She, whose body now lay sprawled on the beach, waiting for an indifferent sea to carry it away.

He ran up the path, moving with long easy strides. The excitement of what he was going to find sent flames licking through his blood, adding to the stimulation he already felt from taking Flijanou's life.

Killing always had that effect upon him—it added to his power as nothing else could. It was magnificent, the swallowing up of the life force of another; dizzying, to bring that heart and pulse and breath under his control, to seize, master, and then end it. Even the life of a feeble old Terran like the one whose pitiful existence he had just snuffed out was delicious. And knowing what was waiting for him in the crude Terran house intoxicated him still more.

The door was locked. One effortless push of his hand sent it flying open. He went inside, glancing around with cold curiosity. A vicious scowl sliced across his face as he passed by the living room and saw the makeshift bed upon the floor.

From reading Flijanou's thoughts he knew the old woman had believed, no, she had been certain, that Galen had not only spent the night in this house, but had moved from those pillows into Meredith's bedroom. Of course, she had not actually seen them, but Anastas did not doubt that her deduction was correct. There were few women—merfolk, much less, Terran—who could resist his onetime kinsman when he chose to make himself charming.

Anastas marched swiftly down the hall to the bedroom, scowling once again when he saw the unmade bed with its tangled covers. An image of Galen's body intertwined with Meredith's rose before him. He pictured his dark-haired cousin covering her sleek form, driving inside her. He saw her long legs wrap around his hips and imagined he could hear her cries of pleasure as they reached the heights of fulfillment together.

The image made him snarl as it invaded his mind as sharply as Galen's flesh must have invaded the landwoman's. It left him aroused and infuriated at once.

With an effort he thrust the picture from his mind and knelt to pull the metal box from its hiding place beneath the bed. The lid bore a heavy lock but it was not fastened, a discovery that had surprised him when he'd seen it in the old woman's mind. Yet Meredith had been keeping the precious box well hidden and there was no reason for her to suspect that anyone knew of its existence.

Anastas grinned. "Foolish unthinking little Terran," he said into the emptiness of the bedroom. His grin faded as a new thought occurred to him. What if she had already shown the scroll to Galen, and that was why the box was unlocked?

No. He dismissed the unpleasant idea almost immediately. If Galen had indeed seen the scroll, it would no longer be there. He would have seized it and fled back to the sea with it at once. Hurriedly, even though logic and the old woman's thoughts told him it would be there, Anastas flung open the lid.

The finely rolled sheets of gold—sun-metal, merfolk

called it—lay there, nestled inside their felt coverings, as undimmed by the passage of time as the sun itself.

Anastas drew in his breath, awed despite himself. Sitting down cross-legged for a closer look, he drew the top sheet out and unrolled it carefully across his knees. He could scarcely believe how well preserved it was, how easily the finely beaten gold unrolled itself, offering what was written on it to his eyes. Frowning impatiently, he studied the characters.

They formed a garbled version of the merfolk language, but he could make out only bits and pieces of what they said. He cursed softly, rerolled the shining metal, and placed it back in the box.

The only thing he had ascertained was that this sheet, as well as the others with it, apparently formed all the parts of a single scroll. However, he knew he would have to sit down at his leisure to fully decipher their meaning. He had never been proficient with obscure languages. Unless there was something tangible to be gained by them, such as the seduction of a woman or the compiling of some sort of power, the study of languages or any other scholarly pursuit held virtually no interest for him.

Now Ladru—Malk's unfortunate brother—had belonged to the Historian Strata. He had derived great enjoyment from such things and would have proven useful just now. How inconvenient of him to have fallen sick with that illness, thus making it necessary for Anastas to dispose of him.

The blond merman rose, the heavy box clutched tightly in his arms. Its weight did not affect him in the least as he strode out of the bedroom and down the hall.

He was beginning to suspect that another of his followers was coming down with the same illness that had afflicted Ladru. Bron—burly, powerful Bron—was not feeling well, although he and the others were going to ridiculous lengths in an effort to conceal that fact from their leader. Clearly they feared he would treat Bron in the same fashion that he had treated Ladru.

Anastas was not deceived, though. He had seen Bron earlier that evening and had formed his own conclusions. Yet it just might be that Bron would have better luck than the ill-fated Ladru had.

Anastas glanced down at the box as he left the house and headed back down to the sea. If Bron indeed had the illness that robbed one of one's gills, and if these golden writings indeed contained a cure, then Bron as the first experimental subject might possibly be the first beneficiary of that knowledge.

Meredith stirred restlessly, emerging slowly out of sleep. She had been dreaming, confused vivid streams of pictures and sensations. Not the all-encompassing state Galen had called a dream-walk, and not the mysterious dream of herself and the faceless man that had haunted her these many months.

That dream, she thought, opening her eyes and staring up at the craggy ceiling, would probably never visit her again. Why should it, now that Galen had come into her life?

As if the mere thinking of his name was a magnet drawing him out of sleep toward her, he shifted his body against hers. He breathed out a soft gusty sigh, then spoke to her. His voice was a husky murmur in the shadowy darkness, so like that of the man in her dreams. Even though she now knew that faceless one's identity, just the sound of Galen's voice still sent shivers up Meredith's spine.

"Why are you awake?" he asked. "You should be sleeping."

She echoed his sigh, nestling so that she rested more comfortably within the curve of his body. "I was dreaming," she told him drowsily.

"Bad dreams?"

"No, not exactly. Disturbing, though, because I seem to understand them and not understand them at the same time."

"They were about the Land of Gifts." He said it as a statement, not a question, and when she did not answer he took her silence as an assent. He held her closer. "What did they show you?"

She was not surprised by his insight, yet she brooded about what to say. "Destruction," she said at last. "And life. With a lot in between. Oh, hell, I don't know, and I don't mean to sound so cryptic. It wasn't like the other one I always have—"

"Other one?" He raised his head slightly so he could see her face. "What are you talking about?"

He didn't know about the dream, Meredith realized belatedly. Of course not, she had never told him. She began to describe it to him, finding that the words came haltingly, with more than a little difficulty.

It was harder than she would have thought to speak of something so intensely private, despite the fact that it was Galen who was listening. She had never discussed her peculiar and haunting dream with anyone before, though she had been tempted to, once or twice, with Flijanou, whose own peculiar brand of knowledge meant she would have probably understood it better than anyone else except Galen.

"And the man," he said when she had finished. "Have you come to know who he is?"

She hesitated, caught in the grip of an unaccountable shyness that verged on embarrassment. How stupid it was to let herself feel this way after everything that had happened between them! Telling that to herself still did not ease the determined hold this awkwardness had taken upon her tongue.

"I thought it would be obvious," she finally said stiffly. Now she was glad for the darkness of the cave, glad that she had her head on his chest and did not have to look at him. "The man in my dream was you, Galen. There isn't any other answer."

She waited for him to say something. He did not. Instead, he put a hand under her chin, lifted her head to meet his, and kissed her.

"I know," he whispered against her mouth, his breath stirring across her lips. "I know."

"You do?" Wanting to see his face now, she drew back. His features were indistinct, his eyes great black pools that pulled at her, luring her into their depths with seductive intensity that promised great pleasure. Wonder mingled with surprise in her voice as she murmured, "How?"

He shrugged. "As you said yourself, there could be no other answer." He reached out, one hand lightly caressing the hair that lay tumbled over her shoulders, dry now but still stiff with salt.

He went on, his voice quiet, reflective. "I think the sea has been trying to tell you all of your life that you belong to Her, or that at least your ancestors did. Only you didn't know enough to listen. These dreams of yours were just another of Her ways to try to speak to you. They were stronger because the scroll make them stronger."

He kissed her again, more determinedly this time, his lips gentle and urging and seeking all at once. Meredith opened her mouth to him, feeling her breasts come alive in his hands, swelling with the anticipation and the wanting of him.

Honey. That was what he did to her inside. He sent a river of rich amber, heavy and sweet as heated honey, flowing from between her legs into her belly and up to her nipples. To make love to him again, now that she knew his secrets, now that they had discovered their mutual heritage, would surely be a sharing more wondrous than anything she had ever known. Still, she made herself pull back. She had one more question.

"Galen, why would the sea send me dreams about you, about us making love? How—"

"Hush." He laid a finger across her lips. In the darkness, his voice came oddly to her ears, a strange mixture of grief overlaid with passion and need.

"Is it not enough that She did? I am carrying grave burdens on my shoulders, *philtate*, and so is Toklat. I can't free myself of the worry I feel for my people, and in the morning, when Toklat is strong again, it will be time to leave this place that has given us all safety. Yet until then, I want to love you, to give you the only gift I can in return for the scroll: myself."

She shook her head, started to speak, but he was already going on. "Tomorrow, after I get the scroll from your house, we must return to our people. Toklat to the Selkies, and I to the merfolk. Before yesterday, I was beginning to think we had no hope. But now, thanks to you and the scroll you have brought us, there just might be a chance to save both our peoples."

Their next kiss was deeper, lasting for a long time before their lips regretfully separated from each other.

Meredith had a sudden thought. "What about Toklat?" she whispered into the hollow of his throat. "Won't he hear us?"

They were no longer beside the pool where the Selkie lay. They had dozed off together there, but Galen had awakened her later and led her to a little alcove at the opposite end of the cavern, where they could sleep in more privacy. Still, Meredith was uneasy. The cave was so large it was doubtful Toklat would be disturbed, yet the idea of making love with him nearby was an embarrassing one.

Galen's returning whisper had a smile in it. "It's not likely he'll hear, but if he does he won't mind. There is nothing unnatural in two people sharing pleasures together if they are both willing, is there?"

"No," she said after a moment, then wound her arms around his neck and arched against him.

His nudity, which she had accepted so casually in her exhaustion, enflamed her now, the heat of his body seeming to burn itself into every single one of her nerve endings. She could feel his erection prodding at her thighs. Her shorts and top, long since dried, became a sudden and irritating impediment, a barrier between them that demanded to be torn off as quickly as possible. She moved back from him only long enough to pull the top over her head, eagerness searing ever more swiftly through her as his hands went to the waistband of her shorts.

Their coming together this time had a profoundly different quality. All the questions and uncertainty that had trembled so frustratingly on the edge of Meredith's consciousness before and after that first lovemaking had bloomed, coming full-blown into her awareness.

Galen was right about her—painfully so. She had no gills, she could not survive unencumbered in the ancient world that was her birthright as much as it was his. Yet for all that, Mother Ocean lived in her, bursting and crashing through her, singing in blood and bone and flesh with a fierce and undeniable exultation.

Before it had been Galen who was like the sea, rocking and moving within her like ceaseless waves. Now that sea was in Meredith as well, and it reached out to welcome him, embracing his body and his soul, drawing him in and out with the rhythm of ancient tides.

His flesh filled her, oh, how it filled her, yet she wanted more, wanted him deeper and deeper inside her. She twisted her legs around him as they lay on their sides facing each other, moaned deep in her throat, and felt the hot wetness of tears upon her cheeks. She was sharing herself not only with Galen, but with Mother Ocean and all Her beauty, a beauty she would never truly know.

The rock floor was smooth but damp and hard beneath their twining bodies. Neither of them minded. Meredith climaxed half a dozen times before Galen finally reached the pinnacle of his own release, driving deep inside her with a series of deep shuddering thrusts, as though he wanted to forge a path up to her very heart.

They lay panting, holding each other tightly, as their breaths merged and quieted. Meredith's tears had stopped. In fact, she scarcely realized that she had even cried. The wetness remained, though, dampening Galen's shoulder so that he could not help but notice.

"You're crying," he said, and she did not have to lift her head to know that he was frowning. She could see in her mind's eye his black eyebrows drawing together in that familiar expression of piercing scrutiny, as if he intended to dig up her most secret thoughts, mining them like diamonds sunk deep within the earth.

"It's nothing," she lied. "I'm not anymore. It was just the emotion, the wonder of making love to you again. It made me so happy."

Galen was silent. She guessed that he did not fully accept her explanation, but he said nothing, only drew her even closer into his arms.

It was not until his soft breathing assumed the steady regularity of sleep that the words he had uttered before they made love came back to Meredith. They sank in with heart-wrenching clarity.

Tomorrow, after he had the scroll, he would leave.

And what about her? Would she be left to deal with this

new wisdom about herself as best she could, knowing her heritage was the sea, yet chained to the land for the rest of her days?

She opened her eyes. In the darkness, a single tear slid slowly down her cheek.

CHAPTER
21

Galen's lips on Meredith's neck awoke her. Struggling to open eyes that felt as if they had been glued shut, she blinked up at him blearily. Tired as she was, it had still taken her a long time to fall back to sleep. Once she had, though, she had slept heavily, without dreams, and for what felt like far too short a time.

Galen's arms were still around her. His touch was tender, but his face had grown serious and preoccupied again, as if all the burdens he had set down when he'd made love to her had returned full force to sit upon his shoulders. "It's morning," he said. "I must check on Toklat, then leave for Karpathos."

Meredith was more awake now, a fact for which she was none too grateful. She had spent the night in some primitive places before, but never on a damp rock floor without so much as a pad beneath her. Now, her body was exacting a keen punishment for her cavalier attitude toward it. Every muscle she knew of, and quite a few whose acquaintance she had never made, ached. She felt stiff as a piece of wet leather left in the sun too long, and could already feel tender places that meant she would carry bruises as payment for her exuberant passion of the night before.

Morning had certainly come quickly, she thought grumpily. All too quickly, though in this deep place where the sun never penetrated, she would have had no inkling of its arrival had Galen not told her.

"How in the world can you tell it's morning?" she grumbled, forcing her vengeful body into a sitting position.

Galen sat up too. His answer did not improve her mood any. "It's an ability we have," he said carefully. "One that we're born with."

An ability that she did not have. He had not said it, but he might as well have. Meredith sighed, and levered herself up to stand on stiff, complaining legs. "Remind me never to sleep on cold rock again," she muttered. "I feel like I'm about two hundred years old."

He rose behind her. "There are far more comfortable beds," he agreed. "But I've slept on more than my share of places such as this. One gets used to them, particularly if one has the gift of you beside him, softening the hard rock with your beauty and your fire.

"I'm sorry, *philtate*," he added as she turned back to face him, her eyes wide and startled and pleased at what he had said. "I wish you had our abilities." His gaze drifted away from hers. "You have no idea how much."

She nodded wordlessly, her own gaze lowered. They began to walk back to the larger cave where Toklat lay. "How old are you, Galen?" she asked suddenly. From her dreamwalk she knew how long-lived the merfolk were, yet his answer still shocked her.

"About seven hundred years, more or less, if you count them in Terran terms."

"My God." She looked at him, her mouth open. But whatever else she might have said went unspoken, for with a loud splashing, Toklat climbed out of the pool and stood, swaying slightly, beside it.

"Toklat." Galen swiftly crossed the cave to him. "How do you feel?"

"Better, better, although I'm grateful for the support of your strong arm, brother-friend." Toklat leaned against Galen, and a smile broke over his face. "I'm also so hungry I could devour a whole school of yellowfin all by myself. What is there to eat?"

Galen smiled down at him in relief. They were speaking in the merfolk tongue; for the moment, both had forgotten Meredith, who was standing behind them.

She did not mind, though. It gave her an opportunity to adjust to the sight of Toklat, who, she was discovering, she still considered a mythological being.

There he was, standing on his feet and, apparently, completely healed. Before, when only his head was visible, he had been less intimidating, easier for the rational part of her mind to accept. Out of the pool, it was another story.

He was much shorter than Galen. In fact, he barely reached to the merman's shoulder. He was shorter than herself as well, Meredith noticed.

However, the Selkie's lack of height was quickly forgotten in the impact of his powerful frame. It gave Meredith pause to think about who or what could have been strong enough to overcome this formidable-looking being and injure him so seriously. He was built like a tank, his body just a solid column of muscle, rock-hard and bulging, overlaid with a thick covering of dark brownish-black hair.

And yet he still looked like a man, a short stocky man. A little more hairy than normal perhaps, but undeniably human. Until one glanced at his face and saw the undeniably *unhuman* eyes that stared back.

Those eyes were gazing at her now. Despite the fact that she had already spoken with him and—on the surface, at least—accepted his reality, now that he was clearly recovered, she was unnerved to find herself his target of scrutiny.

Still, the expression on his face was mild, even benign. He smiled at her, though it was a smile that shook Meredith, for it revealed a number of very pointed, very white teeth.

"We should speak so that Lady Meredith can understand us," he chided Galen in his hoarse voice. "Where are your manners?"

"Where are yours?" Galen returned. "You were speaking our tongue too." His tone was good-natured, in the way old friends have of speaking to one another. Still, he was watching the Selkie carefully, and beneath the light bantering, Meredith could sense the concern he still felt.

Toklat apparently sensed it too, for he smiled up at Galen reassuringly. "I am thinking only of food. Ah." He caught sight of what was left from Meredith's meal the night before. Shrugging Galen's supportive arm aside, he made his way toward the food, a little unsteady on his feet but determined nonetheless to reach it unaided.

Galen watched his progress with relieved approval. "If your hunger has that strong a hold on you," he said, "then you should be ready to leave the cave today."

"I will indeed. No question of it." Toklat's words were a little hard to understand because his mouth was full of spiny lobster. Disdainfully, he pushed the small pile of seaweed aside and eyed the remaining lobsters and sea urchins. "I'll need more fish than this to get my full strength back. Shrimp, snapper, lobster, anything will do, as long as you don't try to feed me these *plants* you merfolk are so puzzlingly fond of!"

Galen laughed. "I'll bring you more when I return."

"Ah." Toklat's expression lost its humor. He swallowed the mouthful he had been chewing, and his face turned grave. "Then you are going to get it now?"

Galen nodded; there was no need to define what *it* was. "Right away. Now that I see you're well again."

The Selkie cast a quick glance at Meredith and spoke quietly, switching back to the merfolk tongue. "I think you should take her with you."

"No." Galen shook his head emphatically. "It's far too dangerous."

"Yes, if they are out there. But if they aren't, then you should take her back. She's still uneasy with me, even though she's doing a good job of hiding it, and it's where she belongs."

Galen looked across the cavern at Meredith. She was frowning at both of them, her eyes blazing as if she understood what they were saying. He turned back to Toklat. "She would argue with you about that. But . . ." He sighed. "Perhaps you are right."

He squeezed the Selkie's shoulder, gently because the newly healed skin was still tender, and walked over to Meredith. Taking her hand, he led her to the mouth of the long tunnel that opened back to the sea. Pausing there, he gazed down at her sternly. "Toklat thinks I should take you back to Karpathos now," he began, "rather than waiting until I return with the scroll—"

"Does he think I'm afraid to stay here with him?" she interrupted.

Galen looked a little surprised, then the severe look returned to his face. "No, it's not that. He thinks you belong on Karpathos, not here, caught up in our troubles. No doubt he is right. However, if I sense the least hint of danger once we are away from here, it's back to this cave until there's a safer time. Do you understand me?"

"Yes, I understand," she said impatiently. "But what danger are you talking about? Who or what are you so worried about harming me?"

Rather than answering her, he held out his arms and said simply, "Come."

When his mouth lowered onto hers in what Meredith now knew as the "Breath of Life," she gave herself up to that strange lassitude willingly, even eagerly. She might not be able to swim through the deep waters as the people of the sea did, but this was the next best thing.

She had thought that this time, now that she understood and was expecting what Galen would do, there might be a sort of eroticism breathing through the power of his mouth—especially after last night. There was none, however. Instead, she felt an intimacy, a sharing of the very flow of life, more riveting than anything she had ever experienced, or realized could even exist.

How was it caused, this feeling of deep and unshakable bonding? She wanted to ask him that, along with a thousand other questions. But the heaviness that had started in her limbs spread to her mind and, in a kind of waking sleep, she felt him lift her in his arms and cradle her protectively against him.

The journey back to the land began.

For Meredith, the trip from the cave to the surface of the Aegean was no less stunning than the trip down had been. That surprised her. She had halfway expected otherwise, had thought that with her new knowledge it would be easier. It wasn't, except in one respect. She was no longer afraid.

Still, although she wanted to see what was around her, to experience more than she had the first time, she could not. The spell Galen had laid upon her was too strong. Above them, drawing closer and closer with astonishing speed, the rippling ceiling of the sea beckoned, shot through with a spangled blanket of sun. Yet when their heads finally broke through that shining ceiling of waves, Meredith was scarcely aware of it.

Dazed both by Galen's spell and the speed of their ascent, it took her several moments to come back to herself. When she did, she realized two things: a fiercely hot sun was beating down on her face, and Galen was towing her swiftly through the tossing sea. Her head was held securely in the crook of his arm so that she did not gulp in water. He had towed the wounded Toklat in just the same fashion the day before.

Her strength was flowing back quickly, and with it, her will. She moved her arms in protest. "I can swim," she said. "You can let go of me now."

"Ah, but you cannot swim nearly so fast as I," the deep voice pointed out above her head. "So relax and enjoy the ride. We will be at the beach below your house very soon."

Meredith did as he said; she had little choice. By now it had been borne in upon her that even with the extra encumbrance she represented, Galen was still traveling at an incredible pace. None born of land could ever, in their wildest dreams, hope to attain such speed.

It was difficult to get her bearings in the position she was in. The hard blue sky flashed above her like a giant wall painted brilliant sapphire. Not a single cloud broke its crystalline monotony, and it made her dizzy as it raced past her eyes, for held as she was, she could do nothing but gaze upward.

She realized that they were passing through the cove he had brought her to the day before and suddenly remembered the caïque they had left anchored there. "What about the caïque?" she asked, struggling to get the words out.

"What about it?"

Galen sounded distracted and utterly indifferent. Obviously he had not given any thought to the abandoned boat, or if he had, he certainly did not have any worries about it.

"Someone may find it," she said, "if they haven't already. There're bound to be questions—"

"So let them ask their questions. No one saw you leave with me yesterday morning, so there's no reason for anyone to think you are connected with the caïque. As for whatever else they may think, it is of no concern to me."

Galen spoke truthfully. With so much else to occupy his thoughts, the whereabouts of a single land vessel held virtually no importance for him. Other matters, however, did.

The moment they had left the protection of the Cave of Secrets, all his senses had come alive. Sharply alert, they had reached out to encompass the whole sea around them. Probing and vigilant, as restless as wind-tossed waves, his instincts had searched for the slightest nuance indicating that Anastas and the rest of the banished ones might be anywhere near.

So far, those keenly attuned faculties had revealed nothing. There was not a single sign of Anastas, no trace—even a faint one—of the twisted hatred that would indicate he or his followers were near. For that, Galen did not know whether to be grateful or more worried. There was a sense of foreboding about the blonde merman's absence, and the more obvious it became that Anastas was not in these waters, the greater his feelings of uneasiness grew.

It made him swim all the faster.

They had left the cove behind and were entering open sea. Here the waves were rougher, flailed into whitecaps by a stiff wind. Yet Galen had no more trouble negotiating

these waters than he had the quieter bay. Swift and powerful, he forged on without the least slackening of his pace.
Soon they were entering the stretch of sea that led to the
beach below Meredith's house.

She had fallen silent by then, having long since given up
any further attempts at speech. Being dragged so swiftly
was taking its toll. She was dizzy and disoriented, even nau-
seated, she who had never been seasick a day in her life.
But then, she had never traveled over the ocean in such a
manner before, either! When Galen brought them into shallower water and stood up, lowering her feet to the sandy
bottom as he did, he had to hold on to her lest she fall over,
so difficult was it for her to get her bearings again.

"You'll be all right in a moment," he assured her. "It's not
easy, being carried along like that for so long."

"I'll say." She shook her head to clear it. The warm
waves were sloshing gently about her thighs and she was already feeling better now that she was able to stand upright
once more. "It didn't seem like very long, though," she
said, marveling at him. "I can't believe how fast you were
going, Galen!"

He nodded absently. "If you have your land-legs back,
we must go up to your house, and quickly. There is little
time."

Although he still could not feel the force of Anastas's
presence anywhere nearby, Galen's sense of foreboding had
sharply increased the instant his feet had touched the land
of Karpathos. Something was wrong, he felt it more and
more strongly, yet he could not put a finger on what it was.
He took Meredith by the hand, both to support her as well
as to hurry her along.

They climbed the winding path to the house. Something
of Galen's urgency had communicated itself to Meredith,
and she walked rapidly, allowing her hand to stay within
his, although she no longer needed it.

Mentally, she was still a bit unsettled by the amazing journey there, otherwise she might have questioned the heightening anxiety she saw in Galen as they neared the house. She knew how serious it was that he obtain the scroll, of course, but there was something else driving him in addition to that.

For some reason the face of Stassi, the blonde tourist who Galen hated, popped into her mind. Why would she be thinking of him now? she wondered. Certainly he had not crossed her thoughts before, not with all these other earth-shattering events to occupy her. Now that he had, though, she found herself speculating over why Galen, a merman, would have conceived such an all-consuming hatred for a man who came of a people he regarded as inferior to his own.

"Galen," she began as they approached the house, then she fell abruptly silent.

The front door hung partly open, its hinges creaking as it swung back and forth in the breeze off the ocean.

Beside her Galen had jerked to a halt. "You closed this door when we left, didn't you?" he asked in a low, harsh voice.

She nodded, frowning. "I always do. I lock it, too, although I might have forgotten to yesterday. You had me pretty rattled, you know."

Galen strode forward. No one was in the house, at least not now. He could feel the emptiness inside. But as he thrust through the doorway he stiffened, every muscle and nerve ending going rigid.

"*He* was here," he hissed.

"Who?" Meredith came up beside him, peering about her.

He spun around, taking her by the shoulders. "Where is the scroll, Meredith? Take me to it now."

She freed herself from him. "This way."

She walked down the hall to her bedroom, Galen right on

her heels. She stumbled when they reached it, jerking back against the solid wall of his chest.

"Oh no," she gasped. She wanted desperately to believe that her eyes were deceiving her, yet she knew with dreadful certainty that they were not. "My God, it can't be."

The box in which she had hidden the gold sheets of the scroll was lying beside her rumpled bed. Its lid gaped open, and she did not need to look inside to know that it was empty, its precious treasure gone.

Slowly Galen knelt beside the bed. He looked into the box, then up at Meredith. The expression in his eyes was awful, a terrifying mixture of desperation and fury and grief and hate. "Was this where you had it?"

"Yes, but who could have taken it? Who would have even known about it?"

He was on his feet and moving toward the door in a single motion. "There is one," he said over his shoulder. "And I know who he is."

He?

Meredith went after him. With startling clarity she understood who Galen was referring to. There was only one person she knew of who could arouse that sort of rage in him.

"It's Stassi, isn't it?" she shouted at his back. "Answer me, Galen, I have the right to know! It's him, isn't it? He's the one!"

"Yes." The single word held a universe of pent-up rage. "And when I find him he'll wish he hadn't. For the short time he'll live after I do."

"He must have stolen it because of the gold it's written on." Meredith slammed a hand against her thigh in rage and frustration. "It's worth a damn fortune!"

"The gold," Galen replied in a voice of ice, "is of absolutely no interest to him."

"But who could have told him about it? It sure as hell

wasn't me, and no one else knew of the scroll's existence. And what do you mean, the gold is of no interest to him? You'd better believe it's of interest. It'd be of interest to anyone in his right mind, except— Wait a minute." Meredith caught herself. "He's not just a tourist after quick money, is he?"

Galen paused in the doorway. "No," he said heavily. "He is not what he told you he is, at all. Why do you think I tried so hard to warn you against him?"

"So Stassi is a mer—"

"That is not his name," Galen broke in harshly. "And he is not one of my people. Not anymore. He has forfeited that right for all time."

"Meredith." He walked back to her and took her hands. "Now that he has the scroll, I don't think you are in danger from him any longer, but I cannot be sure of that. I can't be sure of anything—yet. There is little I can do to protect you until I find him, so in the meantime, you must stay away from the sea. To leave this island would be even better. There are boats—ferries, you call them—that come and go from here. I want you to take one of them, and as soon as possible."

"Galen—"

His hands tightened on hers. "Please, Meredith. I beg you. Take the next ferry. Please."

Against her will, she felt herself accede, felt her head nod in reluctant acquiescence. Briefly she wondered if he was using some of the immense powers she now knew the merfolk possessed to ensure that she did as he wished. There were so many questions she wanted to ask! Instead, she only asked one. "But if I leave, how will you find me?"

His eyes burned into hers. "I'll find you, *philtate*. I will always find you."

He released her hands, kissed her hard on the mouth, and left, heading for the sea at a run.

"Galen." She ran to the doorway and called out after him. "What are you going to do when you find him?"

He whipped around impatiently, halting for just a moment. The look he gave her was not directed at her, not really, yet it made her shudder nonetheless.

"Kill him," he said.

CHAPTER
22

With shaking hands Meredith packed the smallest of her suitcases. In her own mind she had decided on a compromise: she would leave as Galen wanted her to, but only for a night or two.

Ferries to and from Karpathos were infrequent, unless their destination happened to be one of the neighboring islands. There was a ferry—a large caïque actually—that left several times a day to ply the stretch of Aegean between Karpathos and Crete. She had elected to take that one.

Crete was very close, "a mere stone's throw away," Marit's voice reminded her. It would be a good place to wait, and if Galen had not sought her out by the end of the second day, then she would return here. "No matter what he thinks I should do," she muttered aloud.

She slammed the front door behind her, locking it this time—though there scarcely seemed any point to it now—

and, lugging her suitcase, set out down the path for Olympus. In the village she would catch the rickety bus that would carry her over the poor mountain roads into Pigadia, from which all the ferries left.

The bus came and went only once, at midday. Fortunately, it was well before that. In fact, Meredith had been shocked when she had picked up her watch from the bedstand and seen how early in the morning it still was. Barely twenty-four hours had passed, yet her life had been altered so dramatically that even the mundane act of packing a suitcase seemed alien, an act belonging to the customs of another planet.

She had almost reached Olympus, when for the first time, she thought of Flijanou. During her time on Karpathos, it had become habit for her to pay the old woman a visit every day, and she had not been to see her since before the storms of two days ago. Most likely, the old woman was wondering where her American friend was, maybe worrying about her.

Meredith glanced down at her watch. Flijanou had come to occupy a special place in her heart. She could stop by the hut to tell her that she was going to visit Crete for a few days, and still have plenty of time to catch the bus.

She was never to reach Flijanou's hut.

As she entered Olympus, intending to walk through it and take the path that led up to the small house on the cliffs above, she immediately saw that the normally placid village was in an uproar. People were gathered all along the dusty street, gesticulating wildly, their voices raised in a cacophony of agitation and grief and anger. Meredith stared blankly at the confusing scene before her. Before she could approach anyone to ask what was wrong, two familiar figures came hurrying toward her.

"Meredith, Meredith!"

Mrs. Xanapoulos reached her first. Meredith had no time

to reply before the other woman flung her arms around her and caught her up in a breathless hug.

"Thank Jesus and Mary and all the holy saints that you are well," she cried in Greek. "We were so worried, so wor—"

"Where have you been?" Mr. Xanapoulos demanded. "We have been searching for you since sunrise this morning!"

Meredith's mind raced as it tried to manufacture a quick and plausible explanation. She finally settled for saying, "I couldn't sleep, so I went for a walk. Way up into the hills. Then I stopped to make some notes, and I guess I just lost track of the time." She gestured at her suitcase. "I was planning on going over to Crete for a few days to do some research. I came down to catch the bus to Pigadia."

It was pretty lame as excuses went, but fortunately, the Xanapouloses, along with the dozen or so other villagers who had gathered around them, were too distracted to examine the lie too closely.

Mrs. Xanapoulos threw her hands up in the air. "Americans and their crazy ways! And you, a young woman who should be at home raising her husband's children, rather than wandering about like a crazy person." There was a chorus of muttered assent and many vigorous nods from her assembled listeners. "Well, at least you are not dead," the shopkeeper's wife added darkly, and crossed herself. "Like her, God rest her soul."

"Like who?" Meredith stared around her. There was a tightness in her chest suddenly, an ominous feeling, as though a hand had closed about her heart. Its cruel fingers squeezed together, tightening with relentless pressure.

Mr. Xanapoulos was frowning. "You mean you have not heard? Oh, I suppose you wouldn't have, gallivanting about as you've been."

"No, I haven't heard." Apprehension and the effects of her long night were making Meredith short-tempered. "What in the world has happened here? Someone tell me!"

It was not Mrs. Xanapoulos or her husband who spoke, but someone else. A stocky man Meredith vaguely recognized as one of the many who made their living from the sea, going out every morning in brightly painted fishing caïques, and returning later in the day to sell their catch in various marketplaces on the island.

"It is Flijanou," the fisherman said. "I found her floating in an inlet this morning." He fell silent, exchanging glances with the others who flanked him. He crossed himself as fervently as Mrs. Xanapoulos had.

"And?" Meredith prodded. The fingers were squeezing her chest so fiercely it was hard to breathe, to talk in a normal tone of voice. "What about Flijanou, what's happened to her? Is she all right?"

The silence lengthened. Meredith was on the verge of grabbing the fisherman by the shoulders and shaking him, when he finally spoke. "She is dead, Americana. May her soul rest in peace."

"Dead?" She must not have heard him correctly, Meredith told herself. Flijanou dead? No one else said anything, and she glared into the man's dark eyes, waiting for him to take back his words. She had heard that people who hear terrible news often become angry at the teller of that news. That was how she felt, unsettled and furious. It could not be true, it could not!

An image of the kind and wise old woman who had become her friend sprang to vivid life in her mind: Flijanou, smiling at her through the shadows of her cluttered hut, relating some ancient tale as she made coffee. Meredith clenched her hand into a fist and pressed it against her forehead. "But how? How could she be?"

"We think she was murdered," the fisherman said bluntly. "Someone broke her neck."

Galen slashed his way out of the Cave of Secrets and into the sea. He headed west, his body slicing through the water with the dangerous power of a ferociously wielded sword. Toklat, now that he knew what had happened, would follow him later, after he had eaten and rested once more.

For a while Galen had thought he might have to use force to make certain his brother-friend did indeed take the time he still required to recover. Toklat had come as close to being distraught as Galen had ever seen him when he had told him that Anastas had the scroll.

"Our people are doomed!" the Selkie had cried. "He will destroy us all in revenge for his banishment. I told you you should have killed him, I *told* you. Now my folk and yours will have to pay the price for your foolish mercy!"

On and on he had raved, and Galen, who was using all his self-control as it was to remain calm himself, had had a considerable task set for him in calming Toklat down. Finally the Selkie had worn himself out. His distress had eased, replaced by a state of mind that was far more quiet, and far more dangerous.

He had picked up one of the large red snappers Galen had brought him. "I will eat," he had told Galen grimly. "And then I will enter the pool one last time to rest. When that is done, I will emerge from this cave. May Mother Ocean have mercy then on Anastas and those who follow him. For I will not. I have a score to settle with those *creatures*, for myself as well as my people."

"First," as Galen had reminded him, "you must go to Karpathos when night falls and the darkness can shield you, to check on Meredith, to see whether she left as she promised me she would. Somehow," he'd added, stern lines creasing grooves alongside his mouth, "I wouldn't put it past her not to have left."

Toklat had nodded. "I will do it. There is no point in her getting caught up in this any further."

Now, as Galen raced along, over one hundred feet below the sunlit surface of the Aegean, he remembered Toklat's words. And the thought he had had was the same thought he had now: It was too late, she was already caught up in this. Too caught up.

By the Mother, she must not become any more entangled in what was happening to the sea people.

Meredith stuffed a handful of pesatas into the bewildered fisherman's hand. His calloused fingers closed around the bills, accepting the money eagerly, though the look on his face was dubious.

"I don't know about this," he said. "I should really go out with you. Are you sure you don't want me to?"

She shook her head firmly. "As long as there's an outboard on it I'll be fine. I have to go alone."

"Well." The fisherman looked down at the money. He was clearly coveting this extravagant payment for the rental of his boat. Certainly it was more than he could ever hope to make in a full week of steady fishing. It was almost as much as the boat itself cost.

However, it was just as clear that the islander's conscience was still bothering him about the propriety of what he was being asked to do. "I don't know about this, Americana," he repeated. "You've never been out on the sea alone, have you? The currents and the winds of our Aegean, they can be—"

"I'll be all right." Meredith brushed past him to where the little caïque, painted a dazzling shade of red, swayed gently in the shallows, held there by its reluctant owner. "I'm not planning on using the sail, just the outboard, and I know how to operate one of those. Don't worry about me." She threw the fisherman a brief, reassuring smile and gestured at him to step back.

He did, but still looked unconvinced. "I think that this is probably not a good idea," he muttered. "After what happened to Flijanou ..."

Meredith's face changed. "It's because of Flijanou that I do this," she said quietly, and yanked the outboard into sputtering life.

The fisherman stood on the sand, watching her direct his caïque out into the bay. At least she had not lied about being able to operate the outboard, he thought. But he still could not get over the feeling that he was making a mistake. He wondered if he would ever see his caïque again. He wondered if he would ever see *her* again. He shrugged in a gesture classically Greek, then crossed himself.

"Crazy American woman," he muttered, and began to trudge back up the beach. "What reasonable man can ever figure out the mind of a woman, especially a foreign woman? Well, if she doesn't come back, she doesn't come back. I warned her, after all. I did warn her."

Following the long narrow coastline, Meredith headed the caïque in a direction that was becoming almost familiar to her. It felt strange to be on the sea, rather than in it, with Galen holding her tight in his arms. It felt strange to be anywhere near the sea at all, without him beside her.

Yet she'd been perfectly truthful when she had told the fisherman he didn't need to worry about her. She was not worried, although a few days ago she would have been. Then she would have considered it the height of foolhardiness to come out here alone.

In general, the Aegean was a gentle sea, windier than the Ionian Sea, but kind to those who traveled upon her. However, she also had a reputation for capricious winds and sudden squalls that could blow up out of nowhere. And the meltemi was threatening to return. The sky overhead was clear, but the horizon was hazy and the clouds that capped the mountains past which she was motoring proclaimed that this time the wind was going to persist for several days at least.

No, a few days ago she would not have ventured out here alone, without someone who knew the sea to guide her. Things were different now, though. She had to be there. It was the only place she could be. With the news of Flijanou's death, the force that had been born in the Cave of Secrets had come roaring into a new and even stronger life, driving her away from the land and back to the cave, the source of its birth. She did not resist that pull. It did not even occur to her to try.

And capricious though the Aegean might be to others, Meredith sensed that no harm would come to her in these crystal blue waters. She could not have said how she was so certain of that, yet she was. No matter what Galen thought to the contrary, *she* knew the sea was no danger to her, whether the Aegean, or any other of Mother Ocean's vast realms.

If only the same had been true for Flijanou.

Meredith swiped a hand angrily across her eyes, even though they were dry. This was not the time for tears; crying was a luxury that would have to wait until later. Flijanou's death had come from the sea, and so had Toklat's near death.

A face rose before her. Coldly handsome, with pale green eyes that chilled the blood, like a moonless night in the dead of winter. The man who called himself Stassi. The one Galen claimed was no longer a merman. But he was!

Involuntarily, Meredith shuddered, trying to imagine why he had been disowned by his people, what he could have done that would cause such terrible hatred to flame up in Galen's warm eyes at the mere mention of him. That hatred had been present before Stassi took the scroll. Long, long before.

She was nearing the cove, and as she did, thoughts of Stassi, and even Galen, fled from her mind. A kind of euphoria descended upon her as the caïque forged ahead. The steady sputter of its motor made her frown absently. It was an alien noise, disturbing the sacred quiet of these waters, of this holy place that should know only the rushing sound of water and wind and crying birds.

The grief for Flijanou was still with her, but it was overlaid with a new sense now—the realization that that grief, the feelings springing to life within her, and the cave were all jumbled together somehow. Flijanou would be avenged, but she, Meredith, had to reach that cave. Something awaited her there, calling to her, telling her she must hurry.

Without hesitation she passed the spot where Galen had anchored his caïque the day before. In some inner level of her mind, so deep it was almost unconscious, was a clear map of where the Cave of Secrets lay. She brought her boat to precisely the spot where one would have to dive to reach the tunnel, and shut off the outboard.

The resulting quiet spread a balm upon her newly awakened, and just as newly sensitive, faculties. She sat in the caïque, her body swaying as it rocked back and forth on the gentle swells, her mind moving in the same restless but aimless channels as the boat. A sensation of terrible loneliness pounded through her veins, a feeling of separation so keen, it sent a cry trembling up into her throat and out into the rustling silence of the cove.

She did not belong here, sitting in this vessel of wood and iron, this thing that kept her apart, imprisoned and exiled from her true world. It was time to go home, to at least try to return. And even if it meant her death, there were worse things: to live on the land with the sea calling to her every hour of the day and night, to stand on the edge of realms that were hers, yet be unable to enter that kingdom. Yes, those things were worse than death. Worth any attempt to change a fate that would otherwise torment her the rest of her days.

She stood up, spreading her feet apart so that her weight would be evenly distributed and the little boat would not capsize. Then she began to draw off her clothes. There was a deliberateness about her motions, as though she were performing the formal steps of a ceremony. And in reality, she was. A grave ritual, from which she might never return.

Naked, she stared about her. The iodine-scented air, redolent of the smells of laurel and broom and wild thyme from nearby Karpathos, whispered over her breasts, raced down her hips and along her thighs like a trail of kisses. She glanced at the cloud-crowned mountains and then down at the sparkling water. The waves rippled and danced, and she imagined that the cove itself was smiling at her, beckoning, inviting her to join it.

Perhaps there was something important she should say, a prayer or an invocation that should be offered up to Mother Ocean or whatever deity was out there listening and who might be willing to protect her. Only two words came clearly through: Help me. And she could not have said to whom or to what that silent plea was directed.

She spread her arms above her head and dived over the side.

•   •   •

Toklat stirred in the Pool of Healing. He had been asleep, lost deep within the final stages of his healing rest, but a cry had awoken him. It was a sound heard only inside his head, yet it was piercingly clear, vibrating with a world of longing and frustration and fear.

"By the excrement of sea turtles." He muttered the curse in the growling rasp of his own tongue and sat up so quickly, water splashed haphazardly over the sides of the pool.

Was it Galen who had called? No, Toklat dismissed that speculation immediately. His brother-friend would not cry out in such a fashion. Who, then?

A sudden thought struck him, and his eyes narrowed in surprise and puzzlement. Now why would it even occur to him that it was the landwoman called Meredith? "But she is not a landwoman," he reminded himself aloud. "She belongs to the merfolk, or she did once."

Still, the cry he had just heard could not have come from her. Surely she was far from there and safe. No doubt, she was well away from Karpathos by now, traveling on one of those infernal floating monstrosities Terrans referred to as "ferries." Toklat sat back, laying his head against the rim of the pool. He would lose himself once more in the peaceful oblivion of the Healing Rest, he decided. He closed his eyes. But even though he waited patiently, that unique sleep refused to come back and enfold him in its embrace.

By the same token, the presence of the young landwoman who was really a merwoman refused to leave. Try as he might, Toklat could not rid himself of the idea that it was she who had let out that disturbing cry. A few minutes passed, then he opened his eyes and sat up again, sighing.

Galen had enjoined him to protect Meredith, to see that she was kept safe. If there was any possibility at all that she was in danger, it was up to Toklat to remove her from that danger, and as quickly as possible.

He pushed himself up out of the pool and walked to the center of the cavern. The easy way his body responded to his commands pleased him. He stood still for a moment, testing his arms and legs, flexing his muscles, running probing hands along the places where the worst of his wounds had gaped.

Yes, he was fully healed. Strength and power ran through him once more, unchecked by injury or pain. The strange cry had woken him a bit early perhaps, but it did not really matter. He was ready to leave.

He headed for the mouth of the tunnel.

The waters closed over Meredith's head, as cool and soft as chilled velvet, a welcome relief from the relentless blaze of the afternoon sun. She had taken a deep breath when she'd dived out of the caïque. Now she concentrated on holding it as she angled her body downward, toward the deeper depths that glimmered dark indigo where the sun could not reach. What would happen when the last bit of air in her lungs was expended was something she did not think about. Not anymore.

In fact, she had ceased to think about anything, anymore. She only felt, listened, gazed about her with wide eyes, as her body slipped without conscious effort into the undulating motion of her ancient heritage. The salt water stung her eyes, but she did not care. All around her was a universe of wonder and magic. Her world.

Before, when she had followed Galen from the boat, she had been too distracted by the sight of the wounded Toklat to pay much attention to her surroundings. Then, when he had come back for her, she had been so immersed in the power he had laid upon her, there had been no room for anything else.

Now, there was only the sea. And her. She was weightless, lifted from the earthbound heaviness of land into another dimension. She glided, flew, raced in this watery atmosphere, as freely as a bird arcs across the sky.

Always she had heard the gurgling songs of the sea in her blood, but she had listened to them in frustration, dry upon the land, when she had longed to be wet and free, able to touch and feel the ocean. Now she could fill her senses to the brim, experience all she could during whatever brief time was allotted to her. And if in the end, she never reached the cave, she would have at least these few moments of knowing what it had been like to be one with the sea.

Noises came to her ears, rising and fading in the background. The cove's deep waters were a muted symphony of whistles, clicks, and flutters that orchestrated everyday life and death in the sea. It was not a silent world to which she had come.

A gray eel, its skin glimmering like silk, swam past, moving sinuously into a patch of light above her. A small octopus, chased out of the rocks by a larger one, hurled by, both creatures shooting into the depths in a welter of flailing tentacles. The brilliant sponges known as sea orange—their colorful shapes wrapped neatly around the shells of hermit crabs trundling in and out of the nearby reefs—dazzled her with their beauty.

The breath in her lungs was running out.

Black spots were appearing in front of her, darting back and forth across her field of vision. At first she thought they were some tiny creatures of the sea, but she quickly came to know better. Her body was protesting, struggling for the dwindling reserves of air taken in that last great gulp before she had left the boat. Her head felt huge, as though it were expanding at the same time that her lungs were contracting. Still, she forced herself to keep descending, deeper and deeper into the cove.

A shoal of fish, striped crimson and white, swam toward her. Unfazed by her presence, they surrounded her, opening their ranks to let her through, then regrouping in perfect formation to continue on. A shark, no more than eighteen inches long, followed after them. Its sleek body, dark above, pale below, swept gracefully across her path, one luminous green eye turning momentarily in her direction, before the shark disdained her in favor of its original, and considerably smaller, prey.

Meredith herself was no longer graceful. The smooth undulation that had come to her with such mysterious ease was failing her at last. She was almost entirely out of breath. It seemed as though she had been underwater for hours, although in reality it had probably been no more than a few minutes, the maximum time she was capable of holding her breath.

Her arms and legs flailed in an awkward imitation of the two octopuses that had passed moments ago. Strangely enough, although her body was panicking, her mind was not. A detached peace was blanketing her inner self, and the more her limbs struggled, the quieter and stronger that odd tranquility became.

The black spots were no longer tiny; they had grown and spread like great splashes of ink, blotting out the beauty of this new world around her. For the first time since she had entered the sea, she was cold. It was a startling cold, piercing in its intensity, and it was accompanied by a terrible shooting pain that began in her neck and swirled out to encompass her entire body.

So unexpected and awful was this pain, that her mouth opened in an involuntary scream of agony. It was a soundless scream in the indigo depths that pulsed with the noise of other life. Water rushed into her open mouth, choking her, and the pain worsened. The salt water was like fire in her eyes now, a flaming agony echoed by a searing anguish that seemed to run through every vein in her body.

The torture was mercifully brief. Her eyes closed and her body went limp. She was graceful once more as the currents took her up, rocking her gently in their grip. A trail of bubbles drifted from her mouth, popping and fading, as she floated into the distance.

CHAPTER
23

The Aegean is a brilliantly blue sea, scattered with islands that the sun cloaks with a reddish patina. To those who know it, it is like a vast pool without fogs, a pool in which the innumerable islands are stepping-stones bringing a traveler home.

But to those who live in the sea, to whom it *is* home, the Aegean is a great city, a metropolis, in which the islands and the thousands of inlets and bays they spawn are nothing more than suburbs, familiar as the lines on one's face. It was to one of these suburbs that six shadows glided, slicing through the depths at the bottom of the sea, then racing upward to where the pitiless sun lightened the waters to a pale sapphire laced with gold.

Anastas was in the lead, the precious scroll, which he had wrapped in several layers of sharkskin, held tightly under one arm. He glanced over his shoulder. His followers were close behind him. Except for Bron. The burly merman was lagging, and would have been dragging back even farther if it were not for the others, who kept slipping unobtrusively around to help him along.

Anastas smiled to himself. The fools were hoping he would not notice. Little did they realize that he was glad Bron was ill. He increased his pace, eager to reach his destination: a tiny island uninhabited by Terrans and dotted with caves that would shield them from prying eyes, particularly the prying eyes of Galen.

He could not know if his kinsman had discovered the scroll's absence yet, but he was taking no chances. In any case, if Bron was coming down with the same affliction that had killed Ladru, then he would need air around him, not water. The cave was a perfect place. Galen, if indeed he was pursuing, would probably not think to look for them upon land.

The approach to the tiny island was difficult, one of the main reasons landfolk never came there. The island had no inlets, no natural harbors to welcome boats, as did other more hospitable islands in the Aegean. Swimming in was out of the question. No Terran in his right mind would attempt to negotiate the only way to reach the island's one flat beach: by braving a jumbled mass of huge boulders and the small angry waves lashed into a treacherous haze of rough water by the wind that always seemed to visit here.

Anastas hauled himself out onto these rocks like a big seal, clambering easily over the slick, uneven surface and onto the strip of sandy beach. The others came after him just as effortlessly. Malk and Bron were last, the sick merman leaning heavily on Malk's shoulder as he stumbled over the boulders.

Anastas turned, studying the sweep of white- and blue-tossed waves. So far there was no sign of Galen. Or of

Toklat, who was, no doubt, recovered by now. He gestured brusquely at Malk, then at Bron.

"Help him to walk, or we'll be standing here all day waiting for him to keep up with us," he ordered. As he observed the surprised glances that passed back and forth between the other mermen, he added caustically, "Did you think I didn't know he was ill?"

No one answered. However, Anastas had not expected them to. In silence the little procession with Anastas at its head, his rapidly drying hair glinting yellow in the sun, wound its way along the beach and up into the rocky cliffs, dotted here and there with sparse groves of myrtle, wind-gnarled oak trees, and wild olive.

The island was small and it did not take them long to reach Anastas's destination. At the entrance to a cave completely concealed from the ocean by rocks and by the few large trees on the island, he stood aside, allowing his followers to precede him inside while he anxiously watched the sea. Satisfied at last that his enemies were nowhere near, he ducked into the cave.

His merfolk eyes adjusted instantly to the almost total darkness. Malk had already laid Bron down on the flattest part of the rocky floor and was kneeling beside him. Tovash, Gilkon, and Memenon had gathered together in a small hushed group, as far away from the other two as possible.

Anastas could feel their terror; it coiled and writhed like a horde of sea snakes, permeating every inch of the small cave with a restless and unceasing dread. They kept glancing over at Bron, then away again. Their thoughts lay open to him, as clear as a quiet lagoon. Each of them was quaking with the horrified realization that if Bron, strong as he was, could be stricken, any one of them could be next.

Only Malk seemed unafraid, perhaps because he had gone through this once already. Absently Anastas wondered if Malk was planning to defy him in some sort of acknowledgment to the memory of his brother. It would provide keen pleasure to master him as he had done before, but—Anastas sighed inwardly—there was no time for that now.

He walked over to Bron and smiled directly into Malk's eyes. The other merman rose to his feet, standing protectively over the sick one's supine body. "Are you remembering Ladru?" Anastas asked with a deceptive mildness.

"I—" Malk tried and failed to meet that pale gaze. "Bron was willing to help Ladru," he finally mumbled. "He was the only one who was. I do not want to see him suffer as my brother did. But in the end, you will do whatever it is you wish. I know that, Lord."

"Wise of you," Anastas commented. "And what I wish is to see Bron get better. This"—he held up the wrapped bundle—"may ensure that he does."

Every eye in the cave instantly focused on the wrapped scroll. Even Bron, who was barely conscious, forced his heavy lids apart to stare up at his lord. "The scroll," he croaked, his once vigorous voice now barely recognizable. "You will use it . . ."

Anastas studied him without replying. "His condition has deteriorated rapidly," he remarked to no one in particular. "Far more quickly than Ladru's did. Now why is that, I wonder. Bron is stronger by far than Ladru ever was, so it must be that the plague is growing stronger, more able to overcome resistance."

He fell silent as the implications of his own words sank in. Never would he admit it to anyone in the cave, but he had his own apprehensions about this mysterious illness. It would be the height of irony indeed if he were to become afflicted now, when everything he desired was once more within his grasp. So close, he thought, his hands curling into claws around the bundle he held. So close!

Abruptly he turned away. "I will study this scroll," he announced. "And whatever cure it contains we will try out on

Bron here. Soon, none of us need fear this sickness any longer. But"—his voice lowered, throbbing with promise and with menace—"for those who banished us, their fears have only begun."

Bearing the scroll like the precious object it was, he walked over to a corner of the cave. Watching him, Tovash sighed. "In truth," he whispered to Gilkon, who was standing closest to him, "I no longer care about revenge on the merfolk. Right now, the only thing that matters to me is finding a way to keep from dying the way Ladru did, and the way it looks like Bron will."

"Have you forgotten?" Gilkon whispered back. "Ladru did not die of the disease. He died of Anastas."

The afternoon wore on. The shadows lengthened toward evening, and still Anastas sat by himself in the cave, not speaking, poring intently over the scroll. The long fine sheets of gold glittered before him, lit with their own private brilliance, heedless of the narrow bars of light that slanted into the cave's mouth from the lowering sun.

Tovash, Gilkon, and Memenon had sat down hours earlier, making themselves comfortable wherever they could, so long as they stayed far enough away from Bron.

The sick merman was tossing in delirium now, muttering in a monotonous undertone that ate at everyone's nerves. Now and then he let out a cry that caused the others to start sharply. Malk had remained stolidly beside the stricken one, maintaining his vigil in a grim silence that nevertheless seethed with helplessness.

Anastas alone paid no attention to the sick man's cries. In fact, he scarcely heard them. He was utterly preoccupied with the scroll and, though he knew better than to allow his minions to see it, was becoming more and more frustrated.

Reading the scroll was in itself not the problem. The language it was written in was easily decipherable—some sort of primitive imitation of his own language. This simpler ver-

sion of his tongue had come as a surprise to Anastas. It was
even more of a surprise to find that the scroll revealed a fas-
cinating saga of an offshoot of merfolk he had never known
existed.

However, history had never been one of Anastas's great
interests. The only part of the scroll that mattered was what
it contained about a cure for this plague, and the subsequent
power that knowledge would give him.

Yet whatever cure there was in these shining gold pages
had thus far proved elusive. For some unfathomable reason,
the author of the scroll—a woman who called herself
Marit—had hidden it, or perhaps she had not included it at
all.

Perhaps, Anastas thought glumly, smouldering with sup-
pressed rage as he glared at the last remaining gold sheets,
the whole idea of the scroll was a hoax, a colossal joke on
Galen as well as himself. He cursed silently and began to
read again.

It was in these last pages that he finally found what he
was seeking. He announced his discovery by a shouted ex-
clamation and by slamming down the golden scroll onto his
thighs.

"By the teats of the Mother!" he roared.

The others stiffened, staring at their leader, shocked by
his unconcealed rage. Anastas was not one to show his emotions so openly. It indicated a lack of control, and whatever
else he was, Anastas was invariably and always in control.
It was part of what made him so dangerous.

"Lord," Tovash began timidly.

"Shut your maw and let me think." Anastas inspected the
sheet he had slammed down. He was already regretting his
angry display. This was a precious document, a treasure that
must be preserved and desired, not only because of what it
contained but for no other reason than that his enemies coveted it so much.

Fortunately, the sheet was not damaged. A testament to the excellent artisanship of whoever had created it so long ago, and a good omen as well, he thought grimly. Swiftly he began rewinding the shining metal pages, packing them away in the waterproof sharkskin.

Tovash, Memenon, and Gilkon exchanged glances, then watched him nervously. Even Malk, still preoccupied with Bron, looked up, glancing over at his leader before returning his attention to Bron.

Memenon nudged Tovash. "He has found something," he hissed. "What do you think it is?"

Tovash shrugged. "Who can know?" he muttered. "He keeps his own counsel, he always has. He will tell us nothing until it suits his purposes to do so. Why else," he added bitterly, "do you think we find ourselves in this position, exiled from everything we know, with this plague staring us in the face?"

Gilkon leaned over. "But he said the scroll contained a cure, and now that he's through reading it, he must have found something."

Tovash nodded at Bron. "Does he look as though he's been cured?"

Both Gilkon and Memenon looked at their ill comrade. Bron was no longer tossing as restlessly as before, but this was not a change that indicated improvement. The brawny merman's ruddy face had grown lividly pale and a film of sweat covered his entire body. In just the time they had been inside the cave, he seemed to have sunk in upon himself. His powerful muscles had gone slack, and he kept plucking feebly at his neck.

Malk had not stirred from his side. He continued to look on in silence, touching Bron comfortingly every now and then. His own face was grave, almost as white as the sick man's.

Anastas wrapped the last layer of sharkskin around the

scrolls and rose to his feet. Holding the bulky bundle possessively against his chest, he turned his attention at last to his companions. "Come," he said. "We've been here long enough. It's time to go."

"But—"

Tovash hesitated. A flurry of bewildered glances passed between himself and the others. He waited, hoping Gilkon, Memenon, or even Malk would speak up. None of them did, so he resignedly screwed up his courage and plunged on.

"What about the scroll?" he asked. "What have you found in it, Lord? Tell us. Please."

Anastas looked at him thoughtfully. "Very well," he said. "I will tell you this: The scroll has pointed me in a different direction, and we must go there without delay."

Tovash regarded him in bewilderment. "Where?"

Anastas looked out the mouth of the cave to the sea, glittering in the late sun as golden as the scroll. "To Karpathos," he said. "And a certain woman there. Without her, this"—he touched the bundle—"has no power. To heal this illness, or anything else. I will get this woman, and once I have her, I will have everything. Now hurry up, we're wasting time."

"Wait." Malk stood up. He was trembling, his eyes haunted as they fixed themselves upon Anastas. "What about Bron?" he asked hoarsely. "What about *Bron*?"

Anastas paused in the cave entrance. Framed against the fading sun he was only a shape, a black silhouette, looming faceless and sinister.

"Leave him," he said.

Toklat shifted uneasily. Meredith lay before him on the floor of the Cave of Secrets. She was unconscious, and had been since he had found her floating outside in the sea, drifting aimlessly among the fish like a stray strand of sea grass.

But it was an unconsciousness unlike anything Toklat had ever seen. Indeed, if it weren't for the barely discernible rise and fall of her chest, he would have thought her dead. He *had* believed her dead when he first came upon her. She had been so limp, so completely motionless. He'd been convinced she had drowned, until he'd drawn close enough to grab her and had felt the pulse of life beating faintly through her. Slight, so very slight, but there.

As it was, he still had no idea how she could be alive. Terrans could not survive underwater for any length of time, especially at this depth. They needed to weigh themselves down with a whole host of bulky paraphernalia, such as great metal tanks containing air, to help them breathe.

Of course, Meredith was not fully a Terran, but neither was she a merwoman. She did not possess gills, after all, and without gills she could not be of the merfolk, much less reach the depth she had attained before she apparently lost consciousness.

It was a puzzle, Toklat thought bemusedly. One he had not the least clue how to solve.

What had she been doing down there, so far away from the safety of land? He could almost believe she had been seeking the cave, but that was impossible. Surely she knew she could never reach it without Galen to breathe for her.

Had she been trying to kill herself, then? Toklat had heard that landfolk sometimes did things like that, decided to destroy the life-gift given them by the Mother for one reason or another. Meredith, though, had not struck him as a person who would voluntarily decide to stop living. Yet, what other explanation could there be?

He leaned forward and placed his hand on her forehead. She felt cold, even colder than when he had first brought her there, and that had not been very long ago. The rise and fall of her breasts seemed slower, too, coming less frequently than before. She was growing worse.

Toklat dithered, staring down at her with helpless concern. He felt totally inept. Healing, unless it pertained to Selkies, was not a skill he was well versed in. With Terrans it was a complete mystery. He had not the least idea as to what he could do to help her, or even what was wrong with her in the first place.

However, as powerless and impotent as he felt, he had to do something. He just could not sit there and watch as her life faded away in front of his eyes. Suddenly an idea came to him, so dazzling in its simplicity, it was really more of an inspiration.

"Well," he muttered, considering it. "It worked for me, and if it doesn't help her, then most likely it won't do her any harm, either."

He picked Meredith up. Despite the multitude of silly legends that had grown among landfolk about Selkies, Toklat, in all his long life, had never been this close to a Terran woman. In fact, this was the first time he had ever touched one. He marveled at how light she was, how insubstantial, compared to the women of his own race. He carried her over to the pool and lowered her into it until only her head showed. The dark water rippled around her, welcoming her into its embrace.

Seeing the way it accepted her made Toklat feel better. It also made him wonder even more about this strange landwoman. The Pool of Healing was a force that lent its powers only to those who were of the sea. The fact that those powers had wrapped themselves around Meredith said a great deal about her origins. A great deal, he thought, gazing at her pale face.

Thoughtfully he settled himself down beside the pool to wait. Meredith moaned. One arm rose suddenly, striking the pool's surface with a sharp splash before she fell back into silence. Toklat leaned closer, inspecting her face. Her eyelids were flickering, moving wildly, despite the fact that she was so still again.

She was dreaming, he realized. He sat back once more. "I wonder what she's dreaming about," he mused aloud.

Meredith moaned again.

CHAPTER
24

The first earthquake struck the Land of Gifts some time after the sickly moon had sunk back into the sea. It was small, little more than a tremor, but to those who had gathered on the beach, it was an ominous precursor of what was to come.

Marit caught hold of Jeram's hand. "It's beginning," she whispered.

He nodded, his fingers curving around hers in a bruising grip. "I'm glad," he whispered back, bitterness biting through his tone. "I'm tired of waiting. And now that I've killed my horses . . ."

His voice trailed off, and they stood in silence, each suddenly separate, captured in his or her own memories of this land they were about to leave forever.

Marit looked off in the direction of the City of Waves. Her beloved city. In her mind's eye, it rose before her.

Beautiful and serene, dancing with a thousand images of the sea, the sea that she would soon belong to in a way she had longed for but had never thought possible.

And yet, at such a terrible cost. Tears stung her eyes. She put a hand up to her face, savoring the wetness on her fingers with poignant sadness. They were probably the last tears she would ever be able to shed.

Kirta came up beside her. "Yes," the merwoman said, as though she had read Marit's thoughts. "Cry now while you are still able to. Weep for your lost home. For once you have changed, you will no longer have tears. And there is very little time left to us now."

As if to punctuate her words, another tremor shook the sand beneath their feet. It was a stronger one this time, and as it died away, one of the handful of Elders who had accompanied Kirta walked swiftly over to them.

Marit stared at him as he approached. She was swept with awe, a feeling she had had from the moment these elegant men and women, dignified and unbowed despite the enormous number of centuries they must carry, had emerged from the sea.

The majestic presence that surrounded Kirta was enhanced a hundredfold in these, the venerable wise ones of the merfolk. Despite her grief, despite the destruction looming so inexorably over her land, Marit was dazzled, rendered speechless by these magnificent beings who had changed their minds and decided to help their lost kin after all.

"The others have all been changed," the Elder said in a deep musical voice. "And the anger of the sea volcano is growing. These tremors are only the first indication of what is to come. Are there any more of your people who are going to join us?"

Marit shook her head. "No, my lord," she whispered. "No others."

He regarded her sadly. "You think that not even these tremors will change their minds? Ah, well," he added before she could answer. "It does not really matter, for even if more come, they will be too late. Now that the ground has begun to shake we can wait no longer. You two"—his deep gaze included Jeram—"are the only ones who have not yet been changed. Are you ready?"

Jeram's fingers tightened even more around Marit's. "Yes," he said steadily, knowing without having to look at Marit that he spoke for them both. "We are ready."

The Elder stepped forward. "Come, then."

It was over in just a few moments. The Elder placed his long powerful hands on Marit's neck, just below her ears. He stared deeply into her eyes, his own eyes seeming to burn unnaturally bright in the moonless darkness. He said a few words under his breath, so softly she could not make them out.

The saying of those words, or perhaps it was the light pressure of his hands—she could not really say which—made her sway. The night, the beach, and sea all blended together in a wild mix of magic and strangeness. A tumult of sensations swirled through her, each one so varied and complex she could not begin to identify any of them. Then the world steadied once more, and it was over.

So quickly, Marit thought in bewilderment, pressing her fingers against the tender new places pulsating on either side of her neck. Gills. Newly born they were, but gills! Just like those that the merfolk—her true people—had. They did not hurt her, not exactly. They throbbed the way muscles that have never been used do when they suddenly come to life for the first time.

Beside her Jeram was standing in stunned silence, the Elder having just finished with him as well. His hands were resting lightly on his neck, and he was staring at her, the bemused expression on his face a mirror of what her own face must surely look like.

Watching them, Kirta and the Elder smiled tolerantly. Jeram said nothing, continuing to explore the small openings in his neck. But the historian in Marit, never able to remain submerged for long, insisted that she ask questions, that she seek, above all, to understand.

"How?" she asked. "To do this thing so swiftly and without pain? Can you tell me—"

"No," the Elder replied, not unkindly. "For one thing, there is no time. And for another, you would not understand. It is not a method commonly known among us, or one that has ever been used. There has never been a reason to use it, you see. At least, not in my lifetime."

"However, Kirta here"—he laid a hand on the merwoman's shoulder—"convinced us that we should at least try it upon you people of this island, to see if it worked. She believed that because of our common heritage we would be able to change you in a different manner than if you were mere Terrans, and that once changed, you would be able to enter the sea immediately, with your abilities fully awake and functioning. She was right."

"And if she had not been?" Marit looked up at that grave face, sensing already what his answer would be.

The Elder met her gaze, acknowledging her insight. A surge of keen understanding flowing between them. "If she had not been," he said, "then we would have had to leave you to your fate. Only those with the tides running through their veins and the songs of Mother Sea in their blood can be converted back so easily to the true world."

He and Kirta exchanged glances heavy with meaning. "Clearly," the Elder concluded in an emphatic voice, "you are of our kin, no matter how distant that link may be. And while there are others who will continue to say 'They made their choice, let them live with it,' I, for one, cannot leave those of my blood to perish."

Thunder growled far off in the distance, sending out a warning rumble that drifted toward them over the dark sea. For the first time, Marit noticed that the rhythm of the waves washing up onto the beach was different. It was faster, and the waves also carried a sound that she had not heard before. An ominous rushing noise that was almost like a snarl. Had these changes just happened, or was there something deeper taking place? Her heart beat more quickly as she realized it had to be the latter.

More had come alive with the touch of the Elder's hands and his murmured words than just her gills. Voices and feelings she had never been aware of spoke to her now, singing, roaring, and pounding through her with a pulse greater than the beat of life itself. In that moment, she realized she no longer belonged to the sea. She *was* the sea.

"Oh," she said, and looked at Jeram.

He looked back at her, his eyes dazzled, filled with wonder and disbelief. His hands still on his neck, he nodded. "Yes," he whispered. "I feel it too. The sounds and voices, the feelings. The sea is angry."

"She is indeed," Kirta said urgently. "The Mother is warning us that She will not wait much longer."

Both she and the Elder spread their arms, urging those on the beach into the water, like shepherds herding their flock toward safety. The other Elders did the same. The sound of their voices rose into the night, reassuring and commanding at once.

"Come now. It is time to leave. Bid farewell to the land. Hurry, hurry. We must go into the sea."

The several hundred newly changed merfolk met this pronouncement with mixed reactions. Some went willingly, eager to try out in the open sea the skills they felt surging through them. Others, and there were many more of these, hesitated. They were excited by their new status, and by the feelings both familiar and unfamiliar stirring within them. Yet they were ambivalent as well, fearful of taking that first step out into the world that waited for them.

Among the tightly packed crowd on the dark sand, parents clutched their children, mates clung together, and sisters and brothers whispered uneasily. Their fear quavered out into a single trembling question: What will happen to us when we do?

For each of them Kirta and the Elders had the same comforting response: Go out into Mother Ocean and you will see. You are of Her now and cannot be harmed. She will always protect you, as She does us. Always.

There was a compelling force to their words, calming even the most apprehensive and drawing them forward as though the murmured words were hands. Singly, or in the small groups they had first arrived in, people began moving out into the waves.

They went slowly, still cautious, then with more speed as the sea took them in Her embrace. Here and there, exclamations of astonished joy rang out, floating back to Marit and Jeram, who were still standing on the beach.

Yearning, Marit watched the bobbing heads of her people as they darted through the water, guided partly by the instructions of the Elders but more and more by their own instincts, bursting into life now that they were within the sea. The spontaneous cries made her fidget. How badly she wanted to join them! But she and Jeram stayed where they were, having agreed beforehand that they would wait to make certain everyone was safely off the island before they themselves left.

Although she had sought to prepare herself mentally for the changes she knew would take place inside her, Marit was still shocked to realize how drastically her senses had altered. Particularly her vision. It had expanded, so that her eyes could not only pierce the black shadows of deep night with amazing ease, but could see distances she would never have imagined possible.

She stared out at the sea, a dark rippling expanse against the darker night. Only to her it was no longer dark. It was a vivid universe, filled with life and music and sound, calling to her, beckoning, as impatient for her to join it as she was to go.

Finally, the beach was empty, save for herself and Jeram. The last of their people had gone, and Kirta—alone, as was somehow fitting—came to fetch them. Here was where it had begun three short days ago, Marit thought, and here was where it would end. Or begin.

"Come," the merwoman said, and held out her hands. "Everyone is waiting for you. It is time for the journey to begin."

Jeram took Kirta's hand. With his other one, he raised Marit's hand to his lips and kissed her palm. "Are you ready, beloved?" he asked softly.

Marit tightened her hand on his in answer, then took Kirta's other hand with her free one. Together the three of them walked down to the sea.

As the first waves curled around his ankles, Jeram paused. "Is there something we must do?" he asked Kirta, his tone revealing not so much anxiety as the need to do this thing properly, in a manner befitting the gravity of this momentous occasion.

Kirta chuckled. "Do what feels natural to you, what your body and your heart tell you to. Mother Ocean will do the rest. It's a simple matter, really. Now that you have changed, you will be amazed at how simple it truly is."

Hand in hand, Marit and Jeram stepped farther out into the waves, walking steadily forward until suddenly the bottom dropped out from beneath their feet. As if that physical separation from land had been a signal, another burst of thunder rumbled toward them. It sounded closer this time, and more threatening. It was followed immediately by a new and stronger tremor, then a second and a third, each one progressively more powerful.

The sea trembled, lashing at itself and the beach in response to the quakes. The Land of Gifts shuddered mightily, and still tied in some deep part of herself to the land, Marit shuddered too.

The destruction of her home was advancing, and there was nothing she could do about it. Nothing at all. She ached with what was coming for her beautiful island, felt its burgeoning agony in every pore. But she could not afford the luxury of grief. There was no time.

Another crack of thunder rolled deafeningly over them as Kirta's strong arms pushed at both her and Jeram. "Dive!" the merwoman shouted, her penetrating voice carrying easily over the waves. "The volcano is going to explode soon, and we must be well beyond the pull of land when it does. The others are already on their way. Hurry, hurry!"

The urgency in her voice verged on panic. It caught hold of Marit and Jeram, seizing them with the same desperate need to get away from there. It did not occur to either one of them to question whether their gills would work; they knew instinctively that they would. Jeram released Marit's hand and went under first.

In the instant before Marit followed him, she took one last look at the Land of Gifts. To her horror, she saw that the beach was no longer deserted. People were running down to it, converging on the sand from all directions. With her new sharp vision, she could see their faces, terrified white masks staring out of a night black as death.

The fear she saw on those faces was indescribable. Now the people of the Land of Gifts comprehended that all of her and Jeram's warnings had been true, and that there was only one escape from what was coming to claim them.

Voices rang out over the heaving water, and Marit heard them all too clearly.

"Marit! Jeram!"

"Are you still out there?"

"Come back and save us. We beg you!"

"Help us!"

Involuntarily Marit turned around, pulled back by their anguish and hers. But Kirta's fingers closed on her shoulder, as grim and inexorable as strands of iron.

"It's too late," she cried harshly. "It's too late!"

"But, Kirta, they will die—"

"Yes, and you with them if you don't dive. Right now!"

Jeram's head broke through the surface. "Marit!" he called out. "What are you waiting for?"

A new earthquake savaged the island, the strongest one yet. Several of the cliffs overlooking the beach crumbled from its force, and the screams from those caught beneath the falling boulders and trees and earth tore at Marit's ears. The clash in her own soul between the old world and the new abruptly resolved itself in the only way it could, in the way she had always known it must.

She wanted to cry for those she was leaving behind, but she no longer could. Her tears had dried up and there would be none to replace them. Never again. She opened her eyes wide so that she would be able to see all there was to see, and dove beneath the waves.

Galen!

The cry came not from Meredith's mouth, but from some place deep inside her, a new part of herself, calm and powerful, where spoken words were no longer necessary.

She shuddered awake. She was still immersed in water! Was she dead then? Drowned? She kicked her legs out, struggling to move herself upright.

320 JESSICA BRYAN

"Gently, Lady, gently. Rest easy," someone said, and she whipped her head around, blinking at the sound of that hoarse, familiar voice.

Toklat sat looking at her, his round-featured face tight with worry. Tentatively he put out an arm and helped her to sit up. "Well," he said, a distinct note of uneasiness in his voice. "Well, so you are going to live, after all."

She rubbed a hand over her eyes. "I was dreaming," she said hazily, not quite returned from the force of the images running through her mind. "About the Land of Gifts. It was being destroyed, and I was seeing it. There were earthquakes, and cliffs falling. It was so real for a dream, so vivid—"

"It was more than a dream."

Toklat said this so sharply, she gaped at him in surprised silence. She was very awake now, and very aware that she was alone in an underwater cave with a being who—no matter how hard she wanted to be matter-of-fact about it—still struck her as a magical and inexplicable entity, a creature who should not even exist.

The Selkie was regarding her closely. His face wore an expression so solemn she could have almost thought he was awestruck. By her? The thought was laughable compared to what *he* was.

"I found you in the lower depths outside this cave," he continued. "And I brought you here. I didn't know where else to bring you. Just as I placed you in this pool because I didn't know what else to do with you. I've been sitting here watching you, Lady, and you are not the same as you were. Not the same at all.

"I tell you this." He leaned forward, his round dark eyes fastened on hers. "I have seen a great many wondrous things in my life, but never have I seen anything more astonishing than what has happened to you. Both while you were out in the deep sea, alive when you should have been dead, and when you were 'dreaming,' as you call it."

"What are you talking about?" She was so astonished by his attitude that she momentarily forgot to be uncomfortable in his presence. "What's happened to me, Toklat?"

Wordlessly the Selkie pointed at her neck. Puzzled, she frowned at him, then touched her neck. She gasped, her hand jerking away as though it had been burned. It couldn't be true. It couldn't! Shaking, she raised her hand again to her neck. The grooves, small and open, and a tiny bit painful, were still there.

"It happened while you were in the grip of whatever this spell is that came upon you," Toklat said in a low voice.

"H—how?" she stammered. Her fingers were flying over the slits on each side of her neck, probing, exploring. She was still trembling, unable to stop, and she could not have said whether it was from excitement or fear, or a combination of both.

Toklat shrugged. "They simply appeared, Lady. One moment they weren't there, the next moment they were." He gazed at her with a penetrating curiosity. "Do you remember anything at all about how it could have happened?"

"No, no, I don't—wait." She looked away from him, staring into space, her whole consciousness turning inward as the memories came sweeping back.

She remembered now. With such intensity, she wondered how she could have ever forgotten. It was Marit!

When she had watched through dream eyes as her ancestor was transformed on that moonless night so long ago, something had happened to her, as well. The flow of energy and power that had surged from the Elder's fingers into Marit had not stopped there.

Through some means Meredith knew she would probably never understand—aided perhaps, by the Cave of Secrets and this magical pool—that power had traveled across the limits of space and time to transform her too. She, who was Marit's child, her granddaughter, descended down from her through uncounted generations, the two of them linked together by the force of blood and ancestral memory.

"Lady?" Toklat said questioningly. "Have you recalled something?"

She nodded, a smile of wonder spreading over her face. "The gills were a gift," she said softly. "From my foremother. And the merfolk who helped her return so long ago."

Toklat looked uncomprehending, but Meredith was already rising out of the Pool of Healing. Now that she remembered everything, she was discovering that her uneasiness around the Selkie had vanished. Even the fact that she was naked did not bother her.

A host of new sensations were swirling through her, and she marveled at them, taking an awestruck delight in the wonderful strangeness. She cocked her head, listening to the sound of the sea outside the cave, hearing it in a way she had never heard before.

"I feel so different," she said "As if . . ."

"As if you've been reborn?"

She looked at him in surprise. "Yes. How did you know?"

"I've been friends with the merfolk all my life, Lady, as have all my people. I know about Terrans being changed, although as far as I've ever heard, it has always been only the destined mate of a merfolk ruler who is able to be transformed into one of the merfolk." Toklat bent a sharp thoughtful gaze upon her. "This is certainly something new."

Meredith sighed. Some of her euphoria was fading in the cold light of what had truly happened to her, and the implications that it carried. What would become of her, now that she was forever different from what she had been?

She certainly did not want to return to the land, nor did she even know if she could. Would there be a place for her among the people of the sea? They were her own true kindred, but would they accept her?

"I know," she said, and sighed again. "I wonder what Galen is going to think when he finds out . . ."

Her voice trailed off. The mention of Galen's name brought alive yet another memory. She had cried out to him when she was just coming awake, although she had forgotten it until now. And she had called to him in a way that was as deep and unspoken as the waters around this cave. Why had she called to him? And had he heard her?

"Toklat," she said slowly, "I have gills now, which means I can go out into the sea. Like you, and like Galen."

The Selkie's tone was cautious. "It's true you have gills," he said. "Whether or not you are ready to use them is another matter entirely. On a personal level, I have no experience with these things. There should really be a merwoman or merman here to oversee your first venture out into the sea, in case something should go wrong."

"But there isn't." Squarely she met his gaze.

She was curiously unafraid, and in that way, she was still the same. For when she had dived off the rented caïque into these waters, she had not been afraid then either, and look where that lack of fear had gotten her.

It had been a miracle. Who knew what other miracles awaited her in the open sea, not that she had the means to go there and survive? She realized suddenly that she could hardly wait to find out.

"I'm not afraid," she said. "If I didn't die before when you found me floating outside, I certainly won't die now. I belong to the sea, just as you do. She won't harm me, She'll never harm me."

Toklat studied her, his expression still doubtful. "Perhaps you're right," he muttered finally. "By the Mother, I certainly have no other explanation for what's happened to you, or why you're even alive. And it's time for me to go anyway."

"Where?"

"To meet Galen."

As soon as he said it, Meredith knew what she had to do. "I'm going with you."

Consternation spread over Toklat's face. "Lady," he began, "that is impossible —"

She cut him off. "I'm going with you," she repeated. "Don't you see?" There was a note of pleading in her voice. "I have no other choice. I don't belong on the land anymore. I have to find out if I belong in the sea."

Toklat's gaze softened. "Yes," he said quietly. "Perhaps you do at that."

CHAPTER
25

Galen flung himself to a halt. His whole body jerked so violently, it was as though one of the cruel harpoons that Terrans used to murder the whalefolk had struck him. He wanted to go on, yet he couldn't.

Meredith had called to him.

It hardly seemed possible, but he knew his inner hearing had not deceived him. She had cried out for him. What was more, she had done it through mind-voice, something no one not of his people or Toklat's should have been able to do.

He undulated in a big circle, torn by the desire to go on and the desire to turn back, to go to her. In his mind the needs of his own people clashed with that silent call, like waves crashing against rocks, leaving him struggling with the fear that she was in danger, that she needed him too.

Frustrated, he swam in a second circle. By the Mother,

he thought, Meredith, these events and all that surrounded them, had grown as convoluted as the most twisted currents of the sea. As he was in the midst of patterning a third wide circle, still debating over what he should do, his instincts came alive with a new warning.

A shadow against shadows, he darted farther down into the lower depths, racing like a streak of darkness two hundred, three hundred feet down. As he dived, his keen gaze pierced through the sea, searching for what had made him seek concealment.

He saw them. They were still far enough in the distance that he had time to call up all his powers of concealment, cloaking himself from their awareness of him. It was a specialized skill, this ability to cloak himself. Taught to him by Cleonith, it was not something that other merfolk, including Anastas and his ilk, possessed.

He watched as they swam past, far off, too far off for them to sense him. Using his every shred of discipline, he kept his mind focused in the trained blankness that would continue to hide him from their inner eyes.

However, there was nothing they could do to conceal themselves from him. Galen's eyes narrowed. He could see Anastas in the lead, and he saw that the blonde merman was carrying something, a bundle he was holding carefully to his chest as he swam.

The scroll. Of course, what else would it be? Galen fought the urge to charge after them, roaring with rage, killing them all. Instead, he listened, wanting to learn all he could before he acted.

Like rustling in his head, he could hear the two minions that were bringing up the rear. They were communicating with each other in the faintest possible mind-voices, obviously not wanting to attract the attention of Anastas. Galen recognized them; their names were Gilkon and Memenon. He had known them once, before the Banishment, and the death of his parents that had led up to it. He had even liked them. Then.

I still think we should not have left him, Gilkon was muttering. *Not that I wanted to get close to him, mind you. But it was ill-done to just go off and leave him like that. And Malk wanted to stay with him. He was willing to. I think —*

You would do better to stop thinking about Bron and start thinking about yourself, Memenon broke in. *He was barely alive when we left, and if he has not transitioned to the next existence by now, he surely will soon. There is nothing more any of us can do for him. There never was. Not from the first moment he fell ill. Worry about yourself, and about staying alive. I'm not happy with Anastas, just as you aren't. But right now, he's our only hope of avoiding the same fate as Bron.*

But what if someone should find him?

You mean a Terran?

At Gilkon's nod, Memenon let out a soft, bitter laugh. *That is hardly likely. As our lord pointed out, the landfolk never go to that tiny glob of land. They have no reason to, especially since it is so hard for them to get on it. By the time any one of their tribe should ever visit there, poor Bron's shell will have long since decomposed into nothing more than bones and a few strands of hair.*

Memenon's mind-voice fell even lower. *Believe me, Gilkon, I am no more pleased with our lord or what has been happening than you are. But in this matter, Anastas was right.* He sighed. *Poor Bron.*

Poor all of us, Gilkon corrected grimly. *Except for Anastas. With that scroll, he will come out of this plague healthy and with all his powers intact, even though the rest of us are long since dead.*

They swam on.

When the last troubled hint of their presence had faded, Galen released himself from the web of concealment he had thrown about himself.

He knew what he should do now, but he paused anyway. All his senses expanded, straining, as they searched for some trace that Meredith was still calling to him. There was no sign of her presence in his mind, not even a tinge. He worried over whether that boded good or ill.

Yet the path he needed to take lay clearly before him. He knew the waters of this sea that Terrans named the Aegean, and his people called the Blue Sea, very well. He knew equally well all the various islands that floated there. He could picture the small island Gilkon and Memenon had been referring to, and despite himself, he had to admit it was an inspired idea on Anastas's part. He would have never thought to look for the yellow-haired merman and his minions there.

He undulated forward, backtracking swiftly along the route the banished ones had taken. Before he did anything else, he would pay that island a brief visit and see if Bron was still among the living.

At the speed he set for himself, it took him only a short time to reach the small island. Memenon had been right about one thing, he reflected, as its barren, sun-seared shape loomed up out of the sea. It certainly was an inhospitable place, at least to Terrans. He rode the rough water into shore and clambered easily over the huge slippery boulders. The sand comprising this one thin strand of beach was blistering hot beneath his feet, but he barely noticed.

He had felt it almost immediately, the instant his feet touched land—the unique miasma of illness and approaching death that hung heavy and stinking upon the air. It was an emanation that came only from a merman or merwoman who was dying.

Only another member of the merfolk would be able to sense that unmistakable aura. Even though Bron had been declared to be no longer of the sea people, Galen mused ironically, he was at last, in his bones and blood, still a merman.

That fading shimmer of a departing life drew Galen forward, tugging at him with the strength of an undertow. He could almost see its death force glistening at him, like a long ominous rope. He had only to follow it, up the hills and into the tiny cave nestled within the rock cliffs.

He found the banished one, abandoned even by those he had gone into exile with, lying on the floor toward the back of the cave, practically hidden in the darkness.

Just as he had known Gilkon and Memenon, Galen remembered Bron. But the man he remembered bore little resemblance to this wasted figure, who was so still that had it not been for the faint emanation still glowing about him, Galen would have thought him already dead.

Bron had been bursting with health and strength, at one time, so heavily muscled that he could have easily rivaled even the strongest of the Selkie folk. Now those mighty muscles had turned flaccid. He looked emaciated and shrunken.

Galen was horrified to see this, for if Bron had deteriorated to such a terrible state, what of young Alaric and all the others of his people who had been stricken? Had they, too, come to this awful pass? There could be no answer to this disturbing question, not yet anyway. He schooled his mind to concentrate on the matter at hand and walked forward.

"Bron," he said quietly.

Bron's heavy-lidded eyes struggled open, and he looked up at him. The merman was too far gone to be either shocked or concerned by Galen's sudden appearance. His voice came out in an appalling rasp, carrying beneath it the rattle of approaching death.

"There is little time left for me, is there?" he gasped.

Galen gazed down at him. "Very little," he said after a long moment.

It violated the rules of Banishment to speak directly to the dying merman, but considering what faced them all, merfolk and banished ones alike, such restrictions seemed unimportant now. Another unexpected twinge of sympathy for the suffering Bron rippled through him, and he fought it down. He did not want to feel such an emotion for any of these creatures who had willingly chosen to follow Anastas, no matter how ill he might be.

"Where did your master go with the scroll?" he asked coldly. "Share what you know with me before you transition from this life, which you have handled so poorly. It is the least you can do after the way you betrayed your own people."

Bron's voice was faltering. "O-others are ill now, as well?"

"Yes."

"How many others?"

"At this point, I don't know. Answer my question."

"He left me." Bron's eyes, glassy and bloodshot, focused on Galen's face. They turned hard, blazing with fever and bitterness and rage. "After all that I did to serve him, he left me. Abandoned me here on this stinking piece of Terran spit to die. Did you know that?"

"I knew it." Galen's muscles tensed. He could feel them going rigid, aching with the desire to exact punishment. Revenge, he thought longingly, clenching his fists. Revenge for his mother and his father, and for himself. He leaned forward. "Now you tell me," he said savagely. "Where did he go?"

The hardness left the sick merman's eyes and his gaze wandered away. "I'm sorry," he whispered. "I'm sorry for all of it, so sorr—"

"Spare me your apologies." Galen's voice slashed through the cave. *"Where is he?"*

"He went to find her."

A river of ice rolled over Galen's whole body. "What do you mean, her?" He went down on one knee beside Bron when the merman mumbled something unintelligible. Bron's life-force was ebbing rapidly now. Soon he would be gone. Galen *had* to pull whatever it was Bron knew out of him before that happened. "Answer me," he said urgently. "Answer me!"

Bron struggled to speak. "The landwoman," he got out triumphantly. "He called her Mere-Meredith."

A sly expression appeared on his face, ghastly on those twisted dying features. "He probably thought I was too ill to pay attention, or that it didn't matter because I would soon be transitioned from this life." He gasped, and a hideous sound that was something like a laugh rasped out of his throat. "He surely never planned on *you* finding me here. That's for certain."

The effort of saying that much had taken its toll. A tremor that Galen recognized as the ominous and unmistakable precursor of death shuddered through Bron's limbs, and Galen shook Bron's shoulder fiercely. "Why? Why would he want her? For what purpose?"

"He said . . ." The merman's voice was weaker, the deadly rattle in his throat so strong it threatened to drown out speech. "He said she was the key . . ."

His voice trailed off, and Galen shook him even harder. "The key to what?"

"To understanding the scroll." Bron's mouth opened as though he wanted to say more, but the words never came. His eyes rolled up into his head, and he died.

"Lady," Toklat began as they stood at the entrance to the tunnel. He was clearly having second thoughts. "I still say this is not a good idea." He regarded Meredith, his expression distinctly uneasy. "It is far too dangerous."

"Hah," Meredith said with disgust. "After what I've just been through? You sound exactly like Galen."

"That is because he asked me to look after you. After I finished my healing, I was planning to go to the island of seals—Karpathos," he added at her inquiring glance. "To make certain that you had left." He gave her a severe look. "As you had told Galen you would."

"But I did leave," she said calmly. "It's just that I came here instead."

The Selkie made a growling noise. "My brother-friend believes you safely away from Karpathos. He will not be happy to find out otherwise."

He growled again, then said glumly, "I wouldn't like to be you when you meet up with Galen, Lady. If you can live long enough in the sea to meet up with him, that is. And if you don't, he'll have more than a few things to say to me about why I allowed you to do this fool thing in the first place."

"But, Toklat . . ."

Meredith put out a hand and gently touched Toklat's arm. It was the first physical contact she had made with the Selkie while completely conscious. Rather than seeming strange and alien, as it would have been before her second dreaming, it felt completely natural. His arm was very hairy, and as solid as a wooden club beneath her hand.

"I thought you understood," she said. "I have to do this. And," she added with a slight smile, "it's not a question of whether or not you allow me. I'll take full responsibility for whatever happens. But nothing will. You'll see."

He shook his head. "I hope you're right," he muttered. "For by my mother's fur, I don't have any better ideas as to what I should do with you. I'd rather not leave you alone in this cave, safe as it is, for who knows when Galen will be able to come back for you? And I don't have the ability to keep you alive, as he can. So it looks like you'll have to come along. I can only pray to the Mother that you'll be safe."

"I will be," she said confidently. "Let's go."

She looked down into the tunnel mouth, then expectantly over at Toklat, waiting for him to dive first. Still the Selkie hesitated. "Remember," he warned, "once we enter, there is no going back. I won't be able to help you if you get into trouble. I don't even know if the mind-speak used between Selkies and merfolk will work with you, so we may not be able to talk to each other."

"You weren't able to help me before, and I still lived," Meredith pointed out. She was fidgeting with impatience. The sea was like a living presence in her mind, summoning her forward so strongly, she could scarcely contain herself. "We've been over all this, Toklat, and I'm ready. I thought you said you had to hurry."

He squared his wide shoulders. "So I did. Very well, then. Follow me. And be sure to stay close."

His squat body seemed to elongate itself, as with a fluid and strikingly beautiful grace he dove into the dark water lapping at the entrance to the tunnel. Meredith marveled for the briefest of instants, then she followed him.

To her astonishment and joy, her body arrowed into the water, taking on the same grace as Toklat's and doing so under no volition of her own. With the same naturalness she found herself following Toklat as they moved single file through the narrow passage. It was not until they were nearing the mouth that led out into the sea that she realized she had not drawn in a breath of air when she dove into the water.

The observation was so profound, she momentarily faltered. She was breathing water rather than air! Her gills had opened, and though they were still new and a bit tender, they were functioning perfectly. What an odd and astounding sensation it was, to feel the rush of water traveling through the slits in her neck with the same easy rhythm as though she were standing in the sun breathing in the clean summer air.

Just ahead, Toklat paused. He glanced back at her, impatience and worry written clearly on his face. Despite the darkness of the tunnel, she could see him as vividly as she could feel the workings of her gills. Her vision had altered too, she realized. She gave him a great wide smile.

The Selkie's look of concern changed to one of guarded relief as he watched her shoot forward to catch up. He gestured to her, beckoning her onward. Together, with him in the lead and her close behind, they emerged into the cove.

The life of Mother Ocean welcomed Meredith. Dazzled, filled with an unspeakable happiness, she felt her senses widen, growing until it seemed she was encompassing the entire sea.

She felt as though she could look seabirds in the eye, be one with all the wondrous and varied creatures darting through Her depths. She could flit in and out of the tiniest crevices, glide easily over shallow ledges, turn on a dime. In every living cell she seemed to explore anything and hear everything: the breathing of dolphins, the grunting of seals, the sizzle of rain splashing into the waves.

Apparently reassured by her newfound abilities, Toklat, after another careful glance at her, began to swim faster. She kept up with him easily, and soon felt yet another difference all through her body. It was subtle this time, but she understood what it was. They were heading out of the cove and into the open sea.

The ocean in all its vastness stretched before her. It was a limitless universe of which she, at long last, was a part. No boundaries could hold her back any longer, and joy ran through her veins with the sweet wild fire of heated brandy. Laughter rippled exultantly through her heart and her soul. Opening her mouth, she smiled widely, delightedly, in the dark blue depths.

She kept swimming, undulating along at Toklat's side, while new observations smote her like a thousand shining jewels.

Fish were no longer random gray angels and queen triggerfish, but *that* group of gray angels living at the edge of the reef, and *that* queen triggerfish who rested at night in a crevice beside the long tube sponges. She passed by a blue parrotfish, and her newly sharp ears heard the crunching as he grazed noisily on algae from a piece of limestone.

She began to recognize other sounds, too, sounds that were oddly and wonderfully familiar, as though she had heard them all her life.

There were the low-pitched grunts of a dozen or so groupers, the frying-pan crackle of snapping shrimp, the staccato sound of squirrelfish. Other noises rose and faded in the background, the varied concert of whistles, clicks, and flutters she had heard before. Only they were far louder now, and far more intimate.

She began to wonder where Toklat was leading her. He had said he was going to find Galen, but how could he know where Galen was? She looked deep inside herself, trying to summon up some sense of him, even if only the faintest awareness of his unmistakable presence.

Instead, she felt something else. A wash of dread spilled over her, so all-consuming that she wavered in her steady progress. Beside her Toklat pulled up short. He sensed it too! She could feel the rage in him, saw it surrounding him in an aura of dangerous red, and felt the worry in him, as well, as he looked over at her.

Wha-what's wrong?

The question burst out of her unbidden, startling her. She had thought the words rather than spoken them. But they were infinitely clearer than mere thought, and so strong she wondered how Toklat could possibly miss hearing her silent but loud question. He had heard it, and much as it obviously startled him, he was too intent to react to it overmuch, other than to respond in kind.

So you can mind-speak, after all. Good. We are in danger, Lady, great danger.

The Selkie's gravelly voice seemed to come from directly inside her head. It was an astonishing feeling, and if she had not been so worried by her own sense of warning and by his words, which only confirmed that premonition, she would have indulged in the wonder and strangeness of it more.

I feel it too, she told him. *But what is it?*

Not what, he replied grimly. *Who.*

He put a hand on her arm and drew her forward, swimming even faster. *We must hurry before they find us, if they haven't already discovered our presence, as we've discovered theirs.*

Infected by the urgency of his mind-spoken words, Meredith went with him unhesitatingly. As they raced ahead, she heard herself demand in that same queer way of communicating, *Who are you talking about, Toklat? Who means us harm?*

His dark gaze stabbed at her through the depths, and his answer was as urgent as his pace. He spoke only one word: *Anastas.*

CHAPTER
26

Anastas. Meredith glanced over at Toklat blankly, even as her legs pushed her forward with an instinctive powerful grace that she would have marveled at had she not been so preoccupied. The name was like an ice cold hand pressed upon her spine. Yet she did not know why; she had never heard it before.

Who is that? she demanded. *Why should he or she want to hurt me?*

The words Toklat sent into her head were as frigid as the icy feeling on her spine. *He is Galen's enemy, and mine. I suspect he will be yours, too, if for no other reason than that Galen loves you.*

Meredith was struck dumb. Involuntarily she slowed, causing the Selkie to whip around and glare at her impatiently. She raced to catch up. One thing about this way of communicating, she thought distractedly, was that you could easily swim and talk at the same time.

How do you know that? she wondered, more to herself than to Toklat. *Did Galen tell you?*

Her companion's reply was brief and to the point. *More or less, although he may not even realize it himself. But I know him. He loves you, Lady. Now keep hurrying. This is not the time to speak of such things.*

But Meredith could not be silent. *This man you call Anastas,* she persisted. *Is he the one who Galen thinks took the scroll?*

Yes.

The handsome but peculiarly expressionless face of the blonde man, the one who had told her his name was Stassi, infiltrated Meredith's mind. It was a sinister image, as ominous as smoke coiling out from a fire of diseased and unhealthy things.

That's who Galen warned me about!

And with good reason. Toklat's mind-voice was frustrated. *I was worried this was going to happen. I had hoped to find Galen before it did, but now . . .*

He threw a quick look behind him. *Faster,* he ordered. *We must go faster, Lady, if you can manage it.*

I can.

Meredith needed no urging to keep up. The thought of Stas—Anastas, the memory of the expression on his face when he and Galen had confronted each other that morning on the beach, filled her with dread. Galen had asked her, had pleaded with her really, to stay out of the sea, and she had disregarded him. She had not really had a choice; she'd *had* to do what she had done. Yet she was afraid, more afraid than she had ever been.

With her new awareness of the sea and all that moved within Her depths, she understood things with a clarity that had been denied her before. Then it had been only inklings, shadows of what she grasped now. Galen had had good reason for his request. She did not want to see Anastas again. Not ever. Galen had told her that he was dangerous. Now she knew, with gut-wrenching certainty, how right he was.

Suddenly she found herself thinking of Flijanou, remembering the old woman and grieving for her. She heard again her friend's voice on the tape she had been transcribing on the stormy night Galen had visited her. The words came back in Flijanou's creaky voice, as brightly as though Meredith were sitting in her dark little hut, sipping coffee and listening while the old woman expounded on her vast store of knowledge.

"The sea does not belong to us, you know, she only tolerates us. *We* are not her true children, no, not at all. Her true children, well, that is something else again."

Had the Greek woman known about the merfolk? She must have. Had she known the truth about Galen, too, even as she introduced them? Stunned, Meredith pondered both possibilities as she thrust through the depths beside Toklat.

Her body's ease in maintaining the astonishing speed reminded her of something that only added to her grief. In some inexplicable way, Flijanou's tragic death had been the catalyst that had set in motion the final forces driving her to the cove, and thus to the discovery of her heritage.

But at what cost? With a sense of horror, Meredith realized something else, comprehended it as positively as she had ever known anything in her life.

Anastas had killed Flijanou.

She could not have explained how she knew this, but she did. It was a fact, as irrevocable and undeniable as her new gills. For what reason, though? Why murder a harmless old woman? If she had been speaking normally, her voice would have been thick with sorrow and rage as she addressed Toklat.

Galen said that Anastas forfeited the right to belong to the mer-folk. What did he do?

Toklat's pace did not slacken one iota as he answered. *Among other things, he caused the murder of Galen's parents.*

Meredith's eyes widened. Shock upon shock upon shock. First poor Flijanou, then her own transformation, and now this. What else could possibly happen in this new reality that made light of all that had been, from the viewpoint of her old life, logical and sane?

Galen's reactions to the blonde man now made sense, and so did the evil that she herself had felt in him. The notion of murder and violence occurring among her ancient people jarred her. It was an alien idea, one that felt wrong, strikingly out of place within a civilization that she knew in her soul was far superior to anything ever produced upon the land. Yet she did not doubt Toklat's word. She had met Anastas, after all.

Why did he do such a thing, Toklat? she demanded. Her heart felt squeezed between her ribs, a painful throbbing mass of sympathy and anger as she thought of Galen. His mother and father murdered!

The Selkie did not answer her question. Instead he growled. It was a sound different from any he had made before in Meredith's hearing. It was not the mere rumble of disapproval made in response to some comment of hers, but something else entirely.

This was a sound of pure menace, so ferocious that even though they were immersed far below the surface of the sea and the growl was not directed at her, Meredith had the distinct sensation that the hairs on the back of her neck were rising. In a movement so swift that even her newly fabulous vision had trouble following it, Toklat darted behind her.

Keep back of me. The words that came from him were a snarl in her mind. *They are too many and too swift for us to out-run them. No matter what happens, stay behind me.*

Meredith whirled around, striving to see and sense what he obviously had. No sunlight brightened the waters at this depth. Only a single-shaded darkness the color of indigo surrounded them. They were about one hundred and fifty feet down, a depth the Selkie had insisted on. Even though they had left the more crowded waters near the coast of Karpathos, they would be less likely to attract the notice of Terrans this far down.

She strained her eyes, convinced she had glimpsed a shadow coming toward them. It was scarcely visible, nothing more than a black opacity against the indigo background, but she tensed, narrowing her eyes and peering around the bulky shape of Toklat, who had positioned himself determinedly in front of her.

No, she had not imagined it. There was a shadow out there, and another, and another. She stopped trying to count them when she saw how swiftly they were moving, and concentrated instead on trying to control the nameless fear licking along her veins, a fear that was eating away her newfound strength and pride like flames charring paper.

Toklat —

Heed what I told you, Lady. Stay back of me!

Toklat opened his mouth, exposing rows of teeth as pointed as daggers. His canines gleamed with an eerie phosphorescence in the monochrome depths: bone-white, long, and curved like the lethal weapons they were.

He roared, and though it should have come out soundlessly at this abyss, it did not. Or perhaps, Meredith thought, mesmerized by the sight of his fury, it was just her imagination. Yet the sound seemed to surround her, booming inside and outside her head with the resonance of a great bull seal challenging the rivals who had dared trespass on his own private strip of beach.

How dare you come skulking back to threaten me again! Toklat bellowed. *You tried to kill me before and could not. This time it is all of you who will die. For now my rage is even greater than it was before!*

Be on your way, Selkie, a cold and familiar voice said. *It is not you we want anymore, but the one who is with you. Let us have her—and you may swim on to wherever it is you were going, unharmed.*

Meredith could not repress a shudder. Though addressed to Toklat, the words had entered her head as well. She knew who had spoken: Anastas. She recognized that voice only too clearly. It was curious, she reflected irrelevantly, how this strange gift Toklat called *mind-speak* worked. A person's spoken voice sounded the same as his mental one, the one that vibrated inside her brain.

However, hearing the voice of Anastas, whether spoken or unspoken, was having an unexpected effect on her. She was still unnerved and deeply afraid, but something else was stirring inside her. She was amazed that she was feeling it now, in the midst of these events that were clearly beyond the scope of her fledgling abilities. What she was feeling was anger.

You're as deranged as a barracuda that's been gorging on coral, Toklat shouted in that same ferocious roar, *if you think I would leave this woman with you. And what could you possibly want with her anyway? She is of no use to you.*

I will decide, that bone-chilling voice replied calmly, *who is of use to me, and who is not.*

Meredith finally saw Anastas clearly for the first time. He undulated slowly into her field of vision, his unhurriedness advertising more blatantly than any words could have how confident he was. In the water he appeared different too. The danger she had sensed so vaguely in him on land was multiplied a hundredfold in the element to which he truly belonged.

He was naked, and his lean muscular body seemed elongated as it undulated through the water. He swam as Toklat did, and as did Meredith herself, arms at his sides so that his body formed one long sleek line propelled by powerful legs pressed closely together.

To Meredith, though, there was no beauty in him, as there was in Toklat. The sleek undulation that was so compelling in the Selkie, struck her as repulsive in Anastas. He seemed too white in these dark waters, and his long hair writhed behind him, like the snake his eyes had reminded her of the day she met him.

He was staring, not at Toklat, but at her. His eyes were exactly as she remembered: pale green, and with that peculiarly flat look of a reptile. They seemed even paler now in the sea's darkness, and they shimmered at her out of the shadows, glinting and shining like the gaze of a demon.

She was so bedeviled by that frightening gaze, it was a moment before she saw the others who were with him. Four of them, all men, lean and naked like their leader, although that was all she had time to notice before Anastas reclaimed her attention.

So, the blonde man said directly to her, *you have become one of us.*

Meredith's courage found her before she found it. *I am not one of you,* she said before she even realized she was sending out a response. *Nor will I ever be. You are evil things. Unclean. Not like Galen or Toklat. You don't belong in the sea.*

Toklat threw her a surprised admiring glance, but Anastas seemed not to have even heard her. *However did you manage it?* he mused. *It is most astonishing—and yet not entirely unexpected, given what I've read in this.* He tapped the bundle she now saw he was holding under one arm.

She knew instantly what it was. *The scroll!* she cried. *You stole it, you broke into my house—*

He interrupted her impatiently. *Of course I did. How else was I supposed to obtain it? You and your lover were hardly going to give it to me, were you?*

Meredith felt a surge of hatred. It came to life in her belly, stretching upward with fingers of flame until it burned out of her thoughts. *And how did you get it?* She flung the mind-spoken words out like hot coals. *By murdering a defenseless old woman who never harmed anyone in her whole life?*

Anastas beamed at her. *Why, Meredith, how perceptive you are.*

She wanted to kill him. She had never wanted to kill anyone before, but she did now, and so earnestly that in a dim though more rational part of her mind she was shocked at the passion of it. She had always thought the phrase "seeing red" was merely a figurative description. Now she discovered it was not. She could actually see a crimson haze before her eyes, and behind that haze, Anastas smiled at her.

Galen should have killed you the first time he ever saw you, she said.

Ah, but he did not. And now I have the scroll, and you. All he will have is regrets, and more than that, when I've finished with him. Anastas raised an arm and gestured at his silent companions. *We've wasted enough time,* he said curtly. *Take her.*

He wanted to get her away before Galen could discover them! The revelation flashed across her consciousness like a streak of lightning. In its wake she found herself issuing a call that was no more predicted than her understanding of Anastas's urgency had been. It burst out of her from some profoundly mysterious wellspring of need, not in mindspeak, but in some other, deeper form of communication.

Galen! she screamed. *Come to us!*

It was not a cry that was meant for those with her to hear. Yet it seemed as though Toklat sensed or heard some echo of it. His dark eyes questioned her, as for an instant his head swiveled toward her. But so did Anastas's.

I said, take her! the merman shouted, and beneath that angry command, Meredith heard a note of apprehension.

The four other mermen exchanged nervous glances but started to fan out and forward, in obedience to their leader's wishes. Only one of them hesitated, treading water uneasily, until a fierce look from Anastas drove him ahead too. They swam warily, Meredith noticed, as if they had tangled with the burly Toklat before and were not anxious to do so again.

Grimly Toklat watched them approach. His back was to her, but to Meredith it seemed as though he had grown larger and more menacing. She could almost catch glimpses of his seal shape hovering in a dim outline beyond his man form, almost imagine that he was bristling with threat, clothed in fur rather than hair. Distractedly she wondered why he did not change into his animal form; surely he would be swifter and more effective against multiple opponents that way.

I warn you. The Selkie's gravelly voice was so deep a growl, the words contained in it were almost inaudible. *I see that there are fewer of you this time. And you, with your so-called leader, who is too cowardly to face me himself, but must have others do his work for him. Some of you are going to die before I'm through. For your bellies are not in this fight, as they were the other time you faced me. You know that, and so do I.*

Another flurry of glances passed between the mermen as Toklat spoke. But scarcely had his fierce thought-words gone out than the merman who was closest to Meredith lunged forward.

His intention was obvious: to seize her while his companions kept Toklat occupied. But the Selkie was there before him. Shooting forward in a lightning motion, he slashed straight across the merman's throat with those long gleaming canines, then fell back into his protective position in front of Meredith.

Blood sprayed out from the merman's torn throat in a hideously beautiful spiral of crimson so dark that at this depth it looked almost black. It spread and fountained out around his body, forming terrible lacy patterns as he

clutched his stricken throat. Even Meredith, who knew little
of such things, could see at once that it was a mortal wound.

The wounded one's eyes fastened on hers. They were
huge with disbelief, agony and fear reflecting whitely in
their wide gaze. Another emotion was there as well, one
that startled her so much, she wondered if she had seen it
at all. Relief.

Then the man's eyes, though still open, lost their focus.
Blindly he grasped at his severed throat, convulsed once,
and went still. Meredith could almost see the life-force departing from him. The whole thing could not have taken
more than a handful of seconds.

Mind-voices erupted around her from the other mermen.
Gilkon!

Is he dead?

He has killed Gilkon!

Slashing through the babble rose the infuriated command
of Anastas. *Take her and kill that Selkie!*

At his words, something vast shook loose in Meredith.
Power seared through her in a great wave, and cresting
upon that wave was rage. Rage for Flijanou, and Galen and
his parents, and for the indomitable brave Toklat, who was
risking his life against hopeless odds in an effort to protect
her.

With the force of leaves being battered before the winds
of an oncoming storm, it drove away the dread and fear that
had held her so rigidly in place. Her legs propelled her forward in a single powerful kick, and she came up beside
Toklat.

Get back, he told her, though he dared not take his gaze
from the remaining mermen to glare at her, much less try to
enforce his order by shoving her behind him again.

Meredith ignored him. She would not hide timorously behind Toklat while he bloodied himself and perhaps died,
fighting to keep these murderers from her. There was

strength in her; she was only now beginning to realize how much, and she would use that strength.

She stared at Anastas and his followers, and the words she sent out were as clear and cold as a beam of winter moonlight. *One of you is already dead, so the odds have just gone down in our favor even more. And now, you have two of us to fight.*

Toklat stiffened. She could feel the impact of his shock and dismay surrounding her, but she knew he would not be able to take his attention away from his opponents to try to do anything about it.

The remaining three mermen were slowly getting themselves in hand, regrouping under the force of their blonde leader's harangue. Clearly, they were more terrified of him than they were of Toklat, despite the mute evidence of the Selkie's prowess in battle: the bloody corpse of the one called Gilkon, spread-eagled upon the current. However, their gathering of themselves seemed halfhearted, even resentful, a state of affairs that Anastas swiftly noticed.

Must I keep possession of the scroll and fight one-handed, as well? he snarled. *Go! Do as I bid you, or I'll rip your throats open myself.*

Still keeping a careful hold on the bundle against his chest, he used his free hand to push the body of the lifeless merman out of the way. The callous indifference of his action, both to the dead man and to his watching comrades, horrified Meredith. Perhaps the others thought so, too, or at least one of them did. He broke away from his companions and stared at his leader.

No, he sent, and Meredith heard the breathless fear in that one word. She could only guess at the effort his defiance cost him. *We keep doing your killing for you,* the merman went on. *And for it we keep dying ourselves. My brother is gone, Bron is gone, and now Gilkon. Soon we will all be dead, and I do not think it matters to you one scallop shell . . .*

His mind-voice trailed off, and Meredith suddenly no-

ticed Anastas. He was staring at the defiant one, and his
eyes resembled pale green coals. A terrible force was reaching out of those burning fireballs, and it sought to touch all
those around him, drawing them into its flames.

Inside Meredith, a deeply rooted instinct stirred, frantically whispering: look away, look away, don't meet his gaze.
She obeyed that inner voice without thinking, and from the
corner of her eye saw that Toklat had also averted his gaze,
although only from Anastas. He was still keeping a wary
eye on the three mermen. In the next moment she understood why.

Not only the one who had been speaking, but his companions as well were staring slack-jawed at Anastas.
Suddenly, as if a cord bound them all together, they turned
as one man. Meredith saw their eyes, wild and blazing, even
those of the merman who had tried to defy Anastas. It was
all she had time to notice before they threw themselves at
her and Toklat.

The Selkie's roar echoed through her mind. A strong
hand closed brutally around her arm, and a battle cry of her
own tore out of her thoughts. Enraged, not questioning the
strength with which she was able to do it, she jerked herself
free and shoved her attacker away. Determinedly he
whirled back to try to seize her again. Two hands clamped
down on his neck from behind and twisted. The sickening
wrench was accompanied by a bellow of fury that did not
sound like Toklat. It took Meredith a moment to realize
who it was.

Galen.

CHAPTER
27

Galen hurled away the merman—whose neck was clearly broken—like a pile of rags and wheeled to attack the two others, who were single-mindedly trying to kill Toklat. The Selkie already had his teeth sunk into the throat of one, and with another of those terrible, incoherent sounds of rage, Galen seized the other.

Blood was everywhere, staining the waters darker and blacker, as though a giant octopus were releasing flood after flood of ink from its jets. Blood still seeped from the mangled throat of Gilkon, and it gushed out of the mouth of the one whose neck Galen had broken and streamed from the throat of the merman Toklat was battling. So thick was it that it prevented Meredith from seeing who came at her next.

He was swift, swifter than thought itself, and he grabbed her with a strength as demonic as his eyes. Before her mind

could fully register what had happened, he was shooting off
through the blood-smeared water, dragging her with him.

Revulsion swept through her in a wave of fury and disgust. Almost immediately, it gave way to something far
more potent.

Release me! she ordered, and it was as if a voice other than
hers spoke through her mind. A voice that was incredibly
ancient, filled with a wealth of power and mystery beyond
understanding.

The force of it blew Anastas back from her as though a
pair of giant hands had laid hold of him and hurled him
through air rather than water. Meredith caught a glimpse of
his face as he tumbled backward, somehow managing to
keep his grip on the scroll. His expression was one of utter
and complete stupefaction.

The inexplicable force was still surging, though, and it
drove Meredith after him in a blind and fearless pursuit of
the scroll, which drew her like a beacon of shimmering light
in her mind.

But Anastas, his face still a study in stunned incredulity,
whirled and streaked off through the depths. Perhaps not
from her, she realized belatedly, but from Galen and Toklat,
who, having disposed of the last two mermen, had suddenly
realized she was nowhere to be seen.

It was a shock to see Galen racing toward her. He swam
in the same undulating fashion as Anastas and all merfolk,
but the movements that had looked sinister in Anastas were
beautiful in Galen, a melody of strength and grace and
speed that made her heart sing just to see it.

The eerie power was ebbing, leaving in its wake a queer
lassitude. Drifting in place, allowing the currents to push
her to and fro, she watched him approach and wondered
absently if she, too, looked so beautiful when she swam.

Galen reached her. Enfolding her in his arms, he pulled
her to him. She felt the pounding of his heart all through

her body, felt his thoughts, his life-force, his very blood and bones, seeming to merge with hers.

And all from a simple embrace. It was shattering.

What in the name of the Mother and all her waves are you doing here!

His mind-voice was like thunder in her brain, battering at her senses in a river of sound. His presence was an overwhelming force, stunning in its intensity. It was as different from Toklat's as a hurricane is from a rainstorm. Even Anastas's sinister force was eclipsed by it.

Was it because they were lovers that he had this effect on her? She stared at him mutely, the ability to mind-speak seeming to have deserted her.

She felt more tired than ever, though the ease with which her gills were continuing to protect her remained unchanged. Her eyes seemed to have grown even keener as she looked at Galen. His magnificent face and fierce blue eyes stood out as clearly to her as though they were gazing at each other under a sunlit sky.

Answer me! he demanded.

I've told you already, Toklat put in. *She came to the cove by herself, and by some means I can't begin to explain, changed herself to a merwoman. I tried to keep her from coming with me to find you, but she's stubborn. As stubborn as you are, Galen,* he concluded after a moment's reflection.

How? Galen's eyes had never left Meredith's. *How did you do it?*

Meredith finally found her mind-voice. *I don't know, not exactly anyway. It just happened. It's all so complicated ...*

Her thoughts were fading, and Galen gripped her in concern. *What's wrong?* he asked. *Meredith, what is it?*

She shook her head. *Nothing,* she sent with a touch of impatience. *I just feel a little tired, is all.*

Small wonder that she is, Toklat's husky mind-voice noted dryly. *After all that she's been doing.*

Galen was studying her. *He had you,* he suddenly shot at her, and by the way he uttered that pronoun, Meredith knew to whom he was referring. *How did you get away from him? Did he see us coming after him and release you?*

The tiredness was beginning to ebb, but she still felt dazed and strangely distant. She gazed at Galen and Toklat with a detached calm she did not understand herself.

He didn't release me, she explained, trying unsuccessfully to keep the weariness from her mind-voice. *Not willingly. I was so angry and so disgusted just at the touch of him. Then—then a power came up in me. It was like a huge force bursting all through me, and it pushed him away. I think he was as surprised by what happened as I was.*

Suddenly she remembered the scroll, and her detached feelings evaporated in the force of that remembering. Stricken, her gaze went from Galen to Toklat and back again. *The power sent me after him, after I pushed him away, to get the scroll. But he fled, and I couldn't get it. I'm sorry, I'm so sorry—*

Hush. Galen's thunderous mind-voice melted to a gentle rumble. *Don't concern yourself. You're safe from him now, and that's all that matters. We'll get the scroll back. But if he had succeeded in escaping us and taking you away with him . . .*

His face darkened, taking on a look so heated and uncompromising that Meredith nearly shuddered. *Well,* he finished briskly, *he didn't. And he won't get another opportunity to, not with me here beside you.*

She looked off in the direction Anastas had taken. The impact of the merman's attempted abduction was fading, but the memory of the scroll and the shimmering light it had sent toward her was more vivid than ever. She could not put it from her thoughts.

You have to follow him, Galen, she said urgently. *He has the scroll with him, I saw it. We have to get it back, we have to!*

We will. Galen's jaw set. *But I won't risk you in doing it.* He glanced at Toklat, who was treading water with fidgety impatience, plainly eager to be gone from there.

You're not risking me. She glared from him to Toklat. *Don't you understand? The scroll is calling me, it's almost like it's alive.* She stared at Galen pleadingly. *It's as though in some way, it's a part of me.*

I know that, philtate. I have learned more than you realize. Why do you think I showed up here when I did?

A hardness came over his features, calculating and cold. He looked utterly ruthless in that moment, and gazing at him, Meredith wished that Anastas could see him. It would certainly give the blonde merman pause if he did.

Anastas wants you, philtate, Galen went on. *Indeed, he has no choice. He must have you to unlock the scroll. He has discovered that without you it is of no use to him. What he does not know is that I have learned this as well. We do not have to go after him. He will come to us again, and that will be his downfall.* His mouth was like a dagger blade, a thin slash across his face. *When he returns to seek you, as he must, we will be waiting.*

Toklat nodded in approval. *I agree. He expects us to pursue him because he is the one who is outnumbered now. Alone, with no one to do his killing for him anymore.*

He cast a grim look of satisfaction behind him. Meredith followed his glance.

In the distance, the bodies of the slain mermen were floating awkwardly, their grace in the water having vanished along with their lives. Already they were being fought over by a bevy of sharks that had shown up quickly, lured by the rich odor of blood spreading through the water. Meredith could not repress a shiver of disgust intermingled with pity at the sight.

These mermen had unquestionably meant her and Toklat harm, yet had they not been forced into it by Anastas? At least one of them had found the courage to openly defy him, although he had still died for his pains. And in such a terrible way, with him now being torn to pieces by the razor teeth of the sea's most efficient predators. In a short time there would be no trace left of the mermen save some smears of blood and perhaps a few bones.

It was Anastas who should be suffering this fate, she thought savagely. Anastas whose flesh and bones should now be being ripped and crunched and swallowed whole. Anastas, and not these followers of his, who, though not blameless, had been manipulated into the attack that had killed them.

Misunderstanding the cause of her shiver, Galen reassured her. *They will not harm you, Meredith. Sharks are easily controlled, and they're too busy filling their gullets to bother with us, anyway.*

Anastas forced them, you know, she sent to Galen, as the three of them set off in the direction opposite to the sharks and their feast. *He made them attack Toklat and me. They didn't want to.*

Galen cast her a look of surprise, and Toklat grunted in assent. *It's true,* the Selkie said, although it obviously annoyed him greatly to say so. *Not that they still didn't deserve killing,* he hastened to add. *But if left to their own devices, I think they would have gone with the currents and let us alone. They didn't want to take me on a second time; their wounds looked scarcely healed from the first. But he called upon his powers and made them.*

Which reminds me. He peered sharply at Meredith. *You knew right off what he was about, Lady. How did you know to look away from him when he was casting his power?*

More to the point, Galen's mind-voice broke in, pensive and probing, *where did you find the strength? It takes a strong mind, whether among merfolk or Selkies, to resist one like him, much less for one who is a Terr—* He caught himself, and a sort of wonder spread over his face. *Ah,* he said softly. *But you are no longer. Are you?*

A great warmth and peace stole over Meredith. *No,* she told him contentedly, *I'm not.*

They swam on in silence, each occupied with his or her own thoughts. Finally, Meredith sent out a question. *Where are we going?*

It was Galen who answered. *To the abodes of my—our people. First, to the one that is the ancestral home of my clan.*

A thrill of excitement ran through her at his words. To see the merfolk! To enter the ancient places where they lived, places that already seemed familiar to her now that her ancestral memories were burgeoning to life and growing more powerful with every passing moment.

However, her eagerness was tempered by the thought of Anastas. Those pale demonic eyes ate at her, rising up in her mind like the miasma rotting vegetation leaves as it drifts out from a low-lying swamp.

But what about ... she began.

Galen cut her off, knowing immediately what she was about to ask. *I have already told you: he will follow us. He has to, or everything else he has done up until now will be meaningless.*

They descended deeper into the sea as night fell. Precisely how Meredith could sense in this eternal darkness that above their heads the day was ending was unexplainable, a mystery to her. Yet she knew that it was. She could picture the merciless sun dropping into the western horizon, staining the sea orange and purple and red as it disappeared.

They were traveling along nearly at the bottom of the Aegean, and it was some minutes before she thought about the fact that the pressure at this depth was not affecting her in the least. It came as no surprise to her that it did not. She found herself nodding a greeting to the creatures sidling past her along the sandy floor: dozens of pale joint-legged crabs and a multitude of shrimp and graceful sea horses.

A flounder, no more than twelve inches long and colored

as brightly as a peacock, startled her when it jerked out of the sand. It had blended so perfectly into the ocean floor she had not even noticed it. Another bottom dweller, a tiny octopus hidden in a deserted mollusk shell, bobbed out to stare at the three of them as they passed, then secreted itself once more when it saw they were too large to be edible.

Luminous spirals of bamboo coral caught her eye. She gazed at them in fascination, wondering why they pulsed with light—why, indeed, they glowed at all. Other corals, scores of them, entranced her equally with their beauty. It was like swimming through a vast underwater garden where the plants—although she knew that corals were actually animals—bloomed as if by magic, touched by a springtime in which the sun never played a part.

Gnarled green fingers of a sea whip floated on the bottom in the sapphire depths. Coral shaped like trees extended delicate polyps as they gleaned plankton from the wafting currents. An orange- and white-striped clownfish gaped at her as it nestled in the pink embrace of a writhing sea anemone.

Several score of small fish with lavender sides and yellow fins swam past a filigreed tracery of burning bush coral. Tentacles extended, its complex eyes and its speed proving its reputation as an efficient predator, a squid jetted by, shooting up through the depths to the azure waters overhead.

The school of lavender fish turned as a single creature and headed upward too. Toklat paused, marked their progress, then left his companions to race in pursuit, his body moving with the fluid grace of a natural hunter.

Galen glanced after him and gave Meredith a gentle nudge. *Toklat is hungry,* he said. *Let's follow him.*

He led her upward, though they still remained well below the surface of the waves. After watching the Selkie flash here and there, snatching his prey, Meredith turned her attention once more to all that surrounded her.

Night was as wondrous as day in the sea, she thought. She could dive down, then lean back and allow herself to surface faceup, enjoying the between-worlds feeling that came as the blue stars of sea-light washed over her face, blending in perfect harmony with the silver points of the distant constellations in the night sky. And in that distant sky a glittering half moon had risen, leading her to discover that in clear water, even at seventy or eighty feet down, a bright moon and a sky full of stars gave enough light to see by, even without the specialized vision of seafolk.

It was also possible to see the living light of the bioluminescence, the blue glow characteristic of hundreds of small sea organisms. She glanced behind her, dazzled by the glowing wake she and Galen and Toklat were leaving as they swam along a reef face.

It's so beautiful, she sent in a mind-whisper to Galen, and he nodded.

There is a place we call the Phosphorescent Bay that is even more beautiful than this, he told her. *We named it that because the one-celled creatures who live there are so brilliant, they cover moving fish and people with flashing blue sparkles at night.*

Toklat had returned to them, chewing busily as he swallowed the last of his catch. *I know the place,* he said, pragmatic as always. *It's a good spot for hunting. One can never go hungry there at night, that's for certain.*

He gestured at the fish still flitting overhead. *Aren't you hungry?* he asked, directing his question more at Meredith than at Galen. *With what lies ahead of us, it's important to have the strength that comes only from having food in one's belly.*

His words made Meredith suddenly aware of the hollowness in her own stomach. She was hungry all right, starved, in fact. Galen glanced at her, and she understood without his having to ask that he was wondering if she would eat as he and Toklat did. She returned his look with some irritation. Of course she would. Was she not one of them now?

Five large silver-scaled fish with luminous eyes were passing by, arching their gleaming bodies with stately elegance as they traveled on their own search for food. With an ease and speed that was almost negligent, Galen captured one of them.

The fish writhed, but its struggles were cut short by Galen setting his teeth firmly into the spot where the base of its neck joined its spine. Skillfully, with teeth and hands, he filleted the long silver body and held out a chunk of the raw flesh to her.

There was an almost challenging look in his eyes as he offered it to her. She met the challenge boldly, taking the fish from him, her eyes remaining on his. He had left the scales on, but the flesh was still easy to get at. Hunger surged up in her with a primeval force, and she felt eager saliva fill her mouth. She took a big bite, then another.

The fish tasted sweet and tender. It was really no different from the Japanese delicacy sashimi, and like everything else since she had awakened in the pool of the Cave of Secrets, it felt natural and completely right.

Briefly she wondered what they must look like to an observer. Two humans and one who only looked human treading water deep below the surface of the sea, ripping at the raw flesh of a fish so freshly taken, the life in it was practically wiggling as it went down their throats.

She put the thought from her mind. Such speculations belonged to the old world, a world that was no longer hers. She felt not the slightest regret that it was not.

Toklat watched her eat with obvious approval. He himself was engaged in devouring the piece Galen had offered to him, even though he had already eaten a number of the small fish he had pursued a few minutes earlier. It was, as he explained to Meredith, always a good idea to eat whenever food was available, for one never knew where his next meal might come from.

When their appetites had been satiated on the large fish, they continued on their journey. All through the long night they traveled, stopping periodically to rest but only at the insistence of Galen and Toklat, who were both convinced Meredith could not maintain such a grueling pace without occasional letup.

In truth, she found the rest stops, short as they were, more than a little welcome. She was growing tired, although it was a good tiredness, the kind that comes from the exertion of new strengths and abilities.

Indeed, she would have been lost in wonder and exultation over the entire journey, were it not for the ever-present stain of Anastas. He cast a pall over her, and over the magnificence of this trip she was taking. He defiled the entire sea. His very existence was a blemish in the midst of all this beauty.

"Anastas killed Flijanou," she told Galen during one of their stops, which they took on the surface.

She had grown so used to the gift of mind-speak that it felt peculiar to speak in her normal voice again. It was deep night and they were far out to sea. Meredith was lying in the wet warmth of Galen's arms while he floated upon the gentle wash of the night swells. Toklat lay stretched out nearby, utterly at his ease, fast asleep.

Meredith continued, "That's how he found the way to my house and the scroll. He must have pried everything she knew about me out of her, and then murdered her."

It hurt just to say the words, and the memory of Flijanou rose to haunt her. Grief stabbed through her, but it was a dry pain, marking even more profoundly than her eating of the raw fish how greatly she had changed. She could no longer cry for Flijanou; she would never shed tears again.

Galen's expression was compassionate and angry, but strangely unsurprised. Or perhaps it was not strange, Meredith speculated. Who would know better than Galen what Anastas was capable of?

"Yes." Galen's voice was serious and sad. "That would be his way. Poor kindhearted woman. It was an unworthy death she suffered. She was loyal to us who are of the sea, and she tried hard to help us. She came of a family that has been our ally for centuries beyond centuries. There are few—very, very few—Terrans who know of our existence, and now, there is one less."

He sighed, and when he spoke again, the compassion had vanished from his voice, leaving it hard as the underwater seamounts that loomed far beneath them. "I shall honor her memory—and I shall see to it that she is avenged."

Meredith studied him, watching the blue and black shadows driven by the currents wash over his stern features. "Why did he kill your parents, Galen?" she asked quietly.

He did not answer her at once. "He wanted power," he finally said in a voice heavy with remembering. "To rule over the people of the sea without limits. But he was not in harmony. With Mother Ocean, Her people, or himself. It is a rare thing among us for one to be born as he is, with this soul-sickness festering inside him. It makes it even worse when the one so afflicted is heir to the throne of the mer-folk."

Stunned, she stared at him. "Anastas was to be a—a king? I can't believe that you or anyone else among the mer-folk would allow it!"

The idea of it made her sick, set her stomach churning with horror. To take someone so unbalanced, yet with such power living inside him as she had sensed in Anastas, and place him in a position of leadership and influence! It was unthinkable, terrifying.

"We didn't," Galen explained coldly. "However, he was the firstborn of our king and queen. Son or daughter, the firstborn always inherits the rulership. Unless it can be proven that in doing so there would be a danger to the well-being of our people. In his case," he finished grimly, "there was."

Toklat stirred and came awake in time to hear what Galen had just said. "And that was only the beginning," the Selkie said darkly. "It was after he was notified of the decision by King Lugarion and the Elders that Anastas committed the deeds that got him and those you saw with him today banished from the abodes and lives of all merfolk. *I* thought he and his followers should have had their lives taken from them, as they took the lives of Galen's parents. But they were banished, instead. The worst thing that can happen to one of them, they always say. Isn't that so, Galen?"

Galen gave a wordless nod of assent, and brooding on all she had just learned about this tragedy, Meredith silently agreed.

Having been awakened to her heritage, she understood with every beat of her heart the deep and ancient links that bound the sea people to one another. She could imagine nothing worse than having those bonds severed, than being rejected, driven away, forced to live apart from the warmth and connecting closeness of a way of life older than time.

The sea was such a beautiful kingdom, she thought, but for those exiled from kin and abode it must have been a realm filled with loneliness and regret. The face of the banished merman whose throat Toklat had torn open suddenly appeared in her mind's eye. She clearly remembered the inexplicable look of relief that had come over his features as death reached out and took him. Now she understood that expression. It must have been a blessing to him to be able to die at last.

She gazed up at Galen's stony face. She could feel his tension and his pain. His body was rigid against hers, though his powerful arms cradled her as gently as ever. The same arms and hands that had so savagely and effortlessly broken the bodies of the mermen who had attacked her. The burden of his parents' loss had not left him. It probably never would.

"I'm sorry," she said, aching at the inadequacy of the words. "I wish I could have known them."

He met her eyes, accepting her sympathy with a sad smile. "I think they would have ... appreciated you," he said thoughtfully, then his expression changed. "But the time for grieving is past. My mother and father are free from harm now. They have transitioned to a new plane of existence, another world. It is those who are left behind to live in this world who need our concern now."

Meredith was silent. His words had made her think again of Anastas—no difficult task, for he was never very far from her thoughts. Where was he? Why had he not come after them yet?

She dreaded another confrontation with the blonde merman, but the tension engendered by not knowing, by waiting for him to appear, could hardly be worse. She wondered how Galen and Toklat could be so calm and patient about it.

As a matter of fact, she found herself wondering about a great many things: the power that had exploded within her when Anastas seized her, the link between her and the scroll, the way it had called to her.

Most of all—she turned her head on Galen's broad chest and stared out over the silver-black realm of her new home—she wondered how and when this would finally end.

CHAPTER
28

Dawn arrived, heralded by faint slashes of pink over the eastern horizon that soon turned a bloody red as the sun gained strength. The morning stretched itself out into a long flame-bright day, then gave way to another night. And still Meredith, Galen, and Toklat traveled on.

Their way had led them around the last of the Dodecanese Islands and past Crete, that large island, steeped in history, that bestrode the Mediterranean and the Aegean, forming a gateway to both. All the while, they moved along well below the surface, for once dawn had broken overhead, none of them were eager to be glimpsed by any early fishermen who might be about.

With an odd sense of reluctance, Meredith had undulated after Galen and Toklat as they skirted Crete and pushed on, drawn by the great riverlike currents that guided them into the rippling blue infinity waiting beyond.

Her companions were delighted, relieved to be freed from the constraints of the many islands of the Aegean, and invigorated by the limitless depths that surrounded them as they burst out of the smaller sea. Meredith, though, hesitated, struck by persistent pangs of regret that would not leave her.

The Greek islands were well behind them, and the coast of Turkey that lay so near to Karpathos had already been passed long ago. It was time to go on, to leave the old world behind and enter the next phase of the astonishing new life she had gone after so determinedly.

Yet, though she had embraced this life openly, with exultant joy, it was still hard to leave behind the security of the Aegean, this gentle sheltering sea with its palette of sun-washed islands splashed over a brilliant blue canvas of waves. She knew she would never forget these waters. The Aegean, beautiful Greek sea of myth and legend. The lovely land-dotted body of water would always be to her the place where she had been given back to herself.

They had left that sea, however, for the wide expanse of the Mediterranean, of which the Aegean was only a small arm. Meredith was rapidly learning just how small indeed.

To be in a true sea, not one bounded and hemmed in by bits and pieces of land, was an utterly different experience. The Mediterranean, too, was an inland sea, bounded by Africa, Asia, and Europe. But oh, the vastness of it! It left Meredith awed and humbled, even intimidated. She was suspended in a huge, eternally moving openness, an ethereal infinity in all directions.

Above her, below her, on every side, she was immersed in a translucent blue world, indescribable in commonplace terms. Cerulean? Sapphire? Any words in any language seemed hopelessly inadequate. There was no way to describe what open-ocean, deepwater blue was like. It seemed to glow with its own light. They went deeper, and the blueness became distant, a dome over her head that shaded to blue-gray, then blue-black.

And the Mediterranean was still a sea, Meredith reminded herself dazedly. What would it be like to journey into the immense reaches of the Pacific Ocean, or the mighty Atlantic, which the Mediterranean connected to by way of the Strait of Gibraltar?

They were swimming in single file now, with Galen forging eagerly ahead. Meredith was next, and Toklat brought up the rear, his dark gaze sweeping back and forth as he searched for some sign that they were being followed.

In spite of the haste that clearly weighed upon him now that they were in his home waters, Galen dropped back frequently to check on Meredith and speak with her. His eagerness was tinged with anxiety, for it was deep in a remote part of these great waters that their destination awaited.

His ancestral abode, he had explained to her, lay near the Strait of Gibraltar. The merfolk, though, he'd added, had another name for that waterway. They simply—and appropriately, Meredith thought—called it the approach to the Western Mother.

Galen shared other knowledge with her as well, perhaps as much to take his own mind off what he might find in his abode as to instruct her. She listened avidly, her brain soaking up everything he said as tenaciously as the honeycomb sponges he had told her were common in this sea and which merfolk found a variety of uses for.

Millions and millions of years ago, this sea—which merfolk called the Inland Mother—had dried up completely, he told her as they swam. Then, at the end of some distant ice age, great waterfalls had cascaded from the continent of Europe down to the Mediterranean basin thousands of feet below.

Even now, Toklat added, swimming up to join in the conversation, one could see places on the cliffs that descended to the bottom of the sea, showing where water from the land had caused erosion.

Their description kept Meredith silent for some time as she swam along, trying to imagine the long-ago scene created by Galen's words. Those massive waterfalls, paths of water so vast they would rebirth an entire sea, roaring into the parched basin. The rising sea level when that water poured over the Strait of Gibraltar and refilled the vast desert that would one day become the Mediterranean, probably the oldest of all the seas.

What a sight it must have been, one that could only be speculated about, for no human eyes would have been present to witness it in that far distant time. But even the wonder of that ancient and momentous event was eventually eclipsed in the learning of other things, things of a more immediate nature. Such as how to find food.

They were deep in the Mediterranean and Meredith caught herself continually marveling at the lavish use of colors in the denizens who inhabited what was virtually a monochromatic world. Fish in their gaudy finery were everywhere, cruising in leisurely majesty or racing by in bursts of color, all engaged in the one basic rule of the sea: eat or be eaten.

They especially thrived in the areas where upswelling currents brought nutrients from the sea bottom into the sunlit upper waters. As they swam at the same depth, Meredith discovered that she not only possessed, as Galen and Toklat did, the ability to catch and eat the fish while still undulating, but that she had the inclination to do so.

The Selkie was a pure eater of flesh, disdaining anything other than living prey, freshly caught. But the merfolk followed a more varied diet, just as their Terran cousins did. They were omnivores, harvesting the sea's bounty in the form of plants, in addition to eating flesh.

Galen pointed many of these plants out to Meredith, telling her what was safe to eat and what wasn't, where to find the best places for the richest gathering of life, whether sea cucumbers, scallops, shrimp, or lobsters, a myriad of different kinds of fish, or the great waving forests of kelp and sea grass.

Meredith had other questions besides those concerning food. She sensed Galen's reluctance to speak of so many matters that were still a mystery to her, but as they drew steadily nearer to his abode, she finally screwed up her determination to do so. Toklat had darted off in pursuit of a popular source of food for merfolk and Selkie alike—a school of giant clawed shrimp common to the Mediterranean—when she asked Galen something that had been nagging at her for some time.

Galen—they were undulating about sixty feet below the sunlit surface, and she spoke in her increasingly natural mind-voice—*according to the legends, Selkies are supposed to be able to change back and forth between seal and human ...*

She could see the tension in Galen as he turned his face toward her. *And you are wondering why Toklat has not done so,* he finished for her.

Yes.

His features in the uncertain illumination were as grim as his mind-voice. *Toklat has good reason not to change. The plague that has come amongst the merfolk has affected the Selkies, too, only in a different way.* He paused. *When they seek to transform themselves, they cannot. Instead, they mutate into some horrific combination of the two shapes, human and animal, and they die in terrible agony.*

Dear God. She stared at him in horror. *I didn't know. He never said—*

Of course he didn't. It is not his way. Selkies live in the here and now far more than we do, Meredith. But he has a great stake in this, not only for himself, but for all his people. He is the leader of the Selkie folk since his own father died trying to transform himself.

It is his responsibility to save his people, and it is an obligation he takes most seriously. That's why he's been with me in all this, and that's why the scroll is as important to him as it is to us. We both think that the knowledge it contains will cure his people as well as ours.

Remembering what Galen had told her in the Cave of Secrets, that the merfolk who fell ill lost their gills, Meredith felt sick with apprehension. She found herself wondering whether she was sick with mental exhaustion as well. As exhilarating as her momentous Change had been, it had not been without strain. She was realizing only now just how incredible a strain all these events had put her under.

There had been so much to take in, to adjust and adapt to. And now, the burden of what was happening to her new-found kin was descending with an inexorability that refused to be ignored. It pressed down upon her with its full force, made all the more heavy by the look on Galen's face.

What about our people, Galen? she asked.

Galen threw her a quick glance, and the haunted look in his eyes slashed through her heart.

As I told you, he began, *the illness, or plague, whatever you want to call it, attacks our gills, causing them to close up. We may not turn into horrible distortions of ourselves, like the Selkies, at least as far as I know. But our fate is no better for all that.*

Without our gills, we are as helpless as Terrans, we who travel as freely into the deep abysses of the oceans as do our allies and brethren, the whalefolk. We live much of our lives in the great depths we call the Midnight Sea; most of our abodes are located there. A man or woman so afflicted cannot hope to survive, not for any length of time.

But ... Meredith concentrated fiercely, trying with controlled desperation to find some flame of hope, no matter how faint. Something that would provide at least a flicker of faith that this situation could be dealt with, regulated, until a cure could be found. *Even if people's gills are gone, couldn't they just stay in the abodes while we try to find a way—*

No, Meredith. His mind-voice was flat and final, leaving her no illusions. *Now that you are one of us, you must learn this for yourself. Our gills, our ability to withstand the cold and the great pressure of the lower depths, all of these are interconnected, woven together as tightly as the spaces in a honeycomb sponge. If one is affected, they are all affected.*

She was silent. *Has anyone died yet?* she finally made herself ask. She dreaded the answer he might give her, but there was no way she could not ask the question.

He shook his head, his gaze going to a group of sleek blue-gray shapes far off in the distance, beyond the great dark length of a canyon slashing down into the lower depths. They were dolphins, Meredith realized. Their intelligence flitted into her mind, a sleek and graceful intellect that matched their gleaming bodies. Thoughts, as swift and glittering as quicksilver, reached out to touch her consciousness, and dazzled, she thought, Oh, they're like us!

The dolphins flicked their tails, and she felt the exchange of greetings that flowed back and forth over the canyon that separated them from Galen and herself. Then they wheeled with joyous silvery grace and disappeared into the depths. A moment later, they shot upward, heading for the surface until their bodies broke through the glittering dome above.

Galen exhaled, his breath sending a plume of bubbles out into the shadows. Three groupers, so massive each one must have been fully five feet long, were swimming toward them, their huge round mouths gaping open. Galen steered Meredith aside to let them pass, and when they had, moving with stately though ugly majesty, he exhaled again.

In the abodes, I don't know how many of our kin, if any, have died. I left when the disease first appeared in order to seek out you and the scroll. But of Anastas's followers, two have transitioned from this world. I watched one of them as he died. It is not a pleas-

ant way to end one's time in this plane of existence. I care nothing for the fate of those who chose to follow that one, but I worry that those who were sick when I left may have died as well.

Suddenly his hand reached out, tightening on her arm. Meredith felt heat, like a rope of fire, flash from his flesh to hers, binding them together. Her eyes met his in the gloom, and she saw pain reflected there, along with terrible worry.

Now you are exposed to the danger too, he sent out, his mind-voice husky and raw with that pain. *You could become ill—*

No more so than you or Toklat, she reminded him.

He shook his head, scarcely seeming to hear her. *You should not have come. You should have stayed where you were at least reasonably safe. Why, philtate, why did you do this thing?*

Galen. She put out her other hand and laid it against his face. *I had to. I thought you understood that. There are powers, forces, moving inside me. I had no choice.*

He sighed. *I know. But you should not have done it alone. You should have waited for me, let me help you.*

I couldn't. Her mind-voice was calm and emphatic, reflecting a sureness deep within herself. *This was something I had to do myself. And have you already forgotten that you didn't want to acknowledge that I was really descended from the merfolk? You would never have stood by and let me dive into the sea, to live or die as She willed it. You would have used the Breath of Life, and I would be exactly where I was before: living on the land and not belonging there, locked away from a heritage I didn't understand, that I could look at but never share. I would have rather died than go on like that.*

Galen's jaw tightened. *Meredith, my dearest love, you still might. So might we all.*

Cleonith the Elder shifted her weight from one foot to the other as she stared out the great window at the eerie vista of the Midnight Sea.

The abode of Galen's clan was situated near one of the warm-water vents that abounded at many deep levels throughout the realms of the Mother. Near these vents, which often appeared at depths of eight or nine thousand feet, although this particular vent was located at only a few thousand, one could see bizarre forms of life. Giant clams, pale crabs, mysterious white threadlike worms and dandelion-shaped creatures, as well as tube worms—bright red worms, some nearly as big around as a man's wrist, encased in tubes as lengthy as eight feet—clustered on the seafloor near the vent.

Most beautiful—and Cleonith's favorite sight when visiting Galen's abode—was the view out of this particular window. Once, in the long-ago days of her youth, she had spent some time wandering the land Terrans called England. She had seen there what she considered to be one of their more magnificent creations: the famed English rose garden. She had privately named this place, where hundreds and hundreds of red-plumed tube worms grew in vivid and wild profusion, the Rose Garden.

As she watched, crabs tiptoed up to the giant tube worms in her garden and snipped off large bites before the worms could retreat back into their shelters. The crabs were slowly but steadily wearing away at the vitality of their vivid and beautiful prey, sustaining themselves as all sea creatures did, by devouring the strength of another.

It was no less inexorable, Cleonith thought, than the steadiness with which the plague was destroying her people. Sneaking up on them and eating away first their gills, then their very lives, even though they had retreated into their abodes, hiding from it like the tube worms hiding in their shelters from the forays of hungry crabs.

Only the tube worms, given enough time, could regrow themselves. Could the merfolk do the same? Increasingly, Cleonith feared not.

The jungle of strangely glowing life gave her no joy this day. Indeed, watching the unending cycle of eater and eaten, utterly merciless, and at the same time, so utterly beautiful, turned the direction of her thoughts into darker and darker waters.

Where were Galen and Toklat? Had they succeeded in their task? Or, as some of her fellow Elders were beginning to suggest, had the plague struck both of them down so that neither one would ever return?

Cleonith did not want to believe that; she could not bring herself to believe it. "No," she whispered aloud. "It cannot be so. They are coming back with good news, with hope for us. I know it."

"Do you, Cleonith?"

The question came from Satera, another Elder, who had seen Cleonith standing by the window and walked down the long corridor to join her.

They had known each other a long time, for uncounted eons, in fact. Gazing at the other woman, Cleonith saw that her sister-friend's lean face was shadowed with weariness and strain, as were the faces of all of them. As was hers, Cleonith knew, if she were to bother to look in a mirror.

"The souls of two more have departed with the dawn tide," Satera said gravely, not waiting for an answer to her question. "Firta and Toomi. First one and then the other, within a few moments of each other. They were mate-bonded, so perhaps it was to be expected that they would go together."

Cleonith's head bent under the weight of this news, lowering on her slim neck as if even the burden of her thick silver hair was too great. "Ah," she breathed, then lifted her hands, palms open. "May they transition in peace and joy to the next plane," she murmured, reciting the ritual words that sent deeper and longer knives into her heart every time she said them.

"There was nothing peaceful or joyful about their transition from this one," Satera said. Her hoarse voice was edged with the sharpness that came from being completely helpless in the face of tragedy. "Until their last breaths, they struggled, moaning and gasping about the terrible stones crushing their vitals. It was the pressure that killed them. We are too far down—"

"I know that, Satera." Cleonith's own voice was ragged. "Have I not seen the same thing myself, until my soul is torn and bleeding with the pain of it?"

Satera nodded. "I know you have, sister-friend." She paused, then continued tiredly, "Consider this, though. Firta and Toomi were young and strong. Only in the first few hundred of their tides. Personally, I would have guessed that they would be spared, that others would be afflicted before them."

"Yes," Cleonith muttered. "I would have thought so too. But then, look at the youngling Alaric. He was the first to sicken, followed by MoAt, who was also strong. Plainly, this thing which attacks us is no respecter of youth."

"Exactly. Which is why, sister Elder, I think we must face the fact that Galen may not be returning to us. This evil sickness may have captured him in its grip, and if he was out in open sea when it did, there would have been no hope for him. None at all."

"That's not what happened." Cleonith said this with more conviction than she actually felt. She said it nonetheless, for if she could convince Satera, then it was possible she could convince herself as well. And perhaps she could even persuade herself that the pain prickling off and on inside her was only her imagination, that it was not the first stirring of something ominous coming to life.

"Why do you say that?" Satera demanded. "How can you be so sure?"

"For one thing, he was with Toklat. If something like that took place, Toklat would have returned to tell us of it."

Satera was unconvinced. "Unless he fell ill himself. Don't forget that the Selkie folk are in as evil straits as we are."

Cleonith shook her head. "Yes, but Toklat would not be so foolish as to try changing his shape. Not after seeing what happens to those who tried. His own father among them."

Satera brooded, her hands clenching and unclenching as she stared out the long broad window. "So, sister-friend," she said at last, after several lengthy moments had passed. "What would you have us do, you who are the oldest and wisest among us?"

Cleonith set her jaw. "Go on waiting. And have faith. At this point, there is little else we can do."

Galen and Toklat were leading Meredith ever farther and ever deeper into the Inland Mother. And their anxiety was growing along with their pace, becoming more palpable with every fathom they put behind them.

What is it? she finally demanded. *Something is terribly wrong and you're not telling me. What is it?*

It was Galen who answered. *Mother Ocean is too empty,* he told her. His mind-voice was somber and pulsating with concern as he stared ahead of him.

Meredith glanced around her. To her the sea appeared anything but empty. Everywhere she looked life in some form called out to capture her gaze, a profusion of beauty and movement and color that still—even after all this time—left her mind reeling.

I don't understand, she said, her eyes drawn momentarily by a huge school of small fish massing above her in a cascade of sunlit gold. *How can you say She's empty?*

Because it's true. There was a tinge of admonition in Galen's tone. *Look around you again, philtate, and think. Where are the rest of our people?*

And mine, Toklat put in. *There are no Selkies anywhere to be seen.*

Speechless, Meredith stared at both of them. The simple and obvious fact that they had just pointed out made the realization all the more wrenching. There *were* no merfolk, and while she could understand why she might not think about seeing more legendary beings like Selkies, she was ashamed that she could be so oblivious to the presence—or absence, as it were—of her own kin.

Where are they? she asked, keenly chagrined.

We don't know. Galen met her eyes, and his face was suddenly gaunt, drawn with the worry that was gnawing at him. *Merfolk wander all through these waters, and through the depths of every other sea and ocean that make up the Great Mother.*

He exchanged a troubled glance with Toklat, whose own expression was filled with painful anxiety. Unconsciously, they all three increased their speed as Galen went on. *Never, in all my centuries, have I traveled the Inland Mother and not felt the presence of other mer-men and -women acknowledging me. There are only two possibilities as to where they could be. One is that they have all gone into the abodes ...*

And the other? Meredith asked fearfully, when he did not continue.

The other—his mind-voice was almost inaudible—*is that we are too late and that our people, at least in the Inland Mother, are no longer among the living.*

No, she whispered in disbelief. *That can't be the reason. There has to be something else, some other logical explanation for why no one is around to greet us.*

This was unacceptable! She could not, would not, believe that she had gone through all that she had, only to discover that her newfound kin were dead. No! Her heart, with all its force, urged her to deny what Galen had told her, to deny the fear she saw in Toklat's dark eyes.

When she looked into Galen's face, though, there was no deceiving herself. The truth was there, naked and irrefutable. She asked no more questions, and when Galen and Toklat picked up the pace again, she undulated on as fast as she could at their sides.

CHAPTER
29

Another night came on, but neither Meredith nor Galen nor Toklat took any notice of it. They were descending, going down and down and down, heading into the final approach to Galen's abode.

A host of new sensations surrounded Meredith as they dove into enigmatic depths that until a few days earlier, she could never have hoped to see, even with the aid of scuba-diving gear. Even now these deep realms were visited by only a few of those creatures who also spent their lives on or near the surface of the sea. Beings such as the venerable and mighty whalefolk, whom she longed to meet but had yet to encounter, or the joyous and quicksilver dolphins.

The featureless deep blue of the open ocean was gone. The sense she had experienced so often on this journey, that she was almost suspended in space, had been replaced by the feeling that she was now truly entering another land. An entire continent, hers to explore. One whose only physical difference from the lands above and beside the sea was that this land was covered by salt water rather than air.

The friendly coral reefs with their panorama of denizens were gone. But the deep sea floor—the abyss beyond the slopes—was a varied terrain, with plains, steppes, mountain ranges, sea mounts, depressions, and trenches, and a whole new profusion of life.

It was cold in these depths, a deep, bone-numbing chill that wound freezing tentacles around the blood, turning the hot life fluid in a person's veins to liquid ice. Or at least, it should have. Despite all the marvelous changes she had already experienced, Meredith was still shocked to realize that her internal structure had altered so dramatically that even this terrible difference in temperature, one that no human should be able to stand, affected her not at all.

Then she got her first sight of Galen's abode, and all thoughts of the cold or of exploring the sea land around her vanished, swallowed up by the strength of her reaction.

It loomed out of the darkness, a great mass of rock, a gigantic mountain lit from within by hundreds upon hundreds of lights that flickered orange and yellow and gold in this eternal night. To other eyes, such as those of Terrans, it might have looked ominous, forbidding. But to Meredith, the abode was beautiful. And enormous, far bigger than she could have ever conceived of in her wildest imaginings. She paused in her swimming, drifting a little in the deep currents, overwhelmed by the sight of what lay before her.

Only one word stood out in her mind as she stared. One coherent thought, bursting fiercely across her consciousness like a flame in the night. Home.

Galen's big hand closed around her forearm, and casting her an impatient, preoccupied look, he urged her forward. He and Toklat were hurrying, increasing their speed even more as they undulated toward their destination.

Eagerness mixed with apprehension flowed out from their minds, surrounding Meredith and permeating her own thoughts as pervasively as the dense darkness and cold. Yet their anxiety was matched no less by her own state of mind.

Her first reaction to seeing the abode had given way to something else. Uneasiness was swallowing her up like the giant mouths of groupers. Her flesh tingled with the crawling intensity of it. The deep and all-pervading disquiet ran through her with growing strength as they drew nearer to the abode, and try as she might, she could not shake it.

Yet she wanted with all her heart to enter that massive place that beckoned and called to her. Oh, how she wanted to!

Out there in the blackness, the mysterious abode was speaking to her, signaling to her every instinct that here was where she belonged. At the same time, though, her heart had begun battering against the confines of her rib cage, and she found herself shivering for reasons that had nothing to do with the cold.

Something awful waited behind those rock walls lit by countless dancing lights. She knew it with a terrible certainty. Her sudden fear of going inside that awesome structure to confront that horror was as strong as the burgeoning need that made her long to do just that.

Was Galen's fear true, after all? Were their people indeed dead? No! her pounding heart cried. But then she looked at Galen. Her eyes pierced the eerie blackness as easily as they had the sunlit upper levels, and there was no denying what she saw.

The same alarm that was coursing through her veins was mirrored in Galen's face. Not on his features—they were set and hard, completely controlled—but in his eyes.

She touched the hand he still had on her arm. *Something is wrong,* she sent urgently. *I feel it, something is wrong—*

He squeezed her arm reassuringly, but the frightening ex

pression in his eyes did not change. *I know,* he sent back soberly. *I feel it too.* He threw a quick look at Toklat. *And so does Toklat. But come, we must go in. We'll discover nothing, for good or ill, if we stay out here.*

Meredith steeled herself. He was right. And whatever was waiting for them in the abode, she was a part of it. It was inescapable, as much as the forces that had driven her from Karpathos to the cove.

Somewhere inside her head, a distant echo of the power that had surged forth to drive Anastas away from her stirred. *Your fate,* that faint voice whispered, *your fate awaits you. Go to it. Go.*

She shivered again, but Galen and Toklat, preoccupied with their own thoughts, did not notice, and so she said nothing else. She swam with them into a vast outer chamber set into the very face of the mountain, and watched with a strange emotion she suddenly identified as familiarity, as Galen swept over to a trio of levers set into the rock of an inner wall. He pulled one of them.

There was a grinding roar behind them, and the massive outer pieces of the mountain—a rock that was really two doors, she saw—began to groan shut. It should have startled, even frightened her, but it did not. Instead, she floated upright, watching in fascination as the mighty portals ground ponderously toward each other, sending out a rolling thunder that vibrated over the sea floor and through every fiber of her body.

There are other openings set into the rock above us, Toklat said to her. *The chamber will begin emptying itself of water as soon as the doors have closed all the way. When that is done, we can go into the abode.*

She nodded. *I know,* she replied, feeling bemused. *I don't know how I know, but I do.*

The Selkie scrutinized her, his eyes glowing like orange

coals in the unrelieved gloom. *Lady*, he said at last, *you have not yet ceased to amaze me.*

She sighed. *Myself either*, she said as Galen arrowed back across the chamber to rejoin them.

The great doors met, and the huge room built out of rock began to send out the water trapped within. Steadily the water returned to the sea, exiting with a rush and a roar no less dramatic than the thunder with which the massive doors had closed.

Within only a few minutes, Meredith and her companions were no longer floating in the nurturing arms of the sea. Their feet were descending through dwindling layers of water, settling at last onto a rock floor that had been rubbed to the smoothness of tile—the result of eon after eon of waves washing back and forth, mingled with equally numberless generations of bare feet crossing and recrossing on their way to and from the sea.

Soon the last of the water had departed, and the vast chamber stood empty. Dazed, Meredith looked about her. She no longer needed her sea eyes to see. Red-tinted light illuminated the great room, although dimly, coming from intricately fashioned lamps that had been enclosed and set into niches in various places about the walls.

How peculiar it was to no longer be submerged in the sea. It seemed so unnatural. Her legs felt wobbly as a newborn foal's, and her center of balance was off. She wiggled her toes against the hard floor, the feel of it beneath her feet a foreign and distinctly unnerving sensation.

She was struck by a sudden yearning to rush across that smooth wet floor and jerk the lever that her inner knowledge told her would refill the chamber. She could already visualize those massive doors opening, feel the eager relief that would sweep over her when they did, allowing her to return to Mother Ocean, who was waiting patiently just outside.

But Galen had taken hold of her hand. His long fingers, wet and warm, curled around hers in a gesture that was both protective and commanding. He looked down at her. In the dim red light, shadows danced off his high cheekbones, slanting down the firm hard lines of his face and thrusting the set of his jaw into grim focus.

His features seemed etched in the same stone from which the chamber had been carved, except for his eyes. They stared down into hers, as blue and blazing as sapphires thrown into a fire. Yet it was a loving fire, gleaming and burning its way into her soul, warming and welcoming her in the same way the glittering lights of the abode had reached out to beckon her through the darkness. She met his searching stare and allowed herself a small—a very small—smile.

"Are you ready?" he asked.

She knew, without his having to elaborate, what he meant. Was she ready to meet her heritage, her future, no matter what it might hold?

She answered the pressure of his hand with a firm grip of her own, and gave him what she hoped was a look of readiness and self-possession. "Of course," she replied. "What are we waiting for?"

Her back straight and her head held high, she strode to the inner doors. Her hand was still within Galen's, and 'oklat had come over to join them. Stolidly he placed himself on her other side as they walked across the smooth wet floor. In the same position, Meredith thought with a sudden burst of affection for the squat Selkie, that he had occupied during so much of their journey there.

The far wall held a set of inner doors, and in response to Galen's pressing one of three panels set into the stone, they round majestically open. A spacious corridor spread itself out before Meredith's dazzled gaze, curving off into the distance and alive with vibrant hues of coral pink and deep rose.

She barely had time to admire it, though, for a tall, stately woman with a thick silvery coil of hair lying over one shoulder was standing before the doors. Her eyes, large and dark, were fixed gravely upon their faces.

"Elder," Galen said, gladness, relief, and worry all coming together in his tone. He squeezed Meredith's hand and brought her forward. "A great deal has happened, and we have much to tell you. But first . . ." He inclined his head toward Meredith. "Philtate, this is our most venerable and respected Elder, Cleonith—"

He never finished. Meredith met the woman's gaze, and a bolt of something she could only identify as electricity blasted through her. It was devastating, irresistible, as though a jagged streak of lightning had arched down out of the sky and struck her squarely between the eyes.

She staggered forward, hearing a babble of voices: Galen's deep tones, Toklat's hoarse cry, and the Elder's quick concerned question. All they were to her was sound, noises without meaning nearly drowned out by the roaring in her ears.

She reached out for the tall silver-haired Elder. Her arms felt heavy as leaden bars, but the electricity shot them forward with terrific force, so that she grabbed fiercely onto the merwoman's arms. It could have been seconds or minutes or hours; she had no idea, no awareness of anything other than that she had seized this woman and was holding her while that terrible current poured through her.

Then it was over. She caught a glimpse of the Elder' eyes, wide and incredulous, as the electricity shattered ou of her with an abruptness that was like the most acute physical pain. She released the Elder's arms, swaying with agony in the wake of its leaving her.

Galen's voice was ringing in her ears. He had wrappe

is arms tightly around her, but she heard and felt him only dimly. The edges of the shimmering hall had gone dark, and that blackness was rushing forward at her in a great inexorable wave.

She opened her eyes wide, trying to see, trying to seek out the path the power had taken when it left her. The blackness reached her, surrounding and dragging her into a spiral of downward motion. In her head, she felt as though she were falling, vanishing into that black spiral. It was only in the last instant of consciousness that she realized her body was falling as well.

Anastas stopped short in the darkness. Bringing himself upright he sent his gaze lasering through the inky black of the Midnight Sea, focusing on what lay ahead of him. Galen's abode.

It was not far away, nothing more than an easy swim for one of his blood. But for Anastas, it might as well have been at the other end of the Inland Mother, in the smaller Red Sea to the east, or in the great ocean beyond that, which the Terrans, with their annoying passion for naming things after themselves, had long insisted on calling the Indian Ocean.

He could no longer enter this abode, or any other. It was utterly ironic that here, in this very place that was Galen's ancestral home, he would have once received the welcome even to the firstborn of a merfolk ruler. He would have walked through these halls boldly, sure of his position and his power.

To try that now would mean certain death. Galen—blast his name—would be more than happy to remove him from his plane of existence, with Toklat only too eager to help. And there was no way of knowing how many other merfolk were inside his former kinsman's abode to back Galen up. No, he would not have a glimmer of a chance; in fact, even staying in these waters was dangerous. He was openly and foolishly risking detection by any mer-men or -women who might be passing through the Midnight Sea on their way to or from the abode.

But he could not leave, not yet. For *she* was in there. Anastas's teeth bared themselves, gleaming with an eerie luminescence in the thick blanket of deep ocean night that had wrapped itself so closely around him. The scroll had told him Galen and Toklat were bringing her to this abode. It had led him there unerringly, crying out for her presence in his mind, tracking her, almost as if it were alive.

As if it were alive. Gingerly Anastas held the bundle away from him. Ever since his encounter with that accursed woman, the delicately wrought sheets of gold within the sharkskin wrappings seemed to have taken on a spirit and consciousness of their own. And it was not a pleasant one where Anastas was concerned.

In some inexplicable and supernatural fashion, the scroll—inanimate object though it was—was trying to escape him! Repeatedly, it had sent out waves of heat so fierce that he had been forced to yank the bundle away from him and hold it out at arm's length. Even so, that had not saved the smooth skin of his chest from being burned.

He touched the painful marks with his free hand and cursed viciously. His frustrated rage was not aided by th incessant throbbing of the burns, their bite exacerbated by the stinging salt that filled the waters of Mother Ocean.

The wrapped scroll twitched in his hands, or was it just his imagination? Savagely he tightened his grip upon it. *You won't escape me*, he told the bundle in mind-speak. *And after you've served my purposes, I'm going to throw you into the deepest whirlpool in all the oceans I can find. It will suck you down into the bowels of the earth, and that will be the end of you!*

He could swear that the scroll laughed at him, a derisive laugh that excoriated his tightly stretched nerves as sharp as the salt sea lapping over his burns. Was he going mad? Perhaps. After everything that had happened, it would not be surprising if he were.

He still could not believe that all his followers, every last one of them, were dead. He was enraged at them for being dead.

Fools! Incompetent, puling, whining imbeciles! They had deserted him when he needed them most, letting themselves be killed, so that now he had to pursue this thing to its necessary conclusion all by himself.

It was enough to turn anyone's wits into the currents of madness. Much less a man as sensitive and intelligent as he was, Anastas told himself with aggrieved self-righteousness. Well, no matter. He still had the scroll, its resistance notwithstanding, and that alone gave him power over these exkin of his. There was still time for him to set things right. All he needed was Meredith.

At the thought of the landwoman, who curiously enough was a landwoman no longer, Anastas snarled again into the darkness. He could not rid himself of the memory of the expression on her face when she had escaped him. Why, she had broken his hold and shoved him away from her as implacably as a giant whale shark pushing a Terran fishing boat out of its path!

It seemed impossible, yet that was exactly what she had done. There had been a force in her during those moments, a strength as supernatural as the mysterious power that he sensed coming to life in the scroll. He would have to understand this force before he could conquer it and control it for his own ends.

The only way to do that was to recapture Meredith, making sure this time that she did not escape. During the turn of the tide he had spent studying the finely beaten sheets of gold in the cave, he had come to understand enough of the scroll's message to know that bringing the landwoman and it together would result in an awesome unleashing of power and knowledge.

And when those mighty secrets had been freed from the hold of over twoscore centuries, *he* would be the final one to possess them. Added to the considerable abilities he already possessed, ah, how formidable he would then be.

He, Anastas! The one these foolish people of his had had the temerity to banish from home and throne.

I will do it, he assured the bundle, although he still took care to hold it away from his body. *And when I've succeeded, I'll rule, as I always should have done. Yes! A rule of fear and strength and power that none will be able to stand against. Least of all Galen.*

He stared into the distance, at the dancing lights of Galen's abode. With every flicker, their warm brightness emphasized his separation from his world and his people. Power, he repeated to himself in a litany of longing and hatred and desire. Above all, he must have power, for that was the answer, the only answer.

Power.

CHAPTER
30

"She healed her." Toklat's dark eyes were blazing, his husky voice made even rougher with wonder and incredulity. "You heard what Cleonith said. She was feeling the first symptoms of the illness, and Meredith healed her!"

"Yes," Galen eased the door of the bedchamber shut behind them, though were he to have slammed the heavy door, it would have made little difference to the deeply unconscious woman inside.

"She healed her." Toklat could not seem to stop saying it. "Galen, do you realize what this means? The long nightmare for both our people may finally be ending. I *knew* there was something special about that woman from the moment you brought her to me in the Cave of Secrets. If she can heal merfolk, then perhaps she can heal Selkies too!"

"She healed Cleonith," Galen reminded him. "That is not

the same as curing all the merfolk. We don't even know if she can do it again, it may have been a fluke ..."

"You know it was no fluke!"

"And," Galen finished soberly, "you see how she is now." His eyes were haunted, turned inward, as the image of Meredith lying so still and silent she could have been dead was summoned up. "How can we know what will happen to her if she tries this again?" he demanded, asking the question as much of himself as of Toklat. "Or the next time? Or the time after that?"

Toklat stepped in front of him, staring up into Galen's face. "Brother-friend, are you placing this woman above the welfare of your own people, and of mine?"

Galen stiffened. "You know me better than that, old friend," he said in a tone of quiet rebuke. "Remember this, though: Meredith is one of my people now. Her welfare is as important to me as anyone in this abode."

"More," Toklat said. "Because you love her." He did not wait for an answer to this statement, but gestured down the silent corridor in the direction of the interlocking chamber. "You will do what's right, Galen. I know that. As for me, I must go to my own waters now. My people have been waiting for me a long time. They will be anxious for some word of what's been happening. And now, I finally have something to tell them."

Meredith shifted stiff legs and raised a clumsy hand to her fiercely aching temples.

"Ah," a woman's voice said. "So you've awoken at last and come back to us. Are you in your present mind now?"

Meredith got her eyes open with an effort, swallowing a groan as white pain lanced sharply behind her eyeballs. Slowly she became aware of softness beneath her, and realized she was lying on a bed. She stared at the woman who was sitting in a chair that had been drawn up alongside. Her thoughts were foggy, and it took her a moment to recollect who the speaker was.

Cleonith, the Elder. The woman Galen had begun introducing her to, when . . .

She sat up carefully, mindful of her aching head. "You," she said dazedly. "I — I grabbed you, held you by the arms. Something happened, didn't it?"

"Something did, indeed." The other woman's tone was dry and thoughtful. "And you fainted at the end of it. Fell right over into Galen's arms like a sack of freshly picked sea kelp."

Galen. Meredith knew, without having to look around her, that he was not there. She ached for him with a sudden sharpness, wanted desperately to see him. A consciousness stirred deep inside her belly, flowing up to her brain, whispering in a voice without words that there was little time, little time . . .

"How long have I been unconscious?" she asked worriedly.

"Not long, considering how deeply you were away from yourself. One turn of the tide, perhaps a little less."

The Elder watched her, her dark eyes probing and searching Meredith's face with an intensity that reminded her strongly of Galen. "How much do you remember about what you did?" Cleonith asked abruptly.

Meredith thought. "Lightning," she muttered. "It was like electricity, white fire, burning all through me."

Cleonith nodded. "A good description."

"It was so strong." Meredith's eyes closed. "My arms were so heavy, but it lifted them up. It made me grab you."

"It did more than that. Or you did, depending how one might want to look at it."

Meredith opened her eyes to stare at her. "What do you mean?"

"You healed me, girl. You cured the sickness that was beginning to take a hold in me. I owe you my life, and I bless you for coming among us."

"I—I don't understand."

Cleonith sighed impatiently. "The plague, sweeting. Galen has told you about it. It has been attacking our people without mercy, regardless of age or strength or will. Today, not long before you swam into the interlocking chamber, I began to feel it taking a hold in me. The first symptoms, which I have been unfortunate enough to witness in too many others, were putting down their evil roots . . ."

A haunted look came into her piercing eyes. "I sought to hide it, for I am a chief Elder, and the fear and despair in this abode and all the others is very great. The people, lost in their panic over what is happening, look to me for strength. They depend on me. It would be a terrible thing for me to fall ill, deteriorating until I likely met the same fate as others already have."

"But"—Meredith gazed at her in bewilderment—"what did I have to do with anything?"

"I was hoping," Cleonith said, "that you could tell me. Since you can't, I must form my own conclusions."

She turned to a small round table carved from alabaster and picked up a tall delicately shaped ewer. After pouring some of its contents into a goblet that looked to be fashioned from several subtly colored shells, she held the goblet out to Meredith.

"I think," the Elder continued thoughtfully, "that you were in the grip of power, a greater power than even I—who am very old—have ever seen. There are forces at work here. They kept alive the memory of a scroll, even if it was only in the vaguest of legends, they sent you to Karpathos, and then sent Galen to find you. Perhaps they also sent the plague, terrible as it is, for reasons that are not yet clear to us."

Meredith drew herself up against the carved alabaster headboard. "I may not know the reasons for why it's come, but I do know this. The illness was foretold."

Cleonith drew in her breath sharply, but lost in the dream-memories that were never very far from her thoughts and that were now even more powerful, Meredith paid little attention. Holding the goblet, forgotten, in one hand, she began to speak. It was not difficult. Indeed, the words came rolling out of her, as continuously as waves rolling up onto a beach.

She told Cleonith of her dreams, of Marit, and of what her distant ancestress had lived through and done so far back in the mists of time. Lastly she spoke of her own birthright and, most important, of the inescapable legacy that Marit had left her through the golden scroll.

A great silence filled the room when she had finished, a silence that was vast and throbbing, alive with thoughts and words yet to be said.

Meredith ventured a glance at Cleonith. The Elder had not looked at her as she had talked, keeping her eyes fixed instead on those long-vanished events, as if she, too, could see those days that remained so real and alive within Meredith's psyche.

She had not interrupted the tale. She had said nothing, not even once. When Meredith finished, Cleonith sat unmoving in her chair, the long brown fingers of one hand resting absently upon the coil of silvery hair that lay over her shoulder.

Her eyes, though, were on fire, blazing with an intensity that was all the more striking because of her utter stillness. Meredith could feel the force of the merwoman's mind, she could almost see the thoughts racing through her consciousness, heavy and swift-moving, like river currents under winter ice.

"Elder—" she began.

Cleonith raised a hand, cutting her off. "The prophecy," she whispered, her voice barely audible. "So it's true."

Meredith regarded her blankly. "The prophecy?"

Those blazing eyes fixed themselves on Meredith's. "It is so old that few know of it any longer," Cleonith said. "And those who do, discount it. Except for me. But it is the reason that those who left the sea did so in that far-off time, although we've always thought they all died when Mother Ocean destroyed their land."

The Elder's words jarred loose another distant memory in Meredith's mind, as though Marit herself were listening and whispering to her. "Yes, the prophecy!" she said excitedly. "Those born of the sea will one day be menaced by the very world they refused to leave. Marit wrote of that prophecy at the end of her life, when she finished the scroll!"

Cleonith was too lost in thought to be surprised by Meredith's knowledge. To her it was only further evidence of the child's power. She picked up the train of thought. "The landfolk will multiply." She closed her eyes, reciting the ancient words softly. "And not content with their hold on the land, will seek to extend their grip over Mother Ocean as well." She opened her eyes. "It ends there," she said. "There's no question that the part about landfolk's greediness is true, but no one has ever believed that the Mother would turn against the children of Her waters."

"But there's more." Meredith sat forward, pressing a hand to her temples. A faint tingling of that awesome force trickled through her, planting words like fertile seedlings in her brain.

"The landfolk will bring devastation and illness in their wake to all people of the sea. Merfolk will—will lose their gills!" Her eyes widened as she stared at Cleonith. "They will lose their gills. Marit wrote it down in the scroll. And on the last page she wrote"—Meredith was too caught up even to question how she knew this—"that only one who has left the sea and then returned, who has lost her gills and then regained them, will be able to save those of the sea."

She was that one.

Meredith did not have to say it aloud. Neither did Cleonith; the knowledge was reflected in the depths of those burning eyes. They stared at each other in silence, and in that silence the internal voice began to whisper again, battering at Meredith's thoughts with new urgency. *There's no time. There's no time. Hurry!*

She replaced the goblet on the table untasted and shifted uneasily. "I need to get up."

Suddenly it was clear to her what she had to do. The certainty of it flamed across the screen of her mind with the brightness of the abode's lights in the Midnight Sea.

She was supposed to cure all merfolk, in exactly the way she had healed Cleonith. Why else would she have been given this gift? The truth of it glittered in her heart like the gold sheets of the missing scroll. And it was only fitting. She was a merwoman. The people of the sea were her heritage, though it had been kept from her all her life, leaving her miserable and longing for something she had never understood. Now, like some wonderful priceless gift, it had been given back to her. Wasn't it only fair that she give something in return?

She looked at Cleonith, to find the Elder staring at her with an expression of stunned wonder on her aged features, as if she were reading the thoughts in Meredith's mind. "I understand," she said slowly. "But the healing you did for me took a great toll upon you. Will you be strong enough to do what must be done?"

Meredith set her jaw. "I'll have to be." It was her turn to

cast a look as intense and blazing as Cleonith's back at the Elder. "After all, there's no other choice. Is there?"

With smooth grace, Cleonith rose to her feet, the folds of her ankle-length white robe rustling about her. "No," she said briskly. "There is not. Let us go."

Her strong arms helped Meredith from the bed. She accepted the Elder's support gratefully, for in getting up she found that she was still dizzy. It passed quickly, though, pushed aside by the ever-increasing urgency pounding through her head as that inner voice warned her onward.

She paid only scant attention to the chamber she had been brought to, absently noting the uneven smoothness of the polished shell floor and the subdued orange light flowing out of several small lamps set in the walls. None of it made much of an impression on her, so anxious was she to heed the imperative of that whispered voice telling her there was no time. *Hurry, hurry.*

She fidgeted when Cleonith stopped before the chamber door, a beautiful thing made of black coral and rubbed to such a rich sheen that it practically glowed in the dimly lit chamber. "There is one thing I have not said to you yet," she told Meredith gravely.

Meredith strove to hold back her impatience, reminding the persistent inner voice that within this stately and imposing woman resided an accumulated wisdom she could not even begin to imagine. "And what is that, Elder?" she asked respectfully.

A warm light shone out of the depths of Cleonith's eyes. "Welcome."

She pushed open the door and gestured at Meredith to follow. They walked rapidly down the hall, Meredith moving with more assurance as the last vestiges of weakness left her. It was a wide corridor, as spacious as the one she had seen outside the vast chamber that led to the sea.

It looked as though it had been constructed to accommo-

date a great many people, but where were the other merfolk? This abode of Galen's was a large place; it should have
been filled with the sound of voices, with the faces of her
newfound people going about their business. The emptiness,
and the resounding silence in the wake of that emptiness,
was eerie and profoundly unsettling.

"Where is everyone?" she asked uneasily. "Shouldn't
there be other people around?"

"They are here." Cleonith's voice was somber. "Those
who are ill are in their beds. Those who are well are tending
to them as best they can. Others"—her shoulders lifted in a
shrug that bespoke utter weariness—"are huddled here and
there, waiting to either live or die, with no hope that they
can affect the outcome."

Meredith stifled a gasp. The implications of this crisis
were growing ever more staggering. You see? the voice insisted, twining itself through her mind. You must hurry.
"But this is not the only abode!" she said out loud, unconsciously quickening her pace. "Is it like this with other merfolk in other abodes throughout the seas?"

She wanted desperately for Cleonith to answer in the
negative. But she knew, even before the question left her
lips, what the Elder's response would be.

"It is," Cleonith said. "But it's becoming difficult to know
for certain. We are growing ever more isolated from our
people in other abodes. Everyone is afraid to go out into
Mother Ocean, for fear that the plague will strike them
when they are out in the depths and too far away to reach
the safety of an abode in time. Although," she added bitterly, "from what I have seen, to hide in our abodes is
merely to prolong the inevitable."

She sighed. "So we hide, held captive here, just as the
Selkies are held hostage in whatever shape they were in
when the illness struck them, terrified that if they try to
change, they will die in torment."

Meredith nodded her understanding, remembering the conversation she had had with Galen about the terrible affliction attacking the Selkies. Galen. His face and his presence sprang into her heart, fierce and penetrating and loving all at once, as if he had laid one of his large warm hands upon her breast. "Where is Galen?" she asked quickly.

"He stayed with you for a time, and as soon as he was certain you would be all right, he left to see to those who are ill." Cleonith paused. "I'm sure he has told you that this is his ancestral abode. Many here who have fallen sick are of his clan."

Fear uncoiled in Meredith's belly, crawling up into her throat so that she tensed, unable to find her voice for a moment. "But what about him?" she said anxiously. "He's all right, isn't he?"

"For now." Cleonith's face was grim. "Yet none of us are invulnerable, child. Including you, who are now one of us."

"I'm not in any danger of being affected." She said this positively, the words leaping from her lips almost by themselves, as though it were that inner voice that had said them, and not she.

Cleonith frowned. "How can you be so sure of that?"

"I—I don't know." She squared her shoulders as she wondered about the answer to that question herself. "It's all tied up with this—this force inside me," she said tentatively. "I wish I could explain it better . . ."

Cleonith's long, even strides halted abruptly. Turning to Meredith she placed both hands on the younger woman's shoulders. Her face was strained, her eyes blazing with desperation and the beginnings of hope.

"You don't need to explain," she said in a low, throbbing tone. "I am convinced of your power, of the prophecy, and of this gift which the Mother, in Her eternal wisdom, has given you. You are our hope, Meredith. You who once be longed to the land but who now belong to us. Our only hope. The Mother sent you here, and I can only hope that She sent you in time."

"Meredith!"

Galen's tall form appeared around a bend of the corridor. He strode swiftly toward them. His startling blue eyes were hot, his tense features molded into an expression of surprise and disapproval and concern.

"What are you doing here?" he asked Meredith as soon as he reached her. Before she could answer, he swung on Cleonith. "You told me yourself that she should not get up until we know exactly what happened to her," he went on angrily. "Why have you allowed this, Cleonith? The risks—"

"—are great for all of us," Cleonith finished quietly for him. "And we know what happened to her. She cured me, as she may be able to cure every one of us who is ill, or becoming so. If we give her the chance."

Galen looked from her to Meredith. His face was thunderous. Meredith could almost hear the thoughts churning through his brain. Her life as the possible price for the lives of all of them. "It's dangerous," he said to Cleonith, though his gaze remained on Meredith. "You saw the toll it took upon her when she healed you. She nearly died. To use her this way—especially in trying to heal others upon whom the plague has a far greater grip than it had upon you—is a harsh thing, even though it may be our only choice."

"We are not using her," Cleonith replied. "This was her idea entirely. I could not dissuade her if I tried."

The sound of their voices washed over Meredith, echoing off the shimmering walls of the deserted corridor. It beat at her ears, but it was not loud enough to drown out the voice inside her head. Nothing could drown that out.

"Stop!"

She had not realized how loudly she had shouted until she saw the looks Galen and Cleonith turned on her.

"Gather everyone together," she said more softly, hearing a telltale trembling beneath her firmly spoken words. "Everyone. Right away."

She stared into their faces, trying to read their response to what was more a command than a request. Cleonith was eyeing her with a serious expression, nodding in grave approval, understanding at once what was driving her. Galen understood, too, all too well. His features turned so grim, they looked as if they had been carved from stone.

"Elder," he said with cold formality, "I wish to speak to Meredith alone."

Cleonith studied him a moment, then inclined her head and walked farther down the corridor. She had scarcely disappeared beyond the curve of the hall when Galen laid his hands on Meredith's shoulders.

"When I told you about my parents," he said, "and about what *he* did, I did not tell you that the kingship of our people still lies vacant because of his father's transitioning, and his own banishment. A new ruler must be chosen, and even though I've never sought the position, it may fall to me. Do you know what that means? It means that I must do what is best for all my people, not just one of them. No matter how much that one person matters to me."

Reaching up, Meredith laid a hand lightly across his lips. His breath was hot against her fingers, and pain shot through her. How she ached for him, caught as he was between her safety and the safety of their people. For her, there was no such dilemma. She wanted to tell him about the prophecy, but what if he did not believe it, as Cleonith had said many did not? There was no time to convince him. "It's what everything has been leading up to all along," she said instead. "You know that as well as I."

His hands tightened on her until she winced. He shook

his head, his fear for her roughening his voice, firing his
next words with anger. It was a thing that should have been
said gently, softly, murmured in her ear while they lay
wrapped in each other's arms after making love.

But Galen did not say it softly or gently. "By all the forgotten gods," he shouted, "I love you, woman! *I love you!*
And I don't want any harm to come to you. I won't lose
you, not now!"

Meredith made a strangled sound deep in her throat, a
sort of sob, though her eyes were painfully dry. "I love you
too," she whispered through that strangled tightness in her
throat.

She wanted to fling herself against him, bury her face in
the reassuring warmth and strength of his wide chest, kiss
him over and over, lose herself in the force and power of
him until everything else was blotted out. But she could not.
There was a force in her now, too, and it would not be
stilled. That inner voice was pushing at her again, more urgently than ever. She had to heed it. She had to.

She held her hands out at her sides, yearning to touch
him and not daring to. "If I don't do this," she said, stum-
bling, struggling to find the right words, "that we love each
other won't matter. Nothing will matter. Because there
won't be anything left."

Galen was silent. His eyes blazed down into hers, and she
saw the agony reflected in those sea-blue depths as he wrestled with the dilemma that faced him: the awful pain of
watching his folk suffer coupled with the appalling prospect
of what her saving them might mean. He pulled her to him
and lowered his mouth to hers.

All that he was feeling in that moment breathed itself into
Meredith's soul through his kiss: his love, his longing, his
frustration and anger, and, buried deep below everything
else, his fear. He lifted his mouth, and his eyes searched her
face.

"Do you know what you're asking me to let you do?" he asked raggedly.

She nodded. "You've already made your decision," she said through the pain and fear and love that clogged her own throat. "And so have I. Deep down, you know it's the right one. Neither one of us would ever be able to forgive ourselves if we did anything else."

He held her a moment longer, then slowly let his hands drop from her shoulders. "We can gather everyone together in the Great Hall," he said quietly, tiredly. "With all the people who have flooded here since this began, even that hall would have once been too small. But now"—his eyes darkened and he looked down the empty corridor, to where Cleonith waited—"there are fewer of us."

CHAPTER
31

It took some time to bring everyone together. Many could no longer walk, and had to be carried by those who could into the Great Hall whose wide doors Galen had flung open.

Meredith stood alone on a dais in the center of the huge chamber, trembling as she watched Galen and Cleonith walk swiftly through the growing throng of the sick, the well, and the dying. The merfolks' voices filled the cavernous hall, rising to the great arched ceiling. There were questions from those healthy enough to ask them, and groans and murmurs from those who were not.

The sight staggered her, leaving her caught between a state of urgency and anticipation and downright panic. She had wanted so badly to see her people, to glory in the bond that stretched between them and her. Well, now she was seeing them, and it was worse than any imagining.

They were tall and magnificent and beautiful, these mer-folk of hers, even the ones who were ill. But the magical quality that she had seen through the eyes of Marit, and in Galen with her own eyes, was gone, swallowed up by some-thing else. Doom rested on these men and women who were her kin, even upon their children. She could see it coiling sinuously above their heads and wrapping itself around their bodies. Black and powerful, mocking them, mocking her.

She was only one person, small, insignificant, barely awakened to her heritage and this life. How could she pos-sibly fight such a dark power, much less defeat it?

The brave words she had spoken to Cleonith and then to Galen came back to her. The taste of them was bitter, like bile in her mouth. She had been a fool to talk the way she had. Whatever force had healed Cleonith seemed to have deserted her now. She could not even hear that inner voice anymore. And even if she could, what difference would it make? This dark plague was too strong.

She wrapped her arms across her breasts, shuddering, as Cleonith's stately form made its way toward the dais, her long white robe floating gracefully about her. Like most of the others in the hall, Meredith herself was naked. It was a state she had grown so accustomed to over these last few days, she had ceased to notice it anymore. But she noticed now, and she shivered again, though the cold she felt had little to do with the slight chill coming from the stone walls of this vast chamber.

"Child," Cleonith said gravely after she'd stepped onto the dais, "the people are gathered as you asked them to be. You said there is little time, and indeed, for many here there isn't. Are you ready?"

Meredith turned desperate eyes to the Elder. "Cleonith, the power—it's gone. I don't feel it anymore."

Cleonith frowned, then her face cleared. "It will come back," she said serenely. "You would not have been sent here otherwise." Her voice lowered, resonating with a quiet force of its own. "You must clear your mind, Meredith, let it flow through you. You are thinking too much, fearing too much. That is not the way. Remember how it happened before when you healed me. Remember that, and then let it come."

Meredith closed her eyes. By now, the people who were well enough knew why they had been summoned there. She could feel their eyes on her, burning holes into her body and brain with their desperation and, in the case of many, with their skepticism. Voices reached her ears, murmuring that she was not even a merwoman, not really, and even if she were, how could she help them, replace gills that had already closed up, when the most skilled Healers and Elders among them could not?

Their doubts took root in Meredith's mind, mirroring her own. They were right. How could she change this? Change them back to what they had once been?

I can't! She opened her eyes, shaking with grief and pain and rage, at herself and at her helplessness. Then Galen stepped in front of her. He had come up onto the dais without her realizing it, but now his presence enveloped her. He stood very close to her, his eyes like bright blue flames. He did not touch her. He did not have to. His love and concern reached out for her, enfolding her in a cloak as soft and warm as a caress.

"You can," he said deeply, intensely, as though he had heard her frantic unspoken cry. "Listen to Cleonith. Clear your mind and do what you must. What I know you can."

She stared at him. His own doubts, all his anguished reluctance to let her take this step were gone, or else he was hiding his real feelings so well that even she could not see them. *Do what you must.* She loved this man, loved him with all her being. If she did not call upon whatever mysterious power had awakened in her, or if she tried and failed, what would become of him? He was as vulnerable as all the rest of their people.

She took a step back from him and closed her eyes. His presence receded, along with the voices and moans and rustling movements in the packed hall. Thoughts and feelings eddied through her mind, rippling like sea creatures caught in a tidal pool. She concentrated on pushing them away from her, out into the open sea of drifting consciousness. Gradually, ever so gently, her mind stilled until the only sound she heard was that of her own breathing. She felt her inner self growing quieter, emptying itself, waiting, waiting for the power to fill it. . . .

Those closest to her, Galen, Cleonith, and the ones nearest the dais, drew in their breath at the sudden change that swept over her face. Frowning uneasily, Galen stepped forward, as though he meant to take her arm. Cleonith's fingers closed hard around his wrist, and glaring fiercely at him, she shook her head. He could have broken free of the Elder's grip, but he did not. Still, the effort it cost him not to showed in his face, in the muscles that bunched tightly along his jaw.

Meredith was unaware of Galen's attempt to touch her. Emptied, her mind a blank canvas, she was unaware of everything save that eerie sensation of waiting. Arms at her sides, she stood motionless. And then it came.

Spiraling up from some place deep in the center of her being, it broke over her with the force of a tsunami, that towering and beautiful wave born far out to sea that sweeps everything before it as it bears toward land. Lightning roared through her, and thunder, and wind, all of it overlaid with that searing white fire she had experienced when she had healed Cleonith. Only it was infinitely stronger now, a living, breathing force bent on its own mission, with her nothing more than the conduit through which it poured.

Later, those who watched would say that bursts of white light had mantled her like a living cloak, that when she raised her arms, lightning seemed to sear from her very fingertips. But Meredith herself had no memory of it, and never would. To the end of her days she would remember nothing of what happened after the power came. Only what happened after it left.

For its leaving was far more terrible than its coming. It tore out of her, blowing through her like a great wind that leaves a small sapling toppled in its wake, and passes unnoticing and uncaring to its next destination.

Meredith swayed with grief at its desertion. She was hollow, bereft, emptied of everything but the pain of this terrible, beautiful force ripping away from her. Vaguely she realized that her arms were stretched straight out in front of her. Pandemonium was erupting all around her: voices laughing and shouting and exulting in a cacophony of marvel and disbelief and joy.

She realized that Galen's arms had encircled her, anchoring her to him in the tumult. His deep voice rang in her ears: "You did it, *philtate*, you did it!" She leaned against him gratefully and let herself slip into unconsciousness.

Far above the abode, the beginnings of a new day were lighting the sea with a mantle of gold and purple. Though deep in the eternal darkness of the Midnight Sea, Meredith could still sense the approaching morning, see it in her mind, feel the cool of night giving way to the slow, glowing warmth of a Mediterranean dawn.

Her hand in Galen's, she walked down yet another of the wide bending corridors with Cleonith close on her other side. But it was a vastly different corridor that met her eyes today. The emptiness, the unnatural stillness was gone.

The hall was crowded, vibrant with laughter and talk as people greeted the three of them, and one another, joyfully, exchanging stories of their suffering and this incredible healing. Children, fully cured and filled with energy once more, ran past in groups, shouting and calling to each other, smiling at Meredith, touching her shyly as they passed.

Cleonith's eyes glowed as she took in the scene. "The Mother Herself sent you to us, child," she said to Meredith. "It's the only way one can explain this miracle."

"The miracle," Galen interjected, "is that she is still alive."

Meredith glanced at him. His dark face stood out in stark contrast to the happiness around them. He alone did not look joyful, and she knew why. She and Cleonith had told him about the prophecy and their discovery of her place in it. None of it had come as a great surprise to him. He knew of the prophecy and he had already drawn his own conclusions about Meredith.

Overshadowing any such revelations for him was the fact that she had been unconscious longer this second time, and more deeply too. She had also been weaker when she came out of it, so dazed and unaware of her surroundings that not even Cleonith could revive her. Only Galen, with his hands and voice, had been able to bring her back, and he was grimly unhappy over the effort it had taken.

Now he looked across Meredith's head at Cleonith. "Is

this the price we are to pay?" he asked in a harsh quiet voice. "Meredith's life for ours?"

"No one has died," Cleonith reminded him. "Least of all, Meredith."

"Not yet!" he answered. "But you saw as well as I the toll it took upon her. It was far worse than when she healed you alone. How can she go to the rest of our abodes and do this again and again? What will happen to her the next time, or the time after that?"

Meredith sighed. "Will you two stop discussing me as if I weren't here?"

"Of course, child," Cleonith said, then addressed Galen as if indeed she were not there. "I share your worry, Galen. I fear for her well-being too. There has to be a way for her to channel this power and heal us, yet at the same time keep alive herself while doing it. The prophecy—"

"How?" Galen broke in angrily. "We haven't been able to find an answer yet, prophecy or no!"

"Yes," Cleonith said. "But we do not have the scroll yet either."

Meredith stopped in her tracks, bringing Galen and Cleonith to a halt along with her. The awesome and terrible power had so filled her mind, she had completely forgotten about both the scroll and the one who still possessed it.

"The scroll," she whispered, her eyes widening in horror. "But *he* has it. Who knows what he might have done with it by now?"

"He will have done nothing," Galen growled, his eyes as narrowed and glittering as the edge of a sword. "It is the only tool of power he has left. He will not throw it away, especially not without you to unlock its secrets for him."

"I agree." Cleonith's eyes were shrewd with speculation as she looked from Meredith to Galen. "So you must let him think he has a chance of getting her. It's the only way to get the scroll back quickly. And it must be quick. We all know how little time there is for those in the other abodes. As it is, it will take a long while to journey from place to place."

Galen looked down at Meredith. There was a heavy silence, then he said, almost too softly for her to hear, "She's right. But it's dangerous. Anything is where *that* one is concerned."

Meredith tried to smile, forcing the image of Anastas from her mind. She shrugged, although the very thought of those pale green eyes made her skin crawl. "No more dangerous than things are for me right now," she replied with an effort at lightness. "At least with the scroll, there's a chance of figuring out how to control this so I don't go into a coma afterwards."

Galen did not return her smile. "It seems that for you, the discovery of your heritage, of becoming one of us, means only danger, and even worse." That grim stony expression had carved itself into his features again, but by now she knew all too well the pain and worry it revealed rather than concealed. "I would give anything," he added in an undertone, "to make it otherwise."

"But you can't." She gave up her effort at lightness; it hadn't been very convincing, anyway. She tightened her hand on his. "So, let's lure him to us. That's what you're suggesting, isn't it?" she said to Cleonith.

A solemn nod was her answer. After a moment they all three continued on down the hall. Meredith exhaled softly, trying to hide the apprehension that wrapped icy fingers around her throat. But though she might be able to conceal her fear from Cleonith, she could keep nothing from Galen.

He moved closer, his warm naked body brushing against

hers. "I won't let anything happen to you," he said in her ear. "I swear it, philtate. On my life."

Anastas fidgeted, his muscles cramping and growing rigid as he glared out from between the boulders that formed the cave he had been lying up in. Until he had taken it over, it had been inhabited by a large moray eel, the creature's skin leached to an eerie white by the endless darkness of the Midnight Sea, as were the skins of so many of the creatures who made their lives in the great depths.

Moray eels could be fierce when threatened, and this one had not wanted to vacate its property. Anastas had used the power of his mind like a spear, honed to an even harder and uglier sharpness by his frustration, to force the creature from its comfortable home. Then he had moved in, laying the bundled scroll among the rocks, relieved to finally be able to place it away from him so that it could no longer burn his tender flesh.

He had settled himself to wait, distantly aware of the emptiness in his belly although he was too wrought up to satisfy it by hunting himself a meal. In any case, he dared not leave the scroll unattended while he did. Now and then an unwary fish would venture too near the mouth of the cave, and with a motion much like that of the eel that had lived there, Anastas would dart out an arm to capture it, swallowing it down with the fish still struggling. He did need to eat after all, even if it was only a few fish here and there. He would need all his strength for what was sure to come.

He had watched morosely as some time ago, Toklat had left Galen's abode. The Selkie had headed in the direction of his own territorial waters, a development that had made Anastas scowl, his fingers digging so hard into the boulder they were clenching that they left grooves.

It had been easy to ascertain what Toklat's purpose was. Plainly he was going to get help from his own. They might not be able to change their shapes, but they could certainly be effective in the forms they were in, especially if there were enough of them. Anastas did not relish the thought of being tracked and then attacked by a score or more angry Selkies. Beyond a doubt, it was a fight he would have no chance of winning.

A debate had waged inside his head as he'd watched Toklat's powerful shape merge into the black distance. Logic and reason had warned that he should follow the Selkie and kill him before he could come back with help. But the wordless voice of the scroll had kept interfering with that logical course of action, crying out for Meredith, insisting that soon she would come.

In the end, Anastas had listened to that silent plea and stayed. To capture Meredith was what he had come there for, after all. Nothing was more important than that.

Now, it looked as though his long vigil was finally going to be rewarded. He leaned forward until his head and shoulders cleared the cave opening, peering eagerly through the depths at the far distant bulk of the brightly lit abode.

The great stone doors of the interlocking chamber were grinding open, as they had so many times for him in tides past. And, he told himself savagely, as they would for him again very soon. Someone was coming out—no, two people. His heart leaped with expectation. He recognized Galen's broad form and sleek powerful way of moving, even at this distance, but it took him a moment to identify his companion. Then he smiled.

Meredith.

Are you sure Toklat is all right, Galen? Guilt stabbed through Meredith as she slipped into mind-speak. She had not even noticed the Selkie's absence until Galen had brought it up. Though she supposed there was good reason for it, given everything that had taken place since her arrival in the abode, she still felt more than a twinge of remorse.

Toklat had rescued her before her Change—in a way, he had saved her life—and they had traveled on the long journey to this abode together. She was bound to him as both a friend and an ally, bound to see this thing through to its end. It bothered her keenly to realize she had forgotten about him. What if he had tried to change his form and . . . ?

When he left he was fine, Galen told her. *In his body at least.*

He fell silent. How could he describe to Meredith his brother-friend's state of mind when Toklat had departed from the abode: a wild combination of dread and fear at what he might find when he rejoined his kindred and, for the first time, a real glimmer of hope. Meredith had healed Cleonith before his and Galen's eyes. Perhaps she could heal the Selkies as well. It was worth a try, at least. It was possible that they did not even need the scroll after all, he had told Galen exultantly before he left. What a colossal joke upon Anastas that would be!

But Toklat had departed before Galen and Cleonith had realized that Meredith could not control the mysterious power sweeping through her. They did need the scroll, Galen thought with a chill around his heart. Or Meredith, who in her stubbornness was determined to go on healing, would very likely die.

He led her away from the abode, his mind distracted with worry, even though all of his senses remained focused and intent. He sent those senses ahead as he and Meredith undulated through the depths, letting them sweep the black sea like great beams of light as he searched for some indication of Anastas's malevolent presence. Taking Meredith and leaving the abode in an attempt to draw Anastas out had seemed like a good idea when they'd discussed it with Cleonith. Indeed, it was the only idea, the only way to bring the scroll back to them quickly.

Now that they were actually doing it—swimming through the Midnight Sea with Meredith doubly vulnerable because, despite her attempts to hide it, she was still feeling the effects of that awesome draining power—he regretted this decision. And he hated even more the circumstances that had left him no choice but to make it—

The first twinge of Anastas's nearness struck him, jabbing him between the eyes as if someone had punched him. He threw a quick glance at Meredith to see whether she, too, had felt it. She had, or she had felt something. Her face had taken on a strange expression, distant and wondering, almost as though the power were going to visit her again.

No! Galen thought with a fresh surge of trepidation. Not out here!

I—hear—something. Her mind-speak came slowly, the words halting, as if another voice were interrupting her. *It's—calling to me.*

Keep swimming. He gave the order tersely, bumping his body against hers in an effort to bring her back to awareness. *Don't let on that you know he's near. Listen to me, philtate! Pretend you don't hear him!*

You don't understand. Her mind-voice was still dazed. *It's not Anastas I hear ...*

Her mind-voice trailed off, and Galen looked at her sharply. *Who, then?*

She was undulating next to him with surprising obedience, matching her speed to his in spite of that bemused look in her eyes. *Not who,* she sent to him after a moment. *What. It's the scroll, Galen. It's calling to me. I don't understand how, but it is.*

Excitement coupled with dread jolted through him. Here

was yet another new shift to the currents surrounding them, and as with the others, he had no idea how it would affect this woman he loved so much. He could protect her from Anastas, but how could he protect her from powers he could not understand, much less control? Being helpless was not a sensation he was used to. It left him seething, filled with a furious need to take action, any kind of action, so long as it was something.

Keep swimming, he repeated, determined to hide his agitation from her. *We'll sort it out later, but for now, nothing has changed. He still has the scroll, and we must draw him to us.*

The scroll. Despite her outward obedience to Galen's order, Meredith's whole self was in rebellion. The scroll's voice—amazing that an inanimate object should even have a voice!—was so beautiful, chiming in her head with the resonance of a myriad of differently toned bells. Every thread of her being responded to that call, urging her to go in search of it, to swim and swim until she found it. She was wrong to swim away, to put more distance between them. *Come back,* the musical many-timbred voice pleaded. *Come back, come back.*

She longed to. Oh, how she longed to. For a split second she hesitated, on the verge of turning around. Then Anastas's face stole into her mind, spreading like a dirty stain over the clear watery musical presence of the scroll. It stopped her, then sent her rushing to keep up with Galen, moving so fast that she overshot him for a moment.

He was beside her in a heartbeat. But he had seen the hesitation, and his eyes blazed at her in the darkness. *What's wrong?* he demanded. *Why did you pause just now?*

It's the scroll, she began, then fell silent. She did not need to explain why. Galen had already picked up on what she had felt.

He might not be able to hear the cry of the scroll as she did, but he could feel Anastas. The blonde merman had slipped from his place of hiding and was following them, slowly, staying far back, but coming after them at last.

Galen grunted with grim satisfaction. *Hah, it's as I thought. With Toklat gone, he thinks the odds are more in his favor. He'll come to us now. All we have to do is act like the fools he believes we are, and wait.*

What do you think he'll try to do? Meredith attempted to keep her nervousness from rattling through her mind-voice. Anastas was a bone-chilling threat. Still it was almost a relief to distract herself with thoughts of him and what he might do, rather than concentrate on the real fear that was gnawing at her.

He'll try to kill me, of course, Galen said calmly. *And then take you with him.* The calmness in his mind-voice was belied by the cold flames that danced and glittered in his eyes. *But he won't,* he went on as though he were discussing a change in the weather. *The question is whether he has the scroll with him.*

He does. Meredith's tone held no doubt.

Galen gave her a quick, hard glance, then said, *Stay close to me, beloved.* His mind-voice was as soft and gentle as a breath of evening wind. *I've told you I won't let him harm you, and that hasn't changed.*

Gratefully she moved nearer to him, taking comfort from his strength and his fierce protectiveness. She knew that he thought Anastas was responsible for her fear and she was reluctant to tell him otherwise. He had more than enough to worry about as it was. As she undulated forward, though, she felt the struggle in her growing, subtle and yet so deep it seemed as though she were being torn in two. The chiming voice of the scroll continued calling to her. She wondered how long she could go before she had to answer it.

They swam on. Anastas seemed in no hurry to catch up to them, a fact that didn't faze Galen. *He's waiting for a good place to ambush us,* he told Meredith. *And I'm looking for the proper one to give him.*

His words struck an odd jangling chord in Meredith. The wind-chime voices cried out something in her head, and she shouldered against Galen, her sudden calmness bringing his attention back to her.

The whirlpool, she snapped out. *That's where it has to happen. We have to go there. Right now.*

CHAPTER
32

Regardless of the black sea around them, Meredith rea
Galen's reaction clearly. His face wore a look that wa
stunned and speculative at once, although he kept the
swimming, too sharply aware of the danger following the
to allow her to stop. *How*, he asked slowly, *would you kno
about the whirlpool? I never said anything about it. Did Toklat
Cleonith?*

She shook her head. *We have to go there,* she insiste
Please, Galen. We're headed in that direction anyway, aren't we

He nodded, his face still set in a frown. *But how would y*
know—

Please! The voices in her head were painful now, so pier
ing and sweet and pleading that they stabbed at her bra
like a thousand dagger blades of musical torture. Sudden
she could wait no longer. She flung herself ahead of hir

pointing her body toward where those voices told her the whirlpool lay.

With one powerful thrust of his legs, Galen brought himself alongside her. *Very well, then,* he sent quietly. *We'll go there. But we stay together, Meredith. Do you understand me? We stay together.*

She made an abstracted noise of assent and kept moving. Galen studied her sidelong as they slipped through the depths, quickly leaving the Midnight Sea behind for the deep monochrome blue of the upper levels and the even lighter surface waters beyond that.

He was certain that in some way not yet clear to him, the scroll was responsible for what was driving Meredith. However, knowing that did not make him feel any better about it. The menace from Anastas was unabated. His senses told him the blonde merman was still behind them, and now there was this maelstrom of violent water to which Meredith was headed so doggedly.

Merfolk had names for each of these wild spots where Mother Ocean sometimes brought the forces of wind and tide together so that they collided with fierce impact. This one—called the Phoenician Whirlpool—was named for the only landfolk unfortunate enough to have encountered it during one of those times. Thousands of years ago a trading ship of Phoenicians had blundered into it and been destroyed.

There were other places like it in the seas and oceans of the world. All of them were dangerous—spots to be avoided by those who were wise in the ways of the Mother, even by those landfolk familiar enough with the sea to recognize the danger.

This place, though, was one of the worst. Maelstroms were not commonplace occurrences, especially in the Inland Mother. But the Phoenician Whirlpool, secret and known only to the denizens of the sea, was a violent cacophony of sucking, battering water that no sensible being would approach during the rare times it sprang into life.

This was one of those times. Galen's mind raced with plans on how to keep Meredith safe as they ascended steadily toward the surface, with Meredith pulling ahead ever more anxiously as she moved faster and faster.

Their heads broke through the sun-dappled waves. The day was brilliant and windy, the sky a seamless dome soaring above them, its sparkling blue merging into the deeper sapphire of the sea. Although the maelstrom was still a considerable distance away, they could already feel its force and the inexorable pull it exerted upon whatever moving thing—whether alive or inanimate—had the misfortune to be nearby.

Galen's eyes narrowed, assessing the danger. "We dare not go too close," he muttered. "It's bad today. It will suck in anything—a Terran ship, one of the whalefolk, or you and me. It's an evil business, coming here. Power or not, I should not have listened to you."

Meredith stared. The sight and sound of the distant whirlpool was so incredible that it quieted even the piercing voices in her brain, at least momentarily. Her first impression was that, despite the clearness of the sky, a thunderstorm was striking close by. Then she realized that the awesome noise came from a score of waves surging and whirling in giant crescents. They flung themselves up at the sky to crash against the angry wind with a sound similar to that which mountains might make when they tumble into the sea.

She shuddered involuntarily, gripped by a primal reflex of fear. Deeply rooted instincts stirred, rustling frantically across her consciousness. Run away, they whispered. Flee, quickly! She felt dizzy and disoriented, no longer able to remember why it had been so urgent that they come there in the first place. She started to move closer to Galen, seeking the reassuring comfort of his nearness, about to tell him that he was right, that they should leave.

In that moment, several things happened at once.

Galen swung around so fast, his shoulder slammed hard against her. She caught a glimpse of his face, enough to see the terrible expression that had come over it. In the same instant she saw what he had seen. Anastas was rushing at them, his perfect statuelike features twisted into a hideous mask of determination and hatred.

Galen snarled deep in his throat. The snarl transformed itself into words. "Keep behind me, and don't go any closer to the whirlpool." He charged in front of her, blocking Anastas's onward rush and protecting her at the same time.

Then the voices returned, a thunderous chiming that echoed throughout Meredith's entire body like the pealing of ten thousand bells. She flung herself forward, her legs driving her with savage and—she would realize later unnatural speed.

She shot into Anastas's path as he was almost upon them. His face tightened with surprise, and a look of cold pleasure that in any other circumstances would have chilled her to the bone and stopped her in her tracks. But she could not stop. The voices, and whatever force was within her, would not let her stop. Not even for Galen.

"Meredith!" Galen roared, and she heard the frantic note buried deep below that furious shout.

She collided with Anastas.

Anastas was knocked backward, thrown off balance by the force of the impact. By all the tides, where had the woman gotten such strength? The astonished question burst through him at the same moment that the precious scroll flew from underneath his arm. He snatched at it unsuccessfully with one hand while with the other he tried to grab

Meredith around the neck. Then Galen was upon them both.

The scroll went tumbling away, swept up by the currents that were swirling and tugging at everything within reach, pulling it remorselessly toward that giant whirling flux of wind and water and death. Meredith cried out and raced after it.

Behind her she knew that Galen and Anastas were locked in combat from which only one would emerge alive, but she could not spare even a single glance backward to see what was happening. Her gaze was fixed desperately on that wrapped bundle that pulsed and called to her as though it were alive, a precious entity that was being swept to its destruction and was pleading with her to save it.

She reached it, stretching out her arms until the tendons cracked, but able at last to curl her fingers around the smooth sharkskin in a powerful grip that could not be broken except by death. And perhaps that was what was going to happen. For now she found that she, too, was caught up in that terrible pull.

She struggled against it fiercely, knowing it was futile. Then an impossibly strong hand closed on her arm, just a a second earlier her own fingers had closed on the scroll.

It was Galen. With awesome force, as if she weighed little more than a sea gull feather, he flung her back and away from the current's relentless pull. His tossing of her was anything but gentle. In fact, it was exquisitely painful. His fingers bruised her flesh as they gripped her arm, taut with raw and unrestrained power.

Meredith described a complete somersault as she flew up into the air. She landed with a stinging belly flop as she and Mother Ocean met again. Yet she gloried in the awkward fall, caring only that she had held on to the priceless bundle. Without a doubt Galen had saved her life, and what was even more important, the scroll.

Quickly she righted herself. Treading water, the bundle cradled against her breasts, she immediately went on guard, her eyes searching the heaving water for Anastas. It took her less than a heartbeat to grasp what had happened. Somehow, Galen had managed to follow her, dragging Anastas and the battle they were engaged in along with him!

Now they were fighting. Two tall and massively muscled bodies arching and twisting above the waves, each caught up in a single-minded desire to kill the other. Her heart wrenched at the sight, lurching as though it wanted to fly up out of her throat.

All the love she felt for Galen swept over her so fiercely, it drove away even the voice and presence of the scroll. Every cell of her mind and body screamed at her to race across the tossing water to help Galen in any way she could. She started forward, then brought herself up short.

What would happen to the scroll if she did what her heart was commanding her to do? What if Anastas tore the bundle from her and sent it out into the centrifugal force of the maelstrom, on purpose this time, so insane with his hatred that he preferred to see the whirlpool have the scroll rather than the merfolk? Galen had saved her and it once already; he might not be able to do so again.

She dithered, helpless and angry, watching the battle unfold, her heart crying out with the agony of her inability to protect Galen as he and Anastas tore at each other like wild beasts.

Anastas lunged forward, trying to hook an arm under Galen's chin so he could wrench upward and use his mighty strength to break his foe's neck. Galen blocked the move with a savage blow from the heel of an iron-hard palm, a blow that would have killed a man not of the merfolk. It threw Anastas back, but only for an instant before he hurled himself back into the fray.

Once, Anastas would have been reluctant for this fight, wary of facing the man whose parents he had killed, particularly when that man was such a one as Galen. That reluctance was gone now, swept away by the knowledge that all his hopes and plans had deteriorated to the point where there was truly nothing left for him to lose.

The scroll was in the hands of Meredith, at least for the moment. His followers were all dead. The future yawned ahead of him, as bleak and empty as one of the great deserts of the landfolk, as uncertain as the giant whirlpool such a short distance away. If he did not defeat this former kinsman—now his implacable enemy—then get possession of the scroll and the woman who held it, he would have nothing to look forward to, save loneliness and a painful and lingering death when the plague finally decided to visit him as it had Bron and Ladru.

It made him a powerful opponent.

A red haze ignited by fury burned before Galen's eyes. The face of Anastas was framed in that film, wavering maddeningly as Galen sought to kill him. His thoughts were as red-tinged as his vision, but in a tiny corner of his brain where reason still prevailed, he had the presence of mind to realize that he had been caught off guard by the force and savage determination with which his former cousin faced him.

Despite Anastas's size and strength of mind, he had always been a coward when it came to facing those as strong or stronger than himself. Even when they were boys it had been that way between them. Anastas was always eager to plan and mastermind his steadily increasing wickedness, but just as eager to have those weak enough to be controlled perform the physical side of his evil for him.

Anastas had never been eager to take on his cousin's wrath about anything—either before or after the deeds that had led to his banishment—and Galen was all too aware of it. If he ever did have the opportunity to confront his enemy, Galen had often told himself in the late hours of the endless nights he'd spent grieving for his parents, the conclusion would be swift and deadly.

Now all that had changed. The man Galen hated so much was proving to be unexpectedly powerful. They were evenly matched. Both were roughly the same height and carried a similar amount of muscle. Even more telling, both were driven by desires—vastly different desires perhaps, but equally compelling ones, nonetheless. The only similarity between them lay in their hatred, and it formed a strange bond between them in this struggle that could have only one end.

They wrestled savagely, entwined in an embrace that was all the more terrible because they were twisted together as tightly as lovers. His bulging arms locked around Galen, Anastas lunged viciously, struggling to pull him forward. He was trying to yank him toward the Phoenician Whirlpool, Galen realized, and new rage blazed through him as he jerked back with bone-crushing strength.

The hate-filled features so close to his own formed words, spitting them like hailstones into Galen's face. "I was to have been king!" Anastas shouted. "*You* turned my own father against me and then caused the Elders to banish me because you coveted what was mine. *You* stole the place that rightfully belonged to me, and still does!"

It was useless to speak to a Banished One. Doing so acknowledged the existence of one who technically no longer existed. Yet a person was not supposed to kill a Banished One either, and that was precisely what Galen longed to do with every fiber of his being.

"Murderer!" he roared, naming the most unthinkable act of which a mer-man or -woman could be accused. "I did not want to rule then, and I do not seek to now. You banished yourself, you misshapen piece of evil! Your father was wise enough to see that one as out of balance with the Ancient Harmonies as you are could never rule. And you proved it by taking out your sick hatred and frustration on my mother and father!"

Anastas let out an incoherent shriek of unadulterated fury, and plunged at him with new strength. Writhing and striking at each other, neither was aware of how close they had been getting to the enormous maelstrom until the currents suddenly caught them up with a strength that dwarfed their own.

Meredith's voice came keening over the waves to Galen's ears, high and thin, distorted by the roar and rush of spiraling water. "Oh my God, Galen!"

He threw up an arm in a "go back" gesture. "Stay away!" he shouted at the top of his lungs, a terror greater than that of any whirlpool racing through him at the thought that she might not obey. "Stay away!" he yelled again.

The currents spun both him and Anastas around, pounding at them like colossal fists, forcing the two to fight them as well as each other. Suddenly there was a blinding crash on the side of Galen's head, just above the right temple. He had taken his attention away from the battle with Anastas for only the second it took to warn Meredith off, but for the blonde merman, it had been long enough.

Starbursts of red and white light exploded before Galen's eyes from the vicious blow delivered to his head. It stunned him, and as though he were watching through the eyes of a dream, he found his strength fleeing him like wine poured out of a goblet. His arms and legs lost their power and black spots danced between the sparks of light in his field of vision. Distantly he felt Anastas and the current striving together to tug him forward.

Toward the heaving mouth of the whirlpool.

"Galen!" Meredith's cry rang through the salt air, a high

and desperate wail so faint, he might have only heard it in his heart and soul.

Strength poured through in a maddened rush. *No!* He would not leave Meredith to this creature. He would not allow the murderer of his parents to take his life too.

Perhaps it was love for Meredith that restored his wits, driving the star bursts from his vision and the dizziness from his brain. Or perhaps it was his hatred for Anastas. He would never really know for certain. What he did know was that the power that billowed up in him came from some inner resource he had not known he had.

He heard a deep, growling sound and realized vaguely that it was coming from him. He plowed to a halt, his strength so overwhelming in its determination that it stopped Anastas as though a giant boulder had jerked him back. Before the other merman could react to this sudden turnabout, Galen's mighty arms closed about him, one around his legs, the other around his chest. He heaved Anastas up into the air, his teeth bared with the strain and with the intensity of his will. Calling upon every ounce of his strength, he hurled him forward.

Anastas landed farther into the currents, well past the point of no return. Screaming, his legs and arms thrashing and flailing, their strength useless against the awesome power of the Phoenician Whirlpool, he was swept on into the center of the maelstrom.

Galen had one last glimpse of his face—wild-eyed and disbelieving, his coldly handsome features contorted with fear. Then he disappeared, spun straight into the gulping maw of the swirling waves.

CHAPTER
33

Galen could not afford the luxury of watching to make certain his opponent was really gone. He was engaged in a battle for his own life, as the currents sought to sweep him to the same place to which they had taken Anastas. The Phoenician Whirlpool was impartial. Its hunger was as eternal as the sea herself, and Anastas had satisfied that hunger for only the briefest of moments. Now, using the deadly currents as its fingers, the maelstrom stretched out after Galen, snatching and tugging at him with greedy determination.

Galen fought to swim as he had never fought in all the centuries of his life. The waves buffeted him, the currents dragging his body remorselessly toward the lethal center. Scores of fish caught up in the same flow swirled haplessly past, bound for the same crushing death that Galen was so doggedly resisting. The water sucked at him, tumbling him end-over-end like a piece of flotsam. Somehow he managed to right himself, stroking desperately toward Meredith, a tiny distant beacon of safety in this howling mass of wind and water.

Inch by agonizing inch, he freed himself from the terrible pull. The thought of Meredith was the only thing that drew him on. Her face was framed in his mind, burning with such a glow that it eclipsed even the drag of the whirlpool. He had to get to her, he had to.

Abruptly he was free. It happened so quickly, he did not realize it at first. He kept plowing ahead, fighting, struggling, until he became aware of arms pulling at him, of Meredith's voice shouting in his ear.

"Galen! Oh, my love. Thank God!"

No, he wanted to say, the Terran god had nothing to do with this. It was the Mother who had given him back his life, and Meredith as well. He was too tired to speak, though, too tired to do anything but wrap his arms around her and pull her to him as though he would never let her go.

Safely away from the sucking current, they held each other for long moments without speaking, content just to hear each other's hearts beating, to know that they were both safe and alive.

Meredith was the first to find her voice. "I was so scared," she gasped. "When I saw you both being pulled toward the center of . . . of that nightmare, I thought I'd never see you again—"

"Hush." He smoothed the mane of hair that trailed in wet tendrils over her naked shoulders. "It's over now. He'll never hurt you or anyone else again." He made a sharp downward motion with the blade of his hand, and his voice was as implacable and dangerous as the swirling waters of the maelstrom. "It's finished. For all time."

He held her closer, and Meredith sighed. She pressed her head tight against his chest, still half-afraid to acknowledge that he was really safe and reunited with her, that his warm presence was not some cruel deceit, with him lost in the depths of that great whirlpool, battered and broken beyond recognition, as Anastas surely was by now.

She could feel Galen's harsh, uneven breathing against her cheek and knew the effort his struggle with Anastas and then the maelstrom had cost him. Her own body throbbed with weariness, in aching sympathy with Galen's exhaustion as well as in response to her overwhelming relief. Anastas was gone, and the scroll was back in its rightful place.

By mutual consent, they finally began to stroke backward, pressed close against each other as they moved away from the towering whirlpool and its reaching tentacles. They could still feel the pull, however faint, and Meredith knew, without Galen having to say anything, that he felt as she did. Neither of them would be eager to see this particular place anytime soon. She thought of Anastas, of that cold face crushed and battered into nothingness by the whirlpool, and she shuddered. It was a horrible end, even for him. But then she thought of Flijanou, and her mouth hardened.

Galen had felt her shudder and studied her with concern. "Are you all right, beloved?"

She nodded, dredging up a weak smile. "You know," she said musingly, "it was fitting somehow, what happened to Anastas. It was what he planned for the scroll. He was going to throw it into this whirlpool or some place like it, after he had drained me and it of all of its secrets. That's why the voices, or whatever they are, brought all three of us here."

Galen drew back to look at her. "What do you mean?"

For the first time since Anastas had charged them, Meredith suddenly became aware of what she still held under one arm. She pulled the bundle forward, her eyes glowing as she looked up at him. Galen, too, had forgotten about the scroll. His own eyes took on a strange glow as he reached out a hand.

"After all this," he said softly. "To find that it really does exist." Reverently he touched the bundle, and his eyes widened slightly. "Ah." His tone was one of marvel and wonder. "There is power here. I can feel it calling to me." His gaze swung to Meredith sharply. "And to you, philtate. Especially to you."

She met his eyes but said nothing, and after a beat, he held out his hand. "Come."

She laid her hand in his. "Where?"

"To the other abodes. There is a great deal of healing to be done, and now that we have this"—he touched the scroll again—"you will be able to save our people without harm to yourself."

It was what Meredith had been thinking. However, she was surprised to hear him say it. "How are you so certain?" she asked.

He only smiled. "Aren't you?"

And so they left the Phoenician Whirlpool behind, their heads above the water, undulating over the surface of the sea rather than diving beneath it. The sun beat down upon their wet backs, seagoing birds bound for the coasts of the Red Sea cried out above their heads, and a dancing breeze lifted the heavy salt-drenched hair off Meredith's shoulders.

She cradled the scroll close against her as they traveled. It was burdensome swimming and carrying the heavy bundle at the same time, but she could not relinquish the scroll. Not even to Galen, though he had offered to relieve her of the extra weight. Just to feel the scroll gave her a new strength. She could sense its power flowing into her, almost glimpse the protective shield it was throwing up around her as it girded them both for what lay ahead when they reached other merfolk abodes.

She found herself wondering what was written on these

precious gold sheets. Now, with her own change complete, she would be able to read them, to decipher their secrets. But in the end, did it really matter any longer? The scroll was giving her its power, that which it had denied so determinedly to Anastas. It was speaking to her, though the speech was not in words. Or perhaps she was not hearing the scroll at all, perhaps it was Marit who was talking to her, to this daughter she'd waited so many eons for, sharing with Meredith the knowledge she had recorded in gold long ago.

She was so lost in the magic weaving itself around her, she at first failed to notice what Galen had already seen: a double line of dark forms cutting through the waves toward them. When she did realize it she saw immediately that the figure in the lead was Toklat. They met and, treading the swells, she and Galen and the Selkie embraced. While Galen related what had happened to Anastas, Meredith found her gaze drawn to Toklat's companions.

They ringed her in, floating in a tight circle, their great dark eyes fixed both upon her and upon what she held. Some were in human form like Toklat, but others were in seal shape—great animals, far larger than normal seals, and with unnervingly human eyes and expressions.

One of them, a dark-skinned powerfully built woman with short, thick hair the rich color of a seal's pelt, reached out a tentative hand. "Is that it?" she asked in a husky voice that quavered with hope.

At Meredith's nod, a swift exchange broke out in the growling tongue of the Selkies. Toklat swung toward her his eyes ablaze. "At last," he breathed. He squared his broad shoulders. "So, what happens now?"

"I can heal you," Meredith said calmly. "Just as I can heal my own people."

"Without it draining you to the point of death as before?"

Toklat eyed her closely, then looked at Galen, who laid his hand on Meredith's shoulder.

"She can do it," Galen said calmly. "She didn't have the scroll before. But she has it now, and it will protect her."

One of the Selkies who was in seal form growled. The sound of recognizable speech issuing from his animal's mouth was wondrous and jarring to Meredith, although no one else appeared to find it the least bit strange. "But we don't know," he pointed out, "whether its power will help us, or only the merfolk."

Before Galen or Toklat could answer, Meredith spoke. "There's only one way to find out."

She gazed at them steadily, then still holding the bundle with one arm, she held out the other. She had to tread water hard to keep herself afloat, until she felt Galen behind her, his powerful arms steadying and supporting her. She leaned back against his chest and let herself relax.

This time when the power came, she felt in control, could grasp what was happening and channel it, rather than be buffeted and emptied as its helpless tool. It poured through her, so brilliant and white and alive, she wanted to shout and sing with joy. When the power then left her, she sagged a little with its departure, and behind her, despite his outward calm, she could sense Galen's anxiety as his arms tightened about her.

He need not have worried. Far from being left exhausted and reeling, Meredith was exhilarated. The blood was pounding through her veins in hot streams of strength and vitality; her mind was wondrously alive, racing with thoughts and excitement. She felt wonderfully strong, powerful and eager to continue, to go on to the next place and the next healing.

A glance at the Selkies, however, showed her that her mood was not shared. The sealfolk were eyeing her and one another dubiously. She studied them in turn. "What is it? What's wrong?" she demanded.

Galen answered her, his deep voice vibrating against her back. "They are worried that your abilities did not succeed," he murmured. He gazed at Toklat over Meredith's head. "Do you feel any different?"

Toklat shook his head. "We know you can help your own folk, Lady," he said apologetically. "I have seen this with my own eyes. But we are very different from you, both inside and out." He swung around in a slow circle, staring at his people, who stared back at him, a whole range of varying degrees of anxiety, hope, and disbelief written upon their faces. Toklat drew himself up in the sparkling water. "Very well," he said. "I am the king of my people, and so it is for me to do this. I will change my form. And if your healing has worked, Lady, then we will know."

And if it has not? No one voiced this question aloud. Everyone knew all too well what the answer to it would be. In silence, they all watched as Toklat swam an arm's length away from the ring of his people.

Meredith swallowed hard. Her exhilaration was fading in the strength of a sudden apprehension. She shifted the scroll so that she held it in both arms against her chest. It was a comforting presence, and to have Galen behind her with his arms close around her was even more comforting.

"It will be all right," he whispered. "I saw the power flow through you. I felt it pass from your body to mine. I know it worked."

Still she could not get out of her mind what Galen had told her before about the sickness afflicting the Selkies: of the horrible creatures they mutated into upon trying to shapechange. Please, she thought, and was unsure toward whom or what she was directing that unspoken plea.

She didn't know what to expect as she looked at Toklat a waving of arms or the chanting of an invocation, per haps. The Selkie did neither. Indeed, the change, when it came, was so subtle and swift that she had to blink hard several times, not quite sure of what she had seen. Toklat's burly form blurred, softened around the edges, and suddenly, a giant bull seal was looking at her. But with Toklat's eyes!

Around her the Selkies exploded. Elated whoops and barks broke out, ringing over the tossing vista of waves, mingling with exclamations of astonishment and incredulous joy. Selkies could not cry any more than merfolk could, but their happiness was so heartfelt it could not help but be contagious.

Galen laughed, the first true laugh Meredith had ever heard him make. It was like a great roar of pleasure that vibrated through her. It was almost as wondrous as the scroll's healing power, and she laughed, too, unable to stop, weak with joy and relief and love.

Yet another sunset was staining the Inland Mother crimson, the sun dying unchanged as it had for uncounted ages, and as it would for uncounted ages more.

Meredith gazed up at the last fading streaks of color and thought of Marit. So long ago, this sun, indifferent witness to so much on sea and land, had sent another dawn to light the death of Marit's world. But in the death of that world had been born the seeds of a new one, for Marit and Jeram and at least a few of their people. And the seeds of what would one day happen to the merfolk and to Meredith.

It had all come full circle. The prophecy, the scroll, and her. Meredith thought of the time the scroll had been in her keeping before her Change, and of all the centuries before that, its power hidden, locked away, waiting for the right moment to be released. Now it had been, and into her. *She* was the scroll, and it was she. Even Anastas, who had read

more of those golden sheets than anyone, had only understood in part the final piece of the puzzle. That once
Meredith in her new incarnation was brought together with
the scroll, they would meld into a power so great that it
would have destroyed him if Galen had not done so first.

She looked out across the violet expanse of restless water,
the eternal wash and rush of the waves moving ceaselessly
in her ears—as it would for now and always, she realized
with a quiet peace in her heart.

Toklat and the other Selkies had departed hours ago, going to gather the rest of their people and bring them to merfolk abodes, where they, too, could be healed. Galen had left
her to hunt some spiny lobsters for their first meal all day.
He had insisted—no, commanded, really—that Meredith
stay there and rest until darkness fell, then meet him at a
place he had carefully described to her. Actually she had
been glad to obey, and with Anastas transitioned to whatever reckoning awaited him, she had no reason to fear being
alone in the sea any longer.

The moon cast a silver path across the black sea, rippling
and beckoning. She had only to follow it to where Galen
waited for her. She took one last look above her. The stars
had awakened, and they lit the night like a vast canopy of
diamonds flung out over an endless length of velvet. She
waved an arm, bidding the dark sky farewell, and dove.

The waves closed smoothly over her passing, unbroken
and rippling as though she had never been there. A night
bird, beating its lonely way toward land, called out as it flew
past. Then all was still, except for the ancient song of the
wind and waves.

Item from a Greek newspaper on the island of
Rhodes

August 28, 1974   The search for Meredith Alaster, an
American woman missing and believed drowned off the
coast of Karpathos, was finally suspended today, after ex-
tensive efforts organized by both the Greek police and the
American Embassy. The caïque she had rented from a local
fisherman was discovered drifting in the sea one month ago,
but no trace of the woman herself has been found. Foul play
is suspected by the authorities, since only one day before
the American's disappearance, the body of a murdered local
woman was found. No assailant has been arrested in that
case, either.

Miss Alaster was staying on Karpathos while she did research for a book. The American Embassy in Athens is
presently seeking to notify next of kin, as well as the university that the young woman worked for.

"I tried to warn her," one of the villagers in the normally
quiet village of Olympus was quoted as saying. "Staying out
there in that house all alone, with the sea watching her every minute. She asked so many questions about the sea. You
can't ask that many questions about the sea and not expect
the sea to answer."

The woman would not elaborate any further.

ABOUT THE AUTHOR

JESSICA BRYAN holds a master's degree in library science from the University of Wisconsin-Madison and is a martial arts enthusiast who has practiced kung fu for the last 14 years. A native of Milwaukee, Wisconsin, Jessica now lives with her husband near Seattle, Washington.

Don't miss these fabulous Bantam women's fiction titles on sale in September

• A WHISPER OF ROSES

by **Teresa Medeiros**, author of HEATHER AND VELVET
A tantalizing romance of love and treachery that sweeps from a medieval castle steeped in splendor to a crumbling Scottish fortress poised high above the sea. ____29408-3 $5.50/6.50 in Canad

• TENDER BETRAYAL

by **Rosanne Bittner**, author of OUTLAW HEARTS
The powerful tale of a Northern lawyer who falls in love with a beautiful plantation owner's daughter, yet willingly becomes the instrument of her family's destruction when war comes to the South. ____29808-9 $5.99/6.99 in Canad

• THE PAINTED LADY

by **Lucia Grahame**
"A unique and rare reading experience." —Romantic Times
In the bestselling tradition of Susan Johnson comes a stunningly sensual novel about sexual awakening set in 19th-century Franc and England. ____29864-X $4.99/5.99 in Cana

• OREGON BROWN

by **Sara Orwig**, author of NEW ORLEANS
A classic passionate romance about a woman forced to choose between fantasy and reality. ____56088-3 $4.50/5.50 in Cana